The Last Alpha

A ROMANCE NOVEL

A ROMANCE-FANTASY NOVEL

written by Aura Rose (Aurawrites)

Copyright © 2022 Aura Rose

Grace has asserted her right under the laws of Singapore, to be identified as the Author of the Work.

All rights reserved.

No part of this book may be reproduced or transmitted in any form by any means, graphic, electronic, or mechanical, including photocopying, recording, taping or by any information storage retrieval system without the written permission from the copyright holder.

This is a work of fiction. Names, characters, businesses, places, events, and incidents are either the products of the author's imagination or used in a fictitious manner: Any resemblance to actual persons, living or dead, or actual events is purely coincidental.

Design and composition by CRATER PTE.LTD.

First Edition, 2022.
Published by CRATER PTE.LTD.
Singapore

AUTHOR'S NOTE

Dear Reader,

Firstly, thank you so much for purchasing this book. I hope you enjoy it as much as I enjoyed writing it! My name is Aura Rose and I live in Somerset, UK with my husband, daughter, and very lazy dog. I started writing for Stary during the Covid-19 pandemic to try and find a new passion and hobby in life that was just for me! I had no expectations going into it and **The Last Alpha** *is my first novel.*

I was blown away by the amount of love and support I received on this new adventure and this book holds a very special place in my heart. The story of Logan and Alina will always mean so much because it set me on a road of self-discovery and awoke a passion for writing I never knew I had.

This book was inspired by a restless night sleep where I could not shake a crazy dream I had. I locked myself in my bathroom with a pen and paper and started to write it down in the form of a paranormal romance. By the early hours of the morning the first few chapters of **The Last Alpha** *were born!*

The Last Alpha *went on to win third place in the Stary Writing III competition this year and there are now three more books in* **The Last Alpha** *series.*

If you love steamy stories with compelling characters that have complex layers fashioned in dark romance palettes, such as unassailable female leads who have a world of challenges to overcome, enticingly sexy male leads who worship their Queens in all versions and forms, and plot twists that cause you to question your reality, then you might like to try my books!

I love to interact with my readers on social media so please feel free to come and follow my socials for extra content, mood boards for books and characters as well as playlists and upcoming projects.

If you enjoy this book, please leave a review, it will mean the world to me as a new author!

Lots of Love,

AuraRose

Instagram: aurawrites31
Facebook: Aura Rose Between The Lines

Table of Contents

- AUTHOR'S NOTE 3
- Chapter 1 9
- Chapter 2 13
- Chapter 3 19
- Chapter 4 23
- Chapter 5 28
- Chapter 6 34
- Chapter 7 43
- Chapter 8 48
- Chapter 9 55
- Chapter 10 65
- Chapter 11 73
- Chapter 12 80
- Chapter 13 87
- Chapter 14 98
- Chapter 15 103
- Chapter 16 113
- Chapter 17 116
- Chapter 18 127
- Chapter 19 135
- Chapter 20 141

Chapter 21 147

Chapter 22 153

Chapter 23 161

Chapter 24 167

Chapter 25 171

Chapter 26 181

Chapter 27 187

Chapter 28 198

Chapter 29 205

Chapter 30 214

Chapter 31 219

Chapter 32 226

Chapter 33 232

Chapter 34 236

Chapter 35 244

Chapter 36 250

Chapter 37 259

Chapter 38 265

Chapter 39 272

Chapter 40 279

Chapter 41 288

Chapter 42 295

Chapter 43 308

Chapter 44 313

Chapter 45 321

Chapter 46 329

Chapter 47 342

Chapter 48 350

Chapter 49 359

Chapter 50 364

Chapter 51 371

Chapter 52 376

Chapter 53 387

Chapter 54 393

Chapter 55 402

Chapter 56 410

Chapter 57 416

Chapter 58 424

Chapter 59 429

Chapter 60 436

Chapter 61 445

Chapter 62 455

Chapter 63 469

Chapter 64 476

Chapter 65 483

Chapter 66 490

Chapter 67 497

Chapter 68 504

Chapter 69 521

Chapter 70 532

Chapter 71 538

Chapter 72 546

Chapter 73 554

Chapter 74 563

Chapter 75 574

Chapter 76 580

Chapter 77 593

ABOUT THE AUTHOR 597

ABOUT DREAME 598

Sneak Peek - Dark Love 599

Chapter 1

Alina's POV

"Come on, Alina. I hate seeing you still so miserable and crying over that prick. Get up, we're getting you out of this flat."

I was currently lying on my best friend's sofa in my faded Nirvana T-shirt and fluffy pyjama bottoms, stuffing my face with a tub of Ben and Jerry's and watching *Dirty Dancing* for the third day straight. I know, pathetic! But what else do you do when you walk in on your boyfriend of three years in bed fucking the Starbucks waitress that served you coffee that morning?

Urgh, just replaying the scene over again in my mind had my swollen, red eyes threatening to shed new tears again.

"Uh, no. No. No more crying! Get up! It's time for the tough love." my new flatmate and best friend, Chloe said, throwing the blanket off me and pulling at my arm.

"Chlo, please... I just want to lie here and dream about Patrick Swayze coming to my rescue and telling me this was all a nightmare for a few more days."

"As your best mate, I will not allow you to even think about that asshole for even one more minute, let alone days!"

"Huh? Patrick?"

"Nooo, Michael." She sighed. "Here is what we are going to do. You are going to get your butt in the shower, get dressed into something that resembles fashion and I will make you a breakfast that consists of more nutritional value than ice cream," she ordered, prying the tub from my hands. "And then we are going shopping!" she exclaimed, clapping her hands together and turning towards the kitchen.

Chloe and I have been best friends since we met on our first day of high school. She's always been the bossy one, but I know she has my best interest at heart, most of the time. Doesn't mean it isn't super annoying though!

I slowly climbed off the sofa with a groan. There is no point in arguing with her when she is like this. She's a woman on a mission and I knew the only way through it was to do what she said.

As I turned the shower on and the hot water stung my puffy face, I closed my eyes and replayed that last conversation I had with Michael…

"SHIT. Oh! fuck… um… Lina, baby, this is not what it looks like?"

"So you're not fucking a girl in our bed at three PM on a Thursday?" I screamed.

"No… Well, yeah, but I can explain. She came on to me," he said as he scrambled to pull his trousers up and put his shirt on.

"Um, excuse me, but you asked for my phone number when she went to the toilet, remember?" the black-haired girl interrupted. She was trying to get dressed just as quickly.

I looked her up and down slowly. She was pretty in a plain kind of way, but nothing special. Now I come to think of it, I've seen her before.

"Oh my god. She works at Starbucks. You served me coffee this morning!" I shrieked at her.

She just shrugged her shoulders and mouthed "sorry" as she slipped out the door.

"I CAN'T BELIEVE YOU!" I started to throw the first thing in my reach at him, which just so happened to be the teddy bear he bought me on our first Valentines' day, so it didn't quite have the desired effect as it bounced off his head.

"Alina... calm down. Let me explain... I made a mistake. I really fucked up, I know. But you've been so busy recently with studying and your job at the bar. You've hardly spent any time with me."

"Oh, I see. So, it's my fault you're a cheating pig who can't keep his dick in his pants for one afternoon whilst I'm studying. Wow, you really are something. Fuck you, Michael."

I started grabbing my clothes and throwing them into my duffel bag as quickly as humanly possible.

"Alina, listen. It's not your fault, of course it's not."

"I KNOW! ITS YOURS!"

"Yes, well the thing is... we don't really do anything adventurous in the bedroom. It's always so samey and you know sometimes that can get a bit..."

"A bit what?!" I stopped what I was doing to wait for his answer even though I already knew I didn't want to hear it.

"Boring!"

I started to laugh uncontrollably. I don't know where it came from, but I think it is a coping mechanism as I tend to laugh in the most inappropriate situations.

I grabbed the bag and made my way towards the front door.

"Alina, what are you doing? Come back, let's talk about this like adults," Michael pleaded half-heartedly.

I scoffed. "There really is nothing to talk about, Michael. We are done and I really couldn't care less if you think I'm boring in bed because I have more fun thinking of your brother in the shower than having sex with you, so go fuck yourself... or her again. I really don't care."

The last part was a lie. I didn't even find his brother attractive, but I knew that he was always insecure that his brother had everything handed to him on a plate, whereas Michael had to work hard in life. So I hit him where I knew it would hurt. I'm honestly not a spiteful person, but when your heart has just shattered into a thousand pieces, it's the only way I felt anything at that moment…

I turned off the shower and felt refreshed.

I decided Chlo was right.

It was time to stop feeling sorry for myself and move on to better things.

Chapter 2

Alina's POV

"OMG! You have got to try this new iced coffee at Starbu— Oh, shit sorry! I wasn't thinking!"

I rolled my eyes and folded my arms as Chloe stumbled over her words.

"Let's go to Pret instead. They make these chocolate cookies with melt in the middle to die for!"

As we sat down with our orders, Chloe got her iPhone out and started to scroll through Instagram. I leaned back in the leather chair and sipped my hot chocolate. The mall was extremely busy for a Friday afternoon and it gave me the perfect opportunity to sit back and partake in my favourite pastime: people watching. I find the way people walk, the clothing they choose to wear, and how they interact with each other intriguing. Because I don't know them personally, I can imagine a whole life for them. I guess this is one of the reasons I chose to study psychology at university. I find it so fascinating that you can interact with strangers every minute of the day and yet know nothing about their feelings, darkest secrets or the lives they are living. I wanted to know more.

As I was watching a teenage couple, who from their body

language, I could only presume, were loved up and on a date, Chloe pulled me out of my observations.

"I can't believe I forgot to tell you about this, but obvs you've been dealing with your own drama and what not. I have to show you this girl that I met last weekend. I follow her on Insta now and she is drop-dead gorgeous, has the best style, and is freaking hilarious in her stories!"

"Great. That's exactly what I need right now, to socially stalk a stunning woman who has her shit together. I bet she's never been cheated on with a Starbucks waitress." I couldn't help but frown.

"Hey! None of that! Us, women, have got to stick together! Here she is." Chloe flipped her phone around to reveal what I had to admit was a very attractive woman. She had shoulder-length blonde hair and unique grey eyes that popped with the help of clearly immaculate, skilled makeup. I scrolled down to a few more photos and noticed she was a little alternative with her style and a nose ring, lots of ear piercings and a large tattoo down one of her thighs. But what stood out the most was her complexion and lips. They looked so soft and smooth, almost like porcelain.

"Yeah, she is gorgeous," I agreed. "How did you meet her?" Chloe was always meeting new people. She is what you would call a social butterfly.

"Last weekend when I went to that club, Lavish, with Lucy. She was at the bar when this sleazeball tried groping my ass. She turned around and grabbed him by the balls and said, 'How do you like it?' and twisted them! You should have seen the look on his face! Priceless. Anyway, I thanked her for being such a boss bitch and she said, us bitches, have got to look out for each other. She then invited me and Lucy to join her friends at their table and they were wild!"

"Is that the night you got in at 5:30 AM screaming that you had found your girl crush?" I raised my eyebrows at her.

She giggled. "Yea. Well, I love cock too much to go there, but if I was going to, it would definitely be with her! Anyway, she's got a hunk of a boyfriend. Right, come on. I've still got a zillion shops to go to before this place closes."

She dragged me up from the table whilst I shoved the last piece of my cookie in my mouth. I have to admit Chloe was right about the cookies—they are to die for!

"You have got to try this on, Lina! The colour will bring out your eyes and it will suit your tan skin!" She was holding up the smallest bit of material I had ever seen for a dress! It was emerald green, made from a silk fabric, and looked rather expensive.

"I think that is lingerie, Chlo, not a dress!" I turned back to the rack and continued to flick through the rows of stylish clothes.

"No, it's a dress and it's incredible. I will not take no for an answer. You are trying it on!" she demanded whilst pushing me towards the changing rooms with the dress pressed to my chest.

I sighed and gave in, shutting the black, velvet curtain behind me. We were in one of those edgy, urban shops that are full of stylish girls trying to grab the latest trend before they saw someone else in it. I have never really understood it all. I've always been happy in a pair of jeans and a hoody most days and on the rare occasion that I did dress up, it would normally be something I borrow from Chloe. It's not like I didn't like fashion as such, but I worked hard for my money (the little that I had) and refused to splash out on designer clothes.

After my dad left us, it was just mum and me, and between us, we did okay. But when she got ill and could no longer work, I decided to drop out of university and get a full-time job to pay for the house and bills. Unfortunately, after she passed away a year ago, I had to sell my childhood home as I couldn't keep up with the mortgage. I moved straight in with Michael and, well, you saw how that turned out. Here I am, practically homeless, living on my friend's sofa, so spending (I looked at the tag...) £150 for this dress is not a good idea!

"Chlo! Do you know how much this dress costs?"

"Stop your whining and get out here! The anticipation is killing me!"

As I slipped the dress over my head, the delicate fabric fell gracefully into place. It clung to all the right places and stopped halfway up my thighs. It had spaghetti straps that crossed at the back and left my entire back open and bare right down to the top of my tail bone where it scooped around. I have to admit, if I had the confidence to wear this out in public, I would. I loved it. But where on earth would I wear such a thing?

"Hurry up, you are taking forever! I need to see!" Chole squealed, snapping me out of my trance.

I took a deep breath before opening the curtain and stepping out.

"WOAH!" Chloe's mouth hung open as she stared at me.

Suddenly, the cubicle next to mine opened and out stepped a stunning girl in a cropped top and tight figure-hugging jeans. I recognised her instantly but couldn't place how I knew her.

"Madeline! Oh, wow, what a small world! Do you remember me? From Lavish?" Chloe was practically hyperventilating at the poor girl like she was some kind of A-list celebrity.

As she turned to take in my excited best friend, I saw her flawless features and I have to say her photos didn't do her justice. She was curvier than me but in all the right places and gave off this light yet powerful aura. She looked Chloe up and down before breaking into a breath-taking smile.

"Yes, it's Chloe, right? How are you? Did you get home okay after the club?"

I noticed a slight American accent in her voice.

"I'm great, thank you! And yes, I did. It was such a good night. Such a laugh! Oh, sorry. This is my friend Alina," Chloe replied as Madeline looked me up and down. I suddenly felt self-conscious in the little clothing I had on.

"Hi," I replied shyly, holding my arms across my chest, trying to cover the little bit of modesty I had left. "Sorry about this. Chlo forced me to try it on and, well, it's definitely not my style, as you can see."

She gazed at me thoughtfully and smiled. She turned back to Chloe.

"What are you and your friend doing tomorrow evening? My boyfriend and I are throwing a house party and I wondered if you would like to come?" She smiled sweetly.

Chloe practically jumped out of her chair.

"Yes! Of course, we would love to come, wouldn't we, Alina?"

"Um··· I··· er..." I stuttered like an idiot. The last thing I want to do in the world right now is to go to a party full of attractive people.

"On one condition..." Madeline announced, looking from Chloe to me. "You have to wear that dress to the party."

"What?!" I almost choked.

"It looks incredible on you and I know you won't buy it otherwise. And that would be such a shame." She winked at me and then swiftly gave Chloe a kiss on both cheeks and she was gone.

I stood there, dumbfounded.

Chloe looked at me and a mischievous smile stretched across her face.

"No way. Not happening. I don't even want to go anyway!" I tried to reason with her as she made pleading noises and praying hands.

"I am not buying this dress and the last thing I want to do right now is go to a party. I don't even know the girl!"

"Exactly! You won't know anyone there so you can strut in the place looking hot as fuck and be whoever you want to be for the night! You could be anyone for a whole night and forget all the shit you've been through recently. Let go and have some fun!"

She had a point and some small part of me loved the idea of being someone else for a night. A girl who wasn't heartbroken, who hadn't lost their mum and their boyfriend in the same year and wasn't living on their best friend's couch.

"Okay fine," I agreed and Chloe jumped into my arms, knocking me straight back into the cubicle.

"Great, now let's go pay for that dress!"

I was going to have to keep the tag and try and return it the day after.

The life of a student!

Chapter 3

Alina's POV

The next day, I was lounging on Chloe's sofa studying when my phone vibrated, notifying me of a DM.

I opened it to find a message in my other inbox, so it was from someone I don't follow. I froze when I saw the name. Madeline Damaris.

Hey, hun. It was so nice to meet you yesterday. I've messaged Chloe with our address. Looking forward to seeing you rocking that dress later.

I read the message again and I couldn't help but shake my head at it. The girl had so much confidence. I wish I could have even an ounce of her boldness.

I clicked on her profile and an array of cool, edgy photos filled my screen. I scrolled down the page and stopped at one photograph of her with her arms wrapped around a man's neck. I opened the post to get a better look and I swear my heart did a somersault in my chest. This guy was the hottest man I have ever seen on this planet. He had jet-black hair that was short on the side but longer on top and fell forward, curling at the ends just above his eyes. He had chiselled cheekbones and a strong jawline which was decorated with a bit of dark stubble and gave off very masculine vibes. His eyes were looking directly into the camera lens and were such piercing ice blue; it felt as if they were looking straight into my soul. He wasn't smiling and had a pensive expression on his face. His full lips were so inviting that I let my mind drift to what it might feel like to kiss them.

What is the matter with me? This was clearly Madeline's boyfriend!

I looked down at the caption that read, 'My world' with a heart emoji. It was flooded by comments showing appreciation for the couple saying things like 'couple goals' and 'you two are just the cutest.' One comment had tagged Madeline and another name @Logan2u.

Without giving it too much thought, I clicked on the name and there he was. I spent at least half an hour scrolling and scrutinising his profile. It was clear that he was into some dark stuff. A lot of skulls, tattoos, MMA fighting. In fact, it looks like he makes a living from training others in MMA, which I surprisingly found a real turn on.

"What are you doing?!"

I hadn't even heard Chloe enter the room as I was so engrossed in my social stalking.

"Huh What? Uh, nothing. Why?" I spluttered, quickly turning my phone off and throwing it down.

"Why aren't you getting ready? We have to leave in forty-five minutes!"

It was just then that I realised what Chloe was wearing. She had on a short silver dress that barely covered her ass and strappy heels that climbed up her legs. Her brown hair had been curled and bounced just above her shoulders and her makeup was flawless. She looked amazing.

"Oh, Chloe, you look gorgeous. But I really think you should go without me tonight. I'm not feeling great and I don't want to ruin your night." I tried a last-ditch attempt to get out of this nightmare. It would be embarrassing enough that I had to wear next to nothing, let alone be caught drooling all over Madeline's boyfriend. I think I'll pass.

"Alina, please. I am asking you this one thing. Do it for me! I have been there for you through everything because you're my girl. I've supported you, bitch-slapped that two-timing prick for you, cuddled you when you cried yourself to sleep for nights and put a roof over your head. And all I am asking in return is for one night out with my bestie where we get drunk, dance until our feet hurt, and pull some hotties! Is that too much to ask?" She pouted and tilted her head to the side.

"Urgh. Alright, I'll get in the shower now but I am not pulling anyone tonight. That's all on you!"

"YES! You know what they say? The quickest way to get over someone is to get under someone else!" She winked. "Be quick because I need at least half an hour to work my magic on your hair and makeup!"

I showered, shaved, and moisturised as quickly as I could. I mean, if there were to be some fit guys there, I wanted to at least smell nice.

Who was I kidding? Only one man in particular entered my mind.

I cursed myself for my inappropriate thoughts. I was no homewrecker, especially after what I just went through with Michael. And besides, he wouldn't even notice me when he has someone like Madeline in his arms.

Chloe wouldn't let me look whilst she did my makeup and hair, saying that it would ruin the full effect of the reveal. I asked her to keep my makeup simple and natural as I didn't often wear much makeup normally, but I was starting to get nervous at how long that was taking. Not that I didn't trust her. Chloe was an aspiring make-up artist and the girl has skills.

"Okay, nearly ready. Just slip into that sexy nightie and voila!"

"Chloe! I knew it wasn't a dress!"

"Ha-ha-ha, I am only messing with you." She giggled. "It is a dress and a bloody stunning one, so get your hot ass in it now!"

I shimmied into the revealing number and Chloe beamed as she stepped away from the mirror so I could get a look at her handy work.

I actually had to blink a few times to make sure what I was seeing was really there.

Chloe had kept my makeup simple but used a shimmery green eyeliner which made my forest green eyes look bright and vibrant. She had given me a bronze glow which defined my cheekbones and a beautiful stone rose-coloured lip. My sandy blonde hair was straightened and fell just above my tail bone (reminding me I had let it grow too long and it needed a cut soon) and she had given me a side parting that had my hair flipping over with volume and covering part of my face. I loved it.

"Wow, Chlo," is all I managed to say.

"I know, I know. I am a genius! Come on, the taxi is here," Chloe said whilst checking her phone before throwing it into a clutch bag that matched her dress and grabbing my hand.

Chapter 4

Madeline's POV

"OH, yessss... Fuck, yeah... Oh, Goddess...Yes, Logan!" I screamed as he slammed into me repeatedly from behind. He was rampant, fucking me like there was no tomorrow, chasing his climax. I could feel the pressure building but I wasn't there yet. As he picked up the pace, I breathed, "Don't cum yet!" I reached between my legs to bring me closer to my orgasm.

"Urghhhggh!" he growled and I felt him come to a halt and then do one final thrust into me.

"LOGAN!" I cried in frustration.

"Sorry, love. I couldn't help it," was his reply as he pulled out of me swiftly and walked into the bathroom to dispose of the condom.

I huffed in annoyance. Our sex life never used to be like this. He always used to put my pleasure before his own needs, at least making me cum twice before he got his release. Now, it was like he couldn't get it over with fast enough; that is, when we actually got to do it at all!

And the condom thing, that was new. It's not like I want to get pregnant or anything but we'd been having unprotected sex for years and then all of a sudden, he started wearing one. When I questioned him, he raised his eyebrows and said, "Don't you think we've taken enough chances in the past? Better to be safe than sorry" and closed the discussion.

Now watching him foaming and rinsing his athletic and muscular body in the shower, I contemplated joining him and seeing if he would go again or at least finish me off, but I couldn't face the rejection I'd feel if he said no.

Logan was still being his tentative and thoughtful self in every other aspect of our lives. He always kissed me before he left for work and made me breakfast and coffee every morning as he was an early riser (and I'm not). However, over the last few months, something has felt 'off' with us. Or him, I should say. And I can't put my finger on what it is.

We are not like humans in the way that our senses are heightened. Our smell, sight and hearing are advanced, and not to mention our ability to feel when danger or uncertainty is looming. This is why I knew something was wrong.

Logan and I are part of the last group left of our kind. As werewolves, we grew up together in a pack and were always the best of friends. Logan's father was the leader of our pack, the Alpha of Blood Moon, one of the largest werewolf packs in America and my father was his second in command, the Beta. We flourished growing up on the territory's estate, causing mischief and mayhem daily. We were forever laughing. Until that dreadful day.

When we were 17, our pack was brutally attacked by the King of Vampires, Lucius. Everyone was being slaughtered mercilessly—the elderly, the warriors, the defenceless women and children. No one was spared. Alpha James forced me, Logan, and as many of the others our age as he could save into the secret tunnels of our pack house and told us to run. Logan and many of the other males who had already been training to be warriors tried to refuse. They wanted to stay and fight for their pack but Alpha James was insistent. He used his Alpha tone to command us to leave. Before we did, he told Logan and I that our generation was the only chance of protecting our species and restoring the future of our pack. That Logan and I would be the new Alpha and Luna and when the time was right, we would have our revenge. We could not disobey his command as all pack members cannot help but respect and honour the Alpha's authority.

That was eight years ago now. Logan and I were sure that we would end up being destined mates by the Moon Goddess. Mates are soul mates for werewolves. The love and connection between mates are beyond anything you could imagine. My parents were true mates and I remember the unconditional love they shared for each other. They were two bodies, sharing one soul.

So you can imagine how excited I was for mine and Logan's eighteenth birthdays when we would feel the mate bond appear between us. But it never happened. I couldn't fathom why the Moon Goddess would not make me his one true mate. I loved him more than life itself, I still do. Logan was also upset especially as he took his father's final words to heart. We would be the next Alpha and Luna of Blood Moon Pack once we destroyed the Vampire King. So we made a promise to each other. We would take each other as our chosen mates and if our true mates came along, we would reject them. It was the only way.

Luckily, they never have. I suppose with there being only a few hundred of our species left in existence it makes our chances of ever meeting our true mates very slim. Werewolves' mates can be of other species as well such as humans, witches, or even, goddess forbid, vampires. But it is less common and we would prefer to have a strong, pure bloodline than be with them. Don't get me wrong, I like humans. They are fun to play with but they are weak.

After the attack, we laid low and all of the surviving pack members decided to go their separate ways to make it harder for the vampires to track us. Logan and I, as well as a few of our close friends, moved to England and have been living low key amongst the humans to hide our identities. We are still in touch with all the wolves who escaped our pack' s slaughter and they accept and respect Logan as their Alpha even though we are not currently considered a pack. Once we are able to gather enough strength and resources to take down the vampires, I will become his Queen and during the Luna Ceremony, he will finally mark me. I can' t wait!

Even in hiding, we are sociable creatures and have many human friends too, although they do not know our truth. I love the way the humans swoon over our good looks and charisma (perks of being a supernatural being), but what I love the most is how they all think we are the perfect couple. Untouchable.

But recently, I have felt Logan slipping away. Becoming distant. It wasn' t just the sex, but he never cuddled me to sleep anymore. He gave me a peck on the forehead and said 'goodnight, my love' and rolls over! It' s like I' m his 75-year-old wife! In the past, when I felt him withdrawing, I would entice him back with a sexual desire like some BDSM or a threesome with a human. He seemed to like those and especially watching me with another woman.

Suddenly, an idea popped into my head. That is exactly what I will do tonight. I will surprise him after the party with another girl waiting in our bed. I will admit, I don' t like seeing him with another girl (werewolves are known for being very jealous and possessive creatures), but at least I was always there, too. And knowing it turns him on makes it worth it.

Instantly, the image of that cute, timid blonde from yesterday

The Last Alpha

entered my mind. She would be perfect. What was her name? Alaya?

Alina! I quickly grabbed my phone and it didn't take long to track her down on Instagram. I typed out a message and sent it with a grin. I need her to come to the party tonight.

"What are you smirking at?" Logan asked as he walked into the bedroom with only a towel around his neck. What a sight!

"I have a surprise for you."

"Oh, yeah?"

"Yep, and I think you are going to love it... Or should I say her?"

He raised his eyebrows at me in that seductive manner that he has down to perfection.

"Where did you find this one?"

"At the mall. I think you will really like to see what I will do to her later," I said in my most sultry voice.

"Can't wait," is all he said as he chucked on a pair of shorts and strolled out of the bedroom.

Tonight needed to go without a hiccup so we could get back on track. The only problem is, I don't think that girl is the type to just hop into bed with a couple. I will have to play this carefully.

Chapter 5

Alina's POV

"I seriously cannot believe you are wearing flats," scolded Chloe when I got into the taxi.

"I told you I was not wearing heels. It's bad enough that you're forcing me out in this." I pointed to the green, silk dress. "I am not about to make even more of a fool of myself falling ass over tit in a pair of your ridiculous shoes."

"Eek! I am so excited to see Madeline's flat. I wonder what it's going to be like? I bet it's edgy and cool with quirky artwork all over the walls. Did you know that Madeline's boyfriend is an MMA fighter and he trains others? He's, like, really good!"

"No, how would I know that?" I replied a little too defensively.

"Yeah, he's pretty intimidating from what I've heard about him. Not someone you want to mess with. And he loves Madeline fiercely. Apparently, he once beat a man for even ogling at her in a club!"

"What a hero!" I rolled my eyes at her enthusiasm. I couldn't help but be sarcastic. I would be mortified if someone behaved that way because of me. But I will never know what that feels like, I guess, as I am sure no one will ever love me as much as that.

The Last Alpha

After twenty minutes, the car came to a stop and Chloe paid the taxi driver and climbed out. I hesitated for a moment and wondered how pissed off Chloe would be if I quickly slammed the door and tell the driver to take me home. Very pissed! I know I could never do that to her either. There was no way out of this. I suddenly felt a wave of adrenaline rush through my body and I gave myself a pep talk.

I can be anyone I want to be tonight. I don't know these people and will probably never see them again after tonight, so fuck it. I am going to let loose and have fun!

I stepped out of the taxi and the cool evening breeze hit me and sent a shiver through my body. We linked arms and quickly ran up some stone steps towards a vast black door.

"Well, this is it," Chloe said whilst typing the flat number into the intercom. The door buzzed and we waited for an answer. I took a minute to look around my surroundings. We were on a respectable road full of townhouses, most had been converted into flats. I didn't know the area well, but I knew we were on the outskirts of London, away from the hustle and bustle of the city. What caught my attention was that to the right of the building stood the beginning of a large, wooded area. This was quite unusual in a place like London.

BUZZZZZZ

The latch on the door opened and we were met by a giant of a man. He was handsome with brown hair and brown eyes, although a little terrifying.

"Name?" he asked in a gruff tone.

"Oh um… I'm Chloe and this is Alina. We are friends of Madeline's," Chloe answered nervously.

He looked us both up and down slowly with an expressionless face and then opened the door wider for us to pass through.

The flat was on the second floor and was much bigger and homely than the building looked on the outside. It had all of its original features from the Victorian era with an open fireplace in the middle of the living room but also lots of modern designs that made it contemporary yet chic. Chloe was right, it was edgy and cool.

The first thing I noticed was a smell as we walked in. It was a mixture of an earthy pine scent with a masculine aroma of sandalwood. It was divine. The second thing I noticed was that there weren't that many people here for a house party.

There were a few girls huddled together around a built-in bar in the corner of the room sipping their drinks, a couple sat smoking what appeared to be marijuana on the sofa, and a group of five people in the middle of the room chatting.

One of the girls, who was wearing leather trousers and a grey crop top with Doc Martins, threw her head back and let out a laugh that filled the room like music. It was Madeline.

"There she is. Let's go and say hi," said Chloe, pulling me in their direction. "Madeline, hey! Thank you so much for inviting us. Your place is awesome!"

"Chloe, Alina. You guys made it! Welcome." She looked genuinely happy to see us. "You both look spectacular and I see you took my advice, Alina." She winked at me, then scanned my dress. I instinctively started blushing when I realised the rest of the group (who were dressed quite casually might I add) had turned their attention towards me.

I remembered the promise I made to myself and held my head up a little higher, looking her straight in the eyes with as much confidence as I could muster.

"Yes, I did and thank you. I love it. You also look gorgeous yourself, Madeline."

Her eyes gave a little twinkle at my compliment and then she politely changed the topic and introduced us to her friends. What was strange was how good looking they all were. They gave off an aura that was unnerving yet compelling.

All of a sudden, I felt a shift in the air around me. My whole body tensed as the air prickled with anticipation. The hairs on my body stood to attention when I felt a burning gaze at the back of my head.

"Ah, there you are, darling! Come here and meet my new friends," Madeline called to the presence over my shoulder.

My heart started to race as I heard heavy footsteps approaching. When I turned my head, I came face-to-face with those crystal blue eyes and the whole world melted away. His eyes were fixed on mine, encroaching on my soul. I noticed the look of surprise and shock in them and then I watched as his lips parted slightly and his breath hitched. I let out a gasp.

I actually gasped out loud! Kill me now!

"Don't worry, he is used to getting that reaction from women," came Madeline's chuckle, reminding me that we were not the only two people in the room. I felt my cheeks burn with embarrassment. I watched as she snaked her hands through his arm and started to caress his huge biceps.

"This is Logan. My boyfriend." She smiled sweetly.

I glanced back up at his face, but he hadn't reacted to my humiliating behaviour. Instead, he continued to stare at me intensely. I was starting to feel hot and uncomfortable under his penetrating gaze. I immediately looked away and saw a man coming towards us with a few glasses of champagne in his hands. Before I could stop myself, I grabbed one from his hand and downed it in one go and then grabbed another.

"Woah! Calm down there, buttercup!" said the man I had just stolen drinks from. He looked amused with his lips pulled into a sideways smirk. He was also very attractive with auburn hair and chocolate brown eyes. Physically, he was bulky, like all the other men at the party, but not as muscular as that Greek god, Logan.

"Yes, Lina! I like your thinking!" shouted Chloe, also snatching the remaining glass from the stranger's hand and drinking it in one go.

"Wahoo! Let's get this party started!"

Everyone cheered, apart from Logan, and one of the girls in the group that Madeline had introduced as Emma went to the bar and grabbed a bottle of tequila. She started pouring it into shot glasses and handing them out to us. Oh, no! What have I started?

I looked around the group and my eyes rested on Logan again. He had still not taken his eyes off me. What was his problem?

I took the shot glass from Emma, maintaining eye contact with him, and threw it down my neck. As the liquid burned my throat, I fought the urge not to gag.

Madeline stood on her toes and leaned into him, whispering something in his ear whilst peering over at me. I swear I saw his icy blue irises turn a few shades darker at what she said before he dramatically gripped her arms and shouted, "NO!" in her face. In a flash, he was storming out of the room with Madeline in hot pursuit after him.

Everyone was silent.

"Hmm, trouble in paradise!" Emma mumbled and took a sip of her drink.

That was weird. I wanted to know what Madeline said to him to make him react that way, but I had a strong suspicion that it might have involved me and I wanted to stay out of it!

The shot was making my head feel fuzzy and I suddenly wanted to be alone for a moment. I turned around and slammed straight into the auburn-haired man.

"Hey, watch it, buttercup. I don't think you should be stealing any more of my drinks if you are drunk already!" he teased with a cheeky grin.

"I am not drunk." I glared at him. "Just lost my balance for a second and you so happened to be in my way. And please STOP calling me buttercup!"

He laughed and held out his hand. "Alright, what should I call you then?"

"Alina," I said sternly, shaking his hand.

"Darius," he replied whilst turning the back of my hand up to his lips and kissing it lightly.

I couldn't help but smile back and shake my head. I'll give it to him; he was rather charming.

"Darius, would you be so kind as to point me in the direction of the bathroom, please?"

"Oh no, you're not going to throw up already, are you? The night's only just begun!"

"No I am not. I just need a wee if you must know."

"Too much information, buttercup! It's down the corridor and the first door on your left." He smiled smugly.

Wow, he was really annoying!

"Thank you. That wasn't so difficult now, was it?"

"Hurry back now, buttercup! I miss you already," he mocked.

I put my middle finger up at him and stuck my tongue out before walking away. Somehow, I think I have just made a new friend.

Chapter 6

Logan's POV

Madeline had outdone herself with the preparations for this party. She'd stocked the bar with a wide variety of liquor, ordered a mix of drugs to suit everyone's needs, and even hired a DJ for later in the night. I don't know what had her so excited, but her energy was electric. I watched her from the bedroom doorway as she glided gracefully around the room, grabbing bits and pieces she needed to start getting ready. She had always been a pretty girl growing up, but when she turned eighteen and gained her wolf, Nina, she blossomed even more.

I walked up behind her as she sat down at her vanity table to do her makeup.

"You know, love, you really don't need any of that. You are beautiful as you are," I whispered in her ear, making her beam.

It was the truth. She didn't need it, but for some reason or another, she would never leave the house without a full face of makeup.

She turned around and put her arms around my waist. "Well, we have a little bit of time before the guests start to arrive. Why don't you show me just how beautiful I am?" she replied seductively.

The Last Alpha

I carefully removed her arms from my body. "There is still a lot to be done before they arrive, Maddy, and I am afraid I have to go out briefly and deal with something. I won't be long." I gave her a smile that didn't reach my eyes as the look of disappointment was written all over her face.

"Anything to worry about?" she asked, turning back towards the mirror.

"No, I am sure it will all be fine. I will be back shortly." I turned and walked towards the front door. Once I had shut it, I let out a long breath I had not realised I was holding. I don't understand what is going on with me at the moment, but over the last few months, my feelings have started to change towards Madeline. I love her, she is my best friend, but I am not in love with her. I am starting to realise that maybe, I never really have been.

She's still very attractive and I hate the thought of hurting her feelings in any way. So now and again I give in and we have sex. But that is all it is to me... sex. Something is missing.

My wolf, Elias, has been acting up, too. He is always pacing up and down in my head and has even started growling inside my mind any time I get intimate with Maddy, which makes it very hard to focus on anything.

I know she can tell something is up with me. I often catch her staring at me with a blank expression as if she thinks one day, she will be able to just read my thoughts if she tries hard enough. Only true mates can sense your feelings.

Here we go again, those annoying thoughts about true mates.

I am getting so frustrated with myself. I don't care about my destined mate. I hope I never have to meet them. It will save us all a lot of pain. Maddy had never done anything to deserve any of this. She has been a great mate to me so far. She even goes as far as letting me have threesomes with her because she thinks it makes me happy.

I would say it actually makes it harder, as Elias goes berserk. So, normally I sat back and watch her with them, which I have to admit isn't a bad way to pass time.

As my thoughts continued to cause me turmoil, I arrived at the street corner and waited for Fredrik. He is my Beta. Well, technically, he is just another werewolf, but when I manage to restore my pack, I will make him my second in command. He has always been the most trustworthy and loyal friend to me since we were pups.

"Alpha," he greeted me.

"Fredrik, what news from the witch?"

Fredrik was contacted a few weeks ago by a dark witch. She said she had a message for me and needed someone trustworthy to meet with her in secret. It was all very surprising, as the witches tend to keep to themselves and stay away from the ongoing battle between the werewolves and vampires.

"You're not going to like it. She said she had a vision and it involved you and Lucius."

The Vampire King. The very sound of his name caused anger to rise within me.

"Go on," I said through gritted teeth.

"He is coming and you need to be ready. She said that the decisions you make over the next few days and weeks will seal your fate and the fate of our species."

I stared at him, not knowing what to say. How was that useful? I already know that this is all on me, so why is she wasting my time?

"Is that it?" I growled.

"No. There is more to her visions but she was not willing to share anymore at the moment, as she cannot influence your decisions in any way."

I was starting to shake uncontrollably. Just the idea of coming face-to-face with Lucius after all these years and imagining ripping his evil head from his body had me ready to shift. Elias was fighting for control and I could feel him under the surface of my skin.

"He knows you are here in London. It is just a matter of time," I heard Fredrik's voice.

I closed my eyes, trying to get my breathing under control. I hated that if this witch was right, Lucius was two steps ahead of me and could even be here right now.

"Alpha, you need to get to the woods now. Before you expose yourself."

I span on my heels and sprinted to the entrance of the wooded area next to my house. I got there just in time to remove my clothes hastily before I felt all my bones breaking and realigning and black fur replacing my skin. As soon as my paws hit the forest floor, I was running with velocity through the trees, making them blur in my vision. The wind whipped through my fur and I felt the adrenaline pumping through my veins. I ran for miles in my wolf form until I came to our favourite spot. Nestled in the middle of the forest was an idyllic lake. It was the only place that could calm me when I feel out of control. It reminded me of home.

'IT'S TIME.' Elias' deep voice boomed in my mind.

Werewolves were often thought of as monsters in human fiction and films. But the reality is that we are two minds sharing one body. One mind of a human and one of a wolf. Normally, the human mind has the most authority, hence why we rarely shift into our wolves. We can choose when we shift. The rumours about only shifting at full moons are untrue, although our first shift normally happens then. Sometimes, strong emotions like anger or fear can force us to shift because our animalistic side thinks it can protect us better in wolf form.

So, wolves really are a form of defence. That being said, it can be hard to create a good balance between wolf and human and show mutual respect for one another, especially when you do not always share the same morals or ideas.

'I know, Elias. We will get our revenge even if it kills us.'

'NO YOU DO NOT UNDERSTAND. SOMETHING IS COMING. I CAN FEEL IT. WE NEED TO ACT FAST. WE MUST FIND AND BE WITH OUR MATE. SHE WILL MAKE US STRONGER.'

'I do understand, Elias. I won't let anything happen to Madeline.'

'SHE IS NOT OUR MATE!' he roared.

'Elias, she is our chosen mate. We made a promise to remember, and I will not go back on my word. It was my father's dying wish for Madeline and I to be the next Alpha and Luna of the Blood Moon Pack.'

'BUT SHE IS NOT OUR MATE!'

Rustling in the bushes behind me pulled my attention from our argument and Fredrik's grey wolf, Felix, stepped out from the shadows. Even though we are formally not a pack right now, I am able to still mind link with him as we were born in the same pack. He was one of the lucky wolves that escaped with us on that fateful night.

'Sorry Alpha, you need to come back now. Madeline is going crazy that guests are starting to arrive and you are not there.'

We raced back through the woods in wolf form. As we approached the road, I shifted back and put on my clothes I'd disregarded on the floor.

"Where the fuck have you been?" Madeline snarled.

"For a run," I replied, not engaging in her dramatics. I really can't deal with a heated argument right now. I will tell her about the witch's premonitions tomorrow. I did not want to ruin her party.

"Where are you going now?" she shouted as I strolled past her and into our bedroom. I could hear the faint sound of music and chatter in the living room.

"To have a shower so I am ready to greet the rest of our guests." I tried to keep the irritation out of my voice. I heard her huff and stomp off in the direction of the living room. She could be so childish sometimes.

I decided to take my time in the shower mainly because I needed to cool off from my conversations with Fredrik and Elias. Elias had retreated into my mind and shut me out from communicating with him. He only ever did that when he is really pissed.

It doesn't bother me right now as it has given me the opportunity to get my thoughts together. If this witch's visions were correct, then I was out of time. I was going to have to call a meeting with the surviving members of the pack, but it would have to be done discreetly, especially if the bloodsuckers are close.

After five minutes, I noticed Elias lowering the block and started pacing excitedly in my subconscious. He was on high alert, being very active and restless. I had never felt him like this before. I tried talking to him to calm him down but it was no good. He wasn't listening.

I turned off the shower and dried myself quickly.

I picked out a pair of ripped black jeans and a black T-shirt that rolled at the top of my shoulders, showcasing my expressive tattoos. I tousled my hair but it bounced back into the same position, falling forward into my eyes.

"Fuck it," I walked out of the bedroom and was overwhelmed by the most mouth-watering scent. A mix of vanilla and cinnamon invaded my nostrils. Following it towards the living room, I stopped dead when I saw her.

She had her slender, toned back to me, which was completely visible in an open-back emerald dress that hung off the top of her perked and rounded ass. Her legs were long and slim and her sun-kissed skin was a shade of caramel. Sandy blonde coloured hair cascaded down her back elegantly, stopping just above the dip in her dress and swished slightly as she talked to the group in front of her. I hadn't even seen her face yet, but I already knew her beauty would be immeasurable.

'MATE!' Elias roared in my mind.

No. No it can't be. I don't want this. I can't have a mate...

"Oh, there you are darling! Come here and meet my new friends," Madeline beckoned me over.

It took me a few moments to reign in my panic and pull myself together. I had to be strong as I could feel Elias wrestling for control so he could pounce on this mysterious girl in green and mark her in front of everyone.

Steadily, I approached the group and felt an insane pull in the air around me. It sizzled with tension and as I got closer, I could visibly see all the small hairs on the girl's body react to my presence. She obviously felt it, too.

This should be interesting.

When werewolves lay eyes on their mates for the first time, very rarely can they control the urge to run to each other and publicly declare their needs and desires. It was taking every ounce of my self-restraint to not do just that, but if she is feeling the mate bond like I am, why is she resisting? I know I have my reasons, but what were hers? It surprised me at how much her resistance hurt and angered me.

As I turned to face the group, she turned to me and I locked eyes with the most enchanting green irises. They had the same vibrancy as her dress and she had the fullest, plump lips I had ever seen. I wanted to suck, lick, and ravish them.

I parted my lips as my breathing rapidly increased.

At that moment, she let out a gasp. The sound was so sensual and erotic to me, I instantly felt my dick grow hard.

"Don't worry, he is used to getting that reaction from women." Madeline laughed and squeezed my biceps playfully.

I watched as the angel's eyes travelled to the gesture and I swear I saw a hint of jealousy flash across them before it disappeared just as quickly. Then she peered up at me through her thick, dark lashes and her cheeks flushed a faint pink colour. It was fucking adorable.

She nervously broke our eye contact and I watched as she grabbed a glass of champagne and drank it in one go and then took another from Darius' hands. I would have been impressed if I hadn't been so distracted by the drop of champagne that had missed her mouth and was trickling down her neck. I wanted to lick it off.

"Woah! Calm down there, buttercup!" Darius said. I wanted to break his nose for calling her that.

"Yes, Lina! I like your thinking," shouted the small brunette who stood next to her and copied my mate by stealing Darius' last drink.

I couldn't take my eyes off her the entire time. I could feel her awkwardness under my gaze and when she finally glanced back at me, she had a look of determination. She was annoyed. She took a shot that was handed to her by Madeline's best friend and she-wolf, Emma, and held my gaze as she drank it. It was a simple act to show me that I was not intimidating her and it turned me on.

Madeline reached up to me and started to whisper in my ear.

"Do you like your surprise?" she asked in her most seductive tone that no longer had any effect on me. It took me a while to register what she meant as my mind was preoccupied thinking about what a beautiful name Lina was and wondering if it was short for something. Then it hit me like a ton of bricks. This was the girl Madeline brought here for a threesome? NO FUCKING WAY!

"NO!" I thundered and stormed out of the room with Madeline close behind.

Once we were in the corridor and out of ear shot, she jumped down my throat.

"What is wrong with you? Why did you do that? If you don't like her, then pick someone else. I just thought she was cute and innocent. Just how you like them." She gave me a sexy smile and traced her finger down my chest.

I growled at her touch and gripped her wrist to stop her. "I mean it, Maddy. No. I don't want a threesome with her or with anyone. Do you understand?"

"Okay. Okay. I was only trying to do something nice for you!" She sulked but I didn't pay much attention as over her shoulder I saw the girl walk out of the living room and into the bathroom.

Before I could stop myself, my feet were moving towards the bathroom and I called back to Maddy that I needed a piss.

Something took over my body and before I knew it, I had opened the door and locked it behind me. I was engulfed by that enticing scent once more as she jumped from where she stood at the sink from my intrusion.

Chapter 7

Alina's POV

I had just closed the bathroom door and leaned on the sink to steady my shaking body, wondering why Logan had such a physical effect on me, when the door swung open and there he stood. Forcibly, he shut it and locked it behind him.

"Er... um... I-I'm sorry. I must have forgotten to l-lock the door," I stuttered like an idiot. His ocean blue eyes took in my body and returned to my face as if he was regarding me for the first time. I watched as his muscular jaw clenched but he didn't make any attempt to move or speak. I saw some emotions flick across his face. Anger and... lust? I shook my head slowly. I needed to get away from him. I was starting to lose my mind.

"Okay... Well I'll just leave you to it then." I moved around him to reach for the door handle.

In one swift movement, I felt strong hands grip my waist and spin me around so my back slammed against the door. I looked up in shock and his face was inches from mine. It gave me the opportunity to admire his features up close. He really was astonishingly handsome. I could feel his rapid breathing tickling my skin. One of his hands was at the side of my head against the door and the other was still gripping my hip tightly. He pressed his body up against mine, caging me in. I immediately started to burn up at his touch and this strange sensation crawled across my skin from our contact.

"Who are you?" His voice was low and husky and it made my core ache with need.

"A-Alina Clarke," I whispered, so quietly I am sure he couldn't hear me.

Suddenly, he moved his head into the crook of my neck and inhaled. As he did, he tenderly trailed the tip of his nose up my neck, sending volts of electricity through my skin. A shallow growl escaped his chest as I squirmed slightly. Did he just growl? And then he whispered something I was not expecting.

"I can smell your arousal, Alina. Stop before I lose control."

What? Can he smell that I am turned on right now? How? Oh, this is beyond embarrassing. I put my hands on his chest and tried to push him off but he didn't move.

"P-please," I begged as I struggled against his power. He lifted his face and I drew my breath in sharply when I saw that his once beautiful, azure eyes had now turned completely black. Purple veins protruded out around his eyes like twisted jungle rivers. He looked feral and dangerous. I knew at that moment, the logical thing to do was scream at the top of my lungs and get out of here as fast as possible, but I felt oddly calm. Something told me not to be afraid.

Apprehensively, I reached up and stroked the pulsing veins with my fingers, making him freeze under my touch.

"Your eyes... they're... what are you?"

Without warning, he snatched my hand away and growled, "Someone you should stay away from, Alina. You must leave this party. NOW."

And with that, he pushed me aside and bolted out of the door, leaving me wondering if any of that even happened, or did I imagine the whole thing?

I took a few minutes to finish up in the toilet and tried to understand what had just transpired. Being a psychology student, I should be quite good at reading people's emotions and behaviours. His actions suggested he felt something for me, but his words were saying the opposite. He wanted me to leave. But why? What had I done to him?

The more I thought about our encounter, the angrier I got. How dare he come in here and touch me and then tell me to leave! Madeline invited me here, the girlfriend that seemed to have slipped his mind a few minutes ago, and I wasn't going to leave unless she wanted me to.

I opened the door and stepped out into the corridor. The front door was opposite where I stood. I could just slip out without anyone noticing. But then I glanced to my left and saw him watching me from the kitchen. The man who had let Chloe and I into the party was talking to him intensely but his eyes remained fixed on me. I lifted my chin higher, not breaking our eye contact, and gave him my best 'fuck you' smile before turning right and walking back into the living room. I was not going to let this guy or any guy from now on have any control over my life.

I marched over to Chloe who was outrageously flirting with a blonde-haired man.

"Lina, there you are! I was about to send out a search party!" I highly doubted that by the way she had been draped over that stranger a few seconds ago. "Here, have another shot. It looks like you could use it! Also, I made you a Malibu and coke." She giggled as the man nibbled at her ear.

"Thanks," I replied, sinking my shot and taking my drink from her.

"Buttercup! You're back. Come, sit with me," Darius called from the sofa.

I suddenly felt hot under someone's penetrating glare and I knew exactly who it was without looking back. Instead, I walked over to Darius and slumped down on the chair next to him.

"Has anyone ever told you that you could be a Victoria's Secret model strutting in that lingerie?" he flirted.

I giggled and hit his arm playfully. "It is not lingerie. It is a dress and one that I didn't even want to buy in the first place, but your friend, Madeline over there, forced me to."

"Good job she did! You look incredible in it."

I couldn't help but peak over to where I felt daggers radiating from. Logan was leaning in the doorway with his arms folded across his chest. He looked furious.

Good.

I spent the next hour or so laughing and drinking with Darius, Chloe, and some others and I have to admit that I was actually starting to have a good time.

"Everyone, come! Sit in a circle on the floor and let's play truth or dare!" Madeline ordered with a mischievous grin.

"Great idea. I love that game," Chloe said whilst following Madeline to the middle of the room. I was pretty sure Chloe would agree to just about anything Madeline asked of her right now.

"You going to play, buttercup? Or is it not really your 'scene'?" Darius asked with a twinkle in his eye.

I knew he was baiting me and it was working. But I was a new Alina tonight and I was up for anything. I stood up with a smirk and walked over to the group that had formed a circle on the carpet and felt him follow behind me.

"I hope you brought your A-game, buttercup. Maddy can be ruthless." He winked at me whilst sitting cross-legged next to me.

Okay, deep breath, this will be fun, I told myself.

Chapter 8

Logan's POV

FUCK! What the hell is wrong with me? I nearly lost control in that bathroom. I was so close to taking her against that door and making her mine. I needed her to leave. To remove her from my life right now before I did something I would regret.

I hadn't even realised she was human until I was up close to her; feeling her exquisite, soft body pressed against mine. She didn't have the strength to push me away. Why didn't I realise that before? And she saw my eyes change when Elias tried to take control. She didn't freak out though, like most humans would have, but instead she seemed curious.

This was an even bigger mess than I first thought. I had to make her leave but she was still there! I watched her defy me and smirk as she walked straight back into the party. She was feisty for sure and it made my dick twitch.

I followed her and fury rose as she did another shot and went to sit down next to Darius, of all people. He was my cousin and also escaped with us in the attack. We rarely saw eye to eye on anything. His carefree and immature nature irritated me and he thought I was too serious and uptight. If he even lived a day in my shoes, he would see why. But no, here he was flirting with MY mate and making her giggle like a school girl. She was so fucking sexy when she laughed.

Logan cut the crap! I reminded myself. *You don't want her to remember. You want Madeline.*

'NO YOU DONT!' Elias growled back at me.

'Not now, Elias. This is harder than I ever thought it would be. The mate bond is strong and it is taking everything in me not to give in.'

'THEN DON'T FIGHT IT, LOGAN. GO TO HER. MAKE HER OURS. SHE IS PERFECT.'

'She's human!'

'WE WILL TURN HER. SHE WILL BE A POWERFUL SHE-WOLF. I CAN FEEL IT.'

'No, Elias.'

I pushed him back in my mind and blocked him.

Turning away from her and Darius, I stalked back into the kitchen to grabbed a beer from the fridge. Alcohol does not affect us like it does humans, but Maddy had hustled a special blend designed especially for werewolves from a witch friend.

Fredrik was still standing rooted to the spot where I had rudely left him. He had been talking to me about the vamp situation a few minutes ago before Alina left the bathroom.

"Everything alright, Alpha?" he mumbled under his breath.

"Yes. Fine. Sorry. Please call me, Logan. There are humans around. You were saying?" I encouraged him to continue our conversation as I hadn't listened to shit as soon as Alina stepped out of the bathroom.

"I was talking about the king's situation. I would like to lead with you and bring him down. Whatever you decide to do, I am with you every step of the way."

"Of course, Fredrik. You are the first person I would have by my side when we take down that bloodsucker. Thank you for your loyalty."

Fredrick nodded his head and took a sip of his beer. He had also lost everyone he loved in the attack. His parents, younger sister, and his true mate. He was nineteen when it happened and he had just found her. Unfortunately, she lived in one of the cottages on the outskirts of the territory that was attacked first. By the time he got there, it was too late. He nearly lost his humanity that day and survived as a callous rogue for years. I always remember the distressing look of this broken man when we first found him.

My mind started to race. The sudden image of someone hurting or murdering Alina like that had my heart pounding in my chest and my blood boiling. These feelings were so complicated. I knew at that moment that I could never let anything bad happen to her, even if I could not be with her. But what could I do to keep her safe? Mating and marking her was out of the question.

"Come, everyone. Let's play a game of truth or dare." I heard Maddy's voice from the living room.

Shit.

Madeline's POV

I was left shocked and bewildered after Logan's reaction to my surprise. I didn't get it. He doesn't seem keen to have sex with me or have a threesome. What is that about? I'm not arrogant or anything, but I know guys find me attractive and would die to get me in bed with them for one night. Yet Logan doesn't seem in the least bit interested. I would have to think of something else and fast.

As the night proceeded, I noticed Alina getting pretty drunk and coming out of her shell more. She was actually a funny girl with a lot of sass. I like her. I also noticed Logan staring at her intensely a few times throughout the evening. Maybe he was starting to come around to the idea. Perhaps a little subtle foreplay was all he needed to warm up to her.

Then an idea struck me.

Truth or dare!

Once I had everyone sitting in a circle, I decided to ease everyone in first. I picked my best friend, Emma, to go first. She wanted a dare like always, so I made her suck Darius' toes knowing she had a bit of a foot fetish. Everyone cringed and giggled as she went to town on them. Everyone except Logan, who had taken his place on the sofa to observe. I know he wouldn't play. He preferred to supervise than take part in silly games, as he called them.

We slowly worked our way around the circle until we got to Alina.

"Truth or dare?" I asked her sweetly.

"Truth," she answered in a confident voice, but I still detected a slight nervousness. I gave her a reassuring smile.

"Okay. How many people have you slept with?"

She blushed and looked down at her hands. For a moment, I didn't think she was going to answer, but then she looked me straight in the eye and said, "One."

Mmm, I thought as much. I was sure she might have even been a virgin.

"One? One person or one time?" I pried.

"One person," she replied. "Lots of times." she added with a smile.

Good girl, there's that sass!

A raw growl vibrated from Logan's chest, his eyes warning me.

Hah! I knew it. He loved an innocent. Don't worry, my love, my plan is in full swing.

After a few more turns, we got back to Alina. This time, to my surprise, she asked for a dare. It was Darius' turn to choose her fate and I was thrilled when his dirty mind took over.

"I dare you to kiss a girl." Such a perv!

"What?" she gulped.

"Kiss me, it's fine." Her friend Chloe came to her rescue.

No, I couldn't miss this opportunity. I need to give Logan a glimpse of what was to come.

"No, you're her friend. That would be too weird," I said. "You can kiss me instead." I started to crawl towards her seductively and she looked like a deer in headlights. "It's okay," I whispered as I reached her. "I don't bite."

She smiled at me shyly and then closed her eyes. I brushed my lips timidly against hers and softly ease her into the kiss. I reached up and placed my hand behind her neck and pressed harder against her mouth.

She didn't react to start with, but as I start to move my lips in between hers and suck on them, she parted them slightly, allowing me access into her mouth. I darted my tongue into her and feel our tongues dancing together as this kiss becomes more intense. We stayed like this for a couple more seconds before she pulls away.

"You're a good kisser," I said as she blinked rapidly and adjusted to her surroundings again.

"That was hot as fuck!" Darius shouted.

I glimpsed over to Logan as I made my way back to my position in the group. The pupils of his eyes were like discs of dark blue fire full of frenzy and desire. His knuckles were white from gripping the arms of the sofa tightly.

I knew it. It turned him on.

This was all the affirmation I needed to go ahead with my plan.

Alina's POV

I just kissed a girl! I kissed a girl, and not just any girl, but Madeline! Now, I am definitely still into the male sex, but I have to confess that I didn't hate it. In fact, I quite enjoyed it. She made me feel sexy and alive. I wonder what Logan thought about us kissing, but I didn't dare look at where he sat on the sofa.

"Right, your go, Darius." I tried to move the attention onto someone else.

"Oh, dare!" He clapped excitedly.

"Okay, I've got one," Chloe said. "Kiss the person you find the most attractive."

Bitch! She is trying to get him to kiss me. She has been giving me the not-so-subtle thumbs-up and winks from across the room all evening when I was chatting with him on the sofa. I am not sure I am ready to kiss another guy, especially as Logan is staring daggers into the side of my head. Also, I am only just recovering from the last kiss.

"You are on!" Darius replied and turned to face me.

Oh, shit! He lifted his hand to cup my cheek as he inched his way towards me. I froze.

"STOP! The DJ is here. Everyone, move!" I heard a deafening voice shout, making everyone jump out of their skin.

Logan bounded up from the sofa and pulled Darius off the floor and out of the room whilst everyone made way for the man struggling to carry all his gear through the door.

Phew! I breathed a sigh of relief. Darius is gorgeous, but I don't see him in that way. So that saved me from an awkward situation.

An hour or so later and the party was in full swing. More guests had arrived and the living room was now a sea full of bodies grinding on each other to the techno beat blaring from the DJ booth. I was dancing with Chloe and enjoying the music. I have never felt so free. At one point, I had a little steamy dance with Madeline that I giggled my way through. She really was some woman. I admire her infectious zest for life and natural voluptuousness. She could command the whole room's attention without saying a word.

I was starting to really feel the effects of the alcohol I had consumed, so I gave in to the music, swayed my hips to the rhythm and closed my eyes without a care in the world.

My eyes snapped open when I felt sparks erupt on my hips. A pair of firm hands clutched my waist and he started to grind up against me.

What on earth was he doing?

Chapter 9

Logan's POV

What did Maddy think she was doing? I knew this game was just a way of trying to get a reaction out of me. Like I said, she can be very childish sometimes.

"How many people have you slept with?" she boldly asked. I could feel Alina's nerves and hear her heart starting to speed up in her chest.

"One," she replied.

Fuck! She's only slept with one person. She was so innocent. But even the thought of her being touched by another had me seething with jealousy.

"One time or one person?" Maddy continued to question.

"One person," she said with more confidence. "Lots of times."

I couldn't help but let out a deep growl at that. I wanted to be the only one to worship her body, give her pleasure, and have her screaming my name. No one else.

I need to get a grip! I would not accept her as my mate, so I need to stop thinking like that.

Elias growled inside my head.

By the time I had composed myself and my wolf, it was her turn again.

How did that happen?

This time, she said dare! My heart dropped knowing Darius was going to pick it.

"I dare you to kiss a girl."

I gripped the sofa tightly. It's okay. It's not like it's a dude. But what I saw play out before my very eyes had me glued to my seat. Madeline had crawled towards her and started to kiss her very sensually. What surprised me the most was when I saw Alina start to kiss her back. So many emotions hit me all at once.

Anger. Jealousy. Desire.

Yes, my body had let me down as I felt my manhood straining against my stiff jeans. Watching how Alina kissed was making me burn with raw want and need, but also envy that her lips weren't on mine. Finally, they broke away and the room erupted in whistles and cheers. Darius shouted something about how hot it was. He was really getting on my last nerve tonight.

"Right, your turn, Darius," Alina's sweet voice said, trying to move the game on.

"Oh, dare!" His eyes sparkled with mischief.

"Okay, kiss the person you find the most attractive." Alina's friend said whilst staring at her.

Oh, fuck, no. It was one thing having to watch her kiss a girl, but I was not about to sit back and let my aggravating cousin put his dirty hands and lips on her.

As Darius leaned in, I was seconds away from wrestling him to the ground and beating him to a pulp, when the DJ stumbled through the door with his decks and equipment. Perfect timing.

"STOP! The DJ is here. Everyone, move!" I bellowed whilst cutting through the circle and hauling Darius up by his arm. With one quick movement, I tossed him like a rag doll into the kitchen and glared at him. He was a big guy, but luckily, I have Alpha blood running through my body, which gave me immense strength.

"Stay away from her," I demanded.

"Who?" he asked, his eyebrows furrowed in confusion.

"Alina."

"What? Why? What has she got to do with you?"

I was starting to lose my patience.

"As your Alpha, I am commanding you to stay away from her." I hated using my Alpha dominance against other wolves but I was about to lose control.

Darius reluctantly bared his neck in submission before leaving the room.

The party was in full swing and I tried to stay away from as many people as possible by standing against the living room wall radiating 'don't mess with me' vibes. I kept an eye on Alina from my position and watched her dancing with her friend. Any males that came too close to her were met with a fierce, unrelenting glare from me until they backed away. Maddy, on the other hand, was doing everything in her power to get my attention. After inappropriately dancing with Alina for a few songs, she sashayed her way over to me with a flirtatious look.

"Darling, why are you standing over here all alone? Come and dance with me."

"No, thanks."

"Okay. Well, if you don't want to dance with me, then maybe you want to dance with Alina?"

I studied her to see if she was joking but she looked dead serious.

"What? Why would I do that?"

"Because it might make you realise what fun she is." She

fluttered her eyelashes. It was hard to believe that my girlfriend was giving me the green light to dance with a woman that was driving me insane and making my heart race at the sight of her hips swaying with the music. But of course, Maddy wasn't to know any of that. I should refuse. Walk away. But every fibre of my being wanted to feel Alina in my arms, even if it was only for one night. For one song. It would be my closure before I had to do the unthinkable and reject her, leaving her forever.

My wolf whimpered at my thoughts.

The next thing I knew, I was standing behind her on the dance floor. I reached out and gripped her hips, pulling her ass back against my crotch and started to sway. She went rigid at my touch and for a split second, I thought she was going to walk away. But she didn't. She leaned her head back against my chest and covered my hands with her own.

The sparks from our contact travelled through my body, making me moan aloud. Fortunately, the volume of the music drowned it out. She pushed her backside into me more, rotating her hips as we started to grind and I swear I nearly exploded right then and there.

I lowered my head to her neck once more and breathed in her intoxicating scent. I let my lips hover over the crook of her neck, where I would mark her if the circumstances were different, and kissed it gently.

She shuddered and let out the most erotic sigh. I tightened my grip around her waist and started to move more vigorously. I could feel Elias itching to get to the surface and my restraint slipping. I abruptly let go of her and dashed out of the flat like wildfire. I headed for the woods and burst into a flurry of black fur and ran.

Alina's POV

Like in the bathroom, one minute he was there making me feel more alive than I have ever felt in my life and the next, he had disappeared. My body felt cold from the sudden loss of contact.

I stumbled my way through the crowd to look for him and get some answers about his baffling behaviour towards me. My head was spinning and I needed to get away from it all. I wandered down the hallway until I came to the last door at the end. I pushed it open and found myself in a bedroom. The walls were midnight blue and there was a black velvet bed in the centre. This must be their room.

Guilt flooded through me as I realised how close I came to overstepping with someone else's boyfriend. What was I doing here? This wasn't me. He had a girlfriend. An amazing and beautiful girlfriend. I was just embarrassing myself.

I went to leave, but a huge mural on the wall caught my attention. It was an image of a black, lone wolf's face and it had sapphire eyes. Behind it was a full moon and a shimmery, purple night sky. Something about the wolf's eyes spoke to me as if they knew me. They were full of sorrow.

I continued to get lost in the mesmerising painting and didn't hear anyone approaching from behind.

"Beautiful, isn't it? Logan painted it." Her voice spoke with love and admiration.

I turned to see Madeline staring up at the painting, too. Wow, he actually painted this! That's impressive.

"It's magnificent. He is very talented," I agreed.

"Come. Sit with me," she said whilst perching on the edge of the king-sized bed and patting the duvet.

Cautiously, I walked over, feeling very uncomfortable that I had been caught in their room. "I'm sorry. I didn't mean to come in here. I wasn't snooping around, I promise. I was just feeling a little overwhelmed and needed a few minutes to myself," I explained.

"No problem, hun. I get it. My crowd can be a little intense at times." She smiled whilst I fiddled with my hands resting on my lap.

"Tell me, and you can be brutally honest. What do you think of Logan?"

My face snapped up to hers. "Umm… er… He seems nice," I hesitated, not expecting the question.

She chuckled. "Now, didn't I just ask for brutal honesty?"

"Well, I haven't really spoken to him all that much."

She nodded.

"He is very attractive, but of course, you already know that… He seems a bit uptight, though. Stressed maybe? And intense. To be honest, a bit of an asshole." The last bit slipped out before I could stop myself.

Madeline burst out in hysterics and fell backwards onto the bed. A giggle bubbled to the surface and then I found myself led down, laughing with her, too.

"You got him spot on!" she said in between laughs. "He has been very stressed recently. He has a lot to deal with." She suddenly seemed sad. Leaning up on her elbows, she faced me and her grey eyes searched mine. "Which is why I wanted to ask for your help with something."

I was confused. What could I possibly do for her?

"Logan and I have always had an adventurous sex life," she began. I couldn't ignore the knot that formed in my stomach at her words. "And when he is feeling out of sorts, I like to treat him to something new. Alina, did you like our kiss earlier?" She fluttered her eyelashes at me. Was she flirting with me?

"Um, yes. It was… different."

"Different is good. I'd like to do it again and maybe give you pleasure in other ways as well, but in private… in here," she said coyly.

Er, what? First Logan and now her? What was going on?

When I didn't respond, she continued.

"Alina, I am not gay but I know how to please my man. I would like to put on a show for him with you."

Suddenly, everything fell into place.

"You want me to have a threesome with you and Logan?" My voice came out a lot higher than usual.

"Well, technically not. I want us to do sexual things in front of Logan. He will watch and take pleasure from it. He may decide to join us, but that will be up to him."

I gulped, trying to take in all this information. Is this what the whole night had been about? The bathroom, truth or dare, the dancing. It was all foreplay for them and I was their sex toy.

Madeline could clearly see the panic on my face. "Alina, you don't have to do anything you don't want to. Logan doesn't even know I am having this conversation with you. It's a surprise for him."

That confused me. Why has he been acting so strangely to me all night then? I could tell Madeline was really up for this by the eager look she was giving me. I am not so sure Logan would be, though.

"Um… What if he doesn't want me to?" I couldn't hide my insecurity.

"Oh, darling, he does. I can tell by the way he has been looking at you tonight. Don't worry, I am not angry. That's how I knew you were the right one to ask. He only seemed hesitant as he thinks you are too pure and innocent to do it."

I felt fresh anger rise in me. Is that what he thinks?

"WHAT are you doing in here?" His voice boomed into the room.

Madeline and I both jumped and sat up from the bed to see Logan in a pair of shorts, completely shirtless with sweat dripping down his torso. How strange. When did he change? His chest was covered in tattoos that ran down the lengths of his arms and he had the most defined six-pack I had ever seen that ended with a deep V disappearing into his shorts. He was a god.

"Logan, come and sit down." Madeline gestured to the back-winged chair in the corner of the room. "Alina and I were just getting to know each other better, isn't that right?" she said with a sultry voice whilst moving my hair away from my neck. All I could do was nod.

Logan didn't move a muscle but continued to stare.

Madeline leaned in and started running small kisses up my neck. Logan's eyes were fixed on mine and turned completely black when I parted my lips.

"No!" he roared. "Madeline, I told you, no!"

I instinctively cowered at his outburst. Why? Wasn't I good enough? They had clearly done this before, so why not with me?

"Logan, stop being a party pooper. Just sit back and enjoy the show." She smiled sweetly. "Or you can join us if you prefer." With that, she tilted my chin up towards her and her eyes were seeking my permission to continue.

I nodded once and closed my eyes. I felt her soft lips on mine and then she slowly pushed me down onto the mattress. The adrenaline was coursing through my body. Was I really going to do this?

'Why the hell not?' a small voice whispered in the back of my head.

In a flash, I could no longer feel the warmth of her body on top of mine. I opened my eyes to see Logan holding her by the throat. Her eyes were wide with horror and her face was starting to turn red as she struggled against him. I leapt up and ran towards them.

"Let her go!" I screamed. "You're hurting her!" I grabbed his arm and tried with all my might to force him off, ignoring the electricity between us, but he was relentless.

"LOGAN!" I cried in desperation.

He turned his head and looked at me and his face softened slightly.

"Please, Logan, let her go." I whimpered.

To my surprise, he loosened his grip on her throat. She dropped to the floor like a pile of rags.

Madeline wheezed and gasped for air. I immediately bent down to check that she was okay, but stopped when she gave me a shocked look that then turned into pure hatred. I started to shake with fear.

"GO!" she yelled.

I blinked at her, not understanding.

"Get the fuck out of here before I rip your head from your body!" Her eyes turned black like Logan's.

I stumbled to my feet and ran out of the room. I needed to get out of here and away from these people... No. They were not people, they were monsters!

I reached the front door and heard Darius behind me.

"Hey! Hey, Alina! What's wrong? Where are you going?"

"Please, just leave me alone," I said, putting my hands up to stop him from coming any closer. "I need to be alone." He paused and let me go as I ran out into the night. The cold air lashed my face as a sob escaped my lips.

"Alina, what happened? Are you okay?" Chloe came running outside.

I fell into her arms whilst I cried uncontrollably. "I want to go home," I managed to say between sobs.

"Okay, sweetie. I've already called an Uber. It should be here any minute."

A few seconds later, the taxi pulled up at the curb. I dived in and the car pulled away just as I saw a dishevelled looking Logan running down the concrete steps. He watched as I drove away with a broken expression and ran his hand through his hair.

I turned away from the back window and faced forward. I took a deep, shaky breath. I am safe now. Far away from them and I would never have to see him again. Relief flooded me, but at the same time, I couldn't ignore the stabbing pain in my heart.

Chapter 10

Logan's POV

I was shaking uncontrollably as I glared down at Madeline on the floor.

Watching her seduce Alina made me beyond mad. But it was seeing the uncertainty on Alina's face and hearing the fear in her rapid pulse that broke me. Before I knew what was happening, Elias was sharing control with me, and I had Madeline's throat in my hand.

Her eyes widened in shock and hurt at my actions. I had never lifted a finger towards her before and we had only ever been rough during sex. Not like this.

As I felt Madeline's oesophagus closing, she meant nothing to me at that moment. Elias urged me to rip open her throat for touching our mate. It was Alina's touch and hearing my name leave her lips for the first time that brought me back to my senses. When I looked into her pleading eyes, they were full of fear and distrust. It tore me apart and I released my grip on Madeline's neck instantly. But it was too late. From the look on Madeline's face, she knew. She screamed at Alina to get out of the room as her wolf, Nina, fought for dominance. Alina ran from the room, petrified. My instincts kicked in and I went to follow her to check if she was okay but Maddy pulled me back and shoved me against the wall.

"What the fuck was that?" she screeched, her eyes black pits of despair.

"Maddy, I can't do this right now. I will explain everything later. I'm sorry, but I have to go."

"After her? You don't get to strangle me and run after that human slut Logan. Who is she to you?" she screamed whilst hitting my chest. "SAY IT!"

I stood still letting her unleash her anger on my body. When she finally stopped, she looked up at me through tear-stained eyes.

"She's my mate," I said carefully. "Alina is my destined mate."

She slid down to the floor on her knees, sobbing and clutching her chest. I hated seeing her like this and knowing I had caused her pain, but right now, I needed to find Alina. By now, she will know we are not human, and she will be terrified and unsure of everything.

"You will reject her, right?" I heard the tiny voice behind me as I left the room.

I hardly made it into the corridor before I was bulldozed by Darius.

"What did you do to Alina?" His nostrils were flaring as he gave me a menacing stare. Normally, I would put him in his place for challenging his Alpha, but I was more concerned about finding Alina right now.

"What? Darius, where is she?"

"She's gone! She left a few minutes ago. Couldn't get out of here fast enough and she was really messed up," he said, pointing to the open front door.

I raced out of the flat, taking three steps at a time down the stairs until I was outside the building. A few metres down the road, a black car was speeding away, and I could see her small, pale face peering back at me through the back window. I ran my hands through my hair, pulling strands in frustration. She was gone and it was all my fault.

"Alpha, what's going on?" Fredrik caught up to me.

I sighed. "Alina. The human in the green dress. She is my true mate."

Fredrik's face froze in shock before he quickly recovered himself. "Okay… and she ran away?" he asked.

"Yes. I fucked up big time. She knows we are not human, but I am not sure if she knows exactly what we are. Both Maddy and I lost our shit in front of her."

He nodded in understanding. "What do you need?" he asked, ever the loyal friend.

"Right now, I need to go after her and check that she is safe and okay. My wolf will not rest until I do. I need you to tell everyone that the party is over and to keep Maddy here. Do not let her leave the flat or speak to anyone else about this until I come back."

"No problem." He walked back into the building and threw me my leather jacket and bike helmet that was just inside the doorway.

I couldn't help but smile at his care. I'd forgotten I was still only wearing a pair of shorts from my unexpected run earlier. I chucked on the jacket and helmet but kept the visor up. I needed to be able to follow Alina's scent to find her. I pulled my Ducati motorbike out of the side street and sniffed the air around me.

Luckily, her scent lingered, and I was able to follow it easily. They must have had a window open in the taxi because, after around twenty minutes of driving, the scent grew stronger and then disappeared into a building. I pulled the bike over to the opposite side of the road and stood under a large oak tree. The street was deserted and all the lights were off in the houses, making it easy to stay hidden from plain sight.

On the second floor of a tall, white building, a light flicked on, and I saw Alina and Chloe enter what looked to be a living room. I watched as Chloe gave her a hug and went into a different room. Alina glided over to the kitchen and poured herself a glass of water. She drank a large amount and wiped her mouth with the back of her hand and wandered over to the window.

I quickly stepped back into the shadows. The last thing I wanted to do was creep her out even more. She seemed pensive as she stared down the road. Her beauty was out of this world. Even though her eyes were puffy from crying, she was still the most radiant woman I had ever laid eyes on.

As if she could sense someone watching her, she drew the curtains, blocking her from my view. I huffed and clambered back onto my bike before making a note of her address. I didn't know what my next move would be, but all I could be sure of was that her safety had become my main priority.

Now, to return home and face the music.

Unknown POV

The Alpha seemed a broken man as I watched him stare longingly at the young woman from the corner of the street. There was something about his tense demeanour that suggested he was anxious. After following this impressive man for the last few days, he had always seemed to be a threatening, well-respected and dominant character. It was almost a shame that he would be dead soon. But right now, he was having some kind of inner struggle. I had not seen this woman before either. He was normally being doted on by that blonde she-wolf he called his mate. But he had never looked at her the way he was admiring this human right now. She must be important to him. Master is sure to find this information very compelling indeed.

I lifted the polaroid camera and snapped a picture. Suddenly, the girl closed the curtains and Logan jumped back on his motorbike. I promptly shimmied away with a puff of black smoke before he could detect my presence.

Madeline's POV

How could I have been so stupid? All of the signs were right in front of me. She was his true mate, destined by the Moon Goddess. But why would a meek human girl be destined to an Alpha? The last remaining Alpha as well?!

Anger curled hot and unstoppable in my gut, like a blazing inferno that wanted to burn me from the inside out. I had no one to blame but myself. I was the one who invited her here and into our lives. I was the one that pushed her towards him, trying to make him want her when he was already trying so hard to resist her.

At least that gave me some hope. That if he felt the mate bond so strongly, he would have claimed her the moment he laid his eyes on her. But he hadn't. He wasn't interested. All night, he had been trying to keep his distance from her. But now he had gone to her because of my foolish actions. From the moment he left me, I have been a blubbering mess on our bedroom floor. I need to try to be optimistic right now. Maybe he had gone to reject her.

A soft knock on the door broke me from my spiralling thoughts. A mop of brown hair poked around the door. I couldn't help but feel the disappointment wash over me as Fredrik asked warmly, "Just checking how you are doing. Do you need anything?"

Most people were afraid of Fredrik based on first impressions. He was an intimidating guy with scars on his face and a stern expression that rarely lifted. But over the years, I had gotten to know that under that hard exterior was a big teddy bear.

I smiled sadly and shook my head. He nervously edged into the room and sat down next to me with his back against the bed.

"He has a mate, Fred," I whimpered as another sob escaped my lips.

"I know," is all he replied as he let me rest my head on his huge shoulder.

"I can't lose him. I won't let her take him from me."

"Logan cares for you and the future of his pack, Maddy. This is going to be very difficult for him, but just be patient. When you find your true mate, it can be very overwhelming." His voice strained as he tried to keep his own emotions at bay.

"What is it like?" I asked quietly. "To have a mate?"

I felt his body tense at my question. I know he didn't like talking about this after what happened to his own, but I needed to prepare myself.

"Its…" he began. "It's as if the universe made someone completely unique just for you. Their love warms your soul. They have the power to save you or destroy you. Without them, you feel like you cannot breathe, but when you're with them, you forget how to breathe."

As he spoke, my heart broke in two. Is this how Logan was feeling? Did I even stand a chance?

"Do you think he can reject her? Would you have rejected Iona if you had known how much pain her death would cause you?"

He sighed before speaking. "No. I could never have rejected Iona. When I found her, it was like I had found myself, the real me. I never wanted any form of eternity until I saw her. And then, when I lost her, I wanted to die, too. But loving her, for even the short time we had, was better than never loving her at all." A single tear slid down his cheek. "But Logan is not me. He has responsibilities. He has you. His decision will not be easy, but it will be the right one. Just allow him to grieve what he is about to lose, Maddy."

"Thank you," I muttered as I squeezed his arm. I prayed to the Goddess that she gives this man a second chance mate one day.

Suddenly, the bedroom door flung open and Logan looked down at us on the floor. Confusion etched on his face. Fredrik stood up abruptly and nodded at him before closing the door behind him.

We were frozen in time for a few minutes, neither one of us knowing what to say.

"I'm…"

"Are…"

We both started speaking at the same time and smiled wistfully. He took a step forward and sat down in front of me, attempting to cross his legs before giving up and stretching them out at either side of me. I couldn't help but smile at his goofiness. For a split second, it felt like we were Maddy and Logan again before all this craziness began. But just as quickly, the moment had gone, and he cleared his throat whilst running his hands through his hair like he always did when he was stressed.

"Maddy, I don't know what to say. I am so sorry that I hurt you. Something came over me and I snapped. I didn't mean to."

"I know, Logan," I interrupted. "It's okay. You lost control. I know it wasn't you doing that to me but the effect of the mate bond."

He met my eyes as I said 'mate bond' and I saw my pain reflected in his own. I took a slow and steady breath before I continued to say what needed to be said.

"This isn't your fault. Or mine. We always knew there was a

chance one of us would find our true mate. We had prepared for this," I said calmly as Logan rubbed his hands together on his lap, not making eye contact. "We have a duty towards our pack and those who are no longer with us to come together and destroy Lucius. Your father knew we would be strongest together and we must prove him right. She is merely a distraction from our end goal."

"DON'T YOU THINK I KNOW THAT?" Logan roared, standing up and pacing the room. "I understand what must be done, but I just need some time, Maddy. This is a mess. She is human and after that display, she will know that we are not!"

I hadn't even considered that. It is against our codes to expose ourselves to humans unless they are our mates and then we must turn them into one of us. The very few humans that know of the supernatural in this world have made a Blood Oath to protect our secrecy.

"I cannot just reject her without knowing what she saw or thinks she saw. We have to be sure she does not suspect us," he argued.

"Okay," I agreed. "But what if she knows? What then?"

He stopped pacing and looked at me with sorrowful eyes. "I don't know," he whispered.

I just nodded, pulling my knees into my chest.

"It's been a long night. Let's get some sleep," he said, lifting me up bridal style and lowering me onto the mattress before moving over to his side and climbing under the covers. "Goodnight Maddy," he said whilst kissing my forehead and rolling over.

"Goodnight Logan. I love you." I replied in a small voice, only to be met by an aching silence.

Chapter 11

Alina's POV

The pounding in my skull ebbed and flowed like a cold tide, yet the pain didn't disappear. I opened my eyes to a dimly lit room. Although I know it is daytime, no one has opened the thick curtains yet. My mouth feels dry, and I reach over to the coffee table to grab the glass of water. The thirst stayed after each slow gulp and waves of nausea added to my misery. How is it that we can put a man on the moon, but we cannot find a cure for a hangover yet?

"You know what the best cure for that is?" I heard Chloe's hoarse voice as she swayed into the kitchen pointing to what I can only presume is my delicate head in my hands.

"What?" I grumbled, not looking up.

"To stay drunk!" I heard her open the fridge and looked up to see her crack open a can of cider.

"Urgh! That is disgusting. The smell of that alone makes me want to puke."

She strolled over and pushes me upright so she can take a seat next to me on the sofa bed. "So?" she asked, raising her eyebrows as she took a sip from the can.

"So…"

"Are you going to enlighten me as to what the hell happened last night?"

When we arrived home, I'd told Chlo that I was okay, just a bit overwhelmed and that I would fill her in in the morning. When she was satisfied that nothing too awful had happened, she hugged me and went to bed. I am regretting that decision now.

"You wouldn't believe me if I tried." I sighed. How was I supposed to explain everything that happened last night without her thinking I'd had my drink spiked with some hallucinogenic drug or that I had completely lost my marbles?

"Oooh, now I have to know! Come on, try me." She pulled her legs up underneath her and turned to give me her undivided attention. All she needed now was a bucket of popcorn and she'd be good to go!

I started to relay the events of the night from the moment I laid eyes on Logan and the strange feelings I couldn't really describe, up to the point where I ran out of the flat in tears. I decided to leave out the details that led me to believe that these people were not humans, like the fact that they could change their eye colour. I didn't need her shipping me off to a psychiatric hospital just yet.

When I'd finally finished, Chloe's mouth hung open and she stared at me with utter disbelief. "So, wait a minute, you nearly had a threesome with Madeline and Logan?! You, lucky bitch!" she shrieked.

"Of course THAT is what you took from this," I grumbled.

"Sorry, I mean··· no··· well··· bloody hell!" It was a very rare sight to see Chloe struggle to form a coherent sentence. "So let me get this straight. Madeline invited you to the party to have a threesome with her and Logan, but Logan didn't know. But then Logan was coming on to you behind Madeline's back? But then he refused to have a threesome with you and her and went mental and tried to kill her?"

"Um, yeah. That pretty much sums it up," I said, slowly getting my balance to attempt to walk to the bathroom.

"Wow. That guy has clearly got some issues!" Chloe trotted along behind me.

"Yep. Crazy," I said, rotating my fingers on my head.

"So, were you actually going to go through with it? You know, the threesome?" she whispered the last bit like it was some dirty secret.

"I-I don't know. Maybe. I mean, a part of me wanted to try something new, but I don't think I really would have gone through with it even if Logan hadn't..."

"Turned into a psychopath?"

"Exactly. Right... Er, Chloe…"

"Yeah?"

"I love spending time with you, but can you leave me alone now so I can have a shower please?"

She suddenly realised she was standing in the bathroom whilst I was half naked. "Oh, yeah, sorry! I'll make us some breakfast. Then I want to hear all the juicy details."

"I've already told you all..." I heard the bathroom door slam shut, "the details."

This was going to be a long day. I decided I would head to the library to get some peace and quiet and study before my shift at work tonight.

After my shower, I felt one hundred times better and dressed myself in my favourite pair of jeans and an oversized grey hoody. Today was all about comfort.

I pulled my silky straightened hair into a high ponytail and added a touch of mascara. Opening the bathroom door, I immediately sensed there was someone else in the flat other than Chloe. As I turned the corner, I stopped dead when I saw that familiar auburn hair and dazzling smile lounging back on the sofa as if he owned the place.

"Nice place you have here, buttercup."

"Oh, it's mine actually. Alina is just staying with me until she..." Chloe started blabbering.

"Darius. What are you doing here?" I cut Chloe off before she gave him any more personal information.

"Well, good morning to you too, sunshine!"

I rolled my eyes at his chipper mood. Clearly, he was not suffering from a monstrous hangover like the rest of us.

"I came to return this to you." He held up my handbag containing my phone and keys. "Figured they might be useful to you and as you ran away so dramatically last night, I didn't get a chance to give it to you."

"Oh, thanks," I said, taking the bag from him and checking my phone.

"I saved my number in there for you, by the way. You're welcome." He winked.

I wasn't sure I had the energy for him this morning. I stood up and slipped on my trainers before grabbing my keys and laptop bag.

"Are we going somewhere?" he asked, standing up.

"I'm going to study. I don't know what your plans are," I replied, not bothering to keep the agitation out of my voice.

"But you haven't had any breakfast yet!" Chloe cried from the kitchen.

"Don't worry, Chlo, I will grab something on my way. Thanks." I opened the flat door and stepped out, only to be followed by Darius.

"I'll give you a ride," he said, smiling innocently.

"I'll walk, thanks. I could do with the fresh air this morning."

"Oh, good idea," he replied, almost skipping along next to me.

"Don't you have somewhere to be?" I asked.

"Nope. So why did you leave the party last night?"

"So how do you know where I live?" I played him at his own game.

"Touché. But really, are you okay?" He had suddenly turned serious and looked at me with concern.

"Yeah. I am now. I really don't want to talk about it though, if that's alright."

"Okay."

We walked along the busy streets of Piccadilly Circus filled with tourists taking pictures of all the iconic buildings and statues or picking up gifts from the novelty stores dotted along the roads. It was a warm morning but there was a light breezy drizzle starting as people walked with urgency to get to shelter before the downpour. That is the unpredictability of English weather. You can set out of the house armed with an umbrella and a raincoat after a peek at the weather forecast and return home without a drop of rain. But when you decide to leave your new pair of sunglasses and sandals, relying again on your trusty weather forecast, you will come home a drenched, sloppy mess from the sudden rainstorm that hit you. All kinds of weather in just one day. That's the charm of living in London. I have always had a love-hate relationship with my city.

On the one hand, it is breathtakingly beautiful. From its newness and oldness squashed together, the modern, glass buildings surrounded by historic cathedrals and the tiny Victorian houses next to towering apartment blocks. The beauty of the river walks, spacious and pristine parks in contrast with the bustling markets and wide roads crowded with shops, boutiques, pubs and restaurants. But the pace of life here is astonishingly fast. People are always on the move; looking for the next best thing or always in a hurry to get somewhere other than where they are. For such a place full of diverse and interesting people, it can sometimes feel like the loneliest place in the world.

Out of nowhere, a black crow swooped down in front of us to grab a half-eaten sandwich off the floor, causing me to leap into Darius' arms. He chuckled at my irrational fear and stood me upright. The black beady eyes of the bird blinked at me before it flew off again, reminding me of the animalistic eyes I saw last night on Logan and Madeline. I wasn't sure why, but I felt as though I could trust Darius and I wouldn't be judged for my crazy ideas.

"Darius, can people's eyes change colour?" I looked up at his side profile and he seemed surprised by the question.

"Um, well, yeah. I guess so. I mean some people are born with blue eyes and they turn brown, and some eyes can look different colours in different lights or seasons," he rattled on.

"No, I mean… can a person's eye colour change from blue to black when they are angry? Just an example." I peered at him again to study his reaction. He remained expressionless but I did notice his Adams apple vibrate as he gulped.

"Um, that's a strange question. Why do you ask?"

"No reason. I guess I am just starting to think there might be a lot more out there than we know about or can be explained."

He didn't say anything about that, but it didn't go unnoticed by me that he hadn't answered my question. We arrived at the library, and I turned to thank him for the company.

"What are you doing later?" he asked.

"I have work tonight at a bar in Soho."

"Oh, okay. What bar? I might swing by for a drink." He grinned.

"Goodbye, Darius." I rolled my eyes and waved, leaving him standing with his hands in his jeans pocket smiling like a playful puppy.

At least one good thing came out of last night, I thought to myself.

Chapter 12

Logan's POV

The atmosphere was tense as I stood against the wall in my living room trying to stare everywhere but at the others. Madeline was sitting on the sofa with Emma next to her, who she insisted come along to this meeting for moral support. Fredrik was perched on one of the bar stools in the corner of the room on his phone. We were all waiting for Darius before we could begin, but the silence was becoming unbearable.

I had sent Darius to check in on Alina this morning. I despised the fact that I had to ask him to go, but he was the only one Alina might trust right now. It also helped that she had forgotten her bag last night, so I had the perfect excuse to send him. Darius was only too keen to take it to her, which made me feel very uneasy. No one has said a word about last night and I know Darius and Emma will not be overjoyed to hear that Alina is my mate.

The repetitive, painful ticking of the clock on the wall was the only thing that could be heard. Where was he? He should be back by now. It was gone midday. I buried the jealousy that consumed me deep down inside.

"Who died?" his irritatingly happy voice finally broke the

awkward silence as he bounded into the room. He was in a good mood, and it bothered me, knowing it was likely because of Alina.

"Glad you could finally join us. Sit down," I said with a little too much hostility.

"Seriously, what's with all the doom and gloom?" he questioned, taking a seat in the armchair and looking at each one of us.

"I called you all here because we have some important matters to discuss." Madeline's eyes burned into me, and I hadn't even started to talk about Alina yet. "Yesterday, Fredrik met with a dark witch who said she had a vision about our future."

They all remained silent, so I continued. "She said Lucius is coming and that he knows we are in London."

Madeline, Emma, and Darius all started shouting at once, panic rising in the room.

"Enough!" I commanded, causing them all to quieten immediately. "If this is true, it is likely he is already nearby. We need to start making the preparations for our plan now, starting with a meeting of all the existing werewolves willing to fight with us."

"Can this witch even be trusted?" Darius asked.

I nodded over to Fredrik to respond.

"I do not know but what she told me seemed honest. She was quite··· a peculiar woman, but she did seem to have her own hatred against the Vampire King."

"It seems like he is bringing the fight to us, so we have two choices—run and hide again, buying us more time, or end this once and for all." I was giving everyone a choice. I wanted to be the kind of Alpha that led my people rather than dictated to them.

"I say we fight," Madeline surprisingly spoke first. She had a look of determination, and it warmed my heart to know she still had my back.

"I also want to stay and fight," Fredrik agreed.

"Oh, sod it! Let's kill this leech and all his minions," Darius bellowed.

"Emma?" I asked. She was the only one who was yet to speak and looked a little nervous as her eyes darted from me to the others.

"I am not going to lie, Alpha. I am scared… But if you think we are ready, then I am with you."

"It is agreed then, we will stay and get our plan into motion. Lucius is clever, he is likely already close and waiting to attack. The best thing we can do right now is to pretend we are unaware."

They all nodded.

"Fredrik, spread the word discreetly. We need all the existing wolves to meet in Ruislip Woods in one week from now. They must tell no one and come alone."

"On it, Alpha," Fredrik already had his phone out and was typing with purpose.

"So now that is settled, it brings me onto our second matter." I visibly saw Madeline tense at my words. "Last night, at the party, I found my destined mate."

Emma gasped and covered her mouth whilst glancing at Madeline, who didn't react. Darius frowned at me in confusion.

"Who?" he asked.

"Alina."

"WHAT?!" he roared, jumping from his chair.

"Sit down!" I growled with authority, clenching my fists. He slowly obeyed but I could feel the rage radiating from him. "It was a shock to me, too. To all of us." I glanced at Madeline. "But it has happened and at the worst possible time, I know."

"So, what does this mean?" Emma curiously asked, but I noticed her reach protectively over to hold Madeline's hand.

"You're going to reject her, right?"

"It is not as easy as that, Emma. Both Madeline and I nearly exposed our wolves to her last night. I am not sure if she knows what we are, but..."

"She knows," came Darius' voice. It was the first time he had managed to speak since his outburst.

"She knows what?" I asked cautiously.

"That you are not human. She asked me some weird questions this morning about whether human's eyes could change colour to black. She might not know you are a werewolf, but she definitely does not believe you are human."

"This is not good," Fredrik spoke up. "If she knows, you cannot reject her and leave her forever. She could expose us or dig deeper to uncover the truth herself."

"I know," I said, exasperated. "I have to tell her the truth and persuade her to sign a Blood Oath before I can reject her or..." I couldn't bear to say it.

"NO!" Darius yelled. "I will not allow you to turn her against her will and reject her! It could kill her!"

"What other choices does he have?" Madeline spoke softly but with conviction.

"Oh, I don't know. Perhaps he could be a decent person and leave her to continue with her life before we all came into it and messed it up! I am sure she will forget about you in time." Darius was starting to turn the same shade of red as his hair.

"You know we cannot risk that. Trust me, if there was any way to let her live her life without doing any of this to her then I would. But I can't do that without rejecting her."

"Logan will also start to become weaker the longer he is away from her now that their bond has been established. If he does not mark and mate with her or reject her soon, he will not be strong enough to fight Lucius when the time comes. If he rejects her after she has signed the Blood Oath, then he may regain his strength before we have to fight," Fredrik reasoned.

My heart felt like it was being squeezed in my chest at all this talk of rejecting Alina and Elias was snapping at me in my mind.

"Well, what the hell are we waiting for? The sooner we tell her and get her to sign the oath, the better!" Darius stood up again. The man could not keep still.

"I will go to her tonight," I said.

"Can't Darius tell her?" Madeline pleaded. She looked like a lost little girl right now and I felt for her.

"No, it has to be me. She will think this is all a prank if it comes from him."

Darius scoffed and folded his arms across his chest. "One problem. She is working tonight at some bar, so you can't go and see her."

"Then I will go to the bar," I snapped, pulling my phone out of my pocket and calling Jax. He was a professional private investigator for humans, but his talent as the best tracker of our kind gave him an edge.

"Alpha?" he answered after one ring.

"Jax, get me all the information you can on Alina Clarke, including which bar she works at."

"Right away, boss."

"I need it in one hour."

"No problem. I will email it over."

I hung up and slumped back in my chair in the bedroom. I could no longer stay in that room with them. I needed to mentally, emotionally, and physically prepare myself to see her again. It had only been a few hours since I last saw her beautiful face, but I was already feeling the effects of being away from her. She was all I could think about. Her green eyes. Her delicate lips. Her smooth skin. Her warming smell. I needed it like I needed air to breathe. If the mate bond was this intense already, I could only imagine what it would be like once marked and mated.

I sighed. I would never know. Once we reject each other, the bond will break, and we will no longer feel the profound pull towards each other. Does she feel it, too? I know as a human she would not feel it as powerfully as I do, but she must be feeling something for me.

'SHE DOES!' Elias spoke to me.

'How do you know?'

'I COULD SENSE HER LAST NIGHT. SHE WAS LOOKING OUT OF THE WINDOW AND THINKING OF US.'

'What? How do you know that, Elias?'

'I DON'T KNOW. SOMETHING IN HER WAS CONNECTING WITH ME.'

'You're not making any sense. How is that possible when she doesn't have a wolf?'

'I DO NOT KNOW. BUT IT IS TRUE.'

I huffed in frustration with this whole situation. Growing up, I had always envisioned my life with my destined mate by my side ruling our pack together. After my father's declaration, I was convinced he was right, and Madeline was my destined mate. She is a strong wolf and a wonderful person. She would make a great Luna, so I didn't think twice about making her my chosen mate. How naïve I had been to really believe that I could reject my true mate if she came along and someone as perfect as Alina as well. She reminded me of my mother in many ways. She had the same fiery spirit, but I could see there was a soft, vulnerable side to her as well. Telling her everything would be a risk, but deep down, I knew she would try to understand and do what was right. No matter the cost.

Chapter 13

Alina's POV

Three hours had managed to creep by since I had opened my laptop at an isolated table in the corner of the library. Honestly, I had all intentions of studying, but instead of researching Allport's Theory of Personality, I had read the same introductory sentences over and over. Images of Logan swarmed my mind. Memories from the night before had me feeling flustered as I recalled the depths of blue in his eyes, the curve of his lips, his torso dripping with sweat, the heat from his body as we danced, the tender kiss he had placed on my neck, the way he ran his fingers through his hair as I drove away. I guess you could say I was crushing pretty hard. It was strange. I don't remember ever feeling this way about Michael. I fancied him, of course, but not like this. This felt… different. All-consuming. But the bottom line was, he was taken. He could never be mine.

I kept replaying the conversation with Darius this morning. He wouldn't look at me when I asked about Logan's eyes. He seemed nervous and I can't imagine there is much that can make Darius nervous. He was hiding something. Something that I needed answers to. Well, I am in the best place to find them.

Walking through the aisles of books, I wasn't sure what I was looking for exactly. The best place to start was in the human biology section, so I started flicking through books full of facts about the anatomy of the eye and its functions. But nothing was giving me any indication that human's eyes turning entirely black was a common occurrence. Just as I thought, this was something that could not be explained by science.

I continued to walk further down the aisles hoping something would just pop out at me. A sign saying 'Supernatural' sparked my interest. I ran my hand along the spines of many novels with titles about ghosts, witches, goblins, vampires, and werewolves. I lingered on the last section, remembering the mural on Logan's wall of the wolf's head. Pulling out the first book my finger loitered on, I took it back over to my table. It was a fiction book called *Moonlight Howls*.

I skimmed through the first few chapters about a young girl's hardship at home, until something caught my attention. A new boy starts at her school and she feels drawn to him, describing the intensity of her feelings as she stares into his captivating blue eyes. Just like Logan's. He seems just as taken with her and soon they are kissing passionately in the school bike shed. What a cliché! But it was when she pulls away, she sees that 'his eyes are as black as the night's sky.' What captures me even more is the way she describes tingling and sparks at their contact.

I slammed the book shut, my breathing increasing to match my anxiety. A laugh escapes me at the ludicrous thought. A werewolf? I am really losing my mind now. This is fiction. Make believe.

I started to pack up my things as I was starting to feel suffocated in this stuffy building. I needed some fresh air and I clearly wasn't going to get any work done today. Walking towards the front desk, I decided to check the book out anyway. I needed some light bedtime reading.

The Last Alpha

Knowing I had at least another six or so hours to kill until my shift at Lolita's started, I decided to take a nice stroll through St. James Park and grab some lunch from a cute pop-up deli at the corner. It was turning out to be a crisp, mild end of summer's day and the sun was making the occasional appearance from behind the fluffy clouds. I found a free wooden bench to sit on and people watch. My favourite pastime.

After a few minutes, a man who looked no older than thirty sat down at the other end of my bench. He was wearing a tailored grey suit that looked very expensive and he had slick-back black hair. I would have said he would pass as any other London businessman taking a quiet ten minutes for his lunch break but there was something odd about him that had me on edge. He must have caught me staring at him because he turned to face me and gave me a broad smile. It sent a shiver down my spine. His smile wasn't friendly but sly, as if he knew my deepest and darkest secrets. His skin was deathly pale, almost the colour of marble. I gave him a small smile back as not to be rude and returned to staring out across the park.

"Glorious day, wouldn't you say so?" His icy tone did not match his words.

"Hmm. Oh, yes. It is," I replied politely. Not wanting to wait until he said anything else, I rushed to pick up my belongings and walked away.

"Have a lovely day, Miss. Stay safe," He said flatly as I passed him.

I smiled again briefly and made my way across the street. Everything about that man creeped me out.

Taking my time, I made my way back to Piccadilly Circus to hop on the tube over to Oxford Street to do some window shopping. I love browsing the tastefully designed shop windows, not so much for the clothes, but because I love the story they told. Every window was lit up with its very own canvas of life. Christmas in London was the most magical time for this as the whole street would be a window wonderland!

I stumbled upon a chic hair salon that I had never noticed before. Ordinarily, I wouldn't dream of using their services as they cost an arm and a leg, but I really needed a good haircut and after a breakup everyone needs a new look, right? It's like a rite of passage. I'm sure they wouldn't take strays off the street anyway, but there was no harm in asking.

"Hello and welcome to Diamond Blue Salon. How may I help you today?" the pretty receptionist asked with a smile that didn't quite reach her eyes.

"Hello, I know it is a long shot but I just wondered if you have any availability for a cut and blow dry, please?"

"Of course. When were you thinking?"

"Actually, now, if possible. Please don't worry if you can't, though," I quickly added.

She tapped a few buttons on her screen. "You are in luck, lovely. We just had a cancellation today. You can go and take a seat over there and Clarice will be right with you. Would you like tea or coffee?"

"Oh, that's great, thank you! Coffee please," I said as I pulled my hoody up over my head and made myself comfortable. It had been so long since I'd been in a salon, I was rather excited.

A short woman with fiery hair styled in a short, graduated bob comes gliding over and put an apron around my neck.

"Hello, dear. My name is Clarice and I will be your hairdresser today. Tell me, what are we going for?" she said, pulling out my locks from the high ponytail and fanning them around my shoulders.

"Oh, nothing drastic. Just a cut and a style please. As you can

The Last Alpha

see, it's quite long."

"Okay, no problem, dear. How much do you want off?" She held up strands of my hair and used her fingers to measure.

"Just a few inches. Maybe just halfway down my back," I suggested.

"Great idea. It will draw more attention to those babies then." She winked indicating to my breasts that were practically spilling out of my too small strappy top.

I felt my cheeks flame at her remark and gave a nervous giggle.

"So, a gorgeous girl like you must have a boyfriend." Ah, the salon talk. How is it that hairdressers possess the secret power of being able to find out everything about you without you knowing more than their name?

"No, actually I don't. I am single. Very single," I muttered.

"Oh, no. I know that face. He broke your heart, didn't he?" she said as she set about brushing my hair. For some reason, Logan was the first person who came to mind and then I realised I should have been thinking about Michael.

"Yeah, caught him in bed with a Starbucks waitress who had actually served me my coffee that very morning."

"Oh, you poor thing! Well, we had best make this the best haircut you've ever had and make him wish he had never let you go!"

I smiled at her warmly as she picked up the scissors. After a few hours, I had managed to tell Clarise my life story, including the Logan and Madeline saga (sparing her the weird supernatural thing). It felt good to talk to someone older and wiser and, at that moment, I really missed my mum.

"My advice to you, dear, is to always listen to your gut! Everyone tells you to listen to your heart or listen to your head, but I say your gut is never wrong. If your gut feeling is that this Logan guy

The Last Alpha

is the one for you, listen! If it says run for the hills, do that, too!" We laughed together. "It's all done! Go knock 'em dead!"

My hair was exactly how I wanted it. She had taken a few inches off the bottom, so it looked much healthier and she added a few layers to 'frame my face'. She had also blow dried it and curled the ends, giving it a glamorous finish. I thanked her and paid the extravagant price, but it was worth every penny.

The sun was starting to set as I jumped on the tube back to Chloe's. I checked my phone and saw I had a message from Darius.

Hey, buttercup, I stole your number, too. p *Hope you had fun at the library, you nerd. Stay safe tonight.* D x

I smiled, placing my phone back in my bag.

"Chlo, I'm home." I shouted as I entered the flat, throwing my belongings onto the dining table. I checked my watch and calculated I had roughly one hour to get ready and get to Lolita's before my shift started. I couldn't be late as I had already called in sick twice the past week when I was a heartbroken zombie.

Chloe appeared from her room wearing a dress and some heels. "Lina, your hair! I love it. It really suits you. Where did you get it done?"

"Thank you. Oh, some salon on Oxford Street. You look nice. Where are you going?"

"I have a date," she squealed.

"Anyone I know?"

"No, I matched with him on Tinder."

"Okay, well, be safe. You know I always worry when you go on these blind dates."

"They are not blind dates! I know what they look like, silly."

I raised my eyebrows at her. She could be too trusting sometimes.

"I'm jumping in the shower quickly before work. If you're gone before I get out, please be careful and text me when you are on your way home or I will worry."

"Yes, mum," she called back.

My shower turned out to be a little steamier than usual as unprovoked thoughts of Logan filled my mind again. It was like he had awoken some passionate, sexual side of me that needed to be fulfilled and touching myself in the shower did nothing to relieve it. I climbed out and dressed in my bar clothes. I hated the uniform, but we all had to wear one. We had tight PVC leather looking leggings that could have been from a sex shop to be honest, and a black V-neck crop top with 'Lolita's' written across it in red. Sean, my boss, suggested I wear a push-up bra because it would get me bigger tips when I got the job. He is such a sleaze! The work itself is fine, nothing to write home about. Mostly, I just pour drunk people's drinks to make them drunker and then have to swat away unwanted advances from strangers who can't string a sentence together. But it pays well and I needed the money. Luckily, I didn't have to do anything to my hair as Clarice had worked wonders, so I just applied some mascara, blusher, and lip gloss.

As I entered the club, the vile, potent smell of stale alcohol and sweat invaded my senses. I walked behind the bar and started cleaning the sticky tops. I was early and the bar was yet to open to the public. Sean came out of the side door carrying a tray of clean glasses.

"Ah, Alina. Nice to have you back. I'm guessing you're feeling much better?" He eyed me suspiciously.

"Yes, much. Thank you." I smiled sweetly.

"Good because we are in for a busy night tonight. A drag show is playing down the road and will attract lots of lively punters."

"No problem," I said whilst stacking the clean glasses on the shelves behind the bar.

The Last Alpha

"So, you're going to man the main bar with Tiff and Zack. If it gets too busy, well just deal with it, okay, sweet cheeks?"

I smiled and nodded. I quickly learnt that was the best way forward in this job. Just then, Tiffany and Zack came in giggling and canoodling. I see they finally told each other how they felt whilst I was gone.

"Oh, hey girl," Tiffany called when she spotted me. "How are you holding up?" We had a few mutual friends that I am sure would have told her all about Michael and I. I was pleased to see that she had kept it to herself and not told Sean the real reason I didn't make it into work this week.

"Yeah, I am great actually." That wasn't quite a lie. I was feeling much better about the breakup. In fact, since meeting Logan, it was like all my feelings for Michael had just vanished, good and bad. Even the pain from his betrayal was remarkably lessened.

"Well, if you need a minute tonight, like if it gets too much for you, just holla and we can take over," she said sincerely as Zack smiled from behind her shoulder.

"Thanks, but I am sure I will be fine." I gave them a knowing grin. I was pleased they were together. I had been rooting for them ever since Zack had made it embarrassingly obvious that he had a crush on Tiff as he turned into a beetroot every time she spoke to him directly.

A few hours into the night and Sean was right—the bar was packed. There was an electric buzz in the air and people were in great spirits. I only had to sternly redirect a few gentlemen's attentions elsewhere and I'd managed to earn some good tips. I made my way to the side of the bar to take the next order. Without looking up from the sink, I shouted over the music, "What can I get you?"

"Another chance."

My head snapped up to see the familiar face I had woken up to every day for three years.

"What are you doing here, Michael?" I asked, not bothering to keep the disdain out of my voice.

"Like I said, I want another chance. Please, Alina, I miss you."

"Order a drink or leave," I snapped.

"Okay. A Malibu and coke please, your favourite." He smirked as if he had won some brownie points for remembering. It was going to take a lot more than that to get back in my good books. I made him the drink and slid it across the bar to him. He handed me his money and grasped my hand tightly as I tried to take it.

"Can we talk? I will wait until you finish if I have to."

"I really have nothing to say to you, Michael," I said, snatching my hand away.

I carried on serving customers and ignoring him until I finally saw him get up and leave. Thank god.

"Lina, go and collect some glasses now, it's starting to die down a bit," Sean commanded over the music.

I grabbed a tray and made my way through the crowds to the tables that were stacked high with abandoned drinks and empty glasses. Just before I reached them, I felt a rough hand around my wrist and I spun, catching me off guard.

"Lina, please, can we talk now?" Michael pleaded. Urgh, I thought he had left.

"No, Michael. Can't you see that I am working?" I tried to pull away from him but his grasp on my wrist only tightened. Instead, he moved closer to me and forced me into his body, snaking his arm around my waist. That was when I smelled the whiskey on his breath and realised he was quite intoxicated.

"Please… I am nothing without you. Come back to me. I miss

you. Don't you miss me?" he spoke into my ear whilst I struggled to get free.

"No, Michael. Get off me!" I was shouting now, trying to lean back by pushing on his chest.

"Come on, baby," he coaxed.

"SHE SAID NO!" came a powerful voice behind us.

We both whipped around to see a threatening man wearing black jeans and a white shirt that clung to his muscles. He emitted authority as all 6' 2" of him towered over us aggressively.

Logan. He had a murderous expression and he was clenching and unclenching his jaw.

My heart did a somersault in my chest. What was he doing here?

"Stay out of this, man. This has nothing to do with you." Michael didn't back down. He was either feeling brave from the alcohol or had a death wish because it was clear to see Logan was three times the size of him and very angry.

"Actually she has everything to do with me." His words made my core heat up with unexpected pleasure. "I will ask you nicely to remove your hands from her before I do something that will cause you a lot of pain," Logan said calmly but full of dominance.

"Who is this guy?" Michael looked at me thinking I owed him an explanation, but I couldn't answer. I didn't have a clue what to say.

The next few seconds were a blur. One moment, we were all standing there glaring at each other and the next, I heard a loud crunching noise and Michael was rolling around on the floor in agony with blood spurting out of his broken nose and I was slung over Logan's shoulder being marched out the bar.

"PUT ME DOWN!" I yelled, thumping his broad back with my fists.

He continued to walk down the dimly lit road, unfazed. When we reached a very fast looking motorbike, he dropped me down and threw a helmet at me.

"Put it on," he ordered whilst putting his own helmet on.

"I am not going anywhere with you! You can't just storm into my place of work, beat the crap out of Michael and then carry me out like it never happened! What is wrong with you?" I screamed, chucking the helmet back at him. I had lost all control over my emotions now and the fact that he continued to stand there, staring, only annoyed me more. "Who do you think you are? Why are you even here? You have a girlfriend and you tried to chuck me out of your party and refused to have a threesome with me and now you've turned up here and made a massive scene and demanded I get on your bike? So, you can do what, exactly? Take me for a romantic drive around London before you realise that I am not good enough again and cast me away like I am nothing?! I am not playing these games with you anymore, Logan."

I knew I was on the verge of hysterics, but I couldn't help myself. I was panting heavily after my temper tantrum and waited for him to react, but he didn't. He passed me the helmet again and carefully said, "Put it on. Please."

We stared at each other for a few intense seconds and then I lifted the helmet onto my head and climbed onto the back of his bike. He circled my arms around his stomach, and I breathed in that earthy scent mixed with sandalwood and instantly calmed down.

"Hold on," was the last thing I heard before his bike roared to life.

Chapter 14

Lucius' POV

"Baylor!"

"Yes, master?!"

"You have… satisfied me."

The newborn breathed a sigh of relief and his hunched shoulders visibly relaxed. Ever since I had turned him into a vampire two years ago, he had done my bidding without hesitation, or any questions asked. Unlike my disobedient successor. I knew Baylor would make a fine addition to my collection as he was very eager to join our kind.

When I met him in an underground Vamp club, he was a pathetic human allowing us to drink from him. He offered himself to me and I saw the admiration and awe present in his eyes. When I asked why he came to these places and offered himself up to such torture, he replied,

"You are the ultimate species. You are gods and I worship your very existence in this world. My world has never been kind to me and other humans have treated me like I am worthless, damaged, an outcast. I do not belong with them but with your kind as your loyal servant."

I knew at that moment that turning him into one of us would have more benefits than drinking him dry and I was right.

"I live only to serve you, my liege." He bowed respectfully.

"You were right about the girl. She is··· special and very important. You did well to alert me to the situation so promptly. Having this information means I can have a little fun with our wannabe Alpha before I slay him. As a reward, you can choose a treat." I indicated to one of my guards to bring in today's captives for Baylor to select and have his fun with.

Three naked human girls were dragged into the room by chains cuffed at their feet and hands. They stumbled in, all linked together with their heads down and hair cascading like waterfall covering their faces. Hearing their whimpers and cries of terror made me beam from ear to ear. It was my favourite sound. Their bodies were covered in smears of dried blood and dirt and their hair was a matted mess of straw and leaves. The fear that drove their hearts to pump their succulent blood through their veins at a rapid pace had all my men in the room's eyes turning red and licking their lips.

I turned and gestured to Baylor to take his pick.

"That one." He pointed at the pretty brunette girl in the middle. She must have been no older than twenty and her eyes widened in horror. I do not know the process my men go through to take these humans, but as long as it is done discreetly and they clear up their mess without any repercussions, I do not care.

I nodded at the guard who started to uncuff the girl from the others and watched as she begged for mercy. My guard ignored her futile pleas and pushed her in front of me. She fell to her knees before my throne and looked so helpless.

"Be a good little girl now and make sure you give my friend,

Baylor, everything he needs. If you please him, he will make sure your death is quick." I smirked.

"Please··· ple··· don't do this···. to me." Her voice quivered as she struggled to speak between her sobs.

"Baylor, she is boring me now. Hurry up and take her," I said with a dismissive flick of my hand.

Baylor sneered, baring his sharp fangs and grabbed the girl by the hair, dragging her away as she released a blood-curdling scream.

"You're a monster! You all are!" The braver one of the two remaining girls spat at me.

I chuckled at her courage before saying, "Oh, my dear, you have seen nothing of monsters yet. Take her to my quarters. I shall feast on her tonight. Until then, my love."

My guard pushed the girls out of the cellar door and I could hear the clanging of their chains slowly fading into the distance. Today turned out to be a rather exceptional day.

Baylor's name means the 'deliver of goods' and that he was. I picked up the polaroid pictures he had taken of the Alpha's human interest and studied her for a while. She was very alluring. She had an old-school elegance about her that reminded me of the beautiful women of the 1920s. She was sexy but in an unconventional way and clearly had no idea how attractive she was. I can see why this 'Alpha' is so taken with her.

But sitting next to her on that bench today left me baffled. I could not smell him on her, which means he had not imprinted, and my theory may not be correct. She might not be his mate. Surely, he would not be able to resist breeding with her if she was. Werewolves are just horny dogs on steroids at the end of the day.

The Last Alpha

I need to understand more about who she was to him. I thought that curvaceous blonde she-wolf he lived with was his mate. But when I realised she did not bare his mark, it made me question his intentions. I would have Baylor continue to follow him for a few more days. And the new girl. I am sure everything will be revealed soon.

KNOCK! KNOCK!

"Enter," I commanded.

"Father." Arius bowed before striding towards me. I did not bother to stand and greet my son. He did not deserve my good graces.

Yesterday, I caught him offering the human slaves a loaf of bread without my permission. He had felt the wrath of my anger with two hundred lashes upon his back and a night without feeding in the dungeons. He had always been spirited, just like his mother, but he was starting to test my patience with his direct disobedience.

Even after years of rigorous training and trials to prove his worth, he still insulted me by tending to a human's needs. He needed to learn that I was not to be stifled with and learn it fast.

"Have you learnt your lesson, son?"

"Yes, father." he bent his head lower to the ground.

"Excellent. I would hate to have to punish you more."

"I have learnt my lesson. I will not betray you again."

"Good boy. Now, tell me, Arius. What do you make of this?" I held up the polaroid of Logan staring pathetically up at the human in her bedroom window.

Arius furrowed his eyebrows in concentration. "I would say that he loves her," he replied.

My devious smile gave away my happiness at his answer. "I would have to agree with you."

The Last Alpha

"I do not understand what you are waiting for, father. After years of searching, you know where he is now. Why don't you just attack and put an end to this war and their species for good?"

"Because, my child, where is the fun in that? I want to watch him suffer. I want to take my time to slowly sabotage his life and take away everything that he loves and cares for. And then, I want to finally have him beg for my mercy before I rip his heart from his chest."

Arius looked at me with a blank expression. I never knew what he is thinking, it infuriates me.

"I am doing all of this for you, Arius. One day, you will be King, and you will be the most feared and formidable ruler of the supernatural world, thanks to your association with me. Together, we will make history and rid the world of those heinous beasts."

"Sorry, father, forgive my ignorance."

"Forgiven. Now leave me be." I dismissed him.

I think it is time to make that little Alpha sweat.

Chapter 15

Logan's POV

Riding with Alina on the back of my bike felt so natural and euphoric. She would squeeze me a little bit tighter whenever we turned a sharp bend and I fucking loved it. I took the scenic route back to her flat just to prolong the experience.

I slowed the bike until it came to a halt just outside her apartment and removed my helmet as I felt her slide off the back. I shook my head out of habit to reset my black curls and held my helmet in my lap. Balancing the bike expertly between my thick thighs, I rotated my torso slightly to face Alina standing on the curb. She was scrambling with the clip under her chin, cheeks starting to flush at her clumsiness.

"Here. Let me help you," I offered as I reached up and unlipped the clasp effortlessly and lifted the helmet off her head. Just that simple touch of her chin sent sparks tingling through my fingers. She ruffled her hair, trying to restore its volume.

"You've had your hair cut." I kicked myself at my obvious statement.

"Oh… er… yes. Do you like it?" Her cheeks flamed red and she looked down at the ground after clearly regretting her question.

I stretched out my arm to lift her head slowly until she met my eyes and said, "I didn't think you could be any more beautiful, but I was wrong."

She gulped at my confession as I tucked a strand of her hair behind her ear, then leaving my hand caressing her cheek. I know this goes against everything I was here to do but I just couldn't help it. She was stunning.

We stared at each other in silence for a few long seconds before she stepped back on the pavement, leaving my hand hanging in the air.

"Why are you here, Logan? What is this?" she asked in a small voice.

"We need to talk."

"What do we need to talk about?" Her face stayed guarded, but her eyes were searching mine, communicating their longing.

"I think you know. Look, Alina, I don't want to lie to you. Your life is about to get a lot more complicated," I said, trying to subtly warn her about what lies ahead.

"I think it already has." She looked so serious as the moonlight shone directly on her face, illuminating her undeniable beauty.

At that moment, all I wanted to do was lean in and gently kiss her tender lips. To taste her. But what she said next shocked me out of my fantasy.

"Do you want to come in?" She quickly looked over her shoulder at her apartment and then back at me. "I mean, only if you want to. You said we needed to talk and I am getting quite cold out here and Chloe is out, so we will be alone, but don't worry. I don't mean the way it sounds. Actually, forget I said anything," she nervously rambled, not stopping for a breath.

I knew being alone in her apartment together was a terrible idea, but the way she was so nervous made my heart melt and I would do anything to make her happy right now.

"Yes. Okay," I replied.

"Oh, okay. Um, right, it's just this one here," she said, pointing up to the white building that I was already well acquainted with.

I stood back as she fiddled with her keys and then pushed open the door to let me enter first.

"No, please. Ladies first," I encouraged.

She stepped through the door and switched on the light in the foyer. She started to walk the steps in front of us and I could not take my eyes off her ass in those leather leggings.

"So, how did you know where I work and live?" she questioned me, peering over her shoulder whilst I quickly tried to look anywhere else but at her peachy backside. I was momentarily stumped and quickly rattled my brain for a plausible lie.

"Oh, Darius," I said clearing my throat.

"But Darius doesn't know where I work," she continued.

"Er⋯ yeah. You told him this morning."

She looked perplexed as we reached the second floor.

"So, have you lived here long?" I said, trying to change the subject.

"No actually, this isn't my place. It's Chloe's." She shrugged whilst opening the front door to a small but cute living room with an open-plan kitchen. It wasn't to my taste, but it was all very modern and girly with a fake black fur rug on the floor. I internally chuckled at the irony of it. "I am just staying here until I ⋯ er⋯ get back on my feet," she finished. I raised my eyebrows at her turn of phrase.

"What do you mean 'get back on your feet'? What happened?" I know I was prying, but my curiosity about this woman was increasing with every second I spent with her.

She turned her back to me and walked over to the kitchen and took out two wine glasses from the cupboard. "Want one?" she asked.

I nodded and sat down on the grey corner sofa where I noticed a pillow and duvet folded neatly at the end.

"I guess you could say, I, um, had a tough year." That was all she expanded on. It tugged at my insides to hear she had been through something difficult. The mate bond was really doing a number on me.

She came back over to the living room carrying two glasses of white wine in her hands. She passed one to me and when our fingers grazed, she gasped quietly, but my wolf hearing picked it up.

Sitting with one foot under her bum and the other dangling off the sofa, she smiled awkwardly and took a sip of her drink. This was the most time we had ever spent together and I realised that I knew nothing about this woman in front of me.

"Will you tell me about it? Please?" I asked.

"Uh, well, it's not all that interesting really. I mean, I had a normal childhood, everything was great and then my dad just took off one day, out of the blue. He went to the shops and never came back. No explanation. It broke my mum completely. A few years later, we found out that she had cancer. Stage four. Sarcoma."

"I'm sorry," I interrupted as I saw the pain swirling in her eyes.

"It's okay. She was a fighter. She fought every day and tried so hard to hide the agony she was feeling from me. But I knew. I decided to put uni on hold for a while and get a full-time job to help pay for the bills and the house. But when she started to get worse, she needed constant care and I couldn't keep up with it all. The bills started piling up and she was still getting sicker." A lone tear dropped down her cheek onto her lap. "After she passed, I couldn't keep the house.

She had no life insurance and the mortgage was too much for me on my own. So I had to sell it. It was one of the hardest things I have ever had to do, leaving my childhood home full of so many memories."

The need to take away her suffering was almost unbearable. I reached out my hand instinctively and held hers on her lap. She looked down at our entwined fingers as I slowly rubbed my thumb in circles on her soft skin.

"Why does it feel like this?" she asked through sad eyes.

"Like what?" I asked, even though I knew exactly what she was referring to.

"Nothing." She swiftly moved her hand away from my grasp to pick up her wine glass from the coffee table. "Sorry. I haven't spoken about all of this for a while." She looked embarrassed or uncomfortable. I wasn't quite sure.

"Don't apologise. I know what it is like to have to leave a place you call home. You are a very brave person, Alina. I am sure your mother would be very proud of you."

She scoffed at that, which made my eyebrows lift in surprise. I hated that she dismissed herself.

"No she wouldn't."

"Why not?"

"Look at me, Logan. I'm barely surviving. I am juggling working to survive and studying at university, struggling to catch up with what I missed months ago, whilst also sleeping on my best friend's sofa because I couldn't satisfy my boyfriend or keep a roof over my head. I am a mess." She fiddled with the rim of her wine glass, avoiding eye contact. My heart had sped up ten notches hearing the word boyfriend leave her lips. Elias growled in my head.

"Boyfriend?" I asked gravelly. "Was he the guy at the bar?" Flashes of that man's hands all over her had rage and jealousy stirring inside me again. When I had first seen him harassing her, the protective instincts within me suddenly overpowered every emotion storming through my body. Breaking his nose was him getting off lightly.

She casually nodded her head but still would not look at me.

He was her boyfriend?!

"We broke up about a week ago. I found him cheating on me," she whispered.

WHAT? Why in any man's right mind would they cheat on someone like Alina? It filled me with rage to know he could do that to her after everything she had been through as well. I stood up from the sofa and started pacing the small living room trying to get my anger under control.

"Wish I'd done more than break his nose now. The cheating scumbag."

I stopped pacing when I heard the most angelic sound coming from Alina. She had her hand over her mouth and she was laughing. Her laugh was just like the rest of her—sweet and genuine. A slow smile spread across my face as the sound calmed me.

"What?" I asked, amused.

"I'm… sorry…I…, just…" She tried to speak in between her hysterics.

I started to chuckle myself. Her laughter was contagious. How can she make me feel like I am ready to murder someone to feeling giddy like a school kid in just a few seconds?

When she finally took a few deep breaths and calmed down, she tried to explain herself. "I'm sorry. I do that sometimes. You know, laugh at inappropriate situations. But seeing your giant hulk-like body pacing this tiny room just set me off." She smiled the most genuine and dazzling smile I'd ever seen.

"Well, I am glad I have entertained you. And hulk-like?" I laughed, sitting back on the sofa as she swatted my arm.

"So what is it you wanted to talk to me about?" She brought us back to the real reason I was here. I had been so captivated by her that I had completely forgotten about our situation and what needed to be done. This conversation felt so wrong right now and my heart felt heavy.

Suddenly, her phone pinged, breaking the silence. Alina picked it up and read the message with a frown.

"Everything alright?"

"Yeah, it's just Chloe. It looks like her date has gone well and she's going to be staying out for the night," she said with worry in her voice.

"She's a big girl. I am sure she knows what she is doing." I tried to reassure her.

"Yeah," was all she replied before we were catapulted back into silence.

The tension in the air increased as our eyes locked. The atmosphere had changed from easy and laid-back to tense and passionate. It was starting to feel dangerous being here alone. Need and desire filled the void between us and my entire body felt like a magnet being drawn to her. Our heads gradually leaned towards each other and I knew I had to stop this before I couldn't take it back. But the pull was so strong. My desire to feel her plump lips against mine was too much to bear. We were inches away now and her eyes fluttered shut, ready to accept me.

RINGGGGGG RINGGGGGG

We jumped apart at the sudden intrusion. She quickly climbed off the sofa towards the sound of her phone. She walked into the kitchen to give herself some privacy before taking the call.

FUCK! That was too close. What was I doing? I was here for a reason and it wasn't that, I tried to remind myself.

I looked over at Alina marching up and down the kitchen whilst answering the phone. I could tell by the way her demeanour changed that whoever she was talking to, she didn't like very much.

"What the fuck, Alina? Where the fuck are you? You best have a bloody good reason to have walked out of the middle of your shift without so much as an explanation. Well? I am waiting?"

I could hear a male voice bellowing through the headpiece. I didn't even need to use my wolf hearing to know how pissed this guy was and I hated the way he was speaking to her.

"Sean, I am so, so sorry. Something⋯ important came up. It won't happen again. I promise," she apologised and started to bite her nails.

"You bet it won't happen again. I should fire you for being so irresponsible and selfish."

"No, please, Sean. Please don't fire me. I really need this job," she begged. I could see the tears threatening to spill from her eyes.

I couldn't sit back any longer. I stalked across the room and grabbed the phone from her hands whilst she looked at me in shock.

"Hello," I said gruffly.

"Who is this?"

"Alina's boyfriend. I apologise for taking her from work so abruptly but we had a family emergency. I would kindly ask you not to raise your voice or threaten her right now as she is dealing with a lot. Show some compassion or I will not hesitate to not show you any. Goodbye." I ended the call before he could say anything and threw down the phone on the kitchen top.

"LOGAN!" she screamed in disbelief. "What did you do?!"

"I just saved you from losing your job, Alina. But I want you to quit working there anyway. That guy is a dick and he shouldn't talk to you like that," I said calmly even though I could see the anger threatening to explode in Alina with every word that left my mouth.

"You want me to quit? Who the hell do you think you are to tell me what to do? You don't control me! You are the reason I nearly got fired in the first place and now you are trying to act like the hero coming to my rescue. Well, listen up, Logan. I do not need rescuing and you are most certainly NOT my boyfriend!" she yelled.

"Well, it sure as hell looked like you needed rescuing from that asshole ex of yours earlier," I spat, my anger matching hers.

"I can handle my own shit, thank you very much. My life is none of your concern. In fact, I still don't know why you are even here! You still haven't told me. So why don't you go back to your actual girlfriend and leave me alone!" She pushed past me and in a manic moment I grabbed her arms, pushing her against the kitchen cupboards.

We were both breathing heavily and glaring at each other. It was taking everything in me not to kiss her forcefully and rip her clothes off so I could mark every inch of her body and take her on the kitchen island.

She broke my erotic thoughts when she growled, "Let go of me!" with so much venom, I physically recoiled, releasing her from my hold.

She pushed past me again and said, "I want you to leave."

I stayed rooted to the spot and made no attempt to move. Right then, at that moment, it hit me. I need her in my life. I wasn't sure if I would be able to let her go. I would take her in whatever way she would have me.

"Alina, please listen. There are some things you need to know," I started, trying to buy some time in the hope she would calm down and let me stay.

"I said, I want you to leave." She spoke through gritted teeth. I knew if I pushed her too hard right now, I could lose her forever.

I picked up her phone from the counter and saved my phone number in it and placed it back down. I walked carefully towards her until I was staring down into her mesmerising green eyes. "Text me when you are ready for the truth, Alina. I am not going anywhere."

It took everything I had to walk out of the door without looking back.

Chapter 16

Logan's POV

It had been two torturous days since I had last seen Alina at her apartment and her radio silence was infuriating. I knew her curiosity would get the better of her eventually, but she was clearly a stubborn woman. My feelings towards her had grown considerably since that night and I found myself unable to focus on anything for longer than a few minutes before my mind would drift back to thoughts of her. I found myself wondering what she was doing at that very moment or if she was thinking of me. Elias has been unbearable since I left her, constantly pestering me to go and see her.

The only time I feel any peace is at work. I've spent nearly every hour at my gym, training and fighting anyone who was daring enough to get in the ring with me. Even though the mass majority of my clients are humans, so I have to go easy on them, the thrill of the fight occupied my mind long enough for me to forget about her. At least for a few minutes.

The situation at home had become strained as well. Madeline kept saying I am avoiding her, which if I would be truly honest with myself, I am. I was not trying to distance myself from her on purpose, but right now, my feelings were so overwhelming and confusing that I don't even recognise myself. I don't want to hurt her, but I also don't want to give her hope because, truthfully, I didn't have a clue what was going on with me.

After escaping the flat before Madeline woke this morning, I found myself back at the gym. I was now sitting in my office out the back, which had a large blacked-out window overlooking the fighting rings so I could keep an eye on things whilst working. Sweat was trickling down my body after my recent fight with a new client, Daniel. He was turning out to have a natural ability in mixed martial arts and held his own for a good ten minutes against me. That was a new record. Marcus entered the office, throwing me a bottle of water as he sat down opposite me at his own desk.

"Thanks," I breathed, taking a swig to hydrate myself. Marcus was my business partner and one of the only humans that I trusted with my life. We met when I first signed up for his rundown gym as a customer after arriving in London a few years ago. We clicked instantly and soon became good friends and gym buddies. It was hard to watch as the business he had worked so hard to build and clearly had a passion for, was falling apart around him. After his divorce, he got himself into a financial crisis and was struggling to meet the payments of the lease, never mind making the necessary repairs to the place.

So, when I approached him with an idea about starting up MMA training classes with myself as the lead instructor, Marcus leapt at the chance to bring in new clientele. After a year, the gym was booming as word quickly spread about the intensity and success of my classes. It didn't just attract men but women as well who wanted to learn self-defence and I was only too happy to accommodate them. It wasn't quite the same as leading the training of a pack of wolves like I should be doing as an Alpha, but it was the closest thing I had to it.

It also kept me strong and fit. Marcus soon offered me fifty percent of the business, but I would only accept thirty and no more.

"That Daniel is picking it up quick," he observed whilst organising some papers on his desk.

"Yeah, he is. He is keen to train a few times a week and compete as well," I informed him.

"Excellent. Well, he gave you a run around, so he will definitely be an asset to the club." He smirked.

"Behave," I bantered back. "By the way, I might not be around as much next week. I have some other business to attend to." I gave him a knowing look. Marcus was one of the only humans that knew about us and had already signed a Blood Oath, but I wasn't about to drag him into the mess with the vampires. He didn't need to know the extent of my 'other business'.

"Gotcha! Just make sure Dom covers your sessions."

"Already taken care of."

My phone vibrated in my pocket and my heart fluttered when I saw it was a number I don't recognise. Could it be her? I opened the message:

Meet me at Primrose Café in Piccadilly Circus at 3pm. You are right. We need to talk. Alina

Relief flooded through me knowing that she was okay and had finally reached out, but I couldn't help but feel disappointed at the formal and hostile tone of the text. The last two days had given me plenty of time to prepare what I was going to say to her, but just the thought of seeing her in a few hours had my mind spinning. This was possibly the most important conversation of my life and I need it to go well.

Chapter 17

Alina's POV

I spotted him sitting at a corner table as I entered the picturesque terrace café that I often went to in between my lectures. It was one of my favourite spots in London with its delicate flowerpots decorating the outside patio and lilac ivy draping over the veranda. It felt like a little piece of the quaint countryside in the middle of a hectic city. I also picked it today because it was a public place, so I wouldn't need to worry about being alone with Logan again.

He sat with two coffees on the table in front of him and was engrossed in his phone, but as if sensing me approaching, he looked up. My breath hitched as I met his sparkling blue eyes. I couldn't deny that he looked delicious in a casual tracksuit bottom and a white V-neck T-shirt that left his tattooed arms exposed. Nerves started to set in as my feelings overwhelmed me, but I had to concentrate. I am here for answers.

After he left the apartment two days ago, I'd thrown myself into studying and university, barely leaving the library or Chloe's flat. I was trying so hard to distract myself from the anguish I felt at my resolve to never see him again. But when I got an unexpected envelope through the door this morning, my determination dissolved. I needed answers and he was the only one who could give them to me.

In the envelope was a couple of polaroid pictures. The first was of Logan standing on the road outside my house wearing only a pair of shorts and leather jacket. He was looking intensely up at Chloe's flat and I could just make out the silhouette of my body in the window. It must have been the same night as the party. The night we met.

The next was of Darius and I walking to the library the morning after, smiling and laughing. The third was the one that irked me the most. It was of me sitting on the bench in St. James' Park next to that creepy businessman. I was looking down at the ground uncomfortably and he was staring at me from the side. It made me shiver just looking at it.

There was also a smaller envelope inside that was addressed to Logan.

What the hell was this about? Was I being stalked? And why was the letter addressed to Logan and not me? I contemplated opening it even though it was not intended for my eyes. It felt wrong, but I couldn't help myself. I carefully unsealed the envelope, so it didn't rip, and pulled out a cream card with calligraphy writing on it.

Beautiful, isn't she? I am surprised at you, Logan. Not marking your mate. I am sure I could find some use for her if you don't want her? - Lucius.

Marking your mate? Who was Lucius? And what did he want with me? What did any of this mean?

All these questions and more from the last few days swirled around in my mind, which led me to this moment, standing in front of this confusing yet charming man once again.

"Hi," he said carefully and gestured for me to take a seat opposite him.

I sat down without saying anything and pulled my bag onto my lap, rummaging around inside it to find what I was looking for. I did not trust myself to look at him or speak yet, as I needed to make sure we got straight to the point.

"Thank you for asking to meet me. I wasn't sure if⋯" he started saying, but stopped when I placed the envelope on the table in front of him. Confusion laced his face. "What is this?" he asked, not making any attempt to open it.

"That is exactly what I would like to know. Open it," I said as calmly as I could.

He cautiously opened the envelope and took out the polaroids. His face drained of colour as he flicked through them again and again. Fury danced in his eyes as he hovered over the picture of me and the businessman.

"This is for you," I said, sliding the card across the table.

He picked it up and read it. He started to tremble and screwed up the card in his hand. "How did you get this?" he hissed.

"I-it was posted through my door this morning." My voice quivered with slight unease at his reaction.

He dropped the photos and twisted the card on the table and lowered his head to his hands.

"Logan, what is going on? You're worrying me. Am I being stalked? Why?"

He rubbed his hands up and down his face before speaking. "You are not safe, Alina. I am so sorry I got you into all of this. It is all my fault."

I blinked at him a few times, not comprehending. "Not safe? I don't understand, Logan. Got me into what?"

He took a deep breath. "I am not who you think I am, Alina. I am⋯ not human like you, but I think you already know that."

I gulped and nodded slowly. "I think I know what you are, but it's impossible."

His eyes bore into mine. "Nothing is impossible," he said flatly.

I removed the werewolf novel from my bag and placed it on the table. He picked it up and inspected the front cover and the back before a slow smile crept across his face and he raised his eyebrows at me over the book.

"I think you are one of them," I said nervously, not breaking his eye contact.

He leaned in and whispered, "And what is that?"

"A werewolf," I whispered back, the uncertainness evident in my voice.

He leaned back and put his hands behind his head in a relaxed and unthreatening way. "You are correct."

My eyes widened in shock even though a part of me already knew it, I just hadn't wanted to believe it. I continued to stare at him for the longest time, not knowing what to say. This had not answered any of my questions but just created more.

"Are you scared of me now, Alina?" he asked with so much concern etched on his face.

I wasn't scared of him at all. I feared what he was about to tell me, about the fact that this Lucius person was watching me but not him.

"No." I said confidently.

His body relaxed slightly. "Good. Because I would never intentionally hurt you, Alina. I promise."

"Okay." I hesitated.

"There is a lot more that I need to explain to you, but I can't here. There are too many humans. Can we go for a walk?"

I nodded and we stood up to leave as Logan left a £10 note on the table. We walked along the busy roads in a welcome silence. I was

The Last Alpha

grateful as my mind was still reeling from my discovery. So werewolves exist! And he is one of them.

We turned down a narrow side street and down some old, cobbled steps which led to a pleasant stream and riverbank walk. There were very few people around, just the odd dog walker or jogger.

"So, you were born a werewolf?" I need to start getting answers now.

"Yes, both my parents were pure-blooded werewolves. I was born into the pack called the Blood Moon Pack. We were the largest pack in America and my father and mother were the Alpha and Luna. The leaders." He clarified the last bit for me.

"Were?" I asked.

"Eight years ago, our pack was attacked by vampires and nearly all of them were murdered, including my family. Only a few hundred of us escaped."

"WAIT? Vampires? You're telling me that they are real, too?" I couldn't believe what I was hearing.

He chuckled a little. "Yes, and witches and warlocks and goblins and mermaids and…"

"NO FUCKING WAY!" I shouted; my feet rooted to the spot.

He turned when he realised I was no longer walking beside him!

"I love mermaids!"

He laughed and it was the most beautiful sound. I never wanted it to stop. "I don't think you would if you've met one. They are not the friendliest of creatures." He gestured to a spot on the river bank to sit. "I think its best you sit down for the rest of this conversation," he teased. He looked like he was almost enjoying this. "So, as I was saying, my pack was attacked, some of us escaped and went into hiding to protect ourselves. That's how we ended up here in London."

My brain registered 'us'. There were more of them?

"Madeline?" I questioned.

"Yes, and Darius. In fact, most of the people at our party that night were werewolves."

My mouth hung open. I already had my suspicions about Madeline, but Darius? I mean, physically he had a similar build to Logan, so I shouldn't be surprised, but he seemed so… normal.

"Somehow, the Vampire King has tracked us down and now we need to prepare to kill him so I can finally restore my pack and become my father's successor."

I honestly had no words at that point. It felt like I was listening to the plot of a new fantasy film.

"Lucius, the Vampire King who was behind all of the attacks on werewolves, is the one who sent you the pictures."

"But why? What do I have to do with any of this?" I cried.

He took a moment to compose himself before he spoke. Whatever he was about to say was hard for him.

"When I first saw you at the party, my heart knew who you were. When I looked into your eyes for the first time, it was like I was home. The pull we feel towards each other, the sparks on our skin from each touch is all because you are my fated mate, Alina." He turned his face, so he was looking directly into my eyes. The raw emotions that danced within them made them even more hypnotic.

"I-I don't understand. Your fated mate? What is that?"

"Werewolves believe that the Moon Goddess, who created our kind thousands of years ago, also creates a true soulmate for every wolf so they would never be alone. When a werewolf finds his true mate, they often mate and mark with them, creating the most unbreakable bond in existence. They can then never be separated, or it causes immeasurable pain and suffering to both parties." He looked away from me and out across the stream. "Some wolves do not accept their mates for different reasons and reject them, before the bond is cemented. Then both are free to continue their lives apart, but they will forever feel like half of their soul has been torn away."

Wow. This was overwhelming. I was Logan's mate. I was still trying to digest what that meant when another question entered my mind. "But I am human."

"Mmm, that is unfortunate but not uncommon. Most werewolves are mated together but some find mates in other species," he explained.

"Unfortunate?" I said, not able to hide the hurt I felt at his choice of word.

"I just mean that it's harder for humans. If they accept the werewolf as their mate, they will eventually turn into one once they are marked and mated."

"And by marked and mated, you mean…"

"Sex." He smirked at my innocence. I felt a blush forming on my cheeks at his boldness. "And marked means a special kind of bite. It seals the bond between them and makes their feelings more intense."

This was all so complex. For us humans, it's simple. Pick someone, date them, have sex, get married if you want… But all of this, it was a lot. I tried to get my head around my role in all of this.

"So, if I am your mate, would you mark and mate with me? And then I would turn into a werewolf?" I asked, shocked at how well I am taking this right now. I don't know how I feel about any of it but I just needed all the information.

"Well, it's a little more complicated than that for me." I detected a sadness in his answer. "Before I escaped my pack, my father told me that it was my responsibility to avenge our pack and restore it with Madeline as my Luna."

Suddenly, it felt like the world came crashing down around me as the realisation hit me that he didn't want me to be his mate. He wanted Madeline. She was a werewolf after all and an amazingly beautiful woman. She would make a great leader with her confidence and charisma. And she was already his girlfriend! How could I forget?

Logan took my silence as a need to clarify more. "Alina, Madeline and I chose to be each other's mates. We thought it would be best for the future of our pack and we promised that…" He seemed to be at war with himself as he took a few seconds to continue.

"We promised that if our true mates ever came along, we would… reject them."

For some reason, hearing the word 'reject' made my gut twist and bile rose to my throat. My breathing started to become erratic as my heart sped up. He was going to reject me. He had to. I was not made for his life. I was not what he needed.

"I understand," I whispered.

"What? What do you understand?" he asked softly.

"You're rejecting me and it's okay." I struggled to suppress the lump in my throat.

"No, Alina, let me finish. That was all before I met you." He was speaking so gently I could barely hear him.

I looked over at him and could see only pain and turmoil written all over his face. "What does that mean?" I said, shaking.

"It means that I don't know what to do," he said honestly. "But all I know right now is that I need to keep you safe. Lucius knows where you live and has been watching you. He knows you are my mate, so he knows that by getting to you, it will affect me. I can't risk that," he said sternly.

Of course. He couldn't be seen as weakened. He was an Alpha after all.

"So, what do we do?" I asked.

"You need to come back with me. You cannot stay at Chloe's anymore."

"No!" I shouted. "What about Chloe? I can't just leave her knowing there is a vampire out there!"

"Chloe will be safer if you leave. Lucius is only interested in you, not her. Once he realises you are no longer staying there, he will not return to the apartment and Chloe will be safe," he tried to reason with me.

"I can't just come home with you! Where will I live? Because I am not about to play happy families with you and Madeline. You are delusional if you think she is going to let me stay with you."

Logan frowned at me, realising I was right.

"Does Madeline even know about all of this? That I am your so-called 'mate'?" I said 'mate' with a roll of my eyes, earning a low growl from Logan. I must be upsetting his wolf, but right now, the frustration of my situation was infuriating me.

"She knows. You don't need to worry about her. She won't harm you. I won't allow it," he said in a deeper voice than usual.

"Oh, good. At least that is one less person who can kill me," I said sarcastically, the anger starting to bubble inside me. I know I was acting like a child but this wasn't fair. "You know I didn't ask for any of this, Logan. Why don't you just reject me and then we can carry on with our lives? You can kill the vampire and marry Madeline and rule your pack the way you want to and I will no longer be in any danger because I will mean nothing to you. Lucius won't want me if we are not mates!"

Logan wildly turned and pushed me back with so much force that I was momentarily winded from my back hitting the grass. I blinked a few times to regain my senses and realised his body was on top of mine, covering me like a blanket. His eyes had turned completely black and he was breathing heavily. Our faces were so close that I could see every perfect imperfection on his skin.

"Don't ever say we are not mates again," he growled. Something had drastically changed inside Logan and it no longer felt like it was him I was talking to. His heavy, solid body pinned me to the ground and I had no idea what to do. "Alina, did you hear me? We are mates and you are mine."

I moved my head slowly so as not to anger him anymore, my heart pounding in my chest.

"Say it," he ordered louder.

"We are m-mates," I managed to squeak.

"And?" he growled again.

"I-I am yours." I felt him soften at my words and gradually his eyes altered their colour, and I was now staring into piercing blue irises again.

He continued to gaze down at me thoughtfully and said, "You just met my wolf, Elias."

"What?!" I was dumbstruck. He didn't look like a wolf apart from his dark eyes and deeper voice.

He carefully stood up and pulled me up with him. Once we were standing, he shoved his hands into his trouser pockets as if he didn't trust himself not to touch me again.

"I'm sorry about that. I hope he didn't scare you. My wolf, Elias, took control over my body when you said we should reject you. You have to understand, he is borderline obsessed with you." He gave me a shy smile and I couldn't help but go weak at the knees.

"Can he do that? Is that why your eyes turn black?" I asked, intrigued.

"Yes, most of the time I can fight his control, but sometimes he is too powerful. My eyes turn black when he is present on the surface, and I am close to letting him out. But when I am angry, it is harder to keep him back."

I nodded my head in understanding and thought about how Elias just made me feel. His power and possessiveness turned me on hugely and even though he was intimidating, I knew he would never hurt me. It was strange, but I felt like I could trust him, more than I could trust Logan.

"Alina, I don't know what we are going to do about… our situation, but I can't reject you right now. You know about our kind, which puts you and us in great danger. We have certain rules that must be followed to keep you and our identities safe. Once we have dealt with that side of things, we can figure out the rest. But right now, you have to come back with me," he said with authority.

Knowing I really didn't have many other options, I reluctantly agreed. We stopped by Chloe's to grab some of my belongings to keep me going for a few days. Luckily, Chloe wasn't in. She had barely left her new love interest's place in the last few days, so things were obviously going well. I was thankful that I wouldn't have to try and explain why I was packing a bag and going with Logan without her completely losing her shit. I would ring her later, once my brain had finished processing how messed up my life had become, and I no longer felt the need to throw up.

Chapter 18

Madeline's POV

"Please stop with the constant pacing, Emma. You are making me dizzy," I pleaded as I watched Emma's feet pick up speed again as yet another one of her crazy ideas popped into her head. She had been like this for the last twenty minutes since she barged into my room demanding that I get out of bed and do something 'useful' with my day.

"How about giving him an ultimatum? You or her and he has one hour to decide?" she shot at me from the corner of the room where she looked at me expectantly.

I sighed, folded my arms across my chest and stared out of the window. It was not that I didn't appreciate her help, but I had already been through these scenarios numerous times in my head, and they all ended with the same outcome.

Risk.

Risk that Logan would choose Alina. Risk that he would leave me. I needed something else. Something that would take the pressure and choice away from him and make it easier for everyone.

I observed the evening wind wrestle with the branches of the sycamore tree outside my window and longed for a run in the forest.

Dusk was approaching sooner than expected, the last of the sun's rays disappeared behind soft grey clouds. The street took on the look of an old photograph; every aspect turning darker with shadows cast by the moon's glow. I had pretty much spent the day in bed.

After Logan had returned from seeing Alina at the bar she worked at, he was different. Cold and distant. I had waited up for him to check if he was okay, knowing the conversation would not have been easy for him, but as the hours passed by, I grew more and more concerned.

When he eventually tiptoed through the door at 3:00 AM, he went straight into the spare room and slept there. My heart shattered at the rejection, but I tried to tell myself that he just didn't want to wake me.

The uncertainty and panic rising within me had me tossing and turning throughout the night. By sunrise, I had given up on the chance of sleep and decided to get up early and make breakfast for us. When he finally rose, Logan looked as though he had had an even more turbulent night's sleep than me. He'd grunted a 'thanks' whilst scoffing the breakfast and left without a word to go to work.

I'd wanted to confront him about what happened and how it went, but his foul mood prevented me. So, I took the coward's way out and texted him instead. All he replied was a curt, *We will talk later*. That was yesterday morning and I had barely seen him since. He stayed out all day, came home in the early hours of the morning, slept in the spare room again and then he was gone before I even woke up this morning. He was avoiding me. That much was obvious.

Wallowing in my despair, I spent the day in bed, with nothing but the demons in my head to keep me company. Emma turned up an hour ago after I had been ignoring her calls all day and is certain I was depressed. She had always been a fixer, so here she was, trying to think of ways to get me up and win Logan back. No, that was the demons talking. I must keep convincing myself that I have not lost him. Yet.

"Why don't we get rid of her? Fake an accident, a car crash or…"

"Emma! I am not going to murder an innocent girl just because she happens to be my boyfriend's mate. I am not a psychopath!" I yelled at her in disbelief.

"Okay, okay. I know you're right. But honestly, I don't know how you are so calm, Maddy!"

I turned to peer out of the window again, not answering her. I may have looked calm on the outside, but there was a storm of emotions raging within. Unleashing them would benefit no one.

Emma perched on the edge of my bed and squeezed my hand. "At least go and have a shower," she urged.

I pulled back the duvet and got to my feet. "Okay. Thank you, Ems," I said giving her a quick hug.

The hot water burned my skin, waking me from my misery. Emma was right. I couldn't just drown in a sea of uncertainty and allow Logan to drift further and further away. I had to do something. My father had raised me to be a fighter and to never back down from what I wanted in life. I wasn't about to start now. I know my worth. I know that I can make Logan happy and be a wonderful Luna to our people. I just needed to remind him.

I turned the shower off and stepped out with a towel when I heard raised voices coming from the living room. Naturally, my heart sped up and I rushed to get dressed thinking we had an intruder. As I opened the bedroom door, I recognised the voices as the two people I loved most in this world.

"I can't believe you have brought her here, Logan. Do you have any idea what this is doing to Maddy?" Emma shouted.

"It is Alpha to you and need I remind you not to raise your voice at me, Emma? This has nothing to do with you, so leave," Logan gritted back.

"I am her best friend and the only person that seems to care about her right now, so I think you should be the one to leave!" Emma spat.

She was going to get herself killed. No omega wolf can speak to an Alpha that way and live to tell the tale. I heard a ferocious growl and I sprinted into the living room. Logan was advancing towards Emma with ferocity as she backed up against the wall. I managed to position myself between them, bringing Logan to a standstill.

"Emma, leave. Now!" I shouted without breaking eye contact with Logan.

"But…" she started behind me.

"Now!" I said firmly. I knew that look on Logan's face and we had about ten seconds before he snapped completely unless I got her out of there.

"Yes, my Luna," she replied before leaving the flat. I internally smirked at her intentional use of the term 'Luna'. She was reminding Logan of my importance.

Logan turned his back to me and that's when I felt another presence in the room. I glanced over at the sofa where a girl with a terror-stricken face sat as her wide eyes darted between me and Logan.

Alina.

"What is she doing here?" I growled, not tearing my eyes away from her. She gulped at my icy tone and looked down nervously at her hands.

"I will explain everything once you calm down," Logan stated.

I needed to get myself under control. Seeing her again in our apartment brought back so many memories of that night and the feelings I had been trying so hard to suppress. I took a few deep breaths and walked over to the furthest chair from her and sat down. Calm and collected needed to be the way I dealt with this. Like a Luna.

"I am waiting," I said, trying to keep the irritation out of my voice but failing. Logan went on to explain how Lucius sent Alina post and threatened her life, that she knows what we are, and she can no longer stay at Chloe's because it was too dangerous. I listened intently until he had finished.

"So where do you suppose she is staying?" I asked, my eyes had still not left her the entire time. She had managed to shrink lower and lower into the chair with every word and had not made a sound.

"I don't know yet. I hadn't thought that far ahead," he confessed.

I snorted and rolled my eyes. Typical. He always acted before he thought about the bigger picture. That is why we worked so well together I was the strategic one.

"She can stay with Darius," I suggested. "He has a spare room and we already know that they get along." I added the last bit, knowing it would wind him up.

"No way," he snapped.

"And why not?" I asked, giving him a deadpan expression. I was pretty sure I knew his reasons, as the mate bond would not allow her to be around any unmarked males, but I knew he would not admit it. It was fun to watch him squirm.

"I want to stay with Darius," a small voice interjected from the sofa.

"No Alina," Logan said, running his fingers through his hair. I noticed the dark circles under his eyes and his skin looked worn and tired and my heart softened. I'd forgotten how difficult this situation must also be for him.

The Last Alpha

"Please, Logan. I will be safe with Darius," she pleaded. My stomach churned at their familiarity. Whatever time they had spent together had clearly made them closer.

"It is the best decision for all of us," I said, giving Alina a fierce glare.

Logan took a deep breath. "Fuck sake," he muttered under his breath whilst retrieving his phone from his back pocket. He put it to his ear and after a few rings, Darius answered.

"I need you to come over now," Logan growled, glaring from Alina to me.

"What's the magic word?" I heard Darius tease. He was always trying to get a reaction from his cousin.

"I am not playing, Darius. This is serious. Get your ass here in the next ten minutes or I will come and get you myself," he said sharply and hung up the call.

We all waited in excruciating silence until Darius arrived.

After what felt like an eternity in hell, Darius burst into the room like a madman but stopped in his tracks when he spotted Alina. His face softened and he smiled warmly at her.

"Hey, buttercup!" If I didn't know him better, I would have said he was in love with her, but I knew it was more likely just an infatuation.

Alina smiled timidly, but still said nothing.

"Darius, come with me. We need to talk in private," Logan commanded.

They left the room but hoovered in the corridor where they talked intensely in hushed tones. They both kept glancing back at us every now and again, clearly worried about leaving me in the same room alone with Alina. The air prickled with tension and awkwardness. I knew I shouldn't hate her. None of this was of her choosing, but I couldn't help the jealousy and bitterness I felt towards her for being Logan's mate. I didn't trust myself to speak, so I accepted the uncomfortable silence between us. I was flabbergasted when she spoke first. She had more courage than I gave her credit for.

"Madeline. I-I just want to say that I am sorry. About all of this," she said so genuinely that it made it hard to keep up my harsh exterior. I nodded once and looked away.

At that moment, the men entered the room again. Darius looked delighted, whilst Logan looked furious.

"So you're going to be my new roomie?" Darius beamed at Alina.

"Only if you don't mind. I know it has come out of the blue and I don't want to put you out or anything," she replied politely.

"Don't be daft. This is going to be fun. I've always wanted someone to cook me breakfast in the morning." Logan growled in warning at Darius. "Relax, relax! Sorry about my cousin. You have properly become accustomed to his uptight nature by now!" he taunted. If Darius wasn't the only family Logan had left, he'd be dead by now.

"Cousins?" Alina's mouth hung open as she looked between them in surprise.

"I know! Shocking, right? How could I be related to him? I am way better looking," Darius joked. "Grab your stuff then, buttercup, and let's get out of here."

Alina started to pick up her belongings hastily that had been parked by her feet and I studied Logan to see how he was handling this. Not very well by the looks of things. His fists were clenched at his sides and his body was tense. He was staring daggers at Darius, who was pretending to be oblivious. Darius took Alina's bags from her as she walked towards the door.

I watched in horror as Logan grabbed one of her arms to turn her to him and stared intensely into her eyes. I held my breath when I saw so much heat and longing in them. He had never looked at me that way before. He suddenly let go of her and she dashed out of the flat after Darius, leaving me alone with a man I didn't even recognise.

Chapter 19

Alina's POV

Darius' house was everything I expected it to be—a sleek bachelor pad full of character. It was a small, terraced house a few minutes' walk from Logan's. The downstairs consisted of a masculine living room at the front that led through to a dining room and an open-plan kitchen at the back. It had lots of rustic elements with a modern twist. The living room was filled with black furnishings, including a custom-made leather sofa and a cluster of colourful paintings hung on the walls. The kitchen had a polished marble top that contrasted with the reclaimed wood flooring that ran throughout the house. It was cosy but sleek. I loved it.

"Sorry. It's not what you're used to, but please treat it like your home. I don't want you to feel like a guest here," Darius said sweetly whilst shuffling on his feet.

"Thank you, Darius. Really, I love it here already and I promise I won't overstay my welcome. It's just until all this… mess is sorted out."

He nodded, avoiding eye contact with me and started walking up the stairs. "I'll show you to your room and let you get settled in," he said with an unusually formal tone. I got the impression he wasn't too used to having people stay here.

He opened the door to an immaculate spare room and placed my bags on the double bed. It was light and airy for its size and had everything I needed. A wardrobe, bedside tables and a comfy-looking bed.

A bed! It had been well over a week since I had slept in one of those!

I turned to him as he stood awkwardly in the doorway, his broad frame barely fitting through. "Thank you. This is perfect." I smiled.

"I'll just be downstairs. Take your time. If you want a shower or anything, the bathroom is the room next to yours." He pointed down the hall before saluting at me and charging down the creaky stairs.

I fell backwards onto the bed and breathed out a loud, exhausted sigh. What a day! My mind was still trying to catch up with events that had unfolded. I suddenly felt extremely tired. Climbing up the bed until my head reached one of the squishy pillows, I felt the weight of the day consume me. My eyelids fluttered shut as I fell into a deep slumber…

I was strolling through a tranquil forest with trees that stretched to the heavens. I could hear the birds singing their sweet melodies and the sound of running water in the distance. I spun around slowly, taking in these majestic surroundings. Everything is so peaceful, as if I was the only one left to enjoy it. But I know I am not alone. I looked down to my right side and there, standing regally, was a large wolf. Its fur looked so silky and is a milky white in colour. I reached out to run my hand through it. It's velvety under my touch. The wolf's head turned to look at me and its eyes were glowing with a rich gold. There is so much depth to them and I felt as though I had known them my whole life.

Then I heard it. Rustling in the bushes ahead coming from so many different angles. A voice in my head howled, *"RUN!"* and I did. As fast as my legs could carry me, I raced through the trees with my heart hammering in my chest. I looked to my right again and saw the wolf running alongside me looking so graceful as the sun's rays' shimmer on its fur. And then I tripped, and I fell. Falling into darkness. I screamed but no sound left my lips.

I woke with a start, feeling disorientated and bewildered from my dream. It felt so real! Where was I?

Memories of the day before flooded my brain in high definition. My eyes adjusted to take in every ray of light streaming through the window and without a doubt I knew that I had slept too long. I looked down at myself still in yesterday's clothes but noticed a red, wool blanket over the top of me. I smiled as I realised that Darius must have come to check on me at some point.

I quickly grabbed some new clothes and headed for the bathroom. After taking a shower, getting dressed and pulling my hair up in a messy bun in a fraction of the time it normally took me, I headed downstairs to find Darius.

"Good morning, sunshine! How did you sleep?" The gigantic red head asked, putting down his newspaper on the dining table where he was sitting.

"Great, thank you. Some weird dreams but I guess that's to be expected. I think yesterday really took it out of me. I feel bad that I fell asleep as soon as I got here," I said, taking a seat on the chair next to him.

"Don't sweat it. Coffee?" he asked, standing up and walking towards the kitchen.

"Coffee would be amazing. Thank you."

He busies himself with the kettle whilst I sat back and took a proper look around the room. He had a wall of shelves that were brimming with books, old records, quirky ornaments, and a few photo frames. I stood up and wandered over to get a better look.

I could tell none of the photos were recent as they all included a rather youthful looking Darius with bright red hair. One was of him standing between a man and a woman who also had the same auburn curls. I moved along to the next and my heart fluttered as I saw a teenage Logan and Darius with what I presumed to be their parents. They must have been about sixteen when it was taken.

"Cute, weren't we?" He appeared beside me holding out a steaming mug of coffee.

"How old were you here?" I asked, taking the mug from him.

"Seventeen. That was the last photo we took before the attack." He looked at the photo with so much emotion before randomly clapping his hands together loudly, making me jump out of my skin.

"So, what would you like to do today?"

"Um, well, I was hoping to just chill here for the day. Unpack my stuff, bit of studying, maybe watch a film before my shift at work this evening?"

"That sounds perfect. But about the work thing···" he said carefully whilst raising one eyebrow.

"What about work?" I asked, frowning.

"Logan gave me strict instructions not to let you out of my sight and also that you weren't allowed to go out at night." He said the last bit so quickly I almost didn't catch it.

"WHAT?!" I screeched.

"Hey, don't shoot the messenger!" he said, raising his hands in the air.

"So I am a prisoner? What am I allowed to do then?" I berated.

"You can do anything you like as long as it is daylight and you

The Last Alpha

are with one of us." He smiled smugly.

I slumped down in a chair and put my coffee on the table. How did this become my life?

"Logan has good reason for trying to keep you safe, Alina. I don't always agree with his methods, but in this case, I think you should listen."

I didn't respond as I reflected on all that brought me to this moment in time. If I had never gone to that party, none of this would have ever happened and I would be continuing with my life blissfully unaware of all the craziness in this world. But then I would never have met Logan. And for some reason, my life without him in it now seemed dull and without purpose. How could that be when I had only known him a few days? It must be this mate bond thing.

"How long will this last? How long until I get my freedom back?" I asked in desperation.

"The million-dollar question!" he joked, but stopped smiling when he saw I was not amused. "Honestly? I don't know. But I promise you. If you are here with me, you are safe. That's got to count for something, right?"

I knew he was right. My safety was a top priority right now. But I hated more than anything being treated like some fragile human who couldn't take care of herself. I also did not appreciate being told what I could or could not do by men.

I decided to play along with their little game to a certain extent. I would keep a low profile, stay with Darius, but I would still be going to go to work. If I called in sick again, I would most definitely be fired.

"Okay, I'll play nicely," I said, rolling my eyes.

"That's my girl. I would hate it if anything were to happen to you whilst you were in my care," he said shyly. His cheeks started to blush slightly at his confession. Darius had always been flirty, but this seemed like he was trying to tell me that he really cared about me. I knew now was the right time to set things straight between us, especially as we were going to be living together.

"Um… Darius… I really like you and enjoy your company, but just as a… friend," I said carefully.

A deafening laughter bursts out of him as I finish my sentence. His laughter was full of warmth and life. It meshed well with his messy, laid-back appearance.

"What's so funny?" I asked, a little insulted at his reaction to my sincerity.

"You... thought I… sorry." He continued to chuckle between his words and took some deep breaths to calm down.

"What?" I asked in frustration.

"Alina, I don't feel THAT way about you either! I mean, okay, when we first met, I found you very attractive and enjoyed your company, but the moment I found out you were my cousin's mate, those feelings changed. If I am going to be completely honest, I just thought you'd be good in bed and then I'd never see you again." He smirked.

I rolled the newspaper up tightly and started throttling him with it, shouting, "You pig!" as I started laughing to.

"I knew it wouldn't be long until you'd try to kill him," a deep voice boomed from the doorway, forcing us to freeze our playful fight and look up to see Logan leaning lazily on the door, clearly entertained.

Chapter 20

Logan's POV

I couldn't help but smile at the scene before me. Alina was looking adorable in a pair of leggings and a baggy cream jumper that hung off one shoulder. Her ash blonde hair was piled on top of her head in a messy, relaxed style and she was wearing no makeup. But what really brightened my mood was seeing her attacking Darius with a rolled-up newspaper whilst he raised his hands up to protect his face. I had never been more attracted to her.

"I knew it wouldn't be long until you'd try to kill him," I teased, leaning on the door frame.

They both froze mid-fight and a look of shock carved Alina's face whilst Darius used it as a chance to get up and away from her.

"Your mate has a death wish, attacking a werewolf before he's had his breakfast," he joked.

"I am sure you did something to deserve it," I replied.

"Do you want to tell him or should I?" He winked at her and a knowing look passed between them that made me a little uncomfortable as Alina's cheeks flamed.

"Tell me what?"

"Nothing," Alina said far too quickly and Darius chuckled.

The Last Alpha

"What are you doing here?" she asked, folding her arms. I see we are back to hostility. I sighed.

"Actually, I am here to see Darius about some⋯ business," I said, and I could swear I saw a hint of disappointment before her eyes glazed over.

"I will be in my cell," she said to Darius over her shoulder before stomping aggressively up the stairs.

"You've got a feisty one there!" Darius mocked.

"Don't I know it? And cell?" I queried.

"She thinks we are holding her prisoner. She is definitely not a fan of your new rules."

Ah, now the hostility towards me made sense. As long as she is safe, I can deal with her anger.

"So, cuz, what do I owe this pleasure?" he said, leaning against the kitchen cabinets.

I shuffled on my feet feeling vulnerable and uncomfortable with what I was about to do. This was harder than I thought.

After Alina and Darius left last night, Madeline and I lay all our cards on the table, so to speak, and let's just say it didn't end well. She had every right to throw a lamp at my head when she realised I had feelings for Alina. I didn't even get mad. I was expecting way worse, but I knew I had to start being honest with her. I owe her that much. I woke up this morning feeling even more confused after Madeline made some valid points that I needed to hear, but I just kept going round in circles in my mind. I needed to get some advice from someone who knew all three of us. And as much as it pained me to admit it, Darius was the only one who could help me right now.

"Oh, this is serious. Alpha, I rarely get the privilege of seeing you sweat." He grinned, basking in my discomfort.

"This was a mistake," I said, turning to leave.

"No, wait! I'm sorry! Please, continue."

"If I am going to do this, I need you to be on your best behaviour," I warned.

"Do what exactly?"

"I need your… advice." I gritted.

He raised his eyebrows at me and smirked, but quickly recovered himself and raised his hands in apology. "I will do my best," he said seriously.

I sat down on a dining chair and leaned back, tilting my head to the ceiling. "I feel like I am torn between two versions of myself. One where I am a logical, reasonable leader whose loyalty and love for my pack and family means more than anything. I do not want to let anyone down and I feel the weight of the world on my shoulders. But it's okay because we have fought for so long just to stay alive, and we are so close to our end goal and restoring our kind to the way we are meant to be." I took a deep breath.

"And the other version?" Darius asked.

"This new version of myself feels... free. I feel hope for a future I never thought I could have. I'm impulsive. I feel things intensely and it makes me feel alive. I feel like I am truly myself, even though I have never felt this way before. It's crazy yet it feels right. And it's all fuelled by…"

"Love?" Darius finished my sentence for me when I didn't find the word.

I run my fingers through my hair before I continued. "The problem is I no longer know which version of myself I really am or want to be. So how can I make a choice?" I asked, meeting his unreadable expression.

"Why can't you be both?" he asked.

"What do you mean? You know why. My father said…" I

started.

"Forget what your father said for a minute. Why can't you be a loyal and strong leader to your people and have true love?"

"Because love makes you weak. Look at me, I am not the strong, capable leader I was before Alina entered my life and I am not even sure I am fully in love with her yet. And you know it is not as simple as that for me. I gave my word. To my father, to Madeline, to our pack. Alina is human. She is not strong enough to survive the brutality and chaos that comes with our life. That comes with being a Luna. She has been through so much already I can't condemn her to that life."

"You underestimate her. She may be human, but she has a powerful soul and a fighting spirit. You and I both know she would make a fantastic Luna. Don't you think she deserves the choice? And as for your word, it is still good," he argued.

"But Maddy…" I said, feeling the guilt eating away at me.

"Logan, things change. People change. Can you honestly say that things were great with Maddy before Alina came along?"

I slowly shook my head.

"Do you love Maddy? If you reject Alina for whatever reason, will you be able to live a happy, fulfilled life with Maddy? Because if the answer is yes, then I think you should reject Alina. She deserves more than this life and she will be free to live it how she chooses."

I sat still letting his words sink in. Did I love Maddy? Yes. Was I in love with Maddy? No. But I couldn't say that to Darius. Maddy had the right to hear it first.

"If I rejected Alina and chose Maddy, I could be happy to an extent. If it meant Alina lives the life she wanted without me and I have done what is best for my pack. But honestly, I know I will never be whole again. Losing her would leave a void in my soul that could never be filled, but I could live with that, if it is the right thing to do."

Darius sighed and for the first time in my life I saw sympathy in his eyes. "Do you want me to be brutally honest, Logan? You won't beat the crap out of me?"

"Yes, and I won't." I swallowed, trying to prepare myself for his words.

"I don't think you should be with Maddy just because your dead father, no offence to my uncle, told you to be. If that is the only reason, it is not fair to her. She could meet her mate and be loved unconditionally if you weren't together. Would you really want to put her through what you're going through now if she finds him in the future? And as for Alina, she is your destined mate and I am not one to question the Moon Goddess. But human or not, if you have to think this hard about your feelings for her, you don't deserve her and she doesn't deserve to be strung along for the ride. Get the Blood Oath done as soon as possible." His words enraged me, but deep down I knew everything he said was true.

I hung my head in my hands at the sense of doom looming. Apart of me believed talking to Darius would make me see the light, what needed to be done. But now, I feel even more conflicted. He had given me a lot to consider. But he was right. Before I could deal with any of my personal turmoil, the Blood Oath needed to be executed. We were all at risk until it was.

"Will you tell Alina that I am going to be away for a few days?"

"Why? Where are you going?"

"I need to visit the dark witch and ask her to perform the Blood Oath for Alina. She has helped me once before, so I am hoping I have an ally in her. I would send Fredrik but he is still in America gathering wolves for the battle," I explained.

"Well, that's a stupid idea." Darius scoffed.

"Why?" I snapped. I forgot how quickly he could agitate me.

"Because you are being followed, Logan. Lucius has eyes on you and Alina from what you told me yesterday and you will be putting that witch's life in danger too."

He had a good point.

"Alina needs the Blood Oath, or you know I will be forced to turn her before the next full moon. The supernatural council is not very accepting towards humans knowing our kind," I argued and my heart started to race just thinking about what they would do to her.

"I will go." He shrugged his shoulders.

It could work. Lucius wouldn't bother to follow him, I'm sure. And I would be able to stay here with Alina but that left Maddy unprotected.

"Maddy can come with me," Darius said, as if reading my thoughts.

I nodded in agreement. They would be gone for at least two or three days as the witch resides in Sweden and they would need to fly. That meant I would be alone with Alina for all that time. The thought excited but terrified me. How was I going to resist her?

Chapter 21

Madeline's POV

The early morning breeze caressed my fur and soothed my soul. Running through the forest next to our flat before the crack of dawn was my therapy. There was no feeling like it as I darted skilfully between soaring trees. I stopped at a clearing in the middle of the woodland that opened out into a field of long grass and wildflowers.

Being a wolf in a city was hard. We were energetic animals and needed to feel close to nature. I did especially. I am missing home more than ever right now. Growing up in a pack house had its benefits. A huge forest surrounded it and as pups, we were allowed to roam freely. Some of my happiest childhood memories were of Logan, Darius, and I chasing each other and playing hide and seek in those woods. We would spend hours out there and often one of our parents would have to track us down when it was getting dark. But this would have to do for now.

I ambled in my wolf form to the centre of the field. I was not a large wolf like Logan, but bigger than average size and the long grass brushed against my shoulders as I pushed my way through. I stopped when I reached my destination and decided to shift back into my human form as Nina's grey fur didn't provide me with much camouflage. I lay back on the grass naked and looked up at the night's sky.

The sun would start to rise in about half an hour, which didn't give me much time to get back, but Goddess, I needed this. For a moment, I just savoured the moment of complete stillness. Only the twinkling of the stars made any movement. It was the most magnificent painting—alive with raw energy, a feast for the eyes. The stars spoke to me in the darkness, giving me hope that no matter what the new day brings, they would always be there, promising to return at dawn's first light. I hoped Logan's promise was just as trustworthy.

Last night was a mess. Once Alina and Darius had left, I couldn't take it anymore. I was done with being patient and giving him the space he needed. What about what I needed? My feelings? Did he even care? I lunged at him the minute we were alone, screaming and hitting him. He didn't even try to stop me or fight back, as if he saw it coming and accepted it. When my body was spent, I slumped back down on the sofa sobbing with my head in my hands. Strong arms wrapped around me and pulled me to his side. I melted into his embrace, and we stayed like that for a while, just holding each other…

"What is happening Logan?" I finally mustered the courage to ask.

"I don't know, Maddy. I know that is not what you want to or deserve to hear right now, but my head is so completely screwed up. I don't know what I am doing, feeling, thinking from one minute to the next. And I know it is not fair to you. It is eating me up inside knowing you are hurting, and it is all because of me," he said, meaning every word.

I sniffed a few times before responding. "Do you love her?" I asked in a small shaky voice that sounded nothing like my own. The silence that befell spoke volumes.

"I-I'm not sure. The mate bond is strong, Maddy. Stronger than I ever imagined it could be and I care about her and her safety like I do yours," he explained. I stiffened in his hold and then moved away from him and started to pace the room.

"So what does this mean for us, Logan? Are you going to reject her like you promised me you would?" My voice was starting to rise with the unsettling emotions I was feeling. He looked away from me and fell back into the chair, rubbing his hands down his face whilst groaning in frustration. "You're not, are you?!" I screamed.

"You are really going to throw away everything we have worked so hard to build. We are so close to the beginning of the rest of our lives together and just because of a pretty bit of skirt giving you some tingles, you are going to destroy it all!"

I could feel my body trembling as the adrenaline coursed through my veins. I was sure my eyes had turned black as I struggled to keep Nina at bay.

"MADDY…" Logan warned. "You have no idea what this is like."

"No, you are right. I don't. But what I do know is that I would never betray you. Not like you are betraying me!"

"Maddy, I haven't done anything to betray you. You are the reason I am fighting so hard against acting on my feelings for Alina." He stopped abruptly as he realised what he had said.

"So you do have feelings for her. You do love her!" When he didn't say anything but held my gaze, I saw guilt and pity swirling in his blue irises. I lost it. I grabbed the glass table lamp next to me and flung it at his head. I knew it would never hit him as his wolf speed was so advanced, but I needed an outlet for my rage.

"Do you want to be with her? Do you want to forsake everything we have been through and the future of our pack for HER?" I yelled.

"No. I don't know. You know that the pack means more to me than anything, but… it is becoming harder and harder to ignore my feelings," he replied honestly.

I glared at him and then started to walk towards the bedroom. I couldn't bear to be in the same room as him for a minute longer. Stopping at the door, I turned and looked back at the broken man with a mask of sorrow covering his face. "She is making you weak, Logan. You need to make a decision before you bring us all down with you," I said as I slammed the door behind me…

I haven't seen him since. I guess he retreated to the guest room once again.

Now, lying here in the wilderness with only the stars to keep me company, I couldn't help but let the sadness wash over me. Why did this have to happen? Why couldn't it have been me that found my mate? I would have rejected him without hesitation.

'NO, YOU WOULDN'T!' Nina barked in my mind.

Nina and I have never seen eye to eye. Since I was already in love with Logan before Nina revealed herself to me on my eighteenth birthday, I had dismissed her pleas to look for our mate. After years of badgering me, she finally realised I was not going to listen and retreated whenever I was with him. Nina respects Logan as her Alpha, but she does not want me to be with him. She knows how deeply I care and love him, so she has been kind enough to stay out of my head during all this drama, until now.

'Nina, please don't start.'

'WHEN WE FIND OUR MATE, YOU WILL FORGET LOGAN. YOU WILL SEE.'

'I have no interest in finding our mate. Logan is who I want.'

'ARE YOU SURE?'

'Yes, more than anything in this world. Don't you want to be Luna in our pack?'

'YES, BUT NOT LIKE THIS. HE DOES NOT LOVE YOU.'

'He does! He is just under the spell of the mate bond now. Once Alina is out of our lives for good, he will come back to me.'

'YOU REALLY BELIEVE HE WILL REJECT HER? NOT A CHANCE.'

'I have faith in him. And if he doesn't, who's to say that Alina won't reject him? She has a choice to.'

Nina went quiet. She knew that I had just solved all my problems. The key was Alina. She wouldn't work with Logan. She was human and I am sure she wanted to stay that way. I knew from last night that she felt awful about the whole situation. Perhaps I could appeal to her caring nature and make her leave.

I could see the beginnings of the sunrise illuminating the blue and mixing its own blend of the new day ahead with oranges and yellows. I quickly transformed back into Nina and ran home before I would be spotted by the early morning joggers.

Back at the flat, I spent the morning doing housework to busy my mind. Logan had left an hour ago without a word. I heard the ringtone of my phone over the calming melody of music I had playing in the background. It was Darius.

"Hello," I answered.

"Hey, Mads, how you doing?"

"Oh, amazing, thanks. Why wouldn't I be?" I said with sarcasm.

"Well, I have just the thing to cheer you up! How does an all-expenses paid trip to Sweden to see a dark witch sound?"

"You're joking, right?" I scoffed. "What makes you think I would want to do that?"

"Maybe because you are going to go insane if you spend another day cooped up in that flat obsessing over your little love triangle situation and not being able to do a thing about it."

I stopped dusting the blinds and looked down at the duster in my hands. Damn. Why was he always right?

"I need to convince this witch to perform the Blood Oath for Alina and I just thought you might like to help me out seeing as I am not everyone's cup of tea," he continued.

I shook my head at his insecurity. He was a great guy, yes, a little loud and cocky, but he had a good heart. "Okay," I said. "When do we leave?"

"Tomorrow. So, get packing."

I hung up and held the phone to my chest. The sooner the Blood Oath was completed, the better. Logan had said this witch had visions. Maybe she could give me some answers as to what my future holds.

Chapter 22

Alina's POV

After I heard the front door close, I came back downstairs knowing Logan must have left. I hated the way my body reacted around him. I was so mad at him for getting me involved in all of this, but mainly because he was taking away my freedom. Yet, my body longed for his touch and butterflies formed in my stomach every time he looked at me. Darius and Logan had been talking for over an hour and even though I could hear the odd word or my name being mentioned, I had no clue as to what it was about.

"Hey, buttercup, fancy watching a film now?" Darius asked when he noticed me hovering at the bottom of the staircase making sure the coast was clear. "It's alright. He's gone." He reassured me with a smile.

I breathed a sigh of relief but couldn't help feeling a little disheartened that he hadn't wanted to see me. I walked into the living room and plonked myself down on the black leather sofa. Darius followed behind.

"So, you really hate him that much?" he asked as he took a seat next to me.

"No. It's just complicated," I said.

He nodded slowly before changing the subject to what film we should watch. After arguing like siblings, we compromised on a comedy, *Stepbrothers*. I had seen the film before and knew it was hilarious, but my mind was somewhere else and half way through the film, Darius paused it and turned to me.

"Okay, spill. What's up?" He looked at me expectantly.

"What? I'm fine," I lied.

"No one can resist the comedic genius of Will Farrell unless they are having some kind of nervous breakdown," he replied, raising one eyebrow.

I started fiddling with the frayed wool on the sleeve of my jumper and wondered if I should really ask Darius questions about being a werewolf. It had been the elephant in the room ever since I moved in here.

"What is it like… to be a werewolf?"

"Not the question I was expecting, but okay. It's wicked. You have sharper senses like smell and eyesight, but you can also run faster than any human and fight better. Not to mention the sex…" he said, wiggling his eyebrows at me.

My eyes widened slightly. "What about the sex?" Curiosity got the better of me.

"Imagine the best sex of your life." He paused for dramatic effect. "Now multiply it by a thousand. That is what sex with a werewolf is like." He grinned when I started blushing. "And we can go again and again and again and…"

"Okay, I get the picture," I said quickly and I did as images of what it might be like to have sex with Logan entered my mind and my core started heating up. I fidgeted on the sofa, trying to block them out before Darius would notice. "So, you have a wolf, too? Like in there," I said, tapping the side of his head.

He laughed at my question. "Yes, his name is Gunner."

"Gunner. So, can you talk to Gunner in your mind like Logan and can you share control over your body?"

"Yes and no. Yes, I can talk to him in my head. In fact, he rarely shuts up! But I can't share control as well as Logan can. It's an Alpha thing. I can feel Gunner at the surface and my eyes might change colour when I am angry, but I am more likely to shift into my wolf if I don't calm down. Whereas Logan can allow Elias to speak and act in his human form."

I looked at Darius sadly. "So I will never get to speak to Gunner?"

He chuckled. "Afraid not, but I might allow you to give him a belly rub one day."

I smiled at the thought.

"Alina, there is something I need to tell you and I am not sure you will like it very much," he said carefully, removing all the objects that were sitting on the coffee table.

"What are you doing?" I asked.

"Just taking away any objects you could hit me with again," he teased.

"Oh, great. What is it now?" My mind was spinning as to what else could possibly go wrong in my life!

"Well, you know you have to sign this Blood Oath?" I nodded so he would continue. "Well, we need a witch to perform it and I have to go and ask her. Witches like things to be done in person. They are very traditional in that sense."

"Oookay." I wasn't sure where he was going with this.

"She lives in Sweden. So I am going to be gone for a few days. Maddy is coming with me and Logan is going to be staying here. With you."

My eyes nearly popped out of my head. Logan and me. Here, together? For a few days? Alone!

"What! Why can't he go and you stay here?" I asked in panic, even though there was some part of me that was very happy at the thought of spending more time with him. I knew it was wrong.

"Because Lucius has watchful eyes on Logan. We don't need him finding out our plans," he reasoned.

"And what are the plans exactly?" I said, crossing my arms. No one had actually given me any indication of what was going to happen past the point of signing the Blood Oath.

"Don't you worry your pretty little head about that yet, buttercup, and just leave it to us men to take care of everything." He patted the top of my head like an obedient dog. I swatted him away and stood up from the sofa. "Where are you going?" he shouted as I made my way upstairs.

"To have a relaxing bath to destress if that's allowed," I shouted back and got no reply. I was being treated like a helpless damsel who didn't have a single brain cell to think for herself. They clearly didn't know me very well if they thought I was going to put up with it.

I turned on the hot tap and poured in some bubble bath that smelt masculine and peppery. I perched on the side of the tub, waiting for it to fill as I tried to come up with a plan as to how I was going to sneak out of here and get to work tonight when my phone started vibrating.

Chloe. Shit.

I completely forgot to call her last night and then I had fallen asleep as soon as I got to Darius'! I am surprised it had taken her this long to call.

"Hey." I tried to sound upbeat and normal although I was feeling anything but.

"Lina! Where are you? Are you okay? I just got home from Ryan's and some of your stuff was gone and the sofa hasn't been slept on! I was freaking out!" She hyperventilated dramatically.

"It's fine. I'm fine. I am at Darius'," I said calmly as I lowered myself into the soothing water.

"Darius! What?! Why? Oh, my god, are you sleeping with him?" she squealed, unable to keep the excitement out of her voice.

"No. God, no! I just··· er··· He offered me his spare room when he saw I was sleeping on your sofa and I··· decided to take him up on it."

"WHAT?! You're moving in with him?! And you didn't tell me? What the hell, Alina?" She was pissed. I didn't expect that.

"Chloe, it's just a ··· um, trial period. A few days, maybe a week or so to see how it goes. You have been amazing, letting me stay with you, but you have to admit having me on your sofa every night is a bit restricting to your personal life."

"You are my personal life!" she screamed. "Well, I guess it will be nice to be able to have Ryan round and it does seem like a sensible option. But if you have even the tiniest doubt about staying there, you promise you will come straight back here?"

"I promise," I said seriously. "Now tell me all about Ryan. It is obviously going well if you have only just got home."

"Oh, Lina, I think I am in love," she gushed and I couldn't help but giggle.

After half an hour of listening to Chloe drooling over her new boyfriend, we said goodbye and I climbed out of the bath. I was busy drying my body when I heard a knock on the bathroom door.

"Yes?" I called.

"Any chance you could run me one of those?" Darius' booming voice shouted from the other side of the door. I couldn't believe my luck. This was the perfect escape.

"Of course, give me ten minutes and it will be all ready for you," I replied.

I rinsed out the bath and ran a fresh one full of bubble bath and even lit a few candles that I found in a drawer to make it extra relaxing. When I opened the door for Darius, his mouth dropped in shock.

"What did I do to deserve this treatment?" he asked.

"Just a thank you for letting me stay here and taking such good care of me." I smiled sweetly. "Now, get in there before it gets cold and take all the time you need to feel nice and relaxed," I added, shutting the door behind him.

Like the speed of light, I got dressed in my bar clothes and applied a bit of makeup before sneaking down the stairs trying to avoid the creaks.

Reaching the bottom, I blew out the breath I had been holding and smiled. Darius would freak out when he realised I was not here and would most likely alert Logan, thinking I have been kidnapped. I would have to leave a note.

I grabbed a Post-it note pad and scribbled, *Gone to work. Don't tell Logan. I'll be back before you know it. A x* and stuck it to the fridge.

Snatching my keys and phone, I closed the front door as silently as possible and started to run to the tube station. Damsel, my ass!

Logan's POV

Pulling out my phone now seemed like as good a time as any to get an update from Fredrik. I was in the office at work alone and knew I wouldn't be needed for a while. I had sent him back to America to contact and find as many rogue wolves as he could who would be willing to join our fight against Lucius.

"Alpha." Fredrik answered on the third ring.

"Fredrik, how are things going?" I asked, leaning back on my office chair.

"Better than expected, Alpha. Every rogue I have come across so far has agreed to fight with us and has sworn allegiance to you."

"That's great," I said less enthusiastically than I should. This was good news, as we needed all the support we could get, but it meant a lot of these wolves would lose their lives in the battle, especially if they had not been trained in combat. Rogues were known for their ruthless and impulsive natures. They had to be that way to survive on their own. Before Lucius ambushed my pack, he had slaughtered all the smaller packs in America. Many survivors had run away and became rogues or denied their wolf side and tried to live out their lives as humans. It was important to find as many of them as possible to increase our numbers. I was not surprised to hear that they wanted to join us and seek revenge against Lucius.

"Everything okay at your end, Alpha?" Fredrik must have been expecting a more positive reaction to his news.

"Not exactly. Things are becoming more complicated by the day here, but Darius and Maddy are going to speak to the dark witch tomorrow so we can get things moving," I explained.

"Okay. Just warn them that Cora is quite an intense person."

"Will do. They can handle it." My phone started vibrating, notifying me of another call. "I've got to go but I will see you at the meeting in a few days' time. Thank you, Fredrik." I looked down to see the caller ID was my cousin.

"Darius?"

"Hey, um, so, we have a small problem." I stood up abruptly

and my whole body became alert. Darius was nervous. Something was truly wrong.

"What is it?" I gritted. I knew I couldn't trust him to look after her.

"Alina has sneaked out and gone to work," he said quickly.

"WHAT? How the fuck did she manage to sneak out? Weren't you watching her?"

"Well, I was in the bath."

I growled at his stupidity.

"Hey, it's not my fault that she clearly tricked me into relaxing long enough for her to escape. How was I supposed to know she wanted to go to work that badly?!"

I threw a mug on my desk across the room in frustration. Why couldn't the girl just do what she was told?

"It's going to be fine, Logan. Just tell me where she works and I will go down there and get her," Darius tried to reassure me.

"No," I said crossly. "I will go!"

"Is that such a good idea?"

I growled loudly through the earpiece.

"Okay, just go easy on her, Logan."

I hung up, cursing how stubborn Alina was and how idiotic my cousin was. What was it about 'you are not safe' did she not understand?

I grabbed my keys to my Ducati and made my way to the parking lot.

Chapter 23

Alina's POV

It felt so good to have a bit of normality back in my life after the last twenty-four hours of craziness. Sean had avoided me at all costs and only mumbled the odd order here and there. He hadn't mentioned the other night, which was a relief although it didn't stop me from catching him giving me the occasional death stare from across the room.

A steady stream of customers filtered through as the after-work rush started to pick up and, for once, I was quite enjoying the distraction of work. A small group of businessmen sat at the bar in front of me, bantering over who was going to make a partner at their office. I listened in as I washed up some of the bar utensils in the sink.

"I bet it's going to be Phil. He's a jammy git. Always gets everything handed to him on a silver platter," the bold one said before taking a swig of his beer.

"Yeah, and it would have nothing to do with the fact that he is screwing the boss," the most attractive one said. He couldn't be much older than me, maybe twenty-four at a push, and had a charismatic face that made him seem approachable.

"Don't tell me you wouldn't go there? She's a fox and I bet

she loves to take control in bed just as much as she does in the office." The third man winked.

"Nah, she's not my type," the attractive young man said whilst looking directly at me. "I've got a thing for beautiful barmaids instead."

I rolled my eyes at his flirting and smiled.

"You've got no chance, Rob. She is way out of your league." The bold one smirked at me.

"Is that right, gorgeous? Do I really have no chance?" He gave me a smouldering look as he leaned forward on the bar.

I stopped what I was doing and looked into his eyes, leaning slightly forward as well and said with a smile, "I think you have more chance of making partner at your office." My banter earned some hooting from his colleagues and a cheeky grin from him.

"Well, now, I have to get your phone number." He chuckled.

"No. You don't."

I glanced over Rob's shoulder at Logan, who stood behind him. Oh, shit! *I am in so much trouble*, was my first thought, and *I am going to kill Darius* was my second!

Logan's face was serious and the look he was giving Rob was enough to make any man cower. The three men grabbed their drinks and scattered. Rob gave me an apologetic look as he did. He obviously thought Logan was my boyfriend and he had just caused a problem between us. I laughed aloud at the reality of the situation, which only made Logan angrier.

"Get your stuff. We are leaving," he ordered, stepping up to the bar.

"No, YOU are leaving," I replied calmly.

"Alina." His tone was warning me not to push him.

Tough shit, I was in a feisty mood.

"Logan." I stared at him as confidently as I could to show him that he didn't intimidate me.

'Show him who's boss, he loves it really!' I heard a voice whisper to me. It sounded like it was so close, almost like it was in my own head.

My eyebrows furrowed as I whipped around on the spot to see who it came from and Logan watched on perplexed.

"Did you hear that?" I asked.

"Hear what?" He looked just as confused as me.

"Never mind. Look, Logan. I know you're mad that I came to work but if I didn't, I would have been fired and I really need this job. It's the only source of income I have right now." I was almost silently begging him not to throw me over his shoulder again. We both knew he could do it quite easily at any second.

He looked at me with an unreadable expression for a few moments before shaking his head in irritation.

"Fine. But I am going to sit at the bar all night until you finish and no more flirting with men…" He narrowed his eyes at me.

"I wasn't flirting with—" I started, but realised there was no point in continuing as he had already walked away and sat at the end of the bar, brooding.

Great. How was I supposed to work with him glowering at me every time I spoke to a customer?

Halfway through the evening, Tiff approached me and whispered, "Okay, who is mister tall, dark and hot-as-fuck at the end of the bar? He hasn't ordered a drink the entire night and is staring at you like you are a piece of meat he wants to devour."

I peered over her shoulder and saw Logan still sitting in the same spot, watching us intensely. I sighed. "It's complicated." It seemed that was the only response I ever have when it came to Logan.

"Well, I've got to say, girl. You have upgraded." She slapped my ass playfully as she walked away and I could swear I saw Logan nearly stood and clench his fists. I know his wolf thinks I am his property or something, but this possessiveness was getting ridiculous.

Out of the blue, a leggy brunette wearing next to nothing strode over to him and whispered something in his ear. She had her hands all over him and I was mortified when he turned on his stool and spoke to her. My blood boiled and I wanted to rip her off of him.

Now who's the possessive one? I thought to myself.

Tutting at my jealousy, but also unable to watch it anymore, I grabbed a tray of dirty glasses to take out the back. I pushed through the heavy double doors into the kitchen and started to stack the dishwasher. Sean dropped a bag of rubbish at my feet and ordered me to take it out to the bins. Yep, he was punishing me.

I made my way out into the back alley behind the club and threw the bag into the overflowing bin. I turned back but a movement in the shadows had me frozen. My heart was in my mouth as I made out two dark figures standing a few metres away from me, blocking my way back to the bar; my lungs rapidly inflating and deflating with the damp air.

They made no attempt to move but continued to stand steadily like statues. I could feel my heart beating faster with every passing second. Drops of sweat were beading on my forehead as I quickly considered my options—scream and hope someone came to my aid or try and get past them.

Knowing the bar would now be in full swing and no one would hear me over the blaring music, the second option seemed best. I made my way towards them. As I got closer, I could see the men's pale, eerie faces and their eyes glowing red like piercing balls of rage.

'Vampires! Run!' I heard a panicked voice in my head. I

bolted towards them and then swiftly tried to dodge past one, but when I felt icy fingers grip my waist tightly and lift me off the floor, I let out an ear-splitting scream. He slammed me into the wall and held his hand over my mouth when I tried to scream again.

"Now, now, missy, less of that. We don't want to get anyone else killed now, do we?" his voice hissed like a serpent and sent chills down my spine.

"She's a pretty one. She will be fun to play with when we get her back," the second one said whilst running his thin index finger down my neck repulsively as I struggled against them. I was not going to go without a fight. I bit down violently on the first one's hand and he jumped back hissing.

"You bitch!" he shouted as his fangs extended and he slapped me viciously across the face.

My cheek stung from the force, but I was quickly distracted from the pain when I heard a deafening roar that shook the ground. All three of our heads whipped round to see a gigantic, jet-black wolf standing about eight feet tall, growling and baring his razor-sharp teeth.

"You said she was here alone!" the second vampire yelled just before the wolf lunged into the air and landed on his back. I watched in horror as the wolf bit down into his neck and, with a skilful twist, the snapping of bones filled the air and the vampire fell lifelessly to the floor.

The wolf turned, his eyes focusing on the man who was now holding me by the throat, using me as a human shield against his body. Fear engulfed me as the wolf started to stalk around us. I locked eyes with the creature and I knew instantly that it was Elias, Logan's wolf. He was trying to communicate with me through his eyes, reassuring me that I was going to be okay.

Suddenly, I felt a wave of adrenaline and courage pass through me and, without thinking twice, I twisted my body and elbowed the man as hard as I could in the stomach and stamped on his foot. He immediately loosened his grip on my neck and I took my chance to dive onto the floor as the wolf pounced. I scrambled back on my hands and bum whilst the scene before me broke out in chaos. There was blood spraying from all directions, and it was difficult to judge who it belonged to.

Suddenly, the vampire chomped down on the wolf's shoulder, causing him to roar in pain and my heart stopped. But in one swift movement, the wolf locked its jaws around the man's neck and tore his head clean off. The dismembered head rolled towards me and stopped at my feet. I felt bile rise in my throat at the pure horror of it and looked up to see the black wolf slowly approaching me with blood dripping from his jaw. The last thing I saw was deep ocean blue eyes before everything went to darkness.

I could feel myself being lifted and held close against a warm, hard chest and the most amazing scent invaded my nose. Sandalwood and pine. I felt my head swaying with the rhythm of the walk and then I heard car doors opening before the darkness consumed me once again.

Chapter 24

Alina's POV

Everything was black. A pit of nothingness. And then a flicker. Two glowing red orbs in the distance. Closing in on me. Just as I was about to scream, they transformed into rich blue irises that swirled like the tide and I was transfixed.

I sat up with a start, panting heavily with sweat soaking my skin and clothes. Where was I?

It took a moment to realise I was back in Darius' spare room. Darius came running to my side upon hearing me wake up.

"Shh, shh, you're okay. You are safe," he cooed whilst rubbing my arm as I looked around frantically.

"The bar… those men…" I turned to him in panic. "They were…"

"Vampires, yes," he said, helping me to sort my scrambled brain.

"There was a wolf… Logan. Where is Logan?" I started to hyperventilate at the thought of him being hurt.

"Breath, Alina. Breathe for me. Logan is fine. The wolf is fine," he soothed.

Once I had managed to regulate my breathing, I laid back onto the pillows in my bed.

"That wolf… that was Elias?" I asked, turning my face to Darius.

"Yes," he replied.

"Where is he now? Where is Logan?" Panic started to rise again at the fact that he wasn't here with me.

"He's gone back to the bar to deal with… the aftermath. I had to come and pick you both up as a naked man and passed out woman on a motorbike would have looked very concerning." He smiled.

I swallowed as the memory of the disfigured bodies and blood entered my mind. Blood. So much blood.

"Don't worry, he should be back any minute," Darius tried to reassure me.

I nodded before asking for a drink of water.

"Of course. Here," he said whilst handing me the glass I hadn't noticed on the bedside table. "Can I get you anything else?"

"Actually, I'd really like a shower." I needed to scrub every touch from those vile creatures away. I felt dirty knowing their hands had been on my skin.

Darius looked at me with concern, clearly unsure if I was well enough to be left alone.

"Darius, I am fine. It was just the shock, but I would really like to have a shower."

"You're not going to do another runner on me, are you? I will lock the bathroom window." He glared at me before a slow smile crept up his face.

"I promise. I am not going anywhere. I have learnt my lesson," I said, climbing out of bed. He handed me a towel and left me in peace to shower.

I turned the temperature of the water up to an extreme heat and let the boiling water burn away their touch. I scrubbed my skin raw until I felt like the top layer peeled away. As I finally relaxed and let the water calm my nerves, the image of Elias' wolf entered my mind. Now I was no longer overpowered by fear, I could truly appreciate how majestic and powerful he was. I felt such a strong connection to him already and I had only seen him once. Was it just the mate bond? But I don't have a wolf and I read a book on wolves that Darius had lent me earlier when he and Logan had been having their secret meeting that humans don't always feel the connection as strongly with the wolf side of their mate as they do not have one of their own. What bothered me the most was that I was starting to like the irresistible pull I felt towards Logan and now that I had seen Elias, I ached for him even more.

I was still trembling slightly as I pulled on my fluffy pyjama bottoms and faded Nirvana top. My comfort clothes. Opening the door, I collided with Logan's scent and my pulse quickened, knowing he was here. Within seconds, he was striding up the stairs three at a time and almost crashed straight into me as I stood motionless on the landing.

Time seemed to slow down as I gazed up at this enticing man. He looked drained and his hair was a dishevelled mess, but he was still the most gorgeous being alive. Lovingly, he scooped me into his arms and hugged me as if his life depended on it. His muscular arms engulfed my small frame and I pressed my face into his chest and inhaled. I felt him rest his lips and nose on the top of my head and we must have stayed like that for at least five minutes. It was the most intimate moment we've had. To my disappointment, Logan pulled back, still holding onto my arms, and searched my eyes.

"Are you okay?" he asked gently. For some reason, I wasn't expecting that. I was prepared for the scolding of a lifetime.

"Y-yes. Are you?" I stuttered, remembering Elias' howl as the vampire bit him.

"I'll live. We wolves have a very quick healing process," he said with a small smile. "You shouldn't be out of bed. Get some rest, we will talk about all of this in the morning," he said whilst ushering me into my bedroom. I humoured him by climbing back under the covers but instantly sat, bolted right up again when he went to leave.

"Where are you going?" I asked, panic evident in my voice. I knew I must have sounded like a clingy child right now, but I needed him. I wanted him.

"Just downstairs," he said softly, but I could see his own longing in his eyes.

"Don't…don't leave me," I whispered. I knew every time I closed my eyes, the gruesome scene would repeat over and over in my mind and his presence was the only thing that calmed me.

He looked at me with so much worry, but I could also see conflict in the creases of his face.

"I won't leave you," he said. "I will be right back. I just need to speak to Darius. And then I will be back, I promise."

I nodded my head and slid down further under the covers. Rolling onto my side, I curled myself up into the foetal position. I started counting in my head to keep the flashbacks away until I heard heavy footsteps on the floorboards. My heart raced. I felt the bed dip as Logan climbed in behind me and his body moulded around mine. He lowered his arm over my side and the weight of it and the warmth of his body felt so comforting. He leaned in to my ear and whispered,

"Sleep now," and I felt my eyelids flutter closed.

Chapter 25

Alina's POV

Waking up came slow and relaxed as my eyes adjusted to the brightness of a new day and everything softly came into focus. I feel well rested and refreshed as I stretched out on the bed and move my hand up and down the sheets. They were slightly warm under my touch and I could smell that earthy, sandalwood scent lingering.

Everything came flooding back. The bar··· the attack··· fainting and Logan cuddling me to sleep. He must have stayed the whole night.

I sniffed the air and my stomach groaned in hunger as the mouth-watering aroma of bacon drifted up the stairs from the kitchen. Without even bothering to look in the mirror, I ran down the stairs in my pyjamas, expecting to see Darius cooking breakfast. But instead, I was treated to the most delightful sight.

In the kitchen, Logan had his shirtless back to me and was only wearing a pair of baggy shorts that hang low from his hips. He was oblivious to my gawking as he flipped the bacon in the frying pan and all his back muscles flexed whilst he nodded his head along to the beat of the song playing on the radio. He looked so relaxed and carefree as his foot started tapping along.

All of a sudden, he moved his left foot back in a smooth motion, gliding across the wooden floorboards before spinning expertly with the spatula raised high in the air. Through his twirl, he clocked me standing at the foot of the stairs, looking very amused. For the first time, I saw him blush and it felt like I had caught him not as this intense character I've known him to be or a leader of werewolves, but just as Logan. The real Logan. I smiled the widest smile I could manage and after a few seconds, his face mirrored mine. He looked so young and breathtakingly handsome.

"I hope you're hungry." He pointed towards the dining room table that was covered with buttery croissants, platters of fresh fruit, and an array of cooked sausages, eggs, toast and now, bacon. "I didn't know what you liked to eat in the morning so..." His voice trailed off, embarrassed at the gesture.

My mouth hung open. "You did all this?" I asked, astounded by his skills in the kitchen but also at his thoughtfulness.

"Yeah. Well, I was up early so I thought I would make a start and let you sleep in, but I guess I got a bit carried away. Please, sit." He gestured to a chair at the table.

We both sat down and I couldn't help but sneak a look across at his strong chest and impressive six pack. He was in incredible shape and it suddenly made me feel self-conscious as I remembered what I was wearing and how I must look. Quickly, I pulled my hair down from the nest that had formed on top of my head and tried to comb it out with my fingers before smiling nervously and picking up a croissant. The first bite melted in my mouth and it tasted heavenly.

"Hmm. These are delicious. Where did you learn to cook?" I asked, trying to fill the silence between us.

"I pretty much taught myself. I have always loved cooking and helped out a lot in the pack house with my mother. It helps me to relax and Maddy can't cook to save her life, so it was..." He stopped abruptly at the mention of her name. Awkwardness filled the air. I looked down at my plate and pretended not to notice even though my stomach had twisted itself into several knots.

"Where is Darius?" I asked, breaking the uncomfortable silence.

"He has already left for the airport. He stayed with Maddy last night as they had an early flight to catch."

I only nodded, still staring down at my plate of food.

"So, how are you feeling? After last night?" He changed the subject again.

I bobbed my head until I swallowed my mouthful of strawberries before answering. "Yes, I feel much better, thank you. I'm sorry about last night."

"Which part? Ignoring my instructions to stay home? Going out the back of the bar alone? Nearly getting yourself killed? Or fainting at the sight of Elias?" he said casually, but I detected slight anger in his tone. He raised one eyebrow at me whilst he shoved a piece of fruit in his mouth.

That didn't last long, I thought. His cocky, controlling self was back, but I suppose he did have a right to be annoyed.

"All of it," I said slowly with what I hoped was an endearing smile, hoping to gain his forgiveness. If we were going to live together for the next few days, we needed to try and get along.

He continued to stare at me.

"I mean, I didn't ask to get attacked but I understand that if I had listened to you in the first place, none of it would have happened."

His eyes narrowed slightly and he nodded once before taking a bite out of a piece of toast.

"Thank you for staying with me last night," I said quietly without meeting his gaze. "I know you didn't have to and I am sure you would have rather been at home, but I didn't want to be alone and your··· presence made me feel··· safe," I confessed.

He didn't respond but again nodded his head in understanding.

"So, those vampires, were they working for Lucius?" I asked carefully.

"Yes. He must have known I had moved you out of Chloe's, which confirmed you were my mate. So he went after you." His eyes glazed over with some kind of emotion. "Elias wants to know if you were scared of him."

"Did you just talk to him?" I realised that must have been why he looked so vacant for a moment.

"Yes. So, were you? Scared of him?" He spurred me to answer.

"No. I mean, he is quite an intimidating wolf, but I know he was trying to protect me," I said, meeting his gaze. Before I chicken out, I quickly said, "I would like to meet him again and thank him in person for saving my life."

Logan put down his toast and tried to read my expression. "He would like that very much, but I don't think it is such a good idea right now."

"Why not?" I said, disappointed.

"Because Elias feels very strongly about you and if I hand him over complete control, I won't be able to stop him from doing what he wants to you,"

I audibly gulped at his words. "What does he want to do?"

He looked at me cautiously, probably deciding if he should tell me or not. "He wants to mark and mate with you and make you his."

"Oh," I said, looking down at my plate. I suddenly felt an overwhelming urge to ask if that was what Logan wanted to do, but I squashed it quickly. Of course he didn't. That was why we were in this mess.

'Don't be so sure···' a faint voice muttered in my head.

The Last Alpha

What on earth was that?

Logan distracted me as he stood up from the table and took his plate to the sink before turning around to face me and placing his giant hands on the edge of the kitchen tops.

"So what do you want to do today?" he asked.

I couldn't stop my eyes from roaming hungrily down his athletic physique, resting on his hands that I noticed suddenly gripped the kitchen counter firmly. I wondered what it would feel like to have them caressing my skin.

A warm sensation travelled down my body and pooled between my legs unexpectedly. I blushed at how my body was reacting to him and quickly looked up to hope he hadn't noticed. That was my next mistake. His blue eyes had turned a few shades darker and were full of so much heat and desire. My mouth went dry and I wanted to look away as his penetrating gaze made my core ache with need, but I couldn't. I couldn't move. I couldn't speak. I didn't trust myself.

"Alina," he growled deeply, not breaking our eye contact. Just the sound of his husky voice saying my name that way made me want to lunge at him and kiss him. "Stop."

Stop what? I wasn't doing anything. He couldn't read my thoughts, so how would he know my forbidden desires?

I forced myself to look away from him and back at the table of food that I no longer had any appetite for. A few minutes passed before I could feel him coming over to the table again. The moment had passed.

"What do you normally do?" I asked, remembering that he'd asked me a question.

He looked at me puzzled before realising what I meant. "Today? Normally, I would go into work," he said.

The Last Alpha

"Then let's do that," I replied. We could not stay in this house together all day, alone!

"Do you know where I work?" He smirked.

"Yes. In a gym or something. I've been to a gym before," I said defensively.

"Okay then. We will leave in half an hour."

I stood up and climbed the stairs to head for the shower. Luckily, I had actually packed some sports clothes so I wouldn't stand out like a sore thumb. After my shower, I pulled my hair up into a high ponytail, put on my gym leggings and an orange sports bra that complimented my tan skin before throwing my hoody over the top. I met Logan downstairs and was surprised to find he had made us sandwiches and two flasks of iced water to take with us. I was starting to see a different side to him today. An attentive and softer side that only intensified these complicated feelings I was having. I preferred it when he was infuriating because, at least then, I could focus on my anger. We stepped outside and it was a little chillier than I realised. I shivered involuntarily and Logan looked down at me as he was preparing his bike.

"You cold?" he asked.

"A little. I should have grabbed my coat on the way out."

"Here," he said whilst shrugging off his leather jacket and putting it over my shoulders.

"Thanks," I replied as my heart fluttered at the small gesture. I pushed my arms through the sleeves and the heavy material and an explosion of his scent warmed me instantly. We climbed onto his bike and weaved in and out of the London traffic. I had never been a big fan of motorbikes, thinking they were expensive killing machines. But after being on the back of Logan's for the second time, I was starting to understand the appeal. Not to mention Logan looked sexy as hell riding it. There I go again! What has gotten into me today?

We arrived outside a large unit building that didn't look like much from the exterior, but as we stepped through the metal doors, I was blown away. The energy and vibe of the room was exhilarating as people were aggressively lifting weights, striking punch bags, and sparing with each other. The walls were covered with inspirational quotes and mirrors.

In the middle of the vast room was a fighting ring which looked more like a cage with its high ropes and netting. There were two men inside it, beating each other to a pulp, but they seemed to be enjoying it. This place was crazy.

"Logan! I thought you weren't making it in today?" A middle-aged man sauntered towards us. He was wearing a Lycra top with the name of the gym on it and a badge that read: *Manager Marcus.*

"Marcus. Change of plans. This is Alina. Alina, this is Marcus, my business partner." Logan introduced us.

"Hi." I smiled, holding out my hand to shake his. He took it with a broad smile.

"Alina. What a pretty name for a pretty girl. It's lovely to meet you."

Normally I would have found such a compliment cheesy, but he seemed so warm and kind. I liked him already.

He turned back to Logan. "Daniel has just arrived. He was gutted when I said you had the day off. Now you are here, I expect he will want a session."

Logan looked at me, uncertain.

"Its fine. Go ahead. I will just jump on a treadmill or something," I said with a smile that earned a chuckle from him as he passed me one of the flasks.

"I won't be long," he said before walking over to a tall man who seemed to be some kind of body builder from the size of his muscles.

Marcus showed me over to the gym section and I started with a brisk walk on the treadmill. I needed to ease myself into it! After a few minutes, I felt the urge to increase speed and soon, I was sprinting and keeping a good pace with the machine. I have never been much of a runner, but this felt good. Every now and then, I would catch Logan looking my way in between his instructions to Mr. Body Builder. I guess his name is Daniel. Logan was clearly passionate about his work and was a natural leader, shouting commands and giving feedback and praise with respected authority.

After about thirty minutes of intense running, I needed a breather. I switched off the machine and made my way through the gym wondering what I should try next. Suddenly, there was some commotion in the centre of the room and people started gathering around the fighting ring to watch the fight that was about to begin. I strolled towards them to get a better look and I was shocked to see a topless Logan in the ring pacing one side whilst wrapping his wrists with what looked like bandages. His opponent, Mr. Body Builder, was putting a gum shield and a head protection guard on. Why wasn't Logan wearing any of that? Panic rose in me.

Logan glanced at me and he had a wicked glint in his eye. He gave me a wink before he walked to the middle and bumped fists with Daniel to signal the fight had begun. My heart was in my mouth as Daniel's bulky body lunged forward with his fist aiming for Logan's face, but Logan swiftly dodged out of the way with plenty of time. Logan swung and hit Daniel in the ribs and then extended his leg so high and kicked him in the chest. The hulk-like man fell backwards but recovered quickly and charged at Logan again. They

The Last Alpha

punched, kicked, and wrestled each other with so much speed and aggression it was hard to watch.

"Impressive, huh?" A woman who was wearing the same top as Marcus spoke to me whilst watching the fight intensely.

"Uh, yeah. This is real, not like that fake wrestling on the TV!" I said, stunned.

She giggled. "Oh, yes! It's very real. And Logan is going easy on him."

My eyes widened as I realised that Logan was holding back because no one knows that he is a wolf. Knowing he is an even better fighter than he is displaying made him even hotter! The way his body moved so effortlessly, his muscles tensed and expanded with every movement and the look of concentration on his face had my body burning with want and I could feel my wetness building again. Being horny just seemed to be a part of my personality today!

"Have you ever tried it?" The black-haired woman asked, breaking me out of the fantasy of Logan taking me up against those ropes.

"What? That?" I laughed. "No way!"

"We do self-defence classes here for women. You should try it. It's not just about beating the crap out of people, it's about protecting yourself if you ever need to," she replied.

I loved that they taught that here. And that sounded like something I could certainly benefit from at this point in my life.

The crowd erupted in applause as I saw Logan had pinned Daniel to the ground and Daniel had tapped out, signalling the end of the fight.

"AGAIN," Logan's voice boomed as they took their positions.

I turned back to the woman. "Actually, I would love to do that. Are there any classes today?"

"No, but I am happy to do a one-on-one with you. My name is

Hannah, by the way, and I'm an instructor here." She held her hand out to me.

"Alina," I said, shaking it. Her grip was firm just like her toned physique and I knew I was in capable hands. "That would be great, lead the way."

"Follow me," she said, taking me towards a separate studio room with soft mats covering the floor.

After about twenty minutes, we had covered the basics and she was starting to show me what to do if someone attacked me from behind. Unexpectantly, the door swung open and Logan, covered in sweat, was staring at us with an unreadable expression.

Chapter 26

Logan's POV

It was a few minutes into my third round with Daniel when I realised Alina was missing. I grabbed Daniel's fist that had been heading for my stomach and swiftly pulled his arm up behind his back and twisted, bringing him to his knees. I held him there for a few more seconds longer than I should, being careful not to break his arm, so I could quickly sweep the gym for any sight of Alina. When I couldn't see her, my heart stopped. I released Daniel and took a few steps back, buying myself some more time, my eyes searching the crowd frantically.

Without warning, Daniel's fist connected with my right cheek and blood from my mouth sprayed onto the floor. I heard the shocked gasps from the regular onlookers. No one had ever managed to make me bleed before. I felt another blow to my ribs, knocking the air from my lungs momentarily before I realised I needed to end this fight as soon as possible so I could find Alina.

Daniel was unsuspecting as I hunched over from his blow and I used it to my advantage. I skilfully spun around with my leg extended and kicked him with my full force to the chest. He flew across the ring, hitting the ropes and falling to the floor. He looked up at me with a dazed expression and then a sadistic, wide grin spread across his face. He loved it when I went to my full capacity. I smirked and shook my head before exiting the ring. Everyone promptly parted to make way for me and soon, went back to their workouts. I went straight to the main desk where I found Marcus.

"Have you seen Alina?" I asked urgently.

"No. Last I saw her she was on the treadmills. Everything alright?"

I ran past him and out the back to check the CCTV cameras. If she had left on her own or, goddess for bid, someone had taken her, there would be hell to pay. The memory of those bloodsuckers holding her against the wall last night flashed through my mind. I had never felt so much pure rage in my life. Just the thought of her being hurt or taken, had my blood boiling to the point that I would not stop terrorising anyone and everyone who had anything to do with it.

I rewound the tapes until I spotted her. She was at the side of the ring watching the fight with Hannah. They then walked off towards the self-defence studio. I bolted back out past Marcus, reaching the studio in seconds. I pushed open the door and saw Alina in an upright choke hold by Hannah. My instincts kicked in and I was about to rip Hannah off her when something stopped me in my tracks. Alina smiled mischievously at me and, in a sudden movement, gripped Hannah' s arm and leaned forward, forcing Hannah over her shoulder and falling flat on her back. Alina stood upright and gave her the biggest grin.

"I did it!" she screamed with joy.

"That was brilliant, Lina! Make sure next time, you lean back a little more before you flip to give you more momentum," Hannah advised.

She was learning how to fight. What the hell? I realised I was still

The Last Alpha

standing gawking at them when they both turned their attention towards me.

"Alina here is a natural, Logan. She's a quick learner, has picked up everything I've taught her on the first attempt," Hannah gushed, clearly impressed by my mate.

Alina put her hands on her hips proudly and I couldn't help but let my eyes wander down to her breasts as her chest rose and fell with rapid breaths. She had taken her hoody off and was standing in an orange sports bra and tight black gym leggings. Her body was unbelievable.

"We were just about to start sparring," Hannah informed me, snapping me out of my trance. I still hadn't even said a word and must have looked like an idiot who stood ogling her.

Alina picked up some boxing gloves and started to put them on.

"Oh, shoot! I just realised the time. I have a personal training session with a client in five. I'm going to have to bail on you." Hannah's tone was apologetic as she looked over to Alina.

"No worries. Logan can do it," Alina replied, giving me an irresistible smile.

"Do what?" I asked.

"Spar with me," she said, taking me by surprise. "Unless you're too scared." A devilish grin formed on my lips as I accepted her challenge.

Hannah left after Alina had thanked her and promised to come to the self-defence classes this week. I was impressed that Alina was taking such an interest in my world.

I picked up the sparring pads and started showing her how to change her stance to give the most effective punch. Hannah was right, she was a quick learner. After she got the hang of the technique, I pushed her to increase her speed, shouting "One-two, one-two, one,

one-two!" patterns for her to follow. She attacked my pads aggressively with all she had, and I had to admit, I was aroused by her strength and determination. When I sensed her lagging, I paused to give her a break.

She walked over to the bench and took a swig of her water. I took the opportunity to stare at her body again. I couldn't get enough. Beads of sweat trickled down her bronzed skin, vanishing between her delectable breasts and into her bra.

I suddenly had an overwhelming desire to taste her. To lick every drop off her body. My manhood pulsed and hardened at the thought. Turning away from her to hide my compromising situation, I started to put away the gloves and pads.

"Logan?" she called, "Thank you for this. For bringing me here with you. I feel so much better just knowing I have got a few ways of protecting myself now," she said sweetly and my heart melted a little. I hated that she felt like she needed to protect herself, but she was right, there was no harm in her learning how to.

"You've done really well today, Alina. But these aren't just your average attackers on the streets that we are dealing with. They're supernatural. Powerful creatures," I reminded her.

"Okay. Well, attack me then. Let me see if I can do it," she said bravely. I chuckled and shook my head, which only seemed to annoy her.

"You are supernatural, so let me use what I have learnt on you," she continued with a fierce determination. She wasn't going to back down from this.

"Okay," I said. "Whoever wins has to cook dinner." Might as well make this interesting.

"Deal," she said confidently and positioned herself in the middle of the mats with her back to me. Goddess, that ass!

I stalked towards her lazily but stopped inches away from her. The tension in the room was palpable as we felt each other's bodies so close yet not touching. I could hear her heart racing and the hair on the back of her neck stood to attention in anticipation. It reminded me of the very first moment I laid eyes on her at the party.

Without warning, I wrapped my hand around her dainty neck and my other hand around her waist and vigorously picked her up, slamming her back against my chest. Sparks from our contact exploded all over my skin and I heard her gasp in shock and pleasure. I smirked as I think of how she wouldn't have expected me to lift her off the floor and Hannah wouldn't have done this move with her. Was I playing fair? No fucking way.

She composed herself quickly and fixed her hand on top of mine around her neck, pulling my fingers backwards at an awkward angle whilst lifting one leg and kicking me on the shin with her heel. I dropped her to her feet in surprise and she turned to face me and punched me as hard as she could in the gut. Her strength definitely caught me off guard, but it wasn't enough to affect me, so I gripped her shoulders and did my favourite move—using one of my legs to sweep her off her feet and push her backwards so she fell flat on the floor.

Normally, I would let my opponent fall but I didn't want to hurt her, so I kept one hand on her shoulder and cupped the other one behind her head and went down with her. With a thump, she was lying on the mat beneath me, and I was pinning her to the ground with my body, hand still cradling her head.

I got lost in her gorgeous green eyes as we tried to even our breaths. She was so heartbreakingly beautiful. If I just bent my head a fraction, her lips would be mine.

"You cheated," she whispered.

A slow smile formed on my lips. "The first rule in self-defence is there are no rules," I stated, climbing off her and helping her up.

She shook her head but smiled as she brushed herself down. I grabbed our belongings and we strolled out of the room.

"What are you cooking me for dinner then?" I teased as she playfully rolled her eyes.

Chapter 27

Madeline's POV

Sweden was beautiful. Yet I could not get any serenity from its breath-taking landscape. Dramatic mountains could be seen behind the rolling hills and flowing streams that passed the window of the rental car. Darius was driving us further out into the unspoilt wilderness, where pine and birch trees nestled on the winding road. Things had been a little tense between us after he reluctantly confessed that Alina had been attacked last night and that was the real reason he stayed at my flat and Logan did not. Not because we had an early flight like he suggested. To say I was angry would be an understatement. Once again, Logan was putting this human before me.

Since we arrived here, I have felt strange. This setting was beyond spectacular, and I am in awe of the beauty of my surroundings. I feel more at one with nature here than I ever have before. There was something so inviting and calming about this place, but I also felt an overwhelming sense of unease and dread. I knew it had to do with the fact Logan was alone with Alina, but it was more than that. It was as if my body and subconscious were trying to warn me about something to come. Something dangerous. Even Nina seemed on edge as she paced in my mind. I wanted to speak to Logan, maybe hearing his voice would calm my nerves.

I dialled his number but let out a frustrated growl when it went straight to voicemail.

Darius took a quick glance in my direction before concentrating on the road again. "He's fine, Mads. I spoke to him earlier and he was going to work."

Oh, great. So, Logan would talk to the cousin he couldn't stand, but not to me. I slid lower down onto the leather seat and peered out the window again.

Darius brought the car to a halt at the end of the dirt road that led to an enchanted-looking forest. As we climbed out of the car, I couldn't help but gawk at towering, majestic trees. Their knotted arms rose ever upward as far as my head could lift. The leafy paradise before us reeked of age and dark secrets. It felt as if we had stepped through a portal into another realm.

Darius, who clearly was not as affected by his surroundings, pulled out his phone and tutted, "Urgh, no signal. These are the directions Fredrik gave me but there is no road left! I thought I was the only one allowed to play pranks around here."

I continued to spin on my heels, ignoring his moaning, as I listened to the soulful orchestra of the songbirds, running water meeting rugged rocks and rustling of leaves in the breeze. I noticed a moss-veiled trail that seemed to beckon me into the forest's pulsing heart. Feeling an emotional connection to this place, my feet started to move towards the entrance.

"Hey! Earth to Madeline! We are lost! There is nothing here but trees," Darius called behind me.

"Or maybe there is, and you just aren't meant to know about it," I said in a whisper, but I knew he heard me. As I ventured deeper into this primeval forest, stepping over huge roots that spread-eagled on the ground, I could hear the clumsy sound of crunching underfoot as Darius jogged to keep up with me.

"Nope. No, pretty sure we are lost. Let's go back, Mads. I must have driven past it."

I continued to feel spellbound as we walked further on until I spotted a clearing in the distance. The trees stood proudly like guardians around a very impressive building. It seamlessly blended in with the fairy-tale green haven as the walls were covered with plush olive moss and leaves. The only manmade material making it stand out was the enormous, floor to ceiling glass windows along the front of the cabin.

"I think this is it," I said breathlessly.

Darius raised his eyebrows at me as if I was bonkers. "I can't see anything," he replied, perplexed as he scanned the forest. "Have you eaten any mushrooms since being in here by any chance? If so, give me some."

What did he mean he couldn't see it? It was right there in front of us!

Suddenly, a huge gush of wind swept through the forest, sending a blizzard of dust and dead leaves swirling around us. We covered our eyes and coughed until it cleared.

"WOAH!" I heard Darius gasp once the wind had settled. "I can see it now!"

The wooden door flung open with force but no one came out to greet us. I stepped forward to head towards the cabin when Darius grabbed my arm.

"I'm not sure about this, Maddy. There was a cloaking spell on this place, so how could you see it? Something doesn't feel right," he said quietly whilst looking up at the cabin.

I chuckled at his fear. "That's why I'm here, aren't I? To

hold your hand when you get scared," I teased.

His face turned to a frown, and he charged in front of me towards the cabin. I giggled as I ran to keep up.

We entered the cabin with caution and slowly took in the décor. It was a drastic change to the forest as it was immaculately well kept and modern. High walls of glass looked out into the woodland, bringing the outdoors in and everything was white and pristine. I felt very conscious not to touch anything and wondered whether we should take our shoes off, so we didn't leave a mark on the milky marble floors.

In the middle of the expansive room was a large fireplace burning and the embers from the fire were the only piece of colour in the room other than the odd provocative or alarming artwork on the walls.

"You're here," a mystical, haunting voice echoed through the room. Our heads snapped up to where it came from to see a striking middle-aged woman, elegantly dressed in a black silk suit. Her jet-black hair was freely flowing down her back and nearly reached her knees. She had sharp features and the palest, icy blue eyes I had ever seen. They were almost white, giving her a ghostly appearance. She was out of this world and looked nothing like I thought she would.

She glided into the room and sat down on the shaggy sheepskin lounger and gestured her skeletal hands to us to take a seat opposite and join her.

"How did you know we were coming?" Darius questioned.

The witch had not taken her eyes off me for a second and she replied as if I had spoken and not Darius. "I didn't. I can sense you in my visions. I just didn't know who you were." She cocked her head to the side to study me more intensely.

Feeling like that was my cue to introduce us, I said, "My name is Madeline and this is my friend, Darius. We are here on behalf of Alpha Logan."

A small smile formed on her lips at his name. "He is not an Alpha yet," she replied coldly with dark humour.

"He will be very soon. Once we kill the Vampire King and restore our pack to its former glory," Darius said defensively. "But in order to do that we need your help."

Her face regarded Darius for the first time.

"We've run into a little··· problem that needs sorting before we can go ahead with our plans for revenge."

Her eyes flick from Darius to me and back before her smile widened.

"So it is true. He found his destined mate," she replied.

"How did you know that?" I couldn't help my harsh tone on the subject.

"I had a vision that he would. Tell me, what is she like?" Her eyes sparkled with interest.

"She is human," Darius answered.

The witch's face fell instantly and started shaking her head in shock.

"It cannot be," she muttered, more to herself than to us.

"What do you mean?" I asked, but she didn't respond, as if she was having her own conversation in her head.

"That is why we need your help. She needs to sign a Blood Oath before the next full moon or the council will force her to become a werewolf or kill her."

The witch leaned back, still in distress at this information. I couldn't understand why it bothered her so.

"You're Alpha has not marked and mated her?" she asked, surprised.

"No," I said sharply. "He is planning on rejecting her."

She snapped her head at me and studied me carefully again. Her powerful stare had me shifting uncomfortably in my seat.

"And what is your role in all of this?" she asked me directly.

"I-I am the Alpha's chosen mate and soon to be his Luna."

I noticed Darius clearing his throat awkwardly next to me. She scanned my neck and then her eyes flicked back to mine.

"Ah," she responded in a telling way. "But he has not marked you either?"

"No, we are waiting for the Luna Ceremony so we can keep with traditions," I said confidently even though I was feeling anything but confident right now.

Her eyes continued to burn into mine and I could tell she was thinking a lot more about this but she did not voice her thoughts. We all sit in silence for a few moments before her demanding voice filled the room.

"Tell your Alpha I will perform the Blood Oath. However, I want to meet with him in person and his fated mate. I will come to him in three days' time."

I could not help but beam. I was one step closer to getting Alina out of our lives.

"Thank you. Alpha Logan will be in your debt," Darius said, standing up from the sofa. It was clear he was ready to leave and wanted to get out of here as soon as possible. When I didn't stand, Darius signalled his head towards the door, not so subtly telling me to move.

"Darius, can you give me a minute in private with···" I paused to look at the woman before me, realising I didn't know her name.

"Cora." She nodded.

I smiled warmly. "Could you give me a minute with Cora?"

He looked at me as though I had lost my mind, but then shrugged.

"I'll wait outside."

The Last Alpha

Once the door had shut behind him, I turned my attention back to Cora as she sat expectantly, waiting for me to speak.

"I wanted to ask, what did you mean when you said you sensed me in your visions?" I asked curiously.

She fiddled with her gemstone rings decorating her fingers before responding. "I have visions, prophecies, some call them, of the future. Sometimes I see images like a film playing before my very eyes, but other times I just feel others' emotions or their presence. I have seen your Alpha defeat the Vampire King, but I have also seen him fall at the hands of Lucius."

I gasped and my hand covered my mouth. "But how is it possible to see two prophecies? Which one is real?" I asked in panic.

"My dear, prophecies can be changed. They are not set in stone. The choices one makes can change their fate completely."

"What choices? Is it to do with me and Alina?" I hated the thought that I could be the reason he is killed.

"I do not know, as I have never seen you or her in any of the visions. But as that seems to be his biggest choice right now, I would expect it to be so."

"Then how did you know he had met his mate if you haven't seen her?"

"I sensed it. In the vision where he defeated Lucius, he seemed stronger. A strength that could only come from being marked and mated with a powerful Luna. That is why I am so surprised to hear that she is human." she explained.

I nodded my head slowly, trying to understand all this information. Hope started to swell. I must be the powerful Luna he chose to kill Lucius. I came from a strong line of werewolves who have always been Betas. She is human and even if she turned, she would be a weak wolf because of it. If he would choose her, he will be weakened and will not stand a chance against the Vampire King.

The more I thought about it, the clearer it became.

"Let me try something," Cora asked, holding out her bony fingers to me.

I hesitantly place my hand in hers and she gripped it tightly and closed her eyes. She started to chant in a dialect I do not recognise and then her eyes darted open. She looked baffled.

"What is it? What did you see?" I questioned worriedly.

"Nothing," she whispered. "I saw nothing."

"What? I have no future?" I panicked, thinking that could only mean one thing.

"No, no, dear. You do, I can feel your power, but for some reason I cannot see anything. I have never not been able to read someone's future unless they are…" She trailed off.

"Unless they are what?" I urged.

"Family." She looked at me in shock.

"What? I am a wolf and I have no relation to any witches in my bloodline." I almost shrieked.

She shook her head and her hair fell around her face. "I agree, I do not believe we are related but it is very… peculiar."

Suddenly, I felt distrust creep within me. How can I believe anything she is saying? She is a dark witch after all and they are known for their deceptions and selfish ways. The uneasy feeling in the pit of my stomach returned.

"Why should we trust you? Why are you even helping us? You may not look like one, but you are a dark witch after all. Aren't you supposed to be evil and ruthless?" I said, narrowing my eyes at her.

Her deep cackle reverberated around the room. "I may not look like a typical dark witch, but do not be fooled. My darkness lurks within. I am one of the most powerful witches left in this world, but we have the same end goal here. To have Lucius' head on a platter." Her feline eyes were shimmering with spite, and I recoiled at the evil lurking in them.

"B-but why?" I asked nervously.

Her face turned cold and unforgiving. Her reason for her hatred for the Vampire King must be genuine.

"Maybe it is best that I show you, my flower. So, I may gain your trust." She once again held out her hand, but this time, I took it without hesitation.

Suddenly, my mind was immersed in a flashback of her past···

"What are you doing here Lucius?" A younger Cora's voice sounded faint and drowsy as she backed away from him in a red-walled bedroom.

"I don't feel well. What have you given me?"

She stumbled forward, grabbing hold of the edge of the four-poster bed as the pale, vile man stalked towards her. His face reflected the wickedness within as his deep hazel eyes turned flaming red, and his fangs protruded.

"Relax Cora. Why don't you lie down?" He pushed her onto the bed forcefully and climbed on top of her as she struggled to gain control over her body movements from the drugs in her system.

"Lucius··· stop··· please. Why are you doing this?" she cried, a look of pure terror on her face. She lifted her right hand and suddenly, a bright beam of light blasted from it and hit him in the chest, flinging him across the room and into the wall.

He stood with malice and shouted, "Guards!"

Two vampires entered the room at speed and held Cora down on the bed by her arms. In a split second, Lucius was on top of her again, unzipping his trousers and prizing open her legs. She let out an alarming, high-pitched scream as he thrust inside her.

"You will give me what I have lost," he whispered in her ear as he thrust into her again and again whilst she fell in and out of consciousness.

The vision blur and a new scene emerged of Cora in the same bed with women around her holding her hands and legs whilst she screamed in agony. Beads of sweat trickled down her face and her black hair clung to her damp skin.

"One more push Cora," the woman between her legs called out.

She gritted her teeth and bore down with so much might before falling back onto the pillows, panting in exhaustion. A baby was wrapped up in a blanket and taken away to be checked.

"My baby! Where's my baby? Why isn't he crying?" Cora shouted in panic.

"We are just checking him over. He needs some help breathing and then we will bring him right back," the midwife explained.

The vision blur slightly again and then the midwife entered the room with a bundle of blankets in her arms. Her face was full of sorrow as she handed Cora the child.

"I'm sorry," she said. "He didn't make it."

The agonising howl that left Cora was the most chilling sound in the world…

I opened my eyes frantically as I try to calm my shaky breathing. I looked into Cora's pale eyes and saw all the pain I felt her went through at the hands of Lucius. I touched my face and realised my own cheeks were wet from the tears that I didn't know were falling.

"I-I'm so sorry Cora," I managed to say weakly, knowing it would never be enough.

"Now you know," she said coldly and stood up from the chair and disappeared from the room without a goodbye.

The Last Alpha

Chapter 28

Logan's POV

The sensational smell of slow cooked meat wafted into the living room as I took another swig from my beer. Alina had been out there for well over an hour preparing dinner and from the amount of cussing and banging that could be heard from the kitchen, I was expecting to order us a takeaway. But this smell had me optimistic!

If felt surreal, sitting in Darius' living room watching TV with a beer whilst my fated mate that I never thought I would meet, cooked me dinner. I could get used to this.

The thought entered my mind before I quickly dismissed it. It was becoming more and more challenging to think of rejecting Alina after she signed the Blood Oath. I wasn't sure if I could live in this world without her, let alone if I wanted to.

"Dinner is served." She popped her head around the door frame. Her hair wasn't as neatly styled as it was an hour ago and she had smudges all over the apron she was wearing. She looked adorable.

I stood up from the sofa and made my way to the dining room. She had set the table elegantly and there was the faint background noise of a playlist. Alina had also lit some candles on the table and around the room, giving an intimate and cosy vibe. She started to blush when she noticed me looking at them.

"I can blow them out if you think it's too much. I just thought the bright spotlights were a bit glaring for the evening," she explained shyly.

"No. No, I like it," I assured her, taking a seat at the table.

"Okay." She turned and headed back into the kitchen. "Now, I am no chef, so please be nice and I still think you should have been the one cooking as you clearly tricked me. Also, your food probably won't give us food poisoning, but..." she rambled on nervously. She carefully walked back in carrying two plates with a very impressive, stacked burger and chunky fries.

"Woah, this looks amazing," I said as she lowered my plate down in front of me.

She smiled timidly and sat down opposite, taking a few gulps of her wine.

We ate in a comfortable silence and I had to fight back the urge to lick the plate clean when I finished.

"Well, you can cook for me anytime! That was the best burger I have ever eaten and I'm from America!" I said, leaning back in my chair and rubbing my stomach with satisfaction.

She blushed at my compliment. "I'm glad you enjoyed it. It's probably one of the only things I know how to cook well, so don't get too excited," she replied.

"Where did you learn to cook meat so well? The slow cooked brisket on top of the burger was to die for!"

"My dad, actually. He was a big fan of slow cooked meat and you'll be pleased to hear he was American, so maybe that's why they are so good," she explained.

"He was from America? So, you're half American?" I asked, surprised.

"Yes. Well, technically, I am, but I have never been there, so I don't really consider myself to be." She took another drink of wine.

"Do you miss him? Your dad?" I asked carefully. I wasn't sure if she would share such a sensitive subject with me, but I wanted to try.

"Yes. Of course, he was my dad. And then one day, he wasn't. I hate that I miss him. I'm still so angry with him. That he could just take off without a word. My mum was never the same afterwards." She played with her fork on the table as she seemed to get lost in a memory.

"How long ago did he leave? Did you ever think about trying to find him?" I asked, studying her facial features for any sign that I was pushing too hard.

"Um, nearly nine years ago now. I was fourteen when he left. I remember thinking at the time that it must have been because of me and my bratty, teenage ways. He was very strict and protective of me and I always pushed his boundaries. My mum tried to look for him for a few weeks, ringing friends and family, but no one had heard from him. Then one day, it was like she just gave up. I came home from school and found her on the bathroom floor, curled up in a ball and passed out from crying so hard. She had been there for hours. That was when I really hated him. For doing that to her. After that day, it was like a part of her was dead. She had lost her brightness and sparkle that always made her so alluring. When she was diagnosed with cancer, I really believed he would come back. That he would show up when we needed him the most. But he never did."

I listened intently as she spoke about her pain and the betrayal of her father leaving her and my gut twisted, knowing that I had to do the same thing soon. But it was for her own good. Maybe that was her father's reasoning, too. Who knows?

The Last Alpha

"Sorry. I didn't mean to bring the evening to such a depressing state so quickly." She smiled, but it didn't reach her eyes.

"You haven't. I am pleased that you feel like you can talk to me about this," I said honestly.

Her hypnotising emerald eyes darted to mine and I saw so many different emotions swirling in them like a hurricane.

"I feel like I can tell you anything," she said, not breaking eye contact. "I know it is probably just this mate bond, but I feel as though I've known you my whole life and you make me feel like···" She paused, searching for her next words. "Like I am more myself than I have ever been. Does that make any sense?" she asked.

My heart started to pick up speed at the direction this conversation was going.

"Yes. It makes perfect sense because I feel the same way," I replied.

We continue to stare into each other's eyes, really seeing each other for the first time. The raw emotions we both feel thicken the atmosphere.

"Is it?" she asked. "Just because of the mate bond?"

"Probably," I replied, looking away and picking up my beer. I wasn't sure if I would still feel this way without the mate bond, but a small nagging feeling told me I would.

She looked down at the table and seemed almost sad at my answer. Every fibre of my being wanted to go to her and comfort her. But I resisted. Just like I did this morning when she looked at me with so much desire that I still can't believe I managed to refrain myself from picking her up and ripping those ridiculous pyjamas from her goddess-like body and taking her on the breakfast table. I deserved a medal.

I racked my brain, trying to think of something to say to bring back the pleasant ease we had a few minutes ago, but she spoke first.

"What will happen after I sign the Blood Oath?" she asked with a quiet voice. The question hit me like a ton of bricks and I had no idea how to answer.

'TELL HER, YOU FOOL. TELL HER SHE WILL BE OURS!' Elias roared in my head.

'No, Elias!'

I pushed him back into my consciousness. I was about to open my mouth to speak when my phone started ringing in the living room. I didn't move straight away but knew that this was a way to buy myself some time.

"I'm sorry but I need to get that," I said, getting up from my chair.

She nodded and brought her glass to her lips.

Picking up my phone from the coffee table where I left it, my heart sunk when I saw the caller ID.

Madeline.

This was the second time she had tried to ring me today and I had missed the first due to being at the gym. But I really did not want to have this conversation with Alina in the next room. The call ended as I continued to stare at it. Immediately, it started ringing again. She wasn't going to give up.

"Hello?" I said into the headset.

"Finally! Where have you been, Logan?" Her irritated voice boomed down the phone.

"Sorry. I went to work today and I was just eating dinner."

There was a pause before she asked. "So, you haven't been with her?"

I didn't like that she never referred to Alina by her name, but under the circumstances, I let it go.

"Well yeah, she came with me. You know I must make sure she is safe, Maddy. Until this Blood Oath is done, she has a target on her back," I tried to reason with her, knowing how annoyed she was that I was spending all my time with Alina.

"You mean until you reject her, she has a target on her back." She didn't miss a beat.

I sighed, exasperated. "How did it go? With the witch?" I changed the subject.

"Very well, no thanks to Darius. Good job I came with him. She has agreed to perform the Blood Oath. She will come to us in three days."

My mood lifted a little, knowing at least one of my problems would be solved. Now I can concentrate on what to do next.

"Good. Thank you, Maddy," I said genuinely.

There was another long pause.

"Logan?" She spoke softer than before. "The witch told me some things. About her visions."

"Madeline, I really can't talk about this right now. We will talk when you are back," I said, aware that Alina could probably hear every word I was saying.

"You're with her now, aren't you?!" Maddy screeched down the phone. "You want to get off the phone to me so you go and be with her!"

"No, Maddy. That's not—" I start but she interrupts me.

"Fine, Logan. I'll sit back and allow you this time with her whilst I am gone. But very soon, you are going to wake up and realise she is not what you need. And when that day comes, I will be here, waiting. Because I am your Luna and I will not allow you to get yourself killed just to be with her," she snapped.

"Maddy, what are you talking about? Maddy?"

The line went dead.

I threw my phone down on the sofa and ran my fingers through my hair. Turning on my heel, I walked back into the dining room to find all the candles had been blown out and no sign of Alina. Fuck.

Chapter 29

Alina's POV

"Until this Blood Oath, she has a target on her back." I could hear Logan's strained voice from the living room. He was obviously on the phone to Madeline and, for the first time, I felt real envy at the notion that he was hers. Up until now, I had been avoiding the thought of them together and I had been quite successful in doing so. But now, faced with the reality of the situation, I could no longer keep my feelings suppressed. After the near perfect day we had spent together and the intimate dinner, I had let myself get swept up in the idea of Logan and a future with him. Sitting here now, alone at the table whilst he reassured his girlfriend that he was just 'keeping me safe', I felt such a first-class idiot. The sudden realisation of how completely foolish I had been today had tears threatening to spill from my eyes.

"Madeline, I really can't talk about this right now. We will talk when you are back," I heard. He didn't want me listening to their private conversation. He probably felt sorry for me, or worse, they were talking about me.

Blowing out the candles around the room as quickly as I could, I made my way upstairs and locked myself in my bedroom. I started to get undressed and was standing with only my white lace panties on when an urgent knock on the door made me jump.

"Alina?" Logan's deep voice resounded from behind the door.

I stood frozen in the middle of the room as my heart raced. I didn't want to see him. I couldn't keep putting myself through this torture. Because that was what it was like being around him but not having him. Utter torture.

The knocking intensified. "Alina, are you in there?"

I swiftly threw my oversized Nirvana top over my head whilst shouting, "Leave me alone, Logan!"

There was a pause behind the door. "Alina, open the door!" he commanded with his authoritative tone.

Well, too bad. I was not one of his little wolves to order around. I walked closer to the door and said with as much assertiveness as I could in my emotional state. "Leave me alone, Logan. I don't want to see you."

There was another longer pause this time and I sighed as I thought he had given up. The door flung open, shattering the lock and handle to pieces from the brutal force of his kick.

I let out a small scream in surprise as I took a few steps away from him. Logan was glaring at me with a thunderous expression and his fists were clenched at his sides. Any normal reaction to his menacing stature would be to cower away, but rage spiked through my veins at his intrusion. How dare he!

"What the actual fuck, Logan? I told you I didn't want to see you," I shouted across the room at him.

"And I told you to open the door!" he gritted back. His eyes hungrily travelled along my body, taking in my bare legs and up to my chest in the thin, worn fabric of my top. I crossed my arms over my breasts self-consciously when I realised I wasn't wearing a bra. His jaw ticked and the anger in his eyes was replaced with lust. The air prickled around us.

"What's wrong?" he asked in a gruff tone, keeping his heated gaze on me.

I hesitated. Everything was wrong. I was falling for a man who was already taken and would reject me as his mate as soon as I promised to keep their secret. Not to mention he was the leader of werewolves and vampires wanted to kill me because of my association with him.

That was what hurt the most. That he was only protecting me out of duty, and I was just an inconvenience in his life. But how could I admit any of this without being completely vulnerable? I needed to protect myself. I needed to protect my heart from what was about to come.

"You never answered my question." I lifted my head a little higher in determination and I saw slight panic flicker across his face. "What will happen after I do the Oath?"

Logan softened at my question but the tension between us was still abundant. He ran his fingers through his thick curls that I had come to know as a sign of stress, but all it did was make me want to jump him.

"Alina, let's just cross that bridge when we come to it," he said with a sigh.

"No! I am done with secrecy. I want to know! I NEED to know!" I screamed at him, losing my temper.

"What do you want me to say, Alina? I don't even know myself what will happen." He raised his voice to match mine.

"You do know! You just don't want to say it to my face! Why? Because you're scared of hurting my feelings? Well, it's too late for that, Logan. So, please just tell me you are going to reject me so I can prepare myself. I can't keep doing this anymore!" I whimpered as my voice caught at the end. I fought back the tears. I will not allow myself to cry in front of him. I did not want his pity.

He took a step towards me when he saw the control on my emotions falter.

Holding up my hands to stop him, I shouted, "Don't! I mean it, Logan. You need to leave me alone. I think its best we ignore each other until Darius is back. Keep our distance." Every word was like a knife through my heart.

His eyebrows furrowed and he frowned deeply. "I can't do that, Alina." He gritted through his teeth as if he was in pain.

"Why the hell not?" I yelled back.

"You know why." His voice is dangerously low as that heated look returned.

"Because of the mate bond? It is an illusion, Logan. This thing between us." I gestured at the air separating us with a wave of my hand. "It's not real! You don't want me, Logan, and I can't keep doing this with you knowing you will cast me aside once it is safe to do so."

In a split second, he had invaded the space between us and I backed up until my body hit the bedroom wall. His huge frame caged mine as he pressed himself up against me, sending indescribable pleasure through my body at our contact.

His head was bent down to the right so his face was inches from mine and he looked crazed. His hands were on either side of my head, resting on the wall so there was no escape. My heart flipped at the closeness.

"You have no idea what you are talking about." He growled deeply, and I knew Elias must have been close to the surface. "Every passing second of my day is spent thinking of you, about kissing you, touching you, fucking you. Even when I sleep, you consume my dreams. I have never had to fight so hard to resist anything in my life. Everything about you is so fucking addictive."

I swallowed audibly at his words as my core burned with desire that he wanted me as much as I wanted him. But this wasn't right. It didn't change anything.

"Logan. I - We can't. This is just because of the bond. Once you reject me, you won't want me anymore," I almost whispered.

A shallow growl vibrated from his chest, and he pushed his groin against my stomach. I gasped when I felt how hard he was, and my own arousal started leaking between my legs.

"Can you feel how much I want you, Alina? What you do to me? That will never change whether we are mates or not. I will always crave you. You are mine." His eyes turned a few shades darker and I could tell that Logan was struggling to keep control. My heart felt like it was going to explode in my chest at how fast it was beating.

"I-I can't do this, Logan. You are not mine and so I can never be yours."

His eyes blazed with so much turmoil at my words as he realised what I meant and the truth it held.

Suddenly, he pushed off me and turned his back on me. My body yearned for his warmth again and it took everything in me to stay rooted to the spot and not to go to him. His shoulders and back rose and fell with panted breaths and his whole body was rigid. I knew at that moment he was battling Elias to keep dominance and a small part of me wanted Elias to win.

I held my breath as the seconds ticked by, not daring to speak.

Dramatically, he spun around, and I locked eyes with the most beautiful stormy azure irises and my centre tingled. They were sharing control.

His eyes roamed my body possessively once more, but this time, it was more intense. He was no longer trying to hide his desire.

"Fuck this," he roared and in one rapid motion, he closed the space between us and picked me up by my thighs, slamming me hard against the wall and his mouth was on mine.

The intensity of electricity that erupted inside me had all my thoughts, fears and doubts melt away. His kiss was dominating and fierce, making my wetness grow between my legs that were now wrapped around his waist. One of his hands reached behind my head, tangling in my ashen hair as he deepened the kiss. It was the most euphoric moment of my life so far. I moaned desperately against his perfect lips. His tongue licked the centre of my mouth, asking for access.

I parted my lips dutifully and the fireworks exploded within me as our tongues danced together, not able to get enough. He tasted divine.

The world faded away as the raw intensity of the kiss consumed us both. I felt his other hand move up above my baggy T-shirt as his manly hands caressed my bare skin and explored every inch of my body. My hands found his thick hair as I ran my fingers through his soft curls. I never wanted this to end.

The need built as I started to run my hands down his neck, his broad shoulders and then his muscular back. He pressed into me harder, mixing pleasure with pain as I was pinned between his solid body and the hard surface of the wall.

He released my mouth quickly and pulled my top up over my head and then his lips found mine once more. He cupped my breast and rolled his thumb over one of my nipples, causing a muffled moan to escape my mouth. I could feel his manhood growing bigger against my centre at the sound.

He left my lips and his mouth replaced his thumb as he swirled his tongue against my nipple and flicked it expertly, sending a shock of pleasure to my core. I was panting heavily, trying to catch my breath.

"You are so fucking perfect, Alina," he mumbled against my skin. "I need to taste you."

With that, he gripped my thighs forcefully and lifted them effortlessly over his shoulders as he knelt on the floor.

My cheeks turned crimson at the proximity of my soaking centre so close to his face with only the thin lace fabric concealing my modesty. I was about to hesitate when he suddenly plunged his nose into the fabric and inhaled. I froze in shock at the action as he growled in appreciation.

He lifted his hands from where they were gripping my thighs and grabbed the top of my panties, ripping them in half and discarding them on the floor. I gasped and then moaned in pleasure as he plunged his tongue inside me.

My back arched against the wall as I held on to his hair for dear life and threw my head back as his tongue stroked me in long, slow licks, lapping up my juices.

"Fuck, you are the best thing I have ever tasted." He broke away to confess, but immediately after, his mouth was once again devouring me like fire. Only this time, he was more urgent, exploring and tasting every bit of my exposed core.

His hands squeezed my ass, holding me in place as my hips began to buck spontaneously. His rhythm picked up and I could feel the climax in me building. I was a moaning mess as I felt him thrust one finger inside of me, crooking it and matching the movement of his skilful tongue. My moans turned into one long, high-pitched orgasm as my legs quaked on his shoulders.

I closed my eyes as I let my body and mind calm down from the immense pleasure it had just received and when I opened them, I was met with a devilish grin. Before I could react, Logan stood up, still holding my naked body to his and he attacked my mouth with passion. I could taste myself on his tongue and it made me wild with need and want. His tongue claimed me possessively as our kiss became raw and full of emotion.

I pulled at the bottom of his top and he swiftly threw it off and his bare chest rubbed up against mine as sparks ignited all over our skin. He lifted me once again and I cradled his hips with my thighs. I could feel his stiffness bursting through his jeans and rubbing up against my sweet spot, making me cry out at the friction.

I gently bit his lower lip as he groaned in pleasure, and I felt two fingers enter me. They worked inside me, a little uncomfortable at first, but nothing I can't handle. His hardness pushed against my nub as he pulsed his fingers in and out, stretching me.

My eyes rolled back into my head as I broke our kiss and his lips travelled down my neck, sucking and nibbling. I was so close to the edge again. The strength of what was building was staggering.

"I need to have you, Alina," I heard him breathe.

I nodded in cooperation and felt him unbuckling his jeans and releasing his giant erection. I couldn't see it, but my god, I could feel it as it brushed against my leg and was positioned at my entrance. I suddenly panicked that it wouldn't fit.

Logan looked into my eyes and all my worries dispersed. We stared at each other completely still with only our heaving breaths filling the air.

With one sudden thrust, he was inside me. I gasped at the sharp pain.

"Mine," he growled in my ear and slowly slid out, only to thrust back in. This time the pain became a distant memory as the sensation of him filling me fully felt so damn good. Our mouths found each other again as his thrusts gained a steady tempo. He wrapped his arms around my waist and dug himself further into me. His pace increased as his plunges were hard and unrelenting.

"Ahhh⋯ Logan," I cried out. My hands found his soft curls and I tugged at them, causing his head to pull back and look at me.

"Yes, baby. Say my name." He breathed and spun us around and we fell smoothly onto the bed, never releasing our connection. Trapping my body under his weight, he started circling his hips and pounding into me again. His length and speed caused me to see stars.

"Ah, fuck, Logan!" I screamed as I felt myself coming to the edge again. His mouth captured my breasts, playfully biting and licking.

"Come for me," he grunted as my legs began to stiffen and I fell apart beneath him.

The intensity was almost too much to bear. Almost.

He thrust one more time as he reached his own end, calling out my name.

His limp body fell on top of me as we laid, still as one, breathing heavily. I started to regain my senses as we came down from our delirious state.

Shit. What the hell have we done?

Chapter 30

Logan's POV

Inhaling deeply, the scent of vanilla and cinnamon woke my senses and I practically purred into the softest hair that tickled my face. Opening my eyes slowly, I had to hold back laughter at this insatiable woman beside me. Her sandy hair was scattered all over the pillow, her face and mine. Her mouth was partly open as she breathed softly in her sleep. She laid on her back with one arm hanging off the side of the bed and the other one resting on my chest as well as her slender leg pinning my lower half to the mattress. I suppose the best term for her position was star fishing.

I took a few moments to enjoy this feeling and really study her features. Her long, thick eyelashes fanned her rosy cheeks, and her indulgent lips were plump and curved and so bloody irresistible. I considered kissing her awake but she looked so peaceful it felt too mean to wake her, so I fought the urge. She was still naked with only the duvet covering the lower half of her body and the sight of her was making me hard.

My mind filled with erotic flashbacks of the way her body reacted to my touch, her seductive moans and her screaming my name last night. I wanted to do it all over again. I'll never have enough of her.

Never. Last night was something else. It wasn't just sex for me. It was so much more. She made me feel things I had never felt before. Yes, it was an act of passion. It was impulsive, but it felt so right. She felt right.

I sighed as the realisation of how much I have messed everything up dawned on me. From the moment I laid eyes on this woman, I was a changed man. I was trying so hard to fight it, to resist her, that I lost sight of the truth. She was the one. And I nearly fucked it.

This was such a shit show in epic proportions. If I had just given into my feelings straight away and told Maddy I couldn't reject Alina, she would have been devastated but she would have come to terms with it eventually. But now, after what I have just done, she will never forgive me.

A pang of guilt crippled me, and I felt a twisted knot forming in the depths of my stomach. I needed some fresh air.

Carefully, I peeled off Alina's limbs from my body and headed downstairs. I made myself fresh coffee and took a seat on the patio steps that led to Darius' little courtyard. The comfort of the warm coffee slithering down my throat helped me to sort my muddled thoughts. All I knew for certain was that I wanted Alina. No. I needed her like I needed air to breathe. But everything else was still in disarray. What if Alina didn't feel the same way? I mean, she seemed to enjoy last night but maybe it was just lust for her. I am a werewolf after all, and she is human. My world would be terrifying for her. She would have to give up so much to be with me. Would the pack even accept a human as their Luna? What about Maddy? This would break her. Even though I know we are not meant for each other, I will always care deeply for her.

My phone stared vibrating in my pocket and I pull it out with a small smile when I saw the caller ID.

"Fredrik," I greeted.

"Alpha. Everything okay?" His deep voice rippled through the phone.

"Yes. Well, not exactly, but er… let's talk about you." I tried and changed the subject quickly. Fredrik and Maddy had always been close, and I was not sure he would approve of my actions. "Are you back?"

"Yes. Just landed. Many wolves have accompanied me to the UK as they wish to attend today's meeting." His professional tone makes me smile. He was always trying to prove himself to me, but he did not need to. He was already my right-hand man, and he knew it.

"Good. Glad to hear it. You did well, Fredrik. Roughly, how many wolves do you think we have on our side?" I asked.

"It is hard to say. I managed to track down sixty-four whilst I was out there who were all onboard. Most of them had connections to other rogues and said they would spread the word so we could have more. And then we have around one hundred thirty-eight allies from our own pack that survived the attack."

"Okay." I nodded at the numbers even though he could not see me. They were good, but they would not be enough. We were going to have to hope word got out quickly and more would support us.

"Er… Alpha?" Fredrik's voice shook and I sensed his nerves. This was very out of character.

"Yes?"

"There is something I think you should know before the meeting today." The uncertainty was evident in his voice.

"Go on," I encouraged as I put my coffee mug down on the floor.

"When I was tracking the rogues, I… I came across my second chance mate."

The Last Alpha

There was a silence as I registered what he said and then a genuine smile broke out on my face. If anyone deserved a second chance at happiness, it was him.

"Fredrik, that is great! Congratulations. Who is she?" I could barely contain my excitement.

"Her name is Sloane. She is a rogue originally from the Lock Heart Pack in California." His voice was still neutral.

"I remember that pack. They were small but fearless. They were one of the first packs Lucius slaughtered." I flashback to visiting the pack when I was a child. I envied the fact that their pack territory was so close to the beach.

"Yes. She was just a child when it happened. Her parents managed to hide her in trees with her older brother until the attack was over. They have been rogues ever since."

"That is sad to hear but impressive that such young wolves survived the rogue life for so long. She must be a fighter."

"She is," he responded quickly, but he was full of emotion.

There was another long pause and finally I asked, "Fredrik, is there something wrong?"

"I have not accepted her as my mate yet. I am not sure that I can," he said so softly it almost didn't sound like him and I suddenly understood. He felt like he was betraying Iona, his first destined mate.

"I never thought I would have another mate, Logan. I had accepted my fate in living alone. I didn't want anyone else but Iona," he confided.

"I understand, Fredrik. But how do you feel about Sloane? Is there a part of you that wants to give her a chance?" I asked.

"She's… incredible. Strong, fierce, beautiful. But how can I love her the way she deserves when I am a broken man?" His voice was full of sadness.

"Fredrick, do you think you can love her? Really love her?" I asked carefully.

"Yes, I think so," he said quietly.

"Then that is all she needs. Iona would not want you to turn down a chance to be happy in this world. She would want you to have a second chance at love." I said every word confidently, hoping it would be enough for him to let go of some of the guilt he was feeling.

There was a silence at his end as he considered my words.

"Thank you, Logan. For being a friend. You will make a fine Alpha."

I smiled at his compliment. "And you will make a fine Beta."

He chuckled at the end of the line and said, "As your future Beta, may I give you some advice?"

"Of course," I replied.

"Perhaps you should consider taking your own advice when it comes to love." I could hear the smile playing on his lips.

I snickered, "Perhaps I will," before hanging up the call.

"Perhaps you will what?" I heard an angelic voice behind me.

Chapter 31

Alina's POV

I stretched my achy limbs out on the empty bed. The smell of Logan was unmistakable, but he was nowhere in sight. He must have left the room as soon as he woke and the tightness in my chest grew as disappointment took hold. Was he full of regret? Could he not stand to be in the same room as me? My mind spun with all the possible reasons as to why I hadn't woken up next to him, but one stuck out in my mind. Guilt. Of course, he was wracked with remorse because I was feeling it too. It overpowered every other emotion I was feeling at that moment. How could I have done that?

Only a few weeks ago, I was the one being cheated on and now, here I was like the other woman. I was completely disgusted with my behaviour. This wasn't supposed to happen. No matter how entirely blissful being with Logan felt, he wasn't mine and I overstepped because of this inescapable pull I felt towards him. A pull I couldn't try to explain even if I wanted to. What were we going to tell Madeline? Sorry, the pull made us do it! No, I had to take responsibility for my own actions. Oh god, she was going to murder me for real. As I started contemplating who I would rather die—at the hands of a vampire or a werewolf.

The Last Alpha

I heard the faint sound of Logan's voice outside.

I crept over to the window but couldn't see him in the courtyard. Throwing on a pair of grey tracksuit bottoms and a white tank top, I raced down the stairs. Sitting on the step outside the back door was Logan. Only wearing a pair of boxers with his phone to his ear, I could only see the image of his strapping back profile but I could tell whoever he was on the phone was making him laugh. Jealousy spiked as my first thought went to Madeline.

"Perhaps I will." He chuckled and ended the call.

"Perhaps you will what?" I asked, causing him to swivel on his bum in surprise.

His face lit up like a summer's day as he drank in my appearance and my knees went weak. He didn't respond to my question but instead, tapped the concrete slab next to him and said, "Care to join me?"

I casually walked over and sat down cross-legged. The rays from the early morning dawn warmed my skin but there was still a slight chill in the air.

Aren't you cold?" I used it as a chance to look him up and down, admiring his exquisite physique. How I would love to jump his bones again already… *No, Alina. Behave!*

"Perks of being a werewolf," he replied with a cheeky grin.

We sat in silence for a few minutes, neither of us knowing where to start.

"I just wanted…"

"How are you…"

We both said in unison, causing us to stop and smile awkwardly.

"You first," he said politely.

I took a deep breath. I hated what I was about to say but it had to be done. I could no longer be selfish.

"I just wanted to say that I understand if you regret last night and you think it was a big—" I started, but he interrupted me.

"Alina, no. Listen…"

"No, please, Logan. Let me speak and then you can say what you need to."

He sighed but nodded for me to continue.

"I understand if you think it was a massive mistake. I do, too. It should never have happened and I'm not angry at you. I am just angry at myself. For one night, even though that is all it can ever be, I felt a passion I never knew existed and for that, I am grateful. But it was at the detriment of someone else's feelings. I really hope Madeline will forgive you and I will be out of your life as soon as the Oath is completed." My voice quivered as I looked down at the floor. A lone tear escaped my eye and I quickly brushed it away.

Logan grabbed my hands tightly, forcing me to look up at his face, which was burning with a radiant pain.

"Alina, I don't regret last night. The opposite actually. Yes, we may not have gone about it the moral way and I do feel terribly guilty for doing this to Madeline, but that is on me, not you. Do you really think it was a mistake?"

"You have a girlfriend, Logan, who loves you very much. No one deserves that and I am a terrible person for doing it when I know how much suffering it caused. It takes two, Logan, and I am as much to blame as you are. So, yes, it was a mistake." I tried pulling my hands from his grasp, but he held on harder.

"You are not a terrible person, Alina. The fact you even think you are just proves it," he said kindly whilst I shook my head.

"Before I came into your life, you were happy together. I messed everything up for you. I made your life so complicated," I said, choking back the tears.

Logan turned to face me and pulled me between his knees, lifting my chin to meet his gaze. "Alina, listen to me, please. That is so far from the truth. My life was incomplete before you in so many ways. Maddy and I were having problems long before you came along, but I just didn't want to admit it. I have been living a lie ever since the day I escaped my pack. Not because I wanted to, but because I felt obligated to. It seemed like the right thing to do. You must understand that I have been living in the shadow of my father's final words for nearly nine years and I was okay with it because I believed it was my destiny. But now I know it is not. You are, Alina. I honestly have no idea what is going to happen next or how things are going to be and I know it feels messy and impossible, but if it's with you, that's what I want. I want to love you impossibly."

I was speechless as silent tears tumbled down my face and my heart swelled, knowing he meant every word.

"You don't have to say anything. I know this is a lot to handle. I've felt it for so long, but I have been such a coward. Please forgive me."

I blinked a few times, confused. "Forgive you?"

"For not realising it sooner," he explained.

"So, you are not going to reject me?" I said slowly, trying to get a hold on the heaviness of his words and what they meant for us.

"No, Alina. I could never. And I am sorry for ever making you think that I would," he said honestly whilst rubbing small circles on the top of my hands with his thumb. The gesture calmed me as my heart pounded in my chest at the idea that he actually wants me as his mate.

"But what about Madeline? Your pack?" I said, starting to panic.

"I will speak to her in person later. I should have done it a long time ago when I first saw you. I hate that I've hurt her so much." He looked down at our entwined fingers and I could see how deeply he cared for her and it made my heart ache. "As for the pack, they will accept you in time. It will be a shock but they will learn to love you as their Luna."

"Luna?" I gasped, standing abruptly. How can I be a Luna? I don't know the first thing about being a werewolf.

Logan looked up at me from his seated position almost amused, but creases of worry framed his face as he realised my feelings.

"Yes. If you choose to be with me and accept me as your mate, you will be the pack's Luna. They will see us both as equal leaders," he said gingerly, trying to prevent me having a mental breakdown but still needing to give me the facts.

"If I choose? So, I can say no?" I asked quickly. I wasn't sure I would be any good as a Luna. I didn't want to disappoint everyone, especially as they had all suffered so much already. I mean, I am human for goodness' sake! I was not what they would want or need!

"I am not forcing you into anything, Alina. It is your decision. But if we are going to really do this, be together, you will be my Luna," he said calmly but sternly.

I stopped pacing and looked him square in the eyes. "And if I don't want to?" My heart was already preparing for the blow from his predicted answer.

"Then you do not need to. After the Oath, you can reject me if that is what you want and I will leave you alone." His voice was laced with pain and sadness.

"I reject you?" I was in shock. I didn't even know that was an option, not that I wanted it to be!

He nodded gently. "I will not be able to reject you, Alina. So, if you don't want this, you will have to do it yourself."

The Last Alpha

I collapsed back down on the steps with a thud. So if I wanted Logan, I had to be a Luna?

"Can I even be a Luna as a human?"

"No. I will need to mark and mate with you and then you will gain your wolf," he explained.

"But we just… mated. Does that mean I will start transitioning now?" I asked in alarm.

"No, don't worry. It doesn't work like that. I need to mark you whilst mating for the process to begin."

I gulped audibly and nodded as relief washed over me. It was not that I was against the idea of being a wolf, but I wanted to at least have a moment to think about it.

"I can't believe all of this, Logan. I really thought you didn't want me as your mate," I confessed.

"Alina, I am so proud to have you as mine. That was never the issue."

I couldn't help but glance down at his beautiful, almost symmetrical mouth and I wanted to kiss him. As though he could read my thoughts, he leaned in and sparks ignited as our lips caressed. It was a delicate and loving kiss, not like the raw, possessiveness of last night.

I pulled away and got lost in his dreamy eyes. "Can I have a bit of time, Logan? To get my head around all of this?"

Hurt flashed across his face but he quickly concealed it and nodded in understanding.

"I want to be with you, Logan. More than anything. But there is a lot to consider. A lot to digest."

"I know. I will be waiting, however long it takes," he said sincerely and my heart melted at his vulnerability. "As much as I want to, I don't think we should… do anything more until I speak to

Madeleine."

"I agree. When is she back?" I said, even though I know how difficult it would be to keep our hands off each other now that we know our true feelings.

"Today. I will speak with her after the meeting."

"What meeting?" I asked curiously.

He stood up and offered out his hand to pull me up as he said with a smirk, "We, my beautiful mate, are going to your first ever werewolf meeting."

Chapter 32

Madeline's POV

Darius and I headed straight for Ruislip Woods from the airport. It had been a gruelling flight, listening to Darius drone on and on about battle strategies until his excitement caused him to fall asleep and snore like a hog. There was no rest for me as I still could not shake this looming dread that kept catching me off guard. I couldn't relax as I felt I needed to be constantly alert. The encounter with Cora and my argument with Logan last night had not helped matters.

When we arrived in the woods, it was already 9:00 PM and the meeting was due to start. We hurried through the public nature reserve until we found the crumbling stoned wall. Removing decoy stones, we crawled through and found ourselves in the familiar shelter of shady glades and the mossy pillow of the forest floor. It was private land further out than the nature reserve and not accepting of trespassers. Luckily, it was owned by a fellow werewolf who lived successfully amongst humans and often allowed us to conduct important meetings there over the years.

As we walked towards the circle of boulders we used as our assembly grounds, the various scents of wolves mixed with the organic freshness of the forest was quite overpowering. There were rogues, some wolves I recognised from our own pack, and even mated wolves that had clearly once been human, sensing their anxiety. As I looked around the wide glade, it was hard to say how many were present. Many stood huddled together in groups, some alone leaning against tree trunks. Perhaps around a hundred, but there could be more. It was a good turnout.

I spotted Logan in the middle of the boulders, standing next to the centre rock. He had been waiting for us to arrive before he started as he nodded in our direction prior to jumping onto the ragged rock to address everyone. Fredrik stepped to the right side of the rock and, to my dismay, Alina took position on his left. Her petrified face was delicate with fear, as if it might shatter like white china. It made me smirk knowing this proved how she was not the powerful Luna the witch had foreseen.

Everyone hushed their conversations and silence befell as they waited for Logan to speak. He peered down at Alina, and she smiled lovingly at him. When he turned to us, his face was reflecting hers.

What was that?

Logan's POV

Pride swelled in me as I gazed at the unfamiliar faces that had joined our cause at such short notice. Many had travelled from all over the globe to attend and it warmed my heart to know that they had faith in me to bring about justice for our kind.

I noticed Fredrik shuffling uncomfortably next to me and I followed his gaze to a pretty brunette girl who must have only been a few years younger than Alina. She was standing with her arms folded across her chest and her head held high as if she was of high importance. Her stony expression never faltered as she locked eyes with my Beta. Towering over her slight frame was a bulky man with shoulder-length hair who shared a resemblance to the girl. That had to be Sloane and her brother, Niall. I gave Fredrick's shoulder a quick squeeze as I spotted Darius and Madeline entering the clearing at the back. Now I can begin.

I stepped up onto the monumental rock to signal that I am ready and waited for everyone's attention. It didn't take long for their eager eyes to fall on me, and the atmosphere prickled with anticipation. I raised my head to the impressive, glowing waxing gibbous moon illuminating the forest and I fed off its energy. It was in this moment of absolute silence that I felt the Moon Goddess tip the balance of influence to me. The wind died, the leaves ceased to rustle and even the shallow rumble of traffic in the distance faded away. I took a quick glance in Alina's direction to check if she was okay and when she gave me the warmest and most encouraging smile, I felt ten feet tall.

"Fellow wolves. My friends. Welcome. My name is Logan Black for those of you who do not know me, and I am the rightful Alpha of the Blood Moon Pack. I would like to thank you all sincerely for joining me here today. I know the journey has not been easy for some. We are all here because we have something in common. An enemy. The Vampire King has slaughtered our loved ones, destroyed our homes and tried to annihilate our species." I paused, allowing my words to echo through the trees. "But we are still here!" I bellowed.

The wolves' roars resonated through the forest, causing the ground to vibrate at their power.

"The time has come to take back what is ours. To restore our ancestors' traditions and way of life. To rebuild what Lucius took from us. Together, we will put an end to Lucius' reign of terror and give those bloodsuckers a taste of sweet revenge!"

Another loud roar from the collective wolves expressed their approval.

"This is not going to be easy. We should not underestimate our nemesis. He is powerful and ruthless and has many followers. Lives will be lost on both sides, but I am not here to ask you to risk your lives for me. Only to take that risk if you are willing and it will benefit you. Gone are the days where wolves were at war with each other. Under my leadership, I will see all our kind as allies, as family. Every wolf, whether they fight with me or choose not to, will be given safe haven in the Blood Moon Pack if they wish."

Murmurs and whispers erupted around the crowd at my new proposal for our futures.

"So, you are saying that I could fight with you and if I die in battle, you will give my mate and child protection in your pack?" A single man spoke up from behind an oak tree.

"That is correct. I will offer any wolf the chance to rebuild their lives in my pack even if they choose not to fight," I reiterated.

Again, chatter broke out amongst them as I was sure they were all surprised at my generous offer.

"I will fight with you, Alpha," the man who spoke out before he bent to his knee. "I also speak for my brother-in-law and two other rogues from home who will join us."

I bowed my head at him in gratitude.

"We will all fight with Alpha Logan." A woman stepped forward from a group of wolves. The spouting of voices parroted each other as more and more wolves agreed to stand against the vampires.

"My brother and I will be honoured to join the fight," Sloane stepped forward, looking at me directly, but I noticed her eyes quickly darted towards Fredrik before going back to mine. A small smile formed on my lips at her boldness. She was perfect for him.

"Thank you all. I will forever be grateful for your courage and support. My plan is to make Lucius follow me back to America. I feel it is only right to end this where it started. More details will follow about training schedules led by Fredrik and myself as well as battle strategies nearer the time. All who are willing to fight must be in the Blood Moon Pack territory by next Wednesday to prepare. Once Lucius knows where I have gone, he will attack," I said confidently.

Whilst living amongst humans all these years had kept me safe to a certain extent. It was time to head home. Lucius would have no reason to hold back when I am in the secluded burrow of my pack's territory again.

I stepped down from the rock and many men and women approached me to introduce themselves and ask questions. I pulled Alina into my side and snaked my arm around her, keeping her close as I sense her nerves. I could not risk anyone upsetting her just because she was the only human here. She was already doubting whether my people would accept her.

After a few minutes, Darius and Madeline came forward and I felt Alina try and move away from me. Reluctantly, I released her from my hold. Darius wholeheartedly embraced her, lifting her off her feet whilst she giggled and I fought back a warning growl. Madeline's eyes pierced through me and I could feel her rage radiating off her body.

"Good speech, cuz. Uncle James would have been proud." Darius greeted me with a playful punch to my arm.

Before I could respond, a man who had introduced himself as Rohan earlier came running back through the stoned passageway shouting, "Attack! Vampires are attacking the reserve!"

Adrenaline pumped through my system as I realised we must have been followed to the outer wood.

"Everyone, go now!" I roared in my Alpha tone, making some

shift into their wolves and jumping the walls in different directions to escape. Many shifted and sprinted towards the attack to help others. Fuck. Alina.

I turned to see her stunning face had paled and her eyes were wide with fear.

"Darius and Jax, stay here with Alina. If you can get her to safer ground, do. Otherwise, stay here until I return."

I watched as Madeline and Fredrik shifted into their grey wolves and dashed over the wall to join the defence. I took off my shirt and trousers as I felt small hands grip my arm.

"No, please, Logan. Don't leave me. Stay here with me," she pleaded. The worry swirled in her enchanting eyes.

"Alina, I can't. I am their leader and I must help them. You will be safe with Darius and Jax," I said hurriedly and leapt into the air, shifting mid-jump. Elias' oversized paws hit the ground running and I unleashed a ferocious roar to let them know I was coming.

Chapter 33

Lucius' POV

Houses burned as the flames engulfed the roofs and blazed deep red and amber, almost livid purple, as they danced with the wind. The black ash swallowed everything in its wake as it settled on the floor, painting a picture of despair and destruction. I watched on in horror as wolves dart in between them, tearing my people apart without any remorse. The deafening screams of women and children and the hisses and wails of my men who tried so hard to defend their lives filled my ears.

I turned from the castle window to see Celeste pulling out her book of dark magic and flicking frantically through the pages until she found what she was searching for. Her curly black locks fell over her face as her bright blue eyes scrutinised the Latin spells. I ran over to her and gripped her shoulders.

"My love, you must get to the safe room now," I commanded, but her icy eyes challenged me with her stubbornness.

"No. I can help. Let me help!" she said calmly.

"It is already too late, Celeste. It is not just you we must think

The Last Alpha

of," I said, resting my hand on her heavily pregnant belly.

Her face softened and she nodded in agreement. "Then you must come to!" she argued, gripping my forearms.

I drank in her love and concern and shook my head. "What kind of King would I be if I left my people to be mercilessly slaughtered at the hands of those heinous beasts? How could I look you or my son in the eyes ever again?"

The door swung open and two of my trusted warriors entered and start to lead her away to safety as I followed behind. Just before I turned to exit the castle, I took one final look back at her standing at the top of the stairs.

"No mercy." She smiled at me darkly as the evil shimmered in the depths of her eyes. There's the woman I love.

I nodded once with a malice grin and barrelled out into the chaos…

I wipe the beads of sweat from my forehead as I escaped my past. Relieving that haunting night thirty years ago always left me shaken. My flashbacks of that night and dreams of her were becoming more and more frequent and I knew it had everything to do with my current situation. The heir to the Blood Moon Pack.

He had managed to save his little human mate from my vampires, but I never really expected them to succeed. I just wanted to send him a message. However, my flashbacks were concerning and they reminded me of what I may be up against. I could not take any risks this time. I failed at wiping these vulgar savages off the face of the earth nine years ago and I will not fail again.

"No mercy."

Celeste's voice played on repeat in my head as it had done for

The Last Alpha

the past thirty years.

Don't worry, my love. Soon.

I strolled over to my locked cabinet and removed the small silver key from my cufflink where it was hidden. Opening the first drawer, my heart ached at the sight of it. I heaved out the weighty, leather-bound book and blew the dust off the front cover.

The book of Dark Magic.

I trace my fingers over the gold inscription like my wife used to all those years ago. This was the missing puzzle piece I needed to ensure I won this war. But there was only one witch who could handle such spells and she was not going to be pleased to see me.

"Father." Arius entered my chambers and bowed before me.

"What is it, son?" I bit, annoyed at the interruption.

"Baylor has sent word that the Alpha and his mate have left London."

I turned, my eyes widening at this news. Logan has barely left his house in the last few days, let alone the city.

"Where are they headed?" I asked curiously.

"He says they have entered somewhere called Ruislip Woods near a suburb outside of the city. He did not follow them out of fear they would sense him," Arius relayed and his unique eyes fell onto the cover of the book in my hands. They sparkled with interest but he refrained from asking.

"Excellent. Send some warriors to the woods for a little fun. No one is to hurt the Alpha or his mate. I have bigger plans for them, but any other wolves are fair game," I said with a wicked grin.

"How many warriors, father?" Arius asked. His expressionless face was almost robotic. He had his mother's beauty but my coldness.

"Thirty should do the trick. Just enough to warn the Alpha." I smirked.

"Forgive me, father, but is that such a good idea? If there are more than thirty wolves in those woods, we will lose the fight."

My expression turned frosty at his challenging tone.

"Winning the fight is not the goal, Arius. Winning the war is," I hissed.

He bowed his head with respect.

"If you are so concerned about your fellow warriors, why not accompany them?"

"I would be honoured, father," he responded with a twinkle in his eyes. Maybe he was more like me than I thought.

"On one condition. You must command. Oversee. But not fight," I said sternly.

"But, father⋯" he started, but my unsympathetic glare stopped him in his tracks.

"Yes, father. I understand." He bent to the ground before leaving the room.

Now, to summon the witch, although I had no idea where she was.

Chapter 34

Logan's POV

The metallic taste of blood seeped through my jaws after ripping through another vile creature. They were outnumbered by us and in a few minutes, they would all be obliterated. Lucius was playing with us. This wasn't a well-executed attack; it was a warning. Lurking in the darkness of the night, I could feel a pair of eyes watching my every movement. I whipped round, scanning the forest in all directions, but only the flurry of fur colliding with deathly pale skin of men could be seen.

Then I found him.

Standing alone on the peak of a steep, disquieting hill in the distance was a man I had never seen before. He had an air of supremacy and royalty about him as he intensely observed the fighting from the side-lines. Focusing my wolf's eyes to utilise my night vision, I could tell he was a similar age to me, with dark hair swept away from his face and distinguished features. His pale skin suggested he was one of them, perhaps their commander. When his vindictive eyes fell onto my wolf, I was surprised to see his eyes were different colours. One whiskey brown iris and the other a candescent blue. As we continued our outstare, his distinctive eyes flamed red as his hatred for me became evident.

I shifted into my human form and spread my arms out wide and bellowed, "What are you waiting for? Here I am. Fight me!"

His eyes blazed and his face tensed as if an invisible force was holding him back from charging at me.

A painful howl, that I would recognise from anywhere filtered through the air and the man's eyes glanced over my shoulder to see who it had come from. My heart was in my mouth as I saw Madeline's wolf Nina whimpering on the ground with a large gash across her stomach. Her fur was drenched with blood. A vampire hovered over her with sharp nails extended, ready to finish her off. Her wolf clearly could not take any more and she changed back into her human form. The bloodsucker grabbed her by the throat and shoved her against a tree trunk as she struggled to breathe from his choke.

Before I had a chance to rip the vamp's throat out, an ear-splitting whistle that had me crippled over in pain pierced through the forest. The fighting ceased as wolves yelped in agony from the sound and the few surviving vampires turned into puffs of smoke as they retreated. I turned to see where the command had come from and once again locked eyes with the mysterious man on the hill. He lowered his hand and relaxed his pursed lips as the sound faded.

A warlock? After a few seconds, he also disappeared into a puff of purple smoke.

I raced to Madeline who fell lifelessly into my arms and I carefully positioned her on the floor to check her wounds. The one on her stomach was the worst and very deep but not life-threatening. I breathed out in relief.

"L-Logan···" She struggled to speak as she dozed in and out of consciousness.

"Shhh, shhh, it's okay. You're going to be fine," I reassured her, brushing her icy blonde hair from her face.

"I know." She smiled bravely.

I suddenly realised that we are both naked, as well as many other wolves that have shifted back into their human counterparts. Darius, Jax and Alina come running over to us and relief flooded through me when I saw that she was safe and unharmed. Darius handed me my clothes and I put my T-shirt over Madeline's head to cover as much of her body as possible before pulling on my jeans.

I scooped Madeline up in my arms and we all started walking back to the cars. After placing Maddy in the backseat of her car and shutting the door, I turned to the others.

"I'm going to take Madeline home. She will be fine and will have healed in a few hours but needs to be looked after. Darius, will you take Alina back to yours and don't let her out of your sight?"

He nodded and I walked over to her. She was looking down at the ground, avoiding eye contact, and I could tell she was still frightened.

"I'm sorry, Alina. I will speak to her later, once she is feeling better, and then I will come to see you. I promise," I said, squeezing her hand.

"I understand. I hope she will be okay," she replied in a small voice.

I kissed the top of her head before I turned to Fredrick. I was pleased to see he had a protective arm wrapped around Sloane's shoulders, who was wearing a shirt that swamped her small frame and not much else.

"Fredrik, I need to get Maddy home. Can you check on any injured before you leave?"

"Of course, Alpha. So far, I have only counted two fatalities on our side. We had the upper hand."

I nodded and looked across at the girl tucked under his arm. "You must be Sloane. Sorry to be meeting under such circumstances," I said, holding my hand out to her. She looked surprised that I know who she was and glanced up at Fredrik. He gave her a small smile and she shook my hand firmly.

"Alpha, it is a pleasure," she greeted.

"Welcome to the family." I smiled and her face softened.

Climbing into the driver's seat, I looked over my shoulder at a sleeping Madeline. The engine roars to life. As I pulled away from the car park, I peered into the rear-view mirror and saw Alina standing alone watching me go.

Madeline's POV

The damp compress being dabbed against my forehead irked me from my deep sleep. My eyes adjusted and I took in the delightful sight of Logan's face hovering over me. His dark eyebrows were knitted in concern and his hand stopped tending to me when he noticed I was awake.

"How are you feeling?" His tone was soft but cautious.

Pushing my hands against the mattress, I tried to shift my weight to a seated position against the black, velvet headboard and froze as a sharp sting ripped my skin and my hand shot to a bandage on my stomach. I let out a small 'Ah' and winced.

"Careful, Maddy. You are healing well but the wound is deep. Try not to move too much," Logan said, pushing me gently back by the shoulders. Cautiously, I lifted the edge of the bandage and looked at the stitching. He was right. It was healing nicely but it would probably leave a scar. Logan was busying himself with clearing the bandages and bloody sterile wipes he had used to clean me.

"Thank you," I said with a smile.

"You'd do the same for me." He shrugged, as if it was nothing.

"I would," I agree. I took a moment to familiarise myself with his handsome features. Goddess, how I've missed him.

"I've missed you," I said sweetly, reaching for his hand.

He squeezed it and smiled, but it wasn't genuine.

My heart plummets. That was when I noticed it. His scent had changed. It was still earthy and masculine but it was now mixed with a new sweetness. My eyes narrowed at him and I removed my hand sharply. He had sex with her.

His face was laced with confusion at my sudden hostility and then he realised that I knew.

"How could you?" I said lowly with so much venom. I could tell from his shamefaced expression that he was guilty as sin. My body started trembling, but not from the pain of my injury but the pain in my heart.

"Maddy. Please rest. We will talk about everything when you are healed," he pleaded.

"NO! You do not get to walk away from this," I shouted and winced as the agony from my sudden outburst shot through my cut.

"Maddy, please. Let's not do this right now."

I took a deep breath and pushed my emotions down into the dark hole forming in my heart. I needed to stay calm and make him see sense. He was blinded by the mate bond. This wasn't his fault.

"You have to reject her, Logan," I said seriously.

He turned to face the wall and started shaking his head. "I can't."

"You can't or you won't?" I tried to make him see the difference.

"Maddy, I am so sorry. For everything. I care for you deeply and only want you to find happiness in this life, but you will not find that with me. I can't and I won't reject Alina."

Rage boiled inside me. I can't let him do this. "You are wrong. I will find happiness with you and I will be Luna of the Blood Moon Pack. Of our pack," I said with confidence, and he closed his eyes and rubbed his face. I continued. "Do you want to know how I know that?" He didn't respond, so I kept going. I had to make him understand. "The dark witch told me so."

His head snapped up in shock. "What do you mean?"

"Cora, the witch, saw two different visions. One of you defeating Lucius and restoring our pack and one where you are killed by him in battle." I paused, letting my words sink in and his face paled slightly.

"She said that you would only be able to defeat the king if you were marked and mated to a powerful Luna… a powerful she-wolf."

His face registered what this meant as he connected the dots. He stood abruptly and started to pace the room.

"No. That can't be. No. Why would Alina be gifted to me as my mate if she was not the powerful Luna the witch foresees?" he asked more to himself, but I answered for him.

"I don't know, Logan. Who knows why the Goddess does anything? Why did Fredrik lose Iona after just finding her? Why did our parents have to be slaughtered but we escaped? Why is Alina human? The witch was completely shocked when she heard Alina was human. She knew that meant she could not help you to defeat Lucius, so she agreed to do the Blood Oath," I explained. I could see the denial and fury building in his body as his muscles tensed and retracted.

"I don't believe you!" he shouted, and I felt hurt that he thought I would lie.

"Ask Darius." I shrugged casually. "If you choose her··· you will die, Logan. We will all die." My voice hitched as the words left my mouth.

He suddenly became still. His calmness terrified me. He perched on the edge of the bed and gripped my hand in his. His eyes searched my grey irises as if he was trying to bestow his peacefulness to me.

"I know you believe this to be true and you will do anything to protect me. But I know it cannot be true. I can feel it in my bones. I am meant to be with Alina and I am so sorry that this hurts you, Madeline. I cannot deny myself any longer. I wish I could turn back time and make this easier for you, but what's done is done. I only wish for you to find your mate and feel complete happiness in your life. That is what you deserve. I will always be there for you Maddy, but we are not meant to be together."

"No, Logan. I can't let you do this to us!" I screamed from the bed.

He stood and said, "I'm sorry, Maddy, but I've made my decision. And nothing will change it. You must let me go. I have texted Emma to come and look after you."

"Logan!" I yelled after him as he left the room without so much as a glance back.

Tears streamed down my face and my heart shattered into a million pieces. I tried to move from the bed to go after him but fell back down when excruciating pain rippled through me and I cried out in frustration.

I howled and bawled for what felt like a lifetime until there were no tears left to cry.

My door catapulted open and Emma came hurling into the room like a tornado.

"Oh, Mads, I am so sorry." She squeezed me into a tight

embrace.

"He left. Just like that. I don't think anything I could have said would have changed his mind." My voice still cracked and caught in my throat from all the crying, but now, I feel numb.

Logan was right about one thing. I would do anything to protect him. I would do whatever it took.

Chapter 35

Alina's POV

IT had been four hours. Four agonising hours since I had to watch Logan drive away with Madeline. I scolded myself as I start by my nails from the unease I felt. I walked over to the bedroom window for the millionth time and stared out into the dead of night. The moon, a glowing yellowy white, hung low tonight and although it wasn't full, its fluorescent light still irradiated the scene below. Something within me stirred as I became bewitched by its brilliance. It was a need. A need to be released yet consumed all at the same time. It seemed to grow stronger and stronger the longer I stared. I wanted so badly to feel free and this restlessness inside me was growing with each passing second. For some reason, I knew that the only thing that could calm me was Logan. And he wasn't here.

I glanced back over at the alarm clock. Nearly 2:00 AM. What if he had changed his mind? Now Madeline was back, he realised his mistake. I can't lie. Seeing how attentive and worried he was towards her made my heart ache in my chest. Witnessing him carry her through the woods wearing only his T-shirt and cuddled into his naked chest was almost too much to bear. I wanted to run as far away from them as I could but at the same time, I couldn't stop watching.

I had never been the jealous type but when it came to him, everything I once knew about myself seemed to have gone out the window! I feel stronger and fiercer when I am around him yet completely vulnerable and weak by just one glance. And yet I had no right to feel this way. He hadn't even told her what had happened between us yet. Perhaps, he never would. Perhaps, he wasn't coming back like he promised.

My gut twisted at the thought. Turning back to try and take some comfort from the grace of the white-gold moon, I let the powerful pull towards it take over. My eyes scanned the tops of the trees in the distance that indicated the beginnings of the woodland by Logan's house. It was calling to me in a way I could not describe. Maybe I had been spending too much time with these werewolves.

With my mind made up, I thought through my next move carefully. I couldn't go alone. I'm not a complete idiot. After the earlier attack, this world of danger and violence I've been catapulted into had left me feeling less than safe. But I needed this.

Opening my bedroom door, I saw Darius' hefty body slumped against the bannister, head tilted to the side and legs outstretched across the landing floor. He was fast asleep. I guess he took the whole 'don't let her out of your sight' command quite seriously.

I crouched down and shook his shoulder gently at first and then more aggressively as I failed to even raise a stir.

"Urgh. What the—" He sprang up in shock. "What is it? Are you okay?" he asked whilst frantically running into my room to check for any signs of danger.

"Darius, I'm fine," I call out to him.

Once he was convinced there was no intruder, he walked back out onto the landing. "Then why the brutal wake up call, AYE?" He rubbed the sleep from his eyes with his knuckles.

"I want to go to the woods. The one at the end of the road."

His chocolate brown eyes narrowed in confusion and then softened when he realised where I meant.

"You mean the one next to Logan's apartment?" he asked, raising a curved eyebrow at me.

"It's not what you think. I'm not trying to spy on him or anything. I'm just feeling... um... a connection with nature right now and I need to go for a walk in there," I explained the best I could.

"You're an odd one, buttercup. As much as I would love to take you for a moonlit stroll in the woods in the early hours of the morning, the answer is no." He slumped back down on the floor, folded his arms across his chest and closed his eyes.

I fought the urge to stomp my feet and throw a tantrum like a brat knowing it would have no effect. "Please, Darius. I really need this right now. And you said that as long as I was with you or Logan, I would be free to do whatever I wanted. You wouldn't want me sneaking out again, would you?" I smiled innocently under my eyelashes.

He opened one eye, regarding me closely before closing it again and releasing a frustrated sigh. "Fine. But we are going for one hour and that is it. I need my beauty sleep," he whined.

"Yes!" I fist pump the air and ran back into my room to grab my hoody.

***

"So, the woods huh? Normally its only wolves who feel compelled to take midnight runs," Darius mumbled from behind me as we trenched through the barely visible black trails snaking through the undergrowth. The only sound that could be heard was the hooting of owls lurking in the shadows and branches snapping underfoot, especially from Darius' clumpy boots.

"Us humans can appreciate a good forest to. I have always thought that trees remind me that we are only on this planet as their guests. They stand tall and proud rooted to mother earth and can live for centuries, yet it is only the destruction of humankind that they fall." I ran my hand along the rough bark of the tree trunk to my right as I stepped carefully over its raised roots.

"Deep. Not sure I am fully prepared for hugging trees and putting the world to right tonight," he grumbled.

"Someone woke up on the wrong side of the⋯ bannister," I teased over my shoulder as he glared at me.

"I like trees. I like woods. But I like sleep more." He yawned and I stifled a giggle.

We reached a clearing ahead and I gasp in awe as I noticed a large body of freshwater surrounded by small rock pools and mossy bank. Tall shadowed Alder trees stretching up like arrows into the sky decorating it like a frame. The lake looked like a puddle of black ink in the darkness except for the reflection of the stars on its surface like spilt sugar over black marble. It was beautiful and I once again felt that strong urge pulling me towards it.

"Right, it's time to head back now, Alina." I sensed Darius stop behind me but I continued my steady advance.

"I'm going in," I breathed and bent down to start untying my trainers.

"WHAT? Have you lost your freaking mind? It will be freezing! Alina? What are you⋯ stop undressing⋯ Oh, fucking hell. Logan is going to murder both our asses!" he shouted, appalled at my spontaneity.

"Turn around then and you won't see anything you shouldn't!" I shrugged off my bra and pulled down my trousers.

Before removing my underwear, I checked over my shoulder to see if he had listened. I burst out laughing when I saw him hunched forward, practically hugging a tree with his head hidden in his arm, cursing my stubbornness.

I quickly wriggled out of my pants and took a few tentative steps into the glorious lustre of the water until its stillness circled my waist. A high-pitched squeal escaped my mouth as I chuckled at how cold the water was.

"Fuck it!" I shouted as I bravely dived under so my body could get used to the temperature more quickly. When I came up for air, I tilted my head back towards the picturesque sky and gazed in wonder at the millions of stars that sprinkled across it. Every now and then, a twinkle caught my eye.

"Please tell me you can swim. I draw the line at water rescue!" Darius shouted from his position against the tree still avoiding looking in my direction.

I danced my hands across the surface of the water and replied back, "Of course I can swim. You are really missing out, though. This is magical."

"Never been a fan of magic. Witches freak me the fuck out." His tone was serious as he faked a shudder down his spine.

I smiled as I started to swim slow, delicate breast strokes and glided through the lake. Relishing in the tranquillity this moment gave me, I could almost keep Logan from my thoughts.

Almost.

Logan's POV

I had just left my apartment and was walking with purpose down the street towards Darius' house when my phone vibrated in my pocket.

It was nearly half two in the morning so I was confused as to who would need me at this time. I clicked on the text from Darius

Hey, cuz. Just thought I would let you know your mate decided now is the perfect time to take a stroll in the woods. Before you say, I did try and stop her but you know how stubborn she is. Don't worry, I am with her. She is safe. We will be back around 3:00 AM.

Oh, hell no! What were they playing at? Did she not just witness a vampire attack in the woods? Was she trying to give me a heart attack!

Violently, I type out a reply. *Get her home. NOW.*

My body started to tremble as I picked up the pace towards his house and then stopped dead when I realised where they must be. I spun on my heels to retrace my steps as my phone pinged again.

Tried and failed. Apparently, swimming in a lake is too much fun.

I squeeze my phone so hard I nearly crush it. Darius was useless. He was too soft for his own good. Wait until I get my hands on her stubborn ass.

My dick hardened at the thought of it.

Chapter 36

Logan's POV

I see the back of Darius' burly body first as I approached the lake. He sensed my presence and nodded at me over my shoulder, directing my vision ahead. As I brushed shoulders with him and followed his gaze, my breathing quickened, and I was instantly turned on by the image before me.

Alina was standing nude waist deep in the middle of the lake with her toned back to us. She was as still as a picture and seemed to be in a trance as her head tilted up towards the gleaming moon in front of her. Its reflection cocooned around her body on the surface of the water like a halo. Her wet hair cascading down her back and the tips submerged into the darkness. It was the most sensational image I had ever seen, and I knew it would stay with me forever.

"She's been like that for over five minutes. She's going to catch pneumonia if she doesn't get out soon," Darius whisper-yelled in my ear.

"Turn away!" I hissed at him, realising he had full view of my naked mate, even if it was just the back of her.

"Oh, chill out! I haven't seen anything! You should be thanking me for putting up with her insanity!" he bit back, pointing his hand out towards her to prove his point.

Elias gave him a warning growl for insulting our mate. Even so, I did agree. This was insane.

Darius rolled his eyes before asking, "Can you go and get her already so I can go back to bed?"

"Go and patrol the area and make sure we are clear. Mind link me if you find anything, no matter how small. If not, you can go home. We will be back shortly," I said without taking my eyes off Alina.

"Good luck, bro," he said, tapping my shoulder and turning on his heels.

I took a few quiet moments to admire her, feeling like a predator stalking its prey before it pounces. She still had not even moved a muscle as I strolled towards the edge of the riverbank. All my previous anger had dispersed at the sight of her and all I could think about doing was burying myself inside of her and fucking her senseless.

As if she could suddenly sense me, her shoulders tensed slightly and goose pimples adorned her caramel skin, the moonlight making it shimmer.

"Are you coming in?" her voice sounded distant and mythical as she spoke to me without turning around.

"Alina, what are you doing?" My voice came out deeper than usual due to my arousal seeing her this way. Elias was badgering me to let him out. Her raw wildness in his natural environment had him very excited.

She turned gracefully in a circle and I gasp when our eyes met and a glowing ring of gold outlined her bottle-green irises.

"Your eyes!" I shouted in surprise. She immediately looked down at her reflection on the water's surface, but when she lifted her head, they have returned to their usual green vibrancy.

"What about my eyes?" she asked, cocking her head to one

side.

I shook my head, struggling to make sense of what I just saw or if in fact, I saw anything at all. The lack of sleep from the night before and this long-ass day must be getting to me.

"Nothing. I just thought… It doesn't matter. Alina, it's time to get out. Now," I commanded sternly, but her face stayed unaffected, and she made no attempt to move. Irritation ticked in my jaw at her defiance.

I glanced down at her bare tits hovering just above the water. Her nipples pebbled from the cold and drops of liquid glistened on her skin. Fuck. She was a goddess. I could feel my eyes darken as my dick got harder just by looking at her. But she was not reciprocating my lustful gaze. Instead, she seemed unsure, distant.

"You came back." Her voice was quiet, but I still detected slight relief.

"I promised I would," I responded, forcing my eyes back up to her face.

"I wasn't sure you would. I thought… I thought you might have changed your mind." She averted her gaze down to the water as she glided her hands over the top of it.

I sighed. How could I ever make this woman see what she meant to me? Make her trust me. I internally kicked myself for causing her to think I didn't want her for so long.

"Alina. I want you. I'm never changing my mind," I said confidently.

She lifted her head and studied me intensely, trying to judge my sincerity. She slowly nodded and a small smile played on her lips.

"Now, will you get out of there so I can take you home?" I said heatedly, but with warning.

Her eyes sparkled with mischief as she slowly approached the riverbank, seeming more like herself again. Once she reached my feet, she held her hand out for me to help pull her out. I leaned forward to grasp it and as soon as our hands joined, I felt a surprisingly strong tug and I lost my footing, falling headfirst into the darkness.

I gasped out in shock, "FUCK! ITS FUCKING FREEZING!" I shouted. Pissed off was an understatement. My top clung to my muscles and I felt the water droplets from the ends of my hair running down my face as I glared at Alina. She covered her mouth with her hands whilst submerging her body under the water up to her neck, but I could still see the vibrations on the surface as she failed to suppress her laughter.

It didn't take long before she cracked, and the most wonderful sounds burst out of her. It echoed into the silence of the night as birds flew from the trees and, before long, I couldn't help but join her.

I splashed her playfully, sending a mini tidal wave in her direction, and she pretended to act shocked before engaging in a full-blown water fight. We indulged in our childish game for a minute or so until I grabbed her around the waist and pressed her body to mine. She gasped as the sparks zapped across our skin and the warmth of my body spread over to hers. It seemed she was still not used to the sensation. Every part of her body felt so soft and heavenly as I glided my hands up and down her back.

Her hands rested on my drenched chest on top of my shirt and I felt the urge to be skin to skin. I released her body to quickly whip off my top and throw it over to the riverbank. In the time it took me, Alina had taken a few steps back.

"Where do you think you are going?" I asked gruffly, grabbing her wrists and guiding her back into my embrace. She looked up at me through her thick eyelashes and I fought the urge to kiss her.

"We can't. You must talk to Madeline once she's better,"

she said, gripping my forearms, trying to distance herself from me.

"It's taken care of," I said, starting to lose patience, needing to feel her against me.

"You… you told her?" She was stunned.

"Yes, and now I am yours," I said seductively as I stared at her luscious lips. It had been killing me not being able to touch her all day. To taste her again. The need built inside me, threatening to overpower me.

She stared deeply into my eyes as she searched for my soul. I am completely hers. I would protect this woman with everything I am. I would die for her.

I crashed my mouth against hers, not able to hold back any longer. A growl vibrated through my chest as Elias purred in my mind. Our tongues caressed as we gripped each other's hair and deepened the kiss. She was intoxicating. I would never get enough. My dick throbbed against my soaked trousers and I was surprised that I could even get such a hard on in this baltic temperature. But that was what this woman did to me.

I broke away from our kiss and she groaned in protest.

I smirked. "You have blindsided me twice tonight, my little mate. You need to be taught a lesson. And I have just the punishment in mind."

Her eyes widened and lips parted as she digested my words, but I could tell she was excited.

"Later, I am going to take my sweet time to worship and devour every inch of your perfect body and give you more pleasure than you ever knew possible. But right now, I need to fuck you. I'm going to fuck you so hard you are going to beg me to stop," I growled, and she swallowed audibly.

Keeping hold of her body flushed against mine, I undid my

trousers under the water and pulled them down until I could step out of them. My erection sprung free and nestled right between her legs. She bit her bottom lip as she stifled a moan and started to grind her hips against me. She was driving me wild already.

I gripped her hips to still her and started biting, sucking, and kissing her neck and shoulder.

"I'm in control here," I mumbled against her delicate skin as I positioned myself closer to her centre, purposefully brushing against her sensitive spot a few times. I could feel her heart drumming in her chest as she waited eagerly for my next move. My hands roughly roamed her body. When I couldn't wait any longer, I grabbed her ass cheeks and slammed myself deep inside her.

Alina threw her head back and cried out at the sudden intensity as her body rose a few inches out of the water, impaled on my erection. I wrapped her legs around my waist, and she gripped the nape of my neck as I started pounding into her, showing no mercy. The water rolled and frolicked around us as our bodies crashed together aggressively. I assaulted her nipples, biting and sucking as I kept up my relentless thrusts. Her weightless body was so easy to lift up and down, I don't think I have ever been able to go so fast. When I felt her tightening around my cock and getting closer to her orgasm, I pulled out completely, only to replace my thrusts with a painfully slow motion. Her hand tightened around my neck and her eyes shot at mine in annoyance.

"Logaaannn…!" she moaned.

"Yes?" I asked innocently as I moved leisurely inside her.

"Don't stop. Faster. Please," she begged and I smirked. That will not do. I want her to beg me to stop. I need her to not be able to take my teasing anymore.

I suddenly sped up again to let her think I was giving her what she wanted and in a matter of seconds she was a moaning mess, so I slowed my torture right down.

"Ahh, no, Logan! Please!" she cried out, trying to grind herself against me to make me fuck her harder.

I gripped her hips tightly until I felt her coming away from the edge of immeasurable pleasure and thrust into her vigorously once again.

After several more of my torturous teases, I had her exactly where I wanted her and thank fuck because I was struggling to hold on anymore.

"Fuck Logan. I can't! I can't take this anymore!" she cried in my ear, gasping for breath as I pulled her back from the edge once again. I surprised her by turning and lifting her on to the riverbank and climbing out in one swift movement on top of her. I didn't give her a chance to adjust to her whereabouts, as I pushed myself into her warmth and this time I didn't stop. When I felt her centre tightening around me, we both came hard together. Our climaxes called out into the night as we stared at each other, panting heavily. I stayed inside her for a few more moments, enjoying the closeness and turning us onto our sides, so we were facing each other.

"Well, that was mean." She pouted once our breathing had synchronized and calmed. I chuckled and tucked a stray strand of hair behind her ear.

"Now you know what happens when you piss me off."

She rolled her eyes and shivered as a light breeze rolled over our naked bodies.

"You need to get dressed before you catch your death," I said, standing up and throwing her the discarded pile of clothes from the side of the riverbank.

"What are you going to wear?" she asked, amused as she

looked up and down my body appreciatively.

"Well, seeing as my T-shirt is drenched and my trousers are somewhere at the bottom of that lake, I don't have many options." I glowered, faking my annoyance.

Alina giggled as she pulled on her hoody, and it was the most beautiful sound. I wanted to be the one to make her laugh every single day.

"I suppose fur will keep me warm," I said with a half-smile playing on my lips and eyed her cautiously for her reaction.

She stopped tying her shoelaces and blinked up at me.

"Elias?" she asked curiously, her eyes twinkling with excitement in the moonlight. I nodded slowly and could feel Elias prancing around in my mind, eager to meet his mate.

"Only if you feel comfortable," I added.

"Yes! I would love to meet him. Can I talk to him first?" she bounced onto her feet as her face lit up with hope.

I almost felt jealous at how enthusiastic she was. Which was ridiculous. Elias was a part of me! I felt him urging forward in my mind and I allowed him to share control. I still didn't trust him not to do something stupid in our human form if I gave him full control. We shared my body last night, when we first mated with Alina and he was always on the verge of marking her. I couldn't allow it to happen without her consent.

"Elias?" she whispered as she peered up into our eyes. I let him answer her.

"Yes, my mate." His deep voice rumbled.

"Hi," she said in a flirtatious voice with a dazzling smile.

Elias cocked our head to the side to examine her. Our arms snaked around her waist as he pulled her in close. Bending our neck so our face buried into the crook of hers, he inhaled deeply.

"You smell delicious," he growled. Coming up for air, we gazed into her enchanted eyes that carried so much want.

"You are mine," he boomed possessively.

Her smile widened and she replied sweetly, "Always."

Our lips collided as we kissed passionately, but it was all Elias driving it and I let him. After everything I had put him through since meeting Alina and denying him our mate for so long, I could grant him this moment.

After a few minutes, I got impatient. Mind linking him, I told him it was time to shift, warning him not to hurt her in the process.

'AS IF I WOULD!' he growled back at me.

"I want you to see me. The real me," he said to her as she struggled to catch her breath from their kiss.

She nodded and we took a few steps back. Bones cracked and black fur sprouted from my bronzed skin as Elias emerged. Alina's eyes widened in disbelief and ⋯ awe?

Once on all four paws, we still towered above her small frame, but she didn't seem scared.

"Beautiful," she breathed as she stepped forward and reached her hand up to stroke his velvety fur.

Elias leaned his head into her hands as she rubbed his ears and he purred! What a big softy! She chuckled as he continued to act like a lovesick puppy! After a few moments, he bent down onto his front paws, indicating that he wanted her to climb on his back. She did so without hesitation, and we felt her petite hands grip our fur and her legs squeezed our sides as we darted off through the forest. The elated noises that escaped her mouth made Elias' tail wag with happiness.

We have our mate and she is all ours.

Chapter 37

Cora's POV

Packing lightly had never been a strength of mine. I've always lived by the idea that one should be prepared for any occasion and there was no excuse for substandard attire. The atrocities that the younger generations wear and call 'fashion' nowadays had me ready to gauge my eyes out. This trip should keep me for no more than a few days but I had hoped to reconnect with some old friends whilst visiting the UK.

It had been many years since I had travelled anywhere. When you are nearly three hundred years old and had seen the world many times over, there was little desire to explore. I was quite content in my solidarity with the chaos and madness this world has to offer. It helped to keep myself concealed as I had gained many enemies over my lifetime. Many, fortunately, perished long ago, but few remain. In fact, before my visions of the Alpha and··· him, I had not conducted dark magic in nearly thirty years. After that day.

Using my telepathy to relive those excruciating flashbacks reminded me about why this war was so important. I could not sit back and wait to see how it would all play out. I needed to help end him. He had taken so much from me, but I had also gained something in return.

Atonement.

For over two hundred seventy years, I terrorised this world. I had done unspeakable things and committed horrific crimes. I was at one point the most feared dark witch of all time.

But losing my son changed me completely. He was not even granted one day on this planet and it was all because of me. It was my karma for all my terrible past deeds. I know that now. I have barely practised magic since and tried to live a life of virtue in the hope that one day, I may repent for my sins and be granted eternity with my baby boy in the afterlife. Many close to me have questioned over the years why I did not kill Lucius myself. I have the power. It would be as easy as snapping a twig. But after everything, I will not allow him to take away my chance at redemption either.

Luckily, I would not have to as this 'Alpha' was more than obliging. Although I have felt unease since my visit from those two wolves. Things were not playing out how they should. And something about that she-wolf, Madeline, had me shaken. It was infuriating that I could not read her future. I have only ever come across three people I could not do that with. My parents and my sister. It was very alarming. It made this entire situation with the Alpha all the more troubling. Hopefully, I will be able to read Alina's future to help the Alpha make the right choice. If not, perhaps my powers were fading.

I closed my metal suitcase with a thud and zipped it with a twist of my finger. I transported the heavy luggage down to the front door. The perks of witchcraft. As I descended my glass stairs elegantly in my new Manolo Blahnik heels, I noticed a letter on my sheepskin rug by the fireplace.

My plucked eyebrows arched in interest as I made my way towards it. Only a certain type of mail was delivered via the fireplace and has no address or name on the envelope. Those from the enchanted council. I ripped open the letter with a flick of my long, polished nails and read its contents:

Cora,

I hope this finds you well. My friend, I wish I was writing to you with better news, but I must warn you. Lucius came to the council today asking for you. He demanded to know where you were and how to contact you. Of course, the council did not give him any indication of your whereabouts, but I fear this will not deter him. The council do not know that I am alerting you, so please keep this confidential.

Your faithful friend,
Maggie

Creating a flame at the tip of my index finger, I set the corner of the letter alight and watched as the flames engulfed my old friends' scripture before throwing the remains in the fireplace.

A storm brewed inside me, consuming me like the fire to the letter. It was not a coincidence that he was looking for me now. He was scared. Scared of failure. He knew I was the only one powerful enough to help him, although he was a bigger fool than I thought if he genuinely believed that I would.

I sighed. So much for my nice, relaxing vacation. As soon as I went near Logan, he would know. I couldn't risk that. I didn't have a choice but to go to him willingly. At least I would take pleasure in telling him I would rather set myself on fire than help him in anyway.

I pulled out my black marble scrying bowl, crystals, bones and rummaged my safe for the lock of hair I had stolen over fifty years ago. I had an assortment of possessions from enemies over the centuries. You never know when they might be needed for a certain spell.

Pulling one strand of black hair from the bunch and mixing it into the bowl with moss from the north side of a tree and a variety of herbs, before I ran my silver blade along the palm of my hand and squeezed it. Droplets of my blood sizzled as they mixed with the contents and I started to mutter my locator spell in Old Latin. Allowing my eyes to roll back and turn milky white, the image of his whereabouts came to me, vivid and conclusive like a picture. I heard the hiss of the address slither in my mind and the spell was complete.

Picking up my suitcase and taking a final look around the safety of my home, I closed my eyes, concentrated on his location and transported myself there, leaving only a white glow in my wake···

When I opened my eyes, I was in an eerie, narrow hallway. The flickers of candles on the wall were the only source of light. The stone bricks were cold and uninviting, just like their residents.

I walked towards a large, wooden door on my right and see if I could sense any movement from within. Silence. I moved along to the next one. Sensing his evil presence, a shiver ran down my spine and bile rose in my throat. The last time I saw this abomination was the day he violated me.

I swallowed my anger and forced my face into an icy, emotionless mask. With an effortless whip of my hands, the door flew open, sending a rush of wind with it and a flurry of papers from the desk he sat behind floated to the ground like snowflakes. His shocked expression soon turned to a wicked grin as I walked forward into the room.

"Cora." My name slid off his tongue like the hiss of a serpent.

My cat-like eyes narrowed as I raised my chin, not making any attempt to greet him.

"You look... spectacular. I see the mundane life really suits you." He smiled in a way he thought was charming, but I just find it repulsive. "What do I owe this pleasure, dear sister-in-law?"

My stomach churned at the title. The thought that I once considered him as family made my skin crawl.

"You were looking for me so I thought I would save you the bother." My tone was still frosty to match my glare.

"How kind. Please. Take a seat." He pointed to the red, velvet chair opposite his desk. He stood and walked towards his bourbon and started to pour the whiskey into a tumbler. "Would you care to join me?" he asked with a toothy grin.

"I think I'll pass," I said through gritted teeth, remembering what happened the last time I accepted a drink from him.

As if reminiscing a fond memory, he nodded and smiled before saying, "I don't blame you."

My breath ragged as I seethed at his words. I quickly closed my eyes trying to regain control of my emotions before I snapped and broke his neck with a twist of my wrist.

"I must say, Cora, I am impressed. I wasn't sure you would be able to stay so calm in my presence after you know... everything that happened." He took the glass to his mouth and slurped, filling the air with the disgusting sound.

"You mean after you raped me at my sister's funeral? Your wife's funeral," I replied calmly, trying to keep my voice as steady as I could.

"Mmm. Yes. Sorry about that. Grief can do funny things to some people." His eyes twinkled with amusement. He had no remorse.

"Why am I here?" I asked, wanting to end this talk of the past.

"As you are well aware, my ongoing war with the werewolves will be coming to an end very shortly. To guarantee my victory, I shall need a favour."

He heaved out a very familiar book from his desk drawer and it slammed onto the surface between us. My heart pounded at the sight of it. It was once as precious to me as a child, until I had my own, of course. My sister and I created it over one hundred years ago and it held the darkest, most remarkable spells this world had ever seen. Many had tried to get their hands on it over the years, but it was written in such a way that only Celeste and I would be able to decipher it.

"Ah," I said, understanding the role he wanted me to play in his little show. "And why would I ever help you?" I snarled.

"Besides from the fact that we shall be avenging your sister's death?"

He knew for a fact that it held no importance to me.

He leaned back in his chair and touched his fingertips together as a sadistic smile transformed his face to resemble that of a demon about to take a soul.

"Because, my dear Cora, I have something you want."

Chapter 38

Alina's POV

"Where are you going?" I called teasingly from the crumpled hotel bed, leaning on my naked stomach and perching on my elbows.

"To run us a bath. I think it's time we had a break to clean and eat, don't you?" Logan chuckled as he walked towards the bathroom completely nude. The sight of his fine ass and muscular legs had me feeling flushed with need again already. I mean honestly. How can a guy be so fucking tempting?

I grinned and rolled onto my back on the comfy king-size bed as I heard the taps start running for the bath. Once we got back to Darius' last night, it was so early in the morning that we had both passed out. When I woke up around 9:00 AM, Logan had already packed all of my belongings into a bag and it was sitting by the bedroom door next to an unfamiliar leather holdall. I was over the moon when he explained we needed our own privacy, so he had booked us a room at the Claridge's in Mayfair for the next few days. 'A room' was downplayed. It was more like an apartment! Top floor with a view to die for overlooking the buzzing city with a lounge, kitchen and separate bedroom and bathroom. I had never stayed in something so grand in my life and I couldn't help but wonder how he could afford it. A hostel in London was about as much as I earned in a week of shifts at Lolita's, so I dreaded to know how expensive this place was. Especially now that I don't have a job anymore! I had some savings but not much...

"Logan, how much do I owe you?" I shouted towards the bathroom, trying to raise my voice over the gushing water.

"What do you mean?" he called back.

"How much money do I owe you for this hotel?" I shouted back again.

He poked his head around the door frame with an amused expression. "Don't worry about it. And no need to shout I am a werewolf, remember?" He smirked.

I sat up straight and narrowed my eyes at him. "Well, I am worried about it. I'd like to know so I can pay my half," I said defensively.

"Like I said, don't worry. I've taken care of it," he repeated.

I frowned at his refusal to accept my money and fell back on the bed in frustration. "Well, at least let me pay for the room service bills?" I compromised.

"No."

I clambered out of bed with the Egyptian cotton bed sheet wrapped around me and stomped into the bathroom. He stood at the sink, brushing his teeth and I leaned against the his and her sinks, arms folded and glared at him until he finished. He rinsed out his mouth and stood up proudly, beaming at me.

"Alina, I don't mean to be rude, but you don't have the money to spend on flash hotels and I do. So just let me treat you, okay?"

"I don't have any money because someone swooped into my

life, caused it to turn upside down and got me fired from my job." I scowled as he stepped towards me and pushed his hips into mine, caging me against the sink.

"Exactly. It's all my fault, so let me deal with everything," he soothed, and my annoyance faded. No man should be able to have such an effect on a woman like this. It's lethal.

"Well then, thank you," I mumbled, wrapping my arms around his neck.

"I can think of a better way for you to thank me," he replied seductively with a sexy lopsided smile. My swollen centre burned and I felt my wetness seeping between my legs. This was insane. We had already had sex four times today and it was only mid-afternoon yet I still wanted him again. However, I wasn't sure my spent body could handle his manhood again until it had had a good soak in the warmth of the bath, so I decided to do something I'd been fantasising about but hadn't had the guts to do until now. I wanted to take control and be the one to give him immense pleasure like he had done to me countless times already.

Summoning all my courage and giving him what I hoped was my sexiest smile, I said, "Oh really? And what might that be?"

Before he could answer, I leaned up on my toes and started to kiss and nibble at his neck. He groaned in bliss.

"If you keep kissing my neck like that, I am not responsible for what happens next," he growled.

I smiled against his skin and whispered, "Shhhh. I am in control now, my Alpha," using his words from the night before, and continued to trail kisses down his tattooed chest and torso, running my hands along his arousing muscles.

"Say that again," he demanded heatedly, and I peered up into his deep, sapphire eyes which were overflowing with desire.

I placed my hands firmly on his chest and pushed him as hard as I could so he fell back against the bathroom door as I repeated seductively, "My Alpha."

He grabbed the nape of my neck and crashed his lips onto mine. I had lost count of the amount of times we have made out since last night, but the intensity and passion just seemed to grow each and every time. I broke away with my hands still resting on his bare chest. His hooded eyes were filled with lust as I gave him a sultry look and returned to smothering his chest and torso with kisses, nibbles and licks as I made my way onto my knees.

I brushed my boobs against his magnificent erection before taking it in my small hands. I needed both hands to grip it and started stroking it slowly. He leaned his head back against the door as I picked up the pace. I noticed the drip of precum that started to leak out of his tip and leaned over to lick it off with my tongue. Logan hissed at the act. It only encouraged me to take as much as I can of him into my mouth until he hit the back of my throat.

"FUCK!" he groaned as I slowly released him and repeated again. I picked up the momentum, swirling my tongue around his tip as I continued my erotic assault.

"Alina. Fuck. You feel so good," he cried, and I gave him my best performance, knowing he was close. He started squirming beneath me and his legs tense as he yelled, "Oh, ffffuuccck!"

Right on cue, I felt a warm sensation shoot into my mouth and I swallowed while still holding him in place at the back of my throat, making his legs shake. I released him, licking off any of his juices left behind.

"Holyfuckingshit," he panted, looking down at me through dark eyelashes.

I stood embarrassed and kissed his stubbled jawline to hide my blushed cheeks from his view.

He wrapped his arms around me tightly and said, "That was the best thank you I have ever had!"

I pulled back and smiled shyly at his compliment, feeling secretly smug that I could give him just as much pleasure as he gave me.

"Shit! The bath!" He suddenly sprang into action, racing to turn the taps off and pulling out the plug to release some of the overflowing bubbles. I giggled as he flashed me a youthful smile and shook his head.

He climbed in and leaned back, closing his eyes and unleashing a satisfied sigh.

"Coming in?"

I stepped in between his legs and leaned my back onto his chest. His long body didn't fit so he rested his legs on the end of the tub, his feet hanging out whilst I was encased by his body and the balmy water. He wrapped his huge arms around me and nuzzled my neck. This was pure heaven.

"So..." I started playing with his masculine fingers in my hand. "What does a Luna actually do?"

I felt him smile into my neck before he leaned his head back to answer. "A good Luna looks out for her people, checking in on them and their well-being. She's kind, approachable but doesn't take any shit from anyone. She helps to plan large events and ensures any guests feel welcome in the pack. Some Lunas have jobs outside the role but it is quite rare. But the most important thing a Luna does is act as an equal leader, supporting and loving her Alpha."

I listened intently as he described what I presumed was his ideal Luna and I surprisingly felt hopeful. None of that seemed so bad. I like the idea of still having my own life outside of being a Luna. I wanted to be a therapist before all this chaos and perhaps that could still be possible even if it was only for the pack.

"That doesn't sound too daunting," I replied in a small voice.

He squeezed me tighter and whispered, "You are perfect."

I blushed at his flattery. "You said in your speech last night that you were going to go back to America next week." It wasn't a question, but my tone made it seem like one.

He nodded behind me. "Yes, it is time. I need to restore my pack and rebuild the territory."

I gulped and my heart clenched at the thought of him leaving.

"We will leave after the Blood Oath is complete," he added.

I suddenly spun around awkwardly in the small space, in shock. "We?"

"Yes. All of us wolves will go back to start preparing for the battle. You included." His eyes burned into mine. It wasn't a direct command, but it might as well have been.

"But I… My whole life is here. My friends, my university, my job…" I stopped as I remembered the last was not true anymore.

He studied me carefully and it made me feel slightly uncomfortable.

"Alina, I do not want to pressure you into making your decision about becoming my Luna, which is why we're still going ahead with the Blood Oath tomorrow, but you will come with me to America until you decide, because I need to keep you safe. I can't leave you here alone," he explained.

It made sense. And I had always wanted to visit the USA, see where my dad grew up.

"Okay," I said, turning around and falling back onto him. I felt him relax beneath me as he poured water over my breasts with his hands. "So, the witch is coming tomorrow?"

"She is," he answered.

I fidgeted slightly at the thought. I'm not going to lie. I am shitting myself.

Chapter 39

Lucius' POV

"Because, my dear Cora, I have something that you want." I grinned mischievously. To my annoyance, she didn't react but continued her deathly glare without blinking.

"You have nothing that I want, Lucius." Her bitter tone challenged me. I was prepared for her hostility. Hell, I even had another much less powerful witch put a protection spell on me as I thought Cora would at least attempt to harm me, but this calm, composed woman was even more terrifying. Celeste had always been the hot-headed twin and Cora was more grounded, but they both always shared a fiery, vicious nature. Especially when it came to their enemies.

"If you think I would perform any of those spells for you…" She pointed her polished nail towards the *Book of Dark Magic*, "for anything you have to offer me, after what you have done, you are sorely mistaken," she replied coolly but her light blue eyes swelled with hatred.

I sneered, knowing how wrong she was. "Oh, but Cora, you are the one who is mistaken. You see, I have been keeping a very dark secret for many years." I tapped my chin with my fingers, pretending to be deep in thought. "Twenty-nine years, to be exact."

My eyes glistened with devilishness and Cora shifted in her chair, showing the first signs of any emotion since she'd been here.

"Lucius, I do not care about you or your many secrets. I simply came here to tell you that I will never do your bidding or associate myself with you under any circumstances. You are as dead to me as my wretched sister, so kindly leave me the fuck alone. I will not ask twice."

Rage built at the insult towards Celeste as I watched her stand and brush down her satin floor-length dress. With her head bowed forward for a moment, my heart skipped a beat as I could have sworn Celeste, my love, was the one before me. But the moment passed just as quickly and I pulled myself back to the present.

"What a shame. And here I was thinking you would do just about anything for your family," I taunted her, leaning back in my chair.

"You are not my family," she said coldly as she flipped her long, raven locks over her shoulder and headed towards the door.

"Maybe not, but your son is."

She froze, fingers extended to the door handle before glaring back at me with a face only a powerful dark witch could muster. Her skin had paled, and her eyes glowed a stunning lilac colour as black veins bulged under her skin.

"What did you just say?" She gritted through her teeth.

"Please, Cora. Take a seat and let's have a little chat about our son," I said seriously, gesturing to the empty chair she had vacated.

"MY son is dead. What more is there to say?" She spoke slowly and full of warning that she was close to losing control. Even with this protection spell, I did not feel confident that she wouldn't be able to kill me at any moment.

"Your son is very much alive, Cora," I said carefully, rising to my feet.

Her eyes widened at my words but quickly narrowed again with distrust.

"Please sit and I will explain."

She hesitated but I knew she would not be able to refuse hearing me out even if she thought it was a trick. Just as I predicted, she cautiously took her place opposite me once again.

"I can't wait to hear this," she said sarcastically, folding her arms and crossing her legs.

"The day our son was born…"

"MY son." She growled.

I raised my hands in apology. "The day your son was born. What do you remember?" I asked.

"I remember everything," she hissed.

"Do you remember the midwife taking the baby away before you even saw him?" I rested my index finger on the red alarm button under my desk, ready to alert my warriors to my impending danger.

"I… Yes. How did you know about—" she started but she trailed away realising that something terrible had happened.

"The midwife was glamoured by me. She was instructed to bring the baby to me as soon as it was born. She muffled the baby's cry so you would think it was not breathing and needed assistance," I explained clearly.

"But … no! I held him in my arms! He was gone! He wasn't breathing," she screamed, her eyes changing from blue to purple like a two-toned flag blowing in the breeze.

"Yes, you held a dead baby," I said, agreeing with her. "But he was not yours."

A glowing aura started radiating off her body as she gave into her darkness. I pressed my red button just as her hair spread out around her in the air and she levitated off the floor. In a split second, my guards were in the room running towards her only to be thrown back by her power.

"Cora!" I tried to reason with her. "Cora, if you want to see your son you will need me alive."

A few of my guards attempted to grab her again only for them to cry out in agony as their hands were set alight. She slowly lowered herself to the ground, regaining control. Once she had calmed down, she spoke with disbelief, "He's here?"

I nodded my head but really it was to direct my guard behind her, who swiftly injected a drug into her neck to knock her unconscious.

"My… my baby…" she mumbled as she fell to the floor.

Cora's POV

My head throbbed and my mouth was dry like cotton as I adjusted my eyes to my surroundings. The first thing that hit me was the stench of decaying bodies, blood and faeces. I heaved as it consumed my senses. Sitting up on the metal bed, I realised where I was. In a cell. In a dungeon. How did I get here?

I rubbed my head with my hands as I tried to put the muddled pieces of my brain back together. I cried out when I saw a huge rip down the bottom of my Chanel dress. It was my favourite and a timeless piece. I wore it especially because I needed the confidence it gave me to go and see...

Lucius!

Suddenly, memories of our meeting flashed through my mind like a tornado, causing my breath to come out in gasps and terror to run through my veins. Was my son alive? Lucius had had him all this time!

My blood boiled like lava sprouting from a volcano and I raced across the prison cell to use my powers against the bars. Nothing happened. I tried again. Still nothing. Touching the steel bars, I sensed dark magic working against me.

"Surely you did not think I am stupid enough to lock you in a normal cell, Cora?" His sly voice echoed through the darkness as he stepped into the flickering candlelight. Smartly dressed as usual, one would say he could pass as a gentleman. I knew he was anything but.

"Where's my son?" I roared at him through the bars.

"All in good time, Cora. First, we need to discuss the terms of our agreements."

"I have no agreement with you," I spat at him.

"Tut tut, how very unladylike Cora. Now, how about you hearing the conditions before you make any rash decisions?"

I rolled my eyes and put my hands on my hips.

"Much better." He grinned, flashing his vile canines. "Now I will let you see your son and I will even allow him to leave with you. You can make up for the lost time, have that mother-son relationship you've always dreamed of. I promise I will not interfere with you or his life again as long as I live." His eyes twinkled, knowing it was an offer I couldn't refuse.

"And what do I have to do in return?"

"Well, that's simple really. Help me to destroy the werewolves."

Panic rose. I had already pledged allegiance to their cause. I needed Lucius dead but this was a chance to have my son back. The son I never knew I had.

"I want to see him first. Only when I truly know he is my son will I accept," I demanded, folding my arms across my chest.

His wicked smirk widened. "I thought that might be the case."

The Last Alpha

He turned and nodded to the guards. They both disappeared from the dungeon after a couple of agonising minutes, returning holding up a half-conscious man in silver cuffs adorning his wrists. His head of jet-black hair hung low as if he was asleep and his feet stumbled as he was dragged towards my cell.

My heart pounded in my chest, and the love I felt overwhelmed me. I haven't even seen his face yet, but I already knew he was my son.

"What have you done to him? Why is he in cuffs and drugged?" I screamed at Lucius, who was watching on with amusement.

"For all of our protection, Cora. He is a phenomenal being with great power."

I stepped forward and extended my hand out to slowly lift his chin so I could see his face for the first time. My baby's face. My breath hitched as the beauty of him warmed my heart. The heart that I had thought had become frozen when I'd lost him. He had one of my pale blue eyes and one deep brown like his father's. A strong jaw line and chiselled, high cheekbones as well as flawless skin. He could be a model with his good looks. His magnificent eyes tried to focus on my face as I gave him a weak smile, tears brimming at the surface. I reached down and grasped his hand, starting my chant to visualise any sign of his future. Nothing. If I hadn't been certain before, I was now.

"My son, my boy." I stroked the side of his face as confusion creased the lines in his face before he passed out. His head drooped down, and I stared at Lucius over his shoulder, his malice eyes twinkling. I had to save my son.

"Don't even think about trying to harm me, Cora. I have syphoned his life to mine until you complete my requests."

My heart sunk knowing I was backed into a corner. I had to get him away from this monster.

"I will do what you ask," I said to him coldly. He grinned like a Cheshire cat.

"What is his name?" I asked.

Arius."

Chapter 40

Logan's POV

"Alina, try and relax. I promise you it will be over quickly, and the worst part is just a finger prick to write your name on the oath with your blood," I repeated again for the third time as I watched her pacing the softly furnished living room, biting her nails. She nodded as if she was listening, but from the vacant look on her face, I knew she was miles away. I walked over to her, placing my hands on her shoulders to steady her. She looked up into my eyes and all I saw was worry and uncertainty.

"Alina. It will be fine, I promise. And I will be here with you every step of the way," I tried to reassure her.

She finally released a long-drawn-out breath.

"Sorry. It's just I have never met a witch before, let alone the most powerful dark witch in the world." She returned to her incessant nail biting. I slowly pulled her hands away and held them in mine, rubbing her knuckles whilst she gave me a defeated smile.

A knock on the hotel room door made her jump back. She really was a bag of nerves today!

"It's okay. It's just Darius," I said, walking to the door and opening it to my red-headed cousin.

"Morrrrning." He beamed as he waltzed straight past me and into our living room. "Great day for a Blood Oath, don't you think?" He clapped his hands together enthusiastically.

"Alina is feeling a little nervous about meeting the witch," I explained when she barely managed a smile in his direction.

"Aw! I would be to if I were you. She is terrifying," he said unhelpfully, and I scowled at him from across the room. "Fred and his mate are in the lobby with her now. Shall I send them up?" he asked, ignoring my glare.

"No. I will go down and greet them. Alina, stay here with Darius and I will be right back, okay?" She nodded timidly. "Everything will be fine, you'll see."

I pecked her lips hastily before leaving the room. When I arrived in the extravagant lobby of the hotel, I spied Fredrik immediately and approached the group he was with. He stepped to the side and turned to greet me as he sensed my presence.

"Alpha." He nodded, which I returned and then my energy was drawn to the woman standing at the side of him. She oozed importance and looked regal in her tailored purple pantsuit and high heels. Her shiny, black hair nearly touched the floor and people stared at her in awe as they walked past.

"Alpha Logan, it is a pleasure to finally meet you." Her voice was elegant but holds authority.

"The pleasure is mine," I took her outstretched hand and shook it as her eyes clouded over white. I quickly pulled it away as I realised she was trying to get into my head. She smiled warmly at my rejection.

"Sorry. I have just waited so long to meet you and I wanted to see what path you have chosen," she explained, but it put me on edge all the same.

"We are in a public place, Cora, and I would appreciate some warning before you enter my mind," I bit back sternly.

"Of course. Apologies."

I glanced over her shoulder at Sloane who was staring bitchily into the back of the witch's head. It seems I am not the only one who was wary of this woman.

"Shall we?" Cora pointed to the gold-plated lifts to go up to my room.

"Sure, follow me," I commanded as I pressed the lift button.

When we all cram in, Cora's power felt even more intense, and it became hard to concentrate on anything else.

"As you know, Alina is human and is quite anxious about meeting you, so please be considerate of her feelings," I said with a warning tone.

She turned her face to the side to regard me and smiled, "Of course. You seem to know her well." Her cold eyes searched mine.

"She is my mate. Of course, I know her well." I couldn't help but snap back.

She only nodded and then we all remained in silence until we reached the room. I stopped with my card key hovering over the reader and glared at the witch with my most authoritative stance.

"I am trusting you, Cora. Do not disappoint me."

She smiled in understanding and I swiped the card, allowing her in to meet my mate.

Cora's POV

A petite girl with wavy, ash blonde hair whipped around from the window when I entered, and her eyes widened in surprise. That was often the reaction I got from strangers expecting to meet a haggard, old witch in a black cloak and grey hair. I smiled at her warmly as I scrutinise her features. She was very beautiful with her rich, kind eyes, a small nose and full, round lips. But what made me even more intrigued was her aura. It was extremely bright and full of vibrant colours.

"Hello, my dear. My name is Cora, and you must be Alina." I did not offer her my hand as I did not want to upset the Alpha again. He was an intense and intimidating character in his own right, but he was easy to read. He cared for this girl, maybe even loved her already, and he was determined to defeat Lucius. That much was clear, but this human was much harder to read.

She returned my smile and seemed to relax slightly as she took a seat on the plush sofa. I took one opposite in the armchair and glanced around at the group of people who were all glowering at me, watching my every move.

"Is the audience really necessary?" I asked Logan as I glided my hand down the soft satin of my trouser suit.

"Yes," he replied hard-faced.

I rolled my eyes at Alina in amusement and her smile widened.

"Actually, could everyone leave please? I think all the intense staring is making me more nervous." She looked up at Logan with pleading eyes as he contemplated this for a few seconds before he ordered everyone to get out and took a seat next to her on the sofa.

Interesting. She already had a lot of influence over him. This was unheard of between an Alpha and a human.

My eyes darted between the two of them as he leaned back and rested his arm behind her on the back of the sofa protectively. It looked like he had made his choice between Madeline and Alina. If she really was just a mere human, then this would be easier than I thought. He was already sabotaging his own future.

I took out my belongings from my handbag and started to place all the necessary tools on the coffee table. Alina became mesmerised by every enchanted item. I finally unrolled the scroll in old English scripture from the enchanted council.

"Please read this through carefully. Any questions, just ask," I said, pushing it towards her.

She picked it up and read it intensely. Her tongue pokes out in concentration. I started to mix the potion together whilst Logan never took his eyes off me. I expected him to be wary, but his constant attention was going to make what I had to do much harder. I had to remind myself to keep my breathing level and not show any signs of the inner turmoil I was facing. I wanted nothing more than to help him win this war, but now that I had the chance to reunite with my son, I had a different purpose.

"It says here that if I ever break the oath by revealing the truth about the magical world, the highest order will be placed upon me." Alina spoke up. "What does that mean?" she asked innocently.

Logan shifted in his seat and looked pained.

"It means the enchanted council will sentence you to death," I said as a matter of fact. Her mouth hung open and she stared from me to Logan before shutting it again. "Any other questions?" I asked.

She shook her head and I reach out my hands to retrieve the oath from hers. Our fingers connect and I felt a surge of power shoot up through my skin. My eyes widened in shock. I quickly recovered before Logan suspects anything. This girl was anything but human. I needed to get her alone.

"Right, we're ready to begin. Logan, would you mind stepping out of the room for a few minutes whilst I perform the oath?" I asked as sincerely and politely as I could. His eyes narrowed with suspicion.

"No, I am staying," he demanded.

"I am afraid that will not be possible. For the oath to be

successful, I will need to focus all my energy on Alina's presence solely and yours will be a distraction," I lied.

He wasn't buying it.

"Logan. It's fine. I will be okay. I feel a lot calmer now and, like you said, it's only a prick of the finger." Alina smiled lovingly at him and squeezed his knee.

He looked between us both, fighting his own need to control the situation. "You have five minutes and then I am coming in," he growled at me before quickly kissing Alina's forehead and leaving the room.

"Alina, your hands please," I said, outstretching mine. She placed her delicate hand in it and I closed my eyes, not wanting to scare her with my clouded irises. I started my Latin chants, but instead of the Blood Oath spell I was supposed to be performing, I was calling for her future.

What I saw shocked me to the core.

My eyes flew open, and I released her hand immediately.

"Is everything okay?" she asked nervously.

"Yes, my dear. It is just that something seems to be a little off with the spell. Let's try this," I took her index finger and pricked it with my blade, causing a bubble of bright red blood to rise from the incision. "Please sign your name at the bottom of the Oath," I said, watching her every move with new fascination. She pressed her finger on the parchment and started to glide it in swirls along the page. She jumped back when her blood sizzled and evaporated.

"Just as I thought," I said, carefully shaking my head.

"What? What's happening?" she asked in panic. It was clear that she didn't know what she was.

"Alina, I cannot perform the oath on you because, my child, you are not human."

Her face paled as she registered what I said. "What do you mean? Not human. What am I?" she asked in a shaky voice.

"You are a werewolf, Alina. And not just any werewolf. From what I can sense, you came from a very strong bloodline."

She shook her head in disbelief. "But how? I don't understand it. My parents were human. I can't be, I don't have a wolf?!"

"When I touched your hands earlier, I could feel a powerful spell that had been cast upon you. I believe it was to mask your wolf's presence. However, it is starting to fade, probably due to meeting your mate. As for your parents, are you sure they were both human?" I studied her closely.

She slumped back in the chair, bewildered. She was clearly overwhelmed by this news. She really had no idea and I felt pity for her, especially as now this meant her life was in even more danger than before.

"Alina, I know this is a huge shock and you will have lots of questions, but I believe that right now the most important thing is to keep this to yourself," I urged.

If Logan knew her true identity, he would not hesitate to mark her and it would make him unstoppable. I hated doing this, but it was the only way. I had to split them up.

Her eyes snapped up at mine. "Why?"

"Because you will put yourself and Logan in extreme danger if Lucius finds out this information. It is not worth the risk until after the battle."

She nodded in understanding and Logan boomed into the room. He went straight to her side and stroked her cheek, "Are you okay? You look pale." His face is crippled with concern whilst I quickly scrolled up the oath before he could see it.

"I-I'm fine. It's just the sight of blood." She smiled weakly.

Good girl.

He glared at me as I stood.

"It is complete. I will take it straight to the council myself and I will be in touch shortly," I lied once again and gave a knowing smile to Alina.

Logan walked me to the door. It looked like he wanted to say more but instead, "thank you," slipped reluctantly from his lips.

I nodded with respect as my heart flickered with betrayal and I walked out of the room.

As I walked through the hotel reception, I felt a tight grip on my arm, and I spun around. Madeline stood before me, and she looked less than okay since our last meeting. She had dark bags under her eyes and blotchy skin indicating restless nights and lots of crying. My heart went out to her for her heartbreak. There was something about this girl that just connected with me.

"Cora, I need your help," she whispered, and I pulled her into the corner of the room hidden behind a large indoor plant from view.

"What do you need?" I asked, thinking quickly on my feet as to how I could make this work in my favour... or more accurately, Lucius'.

"Logan has chosen her. If your visions are correct, he will die in battle. I need to save him. I will do anything," she pleaded in desperation. My mind races quickly to come up with a plan.

I rummaged around my bag for the right potion and handed her the green liquid in a tiny glass bottle.

"Get him on his own. Give him a few drops of this in a drink. It will knock him out for at least twelve hours. You will need to get creative, Madeline. When he wakes, he won't remember her, so you must make Alina leave before he does," I urged, and squeezed her hands around the bottle before turning on my heels and strutting away.

The Last Alpha

Now to go and get my boy.

Chapter 41

Alina's POV

My shuddering breaths came out in harsh pants as I leaned against the bathroom sink, head sagging to my chest, fighting the panic attack I seem to be having. I haven't been able to control the relentless trembling since the witch left. Making a quick dash to the bathroom to escape Logan's overprotective attention, I've been cooped up in here for the last ten minutes. Her words kept playing in my mind like a broken record. *"You are not human. You are a werewolf, Alina. And from a very strong bloodline."*

I squeezed my eyes shut tightly, trying to get a hold on my emotions and shock. She must be wrong. How can I be a werewolf? I am just me. My parents were human. Unless I was adopted?

I shook my head at the thought. No, I have seen my birth certificate and the photos from the day I was born cradled in my parents' arms. How could they keep this from me? Why was I put under a spell to suppress my wolf? My head pulsated with the endless questions that I couldn't even voice.

A soft knock on the door jolted me from my distress and I quickly splashed my face with cold water.

"Alina? Are you okay?" Logan's enticing voice called from

behind the door and it instantly provided me with the comfort I needed. I long to tell him the truth and it hurt my soul to know I had to keep such a life-changing secret from him. But it was the only way to protect us. In a way, I felt almost useful that I was finally able to do something to help the situation. I could defend this secret if it meant playing a small part in giving Logan a better chance in this war.

"Yes, sorry. I'm fine," I called out, trying to mask the quiver in my voice. I opened the door to his bulky body towering over me, one arm leaning on the door frame whilst the other one tousling his hair. My heart expanded at the concern etched on his face. "Really. I am fine, I just really didn't expect to feel so queasy at the sight of my own blood," I lied, avoiding looking him in the eyes.

"Come here," he soothed, pulling me into the safety of his chest and I inhaled his comforting scent. It relaxed me as I closed my eyes and basked in his warmth. "Are you sure nothing happened? The witch didn't upset you?" he asked and I tried my best to control my muscles as they tensed slightly at his inquisition.

"No, I'm fine," was all I managed to squeak. "Do we have any food? I'm starving," I added, trying to change the subject even though I wasn't sure I would be able to stomach any food right now.

"Order room service. Anything you like." He stepped away from me to reach for the menu on our bedside table.

"Thanks," I said in a small voice.

"Did somebody say room service? I want in on that action." Darius' voice boomed from the living room.

"Of course, he does," Logan muttered and rolled his eyes as I smiled at their banter. They might as well be brothers by the amount they bicker, but deep down, I know they both really love each other even if they would never admit it. It's sweet.

***

It turned out, I really was starving! As soon as I smelt the delicious steak enter the room, I was devouring it like a ravenous beast. Oh, wow, that's exactly what I was! For a moment, joking and giggling with Logan and Darius whilst they squabbled over the TV Guide, I had actually forgotten all about my revelation. Now that I had calmed down and started to accept that I actually could already be a werewolf, I felt strangely serene. I wasn't scared of the idea of being a wolf, in fact, I welcomed it.

Looking between these two lovable men, I smiled, knowing that I finally felt like I belonged somewhere since I had lost my mum. I felt like I had a family again and I was truly one of them, even if they didn't know it yet. I stood up and started to clear the plates, taking them towards the small open-plan kitchen.

"No, I am not watching another episode of *Family Guy*. You're too old for ridiculous cartoons," Logan grunted, trying to snatch the remote from Darius' hands.

"It's better than your depressing shit about the end of the fucking world," Darius bit back, swiping the remote with his other hand out of reach of Logan.

"*The Walking Dead* is not shit! It's bloody brilliant! Tell him, Alina." Logan looked at me for backup as I strolled towards them and placed myself between them on the sofa to stop them from killing each other.

"Hey, keep me out of it!" I said with my hands up in surrender.

Suddenly, Logan's phone pinged and his face creased with emotion that I couldn't quite pinpoint as he read the message. His jaw tensed as he put it down on the sofa and stared at the TV screen.

"Everything okay?" I asked just as it pinged again, alerting him to another text. He swiftly picked it up again and that same emotion donned his face. Was he annoyed? I couldn't be sure, but something was bothering him.

"Yeah, everything is fine. But I think I'm going to have to go out for a bit," he said reluctantly, as if it was the last thing he wanted to do. He was definitely annoyed about something. He turned to me and gave me a small smile, "I'm sorry. I shouldn't be too long. Darius can stay here with you until I'm back."

My chest tightened at him leaving, but I berated myself for feeling so needy. He was an Alpha amid a war and no matter how much I wanted him all to myself, I couldn't be so selfish.

"Don't worry. It's fine. I was actually wondering if I could invite Chloe over to the hotel?" I asked carefully. We had exchanged a few texts over the last couple of days but I was starting to really miss my best friend and I needed to see a familiar face more than ever right now.

Logan frowned but his expression softened when he saw how much this would mean to me.

"Alright, but Darius stays for your safety. And remember, Alina, you cannot tell her anything about what is really happening," he warned me, reminding me that the council would not hesitate to kill me if I broke the oath. Little does he know, I never signed it. Yes, another secret I have to keep from him.

"I know, I promise I won't say anything. But... can I tell her about us?" I asked shyly, looking up at him through my eyelashes.

His smile was so genuine that my heart fluttered and he leaned forward to kiss me before mumbling "Of course" against my lips.

"Urgh. Get a room, guys! I'm trying to relax here," Darius teased.

"We have a room and you're in it. Logan laughed before

standing to get his coat and boots on.

I followed him to the door to see him out. I suddenly felt uneasy, twiddling my fingers as he pulled on his leather jacket. I don't want him to leave, and every fibre of my being wished I would cave and beg him to stay. He made me feel like nobody else could in this entire world. When I'm around him, I feel split in two. A part of me is constantly on fire, burning for him if I'm not touching him. The other half is calm and peaceful just knowing he is mine. Yet, I still couldn't shake the dreaded feeling that he is too good to be true. No one can be this wonderful.

His crystal blue eyes locked with mine and I held my breath as I felt our souls connect.

'Kiss him now.' A voice purred in my head, but before I could react to it, his mouth invaded mine and our tongues entangled in a deep embrace, his arms squeezing me so close to his body, I could barely breathe. When we pulled apart, we rested our foreheads together.

"Come back to me," I whispered.

"Always," he husked and turned out of the door.

"You guys are gross." Darius put his fingers in his mouth, pretending to gag.

"Oh, shut it. You're just jealous that you're still waiting for your mate." I swatted him on the shoulder as I slouched down next to him.

"No way! If I ever find her, she's going to have to get used to my macho wolf. None of that puppy dog shit!" He laughed as I rolled my eyes.

"I'm just going to call Chloe. When she comes over, do you mind if you give us some privacy? She is going to wonder why you're here and not leaving me alone. Clearly acting like a stalker."

I smirked.

"Logan will have my head if I leave this room," he said simply.

"Hang on. Are you scared of him?" I faked my shock, putting my hand over my mouth.

He glared at me with irritation. "I know what you're doing. And it's not going to work."

"I don't know what you mean. I just always thought you were your own man who didn't let others intimidate you, especially not your own cousin. But I guess I was wrong." I shrugged, retrieving my phone from my pocket and dialling Chloe's number. I took a quick peek at him before walking to the bedroom and saw that he was rattled by my comments. Too easy!

"Lina! Ohmygod, I miss you so much! How are you? Where are you? When can I see you?" Chloe's erratic voice bellows down the phone.

"Whoa, Chlo! Slow down," I chuckled. "I'm good. Are you?"

"I hate that I never see you anymore." She sulks down the phone.

"It's only been a few days, Chloe, but I have missed your crazy ass, too," I said.

"Are you sick of it at that odd man's house yet?" she asked hopefully.

"Actually, I'm not staying there right now. I'm in a hotel," I explained, knowing I'm about to be bombarded with a million questions.

"What? Why? Why didn't you come back here if you wanted to leave?" she asked, the hurt evident in her voice.

"It's nothing like that. Look, it's a long story. So I was wondering if you wanted to come over for a girly night and I will tell you all about it."

"Um, yes!" She practically screamed down the phone. "Where are you?"

"At Claridge's. The penthouse." I waited for the dramatics.

"No fucking way! Oh, my god! I am on my way right now! Have you won the lottery or something?" she yelled in disbelief.

I smiled, thinking of Logan. "Something like that. Chloe, could you do me a favour? You know the old box of keepsakes I have stored at yours? Can you bring it with you please?"

"Course. I'll be there in half an hour. Love ya, bye!"

I hung up the phone with the biggest grin. A night with my best friend was exactly what I needed right now.

I walked into the living room and fell back on to the sofa.

"I will wait in the hallway when she's here." Darius pouted, caving into my request.

I leaned over and gave him a sloppy kiss on the cheek.

"Urgh," he said whilst wiping his cheek with his sleeve, but I noted a faint smile playing on his lips.

Chapter 42

Madeline's POV

I put down the pen gently next to the handwritten letter and closed my eyes. I don't know why I felt this way, because everything I had written was the truth. I wasn't exaggerating or even trying to hurt her feelings, but I knew it would.

Opening my eyes, I scanned my writing again, whilst my knee tapped uncontrollably against the table. I was doing the best thing for everyone, right? Then why did it feel so... wrong?

'Because he is not your mate. He is hers!' Nina barked in my head.

I leaned back on the chair and gripped my hair in frustration.

'Mate or not, I can't let him die! We have come too far for all of this to just blow up in our faces because of one girl.' I tried to reason with her even though a part of me knew she was right.

I won't lie and say that the last few days had been a walk in the park. I barely slept or eaten. My mind was in a constant state of panic knowing the outcome of Logan's choice. His rejection hurt. It hurt like hell. We've been together since we were kids and romantically since we were fifteen years old. He had known Alina for five minutes!

But strangely, his decision didn't break me the way I had

expected it to. Instead, all I felt was fear. A crippling sense of doom that I needed to rectify as soon as possible. And no matter how uncomfortable it made me feel, it was my only option.

"Is it done?" Emma asked as she walked into my room.

I nodded slowly, not taking my eyes off the letter, and then sat motionless.

"Here." She handed me an envelope.

I carefully took it from her and folded the letter inside neatly. Emma held her hand out to retrieve it but I hesitated. Taking one shaky breath, I placed it in her hands before I changed my mind.

"You are doing the right thing. For all of us," she whispered and rubbed the side of my arm kindly.

I stood up abruptly and stomped over to the bed only to fall backwards until my back connected with the hard mattress. I hate this room now. It felt suffocating and depressing, filled with memories of my life before. My life with him. Even if this plan worked, I wasn't sure we would ever be the same again. I wasn't sure I could forgive him, let alone be happy in the knowledge that he didn't really want me.

I released a troubled sigh. This was bigger than us. This was about our revenge, our species, and our futures.

"Okay, so I will deliver the letter to Alina in the early morning. If the plan changes, text me," Emma said seriously as she shrugged on her coat.

"Thanks, Ems. I don't know what I would have done without you these last few days," I replied honestly. She had barely left my side since Logan broke up with me and never once complained.

"You know I'd do anything for you, bitch." She smiled cheekily and flipped her hair over her shoulder as she exited my room.

Staring up at the ceiling for the longest time, I finally pulled out my phone to set my plan in motion.

Logan. I need to speak with you. It's urgent. It could affect the future of our pack. Please come over. Alone.

I pressed send and watched as the blue ticks emerged. He had read it straight away. No reply.

After everything, please do not ignore me, Logan. You owe me that much.

I moved from the bed and sat down at my vanity table. I looked like a complete disaster. I combed out my unruly shoulder-length hair, trying to tame the frizz. Curling the ends and then adding a little moose, I sighed at my reflection. There wasn't much I could do about the dark circles under my eyes other than cake my face with as much foundation as possible. I added a touch of mascara and a dab of lip gloss. This was the best I could do right now.

The unexpected sound of a stone hitting my bedroom window jolted me from my thoughts. Strolling over to the window and peering out, I could see nothing but the darkness of the night. I searched the road below for any sign of life but only the screeching of cats having a fight could be heard in the distance. Strange.

The alert of a text had me whipping around and clambering over the bed towards my phone.

Be there in 10.

Shit. I raced through the apartment chucking any mess into cupboards out of sight and ransacking my handbag for the potion the witch gave me. My trembling hands placed it inside a skull vase that Logan and I had bought a few years ago at a market that sat next to our little liquor table.

A couple of minutes later, I heard the front door open and my heart was in my mouth. His heavy footfall increased as he got closer to the living room where I had perched myself on the sofa pretending to read a book.

"Maddy." His deep voice made me look up and I gave him a gracious smile as he stared at me emotionless. He glanced around the room as if he hadn't been here for years rather than days and shifted uncomfortably on his feet.

"Hi, thanks for coming. Do you want to drink?" I asked, standing from the sofa and walking over to the liquor table, needing to do something myself to mask my nerves.

"Uh, yeah, why not? A whiskey please," he replied politely, removing his leather jacket and draping it on the back of the armchair.

My eyes flickered to the skull vase but my courage faltered. I want to give him one last chance before I must resort to that extreme.

"Here you go." I handed him the glass whilst I took a sip of my own. The warmth of the alcohol burned my throat but instantly calmed me.

"So, you needed to speak to me?" He raised his eyebrows above the rim of his glass as he took another sip of his drink.

"Yes. I would like you to hear me out and try to stay calm, so you really listen to the seriousness of what I am about to say." I looked him square in the eyes with a hard expression.

"I will try, Maddy, but please don't ask me to reject her again," he stated.

I swallowed my pain and tried to remain composed. "I understand that you don't want to be with me and you have chosen her, Logan. I really am trying to come to terms with it in my own way. But I still can't sit back and wait for all of this to backfire. I need you to understand the magnitude of your decision and what it will mean for us all." I paused when his nostrils flared and his eyes darkened at my words. I tried to soften my voice. "Logan, I care about you so much, but I also care about our pack. By choosing Alina as your Luna, you will end us all. If you fall in battle against Lucius, what do you think will happen to us? What will happen to Alina?"

I know it was a low blow, but I was sure he hadn't even considered that. His jaw clenched and he looked down into his glass as he twirled the liquid in a circular motion. The silence grew between us as he contemplated my words and hope started to rise in my chest.

"You know I care about you too, Maddy. I feel so terrible for how I have treated you recently and I know Alina does, too. I understand what you're saying, and I know it comes from a place of love and concern. I do. But..." He put the glass down on the coffee table and leaned forward, elbows resting on his knees. "I know with every fibre of my body that the only chance of victory I have against Lucius, the only hope I have for our pack and the only future I have, is with Alina by my side." He spoke so softly and sincerely I couldn't help the tears that threatened to spill. He really wasn't going to change his mind.

I quickly gulped away my emotions and wiped my eyes, so my makeup didn't run. "Okay," I said in a defeated voice, shocking him with my reaction. "I really hope it is the right choice, Logan."

He seemed to be lost for words as we continue to sit in silence, the finality of our relationship polluting the atmosphere.

"Do you know what day it is tomorrow?" I asked in a small voice, peering up at him through my long fringe.

"Of course," he replied before downing the remains of his whiskey. "It will be nine years tomorrow."

I nodded sadly as memories of that day haunted my mind. The tearful faces of my mother and father as they pushed me through the passage door, knowing they would never see me again.

"Shall we have a toast? To the ones that were left behind," I asked softly.

He gave me a sad smile and held out his empty tumbler to me. I climbed up and took our glasses over to the bar. Keeping my back to him, I took the small bottle from the skull vase and added three drops of the green liquid to his whiskey as a treacherous tear rolled down my cheek.

I'm sorry, Logan. You've left me with no choice.

Alina's POV

"I can't believe you kept this from me! You sneaky bitch!"

A pillow flew at me through the air and I held my hands up to cover my face. "I know! I know. I'm sorry, I've wanted to tell you for days, but I just..."

"Having too much wild, passionate sex to make the call?" Chloe mocked and I gave her a guilty smile. "I don't blame you. If I had a hottie like Logan in my bed, I would never let him leave."

A shallow growl escaped my chest involuntarily and my eyes widened in surprise.

"Did you just growl at me?" Chloe asked in shock.

"I - No - uh," I stuttered. Did I just growl? It sounded like it!

She burst out laughing hysterically. "You are brilliant. He must be a sex god to have you acting like this!"

I felt my cheeks burning as a hot flush crawled up my skin. "If you must know, yes, he is. Best sex of my life." I sniggered.

"I bet! Mind you, you didn't have much to compare him with. I mean, Michael?" She laughed even harder, and it was my turn to whack her with the pillow.

Once she got a grip of herself, she suddenly turned serious. That was a talent of Chloe's, she could go from one extreme emotion to another in a split second.

"What about Madeline? How did she take it?"

I lowered my eyes and slid down my seat, fumbling with the zip on my jumper. "I don't really know. Logan doesn't really like to talk about it."

"What? You don't know? Does she want to murder you? Was she upset? Did she beg him to stay with her? You don't know anything?" she cried in disbelief.

I shook my head slowly and she fell back against the pillows.

"Don't you think that's a bit odd? That you haven't talked about it?"

I guess it was, but in the height of our lustfulness, it was like we have been in our own little bubble and suddenly, Chloe had burst it.

"We just don't want to ruin our time together by talking about something we both feel terrible about." I tried to justify our actions and noticed Chloe roll her eyes and fold her arms. "What?" I asked defensively.

"Nothing. I just want you to be careful. They were together for a really long time from what people say and I can't imagine it would be that easy to just let go of all that history. I just don't want you to get hurt, Alina."

I huffed and pretended to watch the TV. I know I should trust Logan and he told me he wanted me, but Chloe had a point. This all happened so fast. I suddenly felt my stomach knotting and a sweep of nausea washed over me. Was I being foolish? Should I be more cautious?

"Oh, before I forget. Here." Chloe grabbed my attention by hauling out my old, tattered keepsake box from her bag. It used to be my mother's jewellery box as a child, and I loved playing with it whilst she would get ready for work. On my sixteenth birthday, she gave it to me. But instead of using it as a jewellery box, I collected memories in it.

The Last Alpha

"Thanks," I said, taking it from her and running my hand over the worn leather lid. The gold clasp was barely hanging on and to anyone else, this would just look like a bedraggled bit of tat. But to me, it meant everything.

"Ohmygod, is that the time?" Chloe looked down at her watch. "Midnight! I better go. I've got work in the morning!" She stood up, brushing herself down and I followed her to the door.

"Thanks for coming, Chlo. I really needed this." I smiled fondly at her before her arms pulled me into the biggest bear hug and I giggled as I squeezed her back.

"I love you, girl. And I'm sorry about what I said earlier. I am really happy for you, but I just want you to be careful. I know I'm being protective," she said, holding my shoulders at arm's length.

"I know, thank you. I love you, too."

After a few minutes, there was a knock at the door. I checked through the peephole to make sure it was who I expected and opened the door to a tired looking man.

"Enjoy yourselves?" Darius yawned as he walked in and fell onto his stomach dramatically on the sofa.

"Yeah! It was good to catch up. Thanks for waiting out there. So, when is Logan going to be back?" I queried, picking up my mother's jewellery box from the coffee table.

"No idea. But he better hurry up because I'm shattered and I want my bed," he mumbled, pressing his face into a cushion.

"Well, you can sleep here. I'll get you a blanket." By the time I've returned with the thick bed throw in hand, Darius was snoring loudly, mouth wide open. I tucked the blanket over him and headed to the bedroom.

Unclipping the gold clasp and opening the lid, I was hit with the familiar, musky smell of my childhood. I tenderly removed each piece of memorabilia, smiling at the fond reminders they brought. There were show tickets, newspaper clippings of me at school fairs, my mum's perfume bottle, a piece of material from my first blanket as a baby, photographs, and much more. But this time, I examined every item with a new curiosity. Did it hold any clues to who I really am? I found a smooth folded note at the bottom that I forgot I had kept. It was a note I found from my dad to my mum saying,

The whole world can become your enemy when you lose what you love. That's why I chose you, my full moon.

I remembered finding it amongst my mums' things when I had to pack up our house and I cried at how beautiful it was. I had no idea when it was written but it was definitely my dad's handwriting.

I read it again and again. He referred to her as his full moon. I always thought it was just poetic, but could there be more to it? Didn't wolves have connections to the moon? I thought of my dad and his large, bulky body that used to chuck me up in the air so effortlessly. He was protective and fierce when he wanted to be, but I just thought all dads were like that when it came to their daughters. Could he have been a wolf?

Something shiny caught my eye at the bottom of the box. I pulled out a tiny, delicate silver key that I swear I had never seen before. Twisting it in my fingers, I studied it from all angles. It was too small to open a door or a safe. What the earth would it be for? As I looked closer, I saw that it had a moon crest engraved into the handle.

I picked up my phone and started to scour the Internet for anything a key like this might be used for, but came up short. I sighed and laid back into the fluffy king-size bed I'd been sharing with Logan. It felt enormous without his exquisite but large body beside me. Where was he? It was nearly half one in the morning. I'd been holding off calling him as I didn't want to interfere with whatever his business was, but I needed to know he was safe. It went straight to voicemail. That was strange. Maybe he had no signal where he was. I tried not to worry as I felt my eyelids sag with heaviness. It had been an eventful day and it was finally catching up with me.

'*He will be back,*' was the last thing I heard in my mind as I fell into a deep slumber, but the voice wasn't mine.

***

I opened my eyes. In the dark stillness. I couldn't see much but the dim glow of the bedside clock. Half asleep, I fumbled with the covers and stumbled to the bathroom without switching on any lights. It was only after I'd emptied my bladder that I realised I could see everything as clearly as if it was the light of day. I rubbed my eyes and looked around my surroundings. Right, I was in a hotel. I'd forgotten in my drowsy state.

Shaking the water off my hands, I plodded across the room, but then stopped abruptly by the bed. An unsettling feeling began welling inside me. There was something wrong with this scene. Even before my mind registered the flatness of the bed, I knew Logan wasn't there.

Flipping on the overhead lights, I glanced around the room. There was no sign that he had come back and it was 5:30 in the morning. I frantically checked my phone for any messages or calls. Nothing. I rushed into the living room and only to find Darius' body spread out on the sofa.

He hadn't come home.

That was when I noticed it. A white envelope by the hotel door. It had clearly been slid under the crack as there was no letterbox. Cautiously, I picked it up and turned it over and was surprised that it was addressed to me. My heart pounded in my chest as I thought about who the last person was to send me mail.

Lucius.

With quivering hands, I ripped it open and returned to my bedroom. It was a handwritten letter and my eyes scanned to the bottom to see who it was from. Madeline. My mouth went dry and I felt panic rise as I started reading.

Alina,

I know I am probably the last person you expected to hear from, but I feel it is only fair to everyone involved that you know the truth. Logan and Darius are walking on eggshells around you and trying to protect you from the danger of our world. But if you are going to be a part of this, it is only right that you have the whole story.

Firstly, I want to say that I don't hate you. Yes, what happened is shitty, but the mate bond is a powerful thing. I am not naïve about that. However, this is bigger than just you, I and Logan.

When we escaped from Lucius' attack nine years ago today, Logan's father, our Alpha, told us that Logan and I would be the ones to seek revenge and restore our pack as the new Alpha and Luna. Over the last eight years, we have worked tirelessly together to make that a reality. Logan has struggled with the intensity and unexpectedness of the mate bond, I know. I don't blame either of you for your actions. But right now, you cannot be selfish. Lives depend on it. What I am sure Logan has failed to mention to you is that the dark witch, Cora, told Darius and me that she had two visions of Logan's future. One where he would overthrow Lucius and bring peace to our kind and one where he would be killed in a battle at the hands of the Vampire King himself.

And it seems that the deciding factor is you, Alina.

If Logan chooses to be with you, he will die. We will all die.

You may not believe me and I wouldn't blame you for that, but you can always ask Darius.

I love Logan and our pack too much to let that happen. So I am asking you, Alina, please give him up.

Madeline

I stared at the last line without blinking, slowly placing my hand on my throat. It felt like my airways were closing and I couldn't breathe. Time suddenly stopped as I allowed those words to sink in. *Please give him up.* So many emotions burned through me, making my whole body trembled in disbelief, fear, sadness, and anger.

"Darius!" I bellowed so loudly I shocked myself. "Darius!"

He came racing into the room in a bewildered fashion. "What? What is it?"

I handed the letter to him as I started pacing the room, waiting impatiently as he took his time to read it carefully.

"Is it true?" I demanded, glaring at him when I saw he had finished and his face paled slightly. "Will he die if he stays with me?"

"We don't know that for sure. Witches and their prophecies cannot always be trusted." He tried to calm me but I was too far gone.

"Why didn't you tell me? Why didn't Logan tell me? Where is he, anyway?" I couldn't seem to stand still as I do laps around the bed.

"I don't know," he muttered, looking confused himself. He reached for his phone and checked it, frowning. "He hasn't called."

"We need to find him. I need to speak to him!" I said suddenly, panicking that Darius didn't have a clue where Logan was either.

Darius put his phone to his ear and after a few seconds I heard a deep grumbling voice. "Fredrik, sorry to wake you, man. Do you know where Logan went last night?"

More mumbling from the other end, but I couldn't quite make out what was being said, but from Darius' dark expression, it isn't good.

"Okay. Thanks, mate." He hung up and picked up his coat.

"Where is he?" I said, running after him as he reached the door.

"Fuck. I can't leave you here alone." He glowered around the room in a rage.

"I'm coming with you, anyway," I said, grabbing my own coat. "Where are we going?"

"To Maddy's," he said in a cold tone. My heart plummeted.

Chapter 43

Logan's POV

"To our loved ones. Forever in our hearts," Maddy raised her glass and clinked it together with mine as her unique grey eyes shone with sadness.

I took a few gulps of my favourite whiskey and revel in the honey-warm essence and allowed it to glide deliciously down my throat. When I first arrived, I had never felt so uncomfortable in my own home. It was as if everything that belonged here was from another lifetime. I no longer felt a connection to any of it. But now, the awkwardness had dissipated and the effects of the strong liquor were lessening the tension, I was starting to relax. I was still stunned that Maddy had given up so quickly after trying to make me see the errors in my ways, but I'm not complaining. I wish more than anything that one day, we would be able to put all of this behind us and be friends. Her attitude right now was giving me hope that we were moving in the right direction.

"It wasn't that terrible, was it?" she asked whilst deliberately tracing the rim of her glass with her finger.

"What?" My eyebrows lowered in confusion.

"Our relationship. Being with me?" Her eyes flickered up to

meet my gaze as she looked like she was on the verge of tears.

"No, of course not, Maddy. I am so grateful to you and everything you have done for me over the years. You have helped me to be who I am today and I wouldn't be in this position if it wasn't for you," I said with complete sincerity. It was true that in any of my times of doubt or depression over the last eight years, she was the one who always picked me up and pushed us to keep going. To never give up.

She gave me a weak smile and looked back down at her glass. "You know, I used to joke with my dad when I was a little girl and say that I was going to marry Darius because my favourite colour was red!" She chuckled but a single tear slipped down her cheek. "If I had listened to that little girl, perhaps things would be very different," she added sadly.

I give her a warm smile and nodded. "I really am sorry for hurting you, Maddy. If I could have changed the way things happened, I would have."

She nodded in understanding and once again, I was blown away by how well she was taking all of this.

"We've all done things we're not proud of," she said in a quiet voice, still focusing on her drink.

I checked my phone and saw that it was already nearly 11:00 PM. I didn't want to be away from Alina for too much longer. I took a swig of the last of my drink and put the glass down on the coffee table.

"Do you mind if I go and grab some more clothes?" I asked awkwardly. I hated to remind her that I was no longer living here, but I barely packed anything when I left that day.

"Go ahead," she said coldly, not moving from the sofa.

I stood up too quickly and felt all the blood rush to my head. I put my hands out in the air in front of me to balance myself until the dizzy spell passed.

"Are you okay?" I heard Maddy ask but her voice sounded miles away.

"Uh, yeah. I- ah- just stood up too quickly."

I started to make my way down the corridor towards the bedroom but when another attack of dizziness hit, I gripped the wall to support myself. Once it passed, I walked to the wardrobe and started pulling tops and jumpers off their hangers aggressively. I wanted to get out of here. I had a sudden urge to see Alina as quickly as I could.

Unexpectedly, my vision blur and the room started spinning as I fell on to my knees, dropping all the clothes in the process.

"Logan! Are you okay?" I heard a voice came from somewhere behind me but the ringing in my ears was making it hard to focus. I felt soft hands around my waist trying to help me up. I stumbled as I was hauled off the floor to the edge of the bed, my vision blurring and clearing simultaneously.

"Logan?" A concerned, gentle voice called my name, but this time, it was closer. Right in front of me. I looked forward as my vision hazed again and I could just make out the faint outline of a woman's face. I saw blonde hair and kind eyes but the other features were distorted.

"Alina?" My voice came out cracked and husky.

"No, Logan, it's me. Here, lie down," the voice said and I instinctively obeyed.

My head started pulsating and it felt like sharp pins were being stabbed into my forehead. "Ah," I said clutching my head in my hands and rolling around on the bed in agony. My wolf, Elias, started howling in my mind as he could feel the intense suffering, which only made the feeling more unbearable.

"Shhh, Logan. You're going to be okay. I promise." That

voice echoed around the room as if it was bouncing off the walls.

I tried to open my eyes, but the pain was too much. "What's happening?" I shouted.

"I'm sorry, Logan. It was the only way. You won't listen," the voice whimpered and panic overwhelmed me.

Before I could open my mouth to speak again, darkness dragged at the corners of my mind and the pain eased. Everything went black and I felt numb.

Madeline's POV

He had passed out. I leaned over his muscular body and checked for his pulse. Thank fuck! He was still alive. Relief flooded through me. That bloody witch! She didn't tell me that would happen. I thought he would just fall asleep!

I stood up and put my hands on my hips. Okay, what now?

The tightness in my chest was still unmistakable, but there was no point in dwelling on what had been done. He was not going to wake up for at least twelve hours, the witch said, so I have got plenty of time to compose myself. If the potion worked, he wouldn't have any memory of Alina or anything connected to her. But that didn't mean she would be out of our lives. I am really praying that my letter would be enough to keep her away and perhaps she would leave before anyone even realised that he had lost his memory. But if she didn't, I needed a backup plan. I have no idea what would happen if he was to see her again and I couldn't risk it.

I walked into the living room to pour myself one more large glass of whiskey and looked around the room. I could make it look like we had had a cosy night, in case she came over searching for him. I turned the TV on but put the volume down low and rumpled the cushions on the sofa. Logan's glass was still sitting on the coffee table and his jacket was on the back of the armchair from earlier.

Once I had finished my drink, I strode back into the bedroom to find Logan in the same spot, lying sideways across the bed. If this was going to work, it needed to look authentic. I kneeled on the bed beside him and started to remove his black top. It wasn't easy as the material clung to his muscles in all the right places like a second skin. Then I unbuckled his belt which I noticed was the one I bought him for his birthday last year and pulled off his jeans. I stopped what I was doing to take a deep breath.

I hated doing this, knowing how much pain this would cause her if she ever saw it. Even though she didn't have a wolf she would still feel the betrayal tenfold. But it was the only way she would truly leave. I flung the jeans carelessly on the bedroom floor and discarded the top in the hallway. Next, I did the same with my own clothes.

Pulling back the covers, I used all my strength to hoist Logan up the bed and onto the pillows. He was such a wall of muscle; it definitely gave me a good workout. Lastly, I took off both underwear and threw them up in the air to see where they would land.

I cruised into bed next to Logan, he looked so peaceful, completely oblivious to the fact his mind was about to rewind the last two weeks. I cuddled up into his chest and inhaled his masculine scent, but it didn't quite have the same effect it used to. Probably because I could still smell the sweetness of Alina mixed in.

Lying here in his arms, our naked bodies next to each other, it felt so false. Like I was playing a role in a movie. I didn't know if I would be able to look him in the eye tomorrow, knowing the level of deception I had committed, but I had to try.

I closed my eyes and prayed for a dreamless sleep to welcome me.

Chapter 44

Alina's POV

Darius and I stayed in absolute silence the entire way to their apartment. I knew that wasn't a good sign, as I don't think I have ever seen Darius so tense and distant. He let us into that building with his spare key and my heart raced a million beats a second as we climbed the lobby stairs. This place was full of terrible memories of the night we first met and when Logan brought me here after revealing his identity. Not to mention, the bile rising in my throat, just at the thought of them in there together.

Why was he here? I didn't want to believe that he was. Fredrik must have been mistaken or maybe he came here first to get some more clothes and then he went somewhere else on werewolf business. Yes, I am sure that was it. He kept complaining yesterday that he had no clean clothes.

We reached the black apartment door and Darius hesitated, key in hand.

"Maybe I should go in alone?" he said in a low whisper. It didn't take a fool to know why. He didn't want me to have to see something upsetting, but I had to know what was going on. Even if it killed me.

I snatched the key from his hand, and he stood back reluctantly as I opened the door to silence. The first thing that hit me was his overpowering scent. He was here alright. I could hear my heartbeat pounding in my ears as I stepped cautiously into the hallway, Darius behind.

I walked into the living room whilst Darius checked the kitchen. The flickering glow of the TV illuminated the room and I noticed Logan's jacket on the back of the armchair. I walked over and ran my hand over the cool leather. On the coffee table, two glasses were empty but an open bottle of whiskey sat beside them.

Darius entered and scanned the room, his eyes falling on the glasses. We exchanged a knowing look as it was clear we had found him, but dread was starting to creep over my skin as we turned back into the hallway. We got as far as their bedroom door when I noticed a black piece of fabric on the floor. Picking it up, I recognised it as Logan's and my eyes snapped up to a shocked Darius.

"Alina, I don't think we should..." he started, but it was too late. I pushed the bedroom door wide open and my hand went to my mouth in disbelief. My world froze at the image before me.

There in the bed were Logan and Madeline's naked bodies entwined with a disarray of shed clothing items scattered around the room. She was nestled in his arms with her head on his chest and he had his arm around her waist, resting on her naked ass cheek. They were both fast asleep, oblivious to our intrusion.

Something inside me broke, snapping off any happiness I dared to wish I could have with this man. I felt like I've stopped breathing altogether as I continued to stare at the two of them, stuck in this moment in time. A hole in my heart formed at the betrayal. It was a pain that I had never felt before, even with Michael.

A firm grip on my arm pulled me back to the present and I turned to look into Darius' eyes, which are full of rage and pity, and that hole burned even deeper. I felt him wrap his strong arm around my waist and guided my frozen body out into the stairwell.

"FUCKING ASSHOLE!" Darius exploded once we were out of the flat. If I wasn't in such a shocked state, I would have tried to calm him down as he turned and punched a stone wall.

My legs kept moving until the chilly morning air hit my face and a shuddering breath escaped my lips. My knees buckled and I crashed down hard onto the uninviting gravel of the pavement, but the pain was nothing like what I was feeling inside. My tears came uncontrollably as the heartbreak consumed me. It felt like someone was ripping pieces of my heart from my chest over and over and over. I leaned forward, hugging my body, not able to bear the loss.

I felt completely stupid. How could I have gotten swept up in all of this? To believe that what Logan and I had was something special. How could I mean so little to someone who meant the absolute world to me?

I felt Darius' comforting arms lift me onto the bottom step outside the building as he wrapped them around me and cradled me to his chest whilst I continued to unleash my pain. He didn't speak but waited patiently for me to contain myself. Once the sobs have simmered down to a few shaky breaths, he said softly, "I am so sorry, Alina. You don't deserve that."

A shiver rippled down my spine as I realised how wrong he was. No, that was exactly what I deserved. I stole him from her first.

"I think we should go back in and confront him. He can't get away with that," he growled.

I shook my head violently. "No. I can't face him or her. This is for the best, leave them to it," I sniffled, rubbing my nose with the back of my hand.

"How can you say that? Just give up on your mate?" Darius argued, loosening his grip on my body.

"Because you know what the witch said. He isn't even meant to be with me, anyway. This is fate, ending it before it could even begin." My heart shattered with every word but I was confident in my resolve. "Can you take me to Chloe's, please?"

"Of course. But I'm coming back here later to give him a piece of my mind... and a black eye."

I smiled flatly, hoping he was joking. But knowing him, he was probably not.

When we let ourselves into Chloe's, I strolled straight over to the sofa that was once my bed before all of this mess. I sat silently as Darius busied himself opening every cupboard in frustration, looking for a glass. I don't have the energy to tell him Chloe keeps them all in the lower cupboards because she is so short. I laid down facing away from him and hugged a pillow for comfort.

After a few minutes, I heard him approaching. "Here's some water. Who keeps glasses in the bottom cupboard? Weirdo!" he said light-heartedly as he took a seat next to me and gave me a sympathetic smile, but I couldn't entertain his attempt at humour right now.

"Why did he do it? Was he really that scared?" I whispered, fresh tears welling up in my eyes.

"Because he is a first-class prick! He's one confused man. But I honestly thought he had made his mind up." He shook his head as he struggled to understand his own cousins' actions.

"No. I mean, was he really so scared I wouldn't sign the Oath that he had to pretend he wanted me? That he wanted a future with me but really it was all a lie?"

"I don't think that is what—"

"How else do you explain it, Darius? The minute I signed that

Oath, he ran back to her." My voice cracked as the pain pulled at my heart once again. Thank god I never told him I was a wolf. Who knows what he would have done?

Darius sighed and shook his head. "I don't know, Alina. He was always unsure about your future in the pack because you are human, but I didn't think he would do that. I'm not defending him, but maybe he is just an idiot with a lot going on right now and not knowing how to handle it."

And maybe I'm just the idiot who fell in love.

Logan's POV

The pounding headache gathered strength beneath my temples as I stood up from the bed. It made it hard to walk in a straight line as I made my way to the bathroom. Turning on the light, I blinked rapidly under the brightness as the pain flared hard and hot. I felt like I had the mother of all hangovers! I must have drunk way too much whiskey last night. I couldn't even remember the last time I had such a long lie in.

I splashed my face with freezing water from the sink in the hope that it would soothe my fragile head and turn on the shower. Basking under the scorching downpour, the fog in my brain slowly cleared and I sighed in relief. Good job wolves' hangovers are half as bad as humans'. I couldn't even really remember last night. I know Maddy and I had a few drinks to toast our loved ones we'd lost nine years ago today, but then everything became fuzzy.

"Oh, you're up! How are you feeling?" Maddy eyed me with concern from the bathroom door. She looked cute in her knee-length fluffy dressing gown and messy icy locks sticking up in all different directions.

"Yeah, not too bad. Pounding headache though! How much did I have to drink last night?" I said as I pushed my soaking hair off my face.

A flash of relief spread across her face and she smiled broadly. "Quite a bit. I've made us brunch, but take your time. I'll be in the kitchen." She practically skipped out of the room.

"What's the occasion?" I shouted, feigning shock at her unusual gesture.

"Just felt like it," she yelled back as I raised my eyebrows and wrapped a towel around my waist.

Suddenly, I heard Darius' aggressive voice from the hallway. "Where is he?" he bellowed at the top of his lungs.

Oh fucking hell, what had he got a bee in his bonnet about now? I strolled out of the bathroom just as he barged into my bedroom, his face thunderous. He was ready for a fight.

"Darius, what···" I started but I was quickly silenced by his fist connecting with my cheek. My face turned from the brutal force and I tasted the coppery flavour of my own blood from a cut on my lip.

"What the FUCK, Darius?"

"I should be saying that to you," he bellowed, spit flying from his mouth in his blind rage.

"Darius, what are you doing?" A panicked Maddy came running to my side.

"I can't believe you would do that to her! You really are a piece of shit!" he snarled, ignoring Maddy completely.

"Do what? To who?" I shouted back, getting more and more frustrated at his vagueness.

"Alina, who else?" He raised his arms out like it was obvious. I continued to stare at him, completely baffled. "She saw you this morning··· in bed together." Maddy's eyes widened but I was still none the wiser as to what he was talking about.

"Alina who?" I replied in an irritated voice. It was obviously the wrong thing to say as his fist connected with my cheekbone once again, but this time I saw red. I lunged at him, tackling him to the floor and punched him square in the jaw.

"STOP! Logan, stop!" Maddy screamed behind us, grabbing my shoulders and trying to hoist me off Darius, but she was not strong enough.

I eased off my punches but held him by the collar of his top. "I don't know what has gotten into you, Darius, but you need to get the fuck out of my house. Now!" I roared at my Alpha command.

He pushed me off him and stood wiping the blood from his mouth. "Gladly," he snarled and bolted out the door.

"Are you okay? Let me get a towel." Maddy fussed as she dashed into the bathroom to get a wet towel to clean off my face.

"Yeah, I'm fine. Just pissed. Who the fuck does he think he is?" I growled.

She didn't answer but started to attend to my cuts and bruises tenderly, which we both knew was pointless. I would be healed in an hour or two.

My mind was racing trying to connect the dots as to what the hell just happened, but it just felt completely random. I looked up to search Maddy's eyes for any sign of understanding and she stopped her nursing when our eyes locked. I was surprised when I saw so much emotion swirling within her stunning grey irises and I could swear I saw a flash of guilt. She looked so sad and, at that moment, I felt the need to comfort her.

I leaned forward to gently kissed her lips, but I was shocked to find that I felt no desire or passion as our lips caressed. She pulled back quickly and looked away as she gathered up the towels and walked into the bathroom. That was strange.

I couldn't seem to focus on it for long as a nagging question started playing on my mind.

Who the hell was Alina?

Chapter 45

Lucius' POV

"Arius, sit down!" I commanded as he kept up his steadfast glare at the door of my office. He had been giving me the silent treatment since I had revealed why I had impulsively drugged him the other day. Which he was also not thrilled about.

He continued to hold my eye contact, toying with the idea of defying me. It wasn't long until he sauntered over to the red, velvet chair opposite my desk, probably due to the fifty lashes I gave him yesterday for raising his voice at me. He was always much more submissive after a brutal reminder of his place.

He flopped down in the chair like a moody teenager, but the relentless glaring persisted. He didn't take the news that I drugged him to use him as bait for my own gain all that well.

"Have you calmed down yet?" I challenged him but used an authoritative tone as a warning not to act up again.

His eyes narrowed and he gritted through his teeth as if it caused him pain. "Yes, father."

"Good. So, as I explained yesterday, before your temper tantrum, Cora is your aunt. But I have led her to believe you are her son, so she will help us to win this war."

"You mean you deceived and blackmailed her," he interrupted, and my eyes turned red in warning.

"Yes, because she is the most powerful dark witch remaining and we need her on our side."

"Why? You said she wouldn't get involved in the war," he asked in a bored tone, but I could tell he was genuinely curious.

"She has the gift of precognition, so she will be able to find out what it is that I need in order to win this war. And an added bonus is that she will be able to train you to use the book of dark magic."

His eyes scintillated with excitement. Ever since he came into his magical powers at the early age of six, it had been difficult to challenge him. He taught himself most of the basics of witchcraft from my library. But when he turned sixteen, I allowed him to be tutored by some common dark witches, but it never ended well. He was always left unsatisfied or jaded by their teachings and would often play pranks or use his own spells against them just for amusement. After he set one witch's hair alight and nearly the entire library, I restricted his use of magic and stopped his tuition. So, to hear he may be taught by the most talented dark witch there has ever been definitely sparked his interest. I had him right where I needed him.

"I still don't understand why I must pretend to be her son," he sulked whilst looking at his fingernails as if he was barely paying attention.

I sighed, exasperated. "Because, Arius, she despises me and the only way she will even contemplate helping me is if she thinks the one thing that she loved and lost in this world is still alive. So, all I need from you is to play along and in return, you get to learn from the very best."

He grinned mischievously. "I think I can manage that."

"Good. But there will come a time when she wants to leave. She will not stand with me in the battle. I know that for a fact. When she does, she will ask you to leave with her." I gave him all the information I needed to make him think I was putting my trust in him. He nodded carefully. "I will seem like I am okay with you leaving, but you must refuse her." I could not have my only heir leave with that woman and have her turn him against me.

"Of course. Why would I even consider going with her?" he asked, as if I was treating him like a fool.

"Excellent. This is your first opportunity to prove yourself as the next leader of our people," I added for good measure.

His face turned serious and he sat up a little straighter in his chair. "Yes, father." He bowed his head with respect.

"You are dismissed. I will call upon you again once Cora has returned."

He stood and exited the room, but I noticed his right arm extended forward slightly and subtly fist bumped the warrior on guard at the door. I rolled my eyes at his friendliness with the men. I have warned him before that if he wanted to be taken seriously as a king and rule successfully, he must be feared above all else. It seemed he hadn't listened. Maybe Cora would have more luck with him.

I almost felt bad for lying to him about his own mother, but I could not risk losing my protégé to that woman. I hadn't put in all this work in raising the boy just to hand him over to her when I needed his powers the most. I was known for being the most successful and ruthless leader of our chaste for centuries and I needed to continue that legacy through my own bloodline. I have never really seen Arius as a son, which had helped me to mould him into the heir I needed with an iron fist. My true son died with his mother at the hands of that beast thirty years ago. And I wouldn't stop until I have my revenge.

I lowered myself further into my brown leather chair and rested my head in one hand. Seeing Cora recently had meant nightly torments of memories of Celeste and our unborn child. Watching her lifeless body fall from the balcony after the dagger had been plunged through her heart still had me screaming out in the middle of the night. Even in death, my love was a fighter. Managing to perform a syphoning spell to link the Alpha' s life with her own, knowing he was about to kill them both.

My office door flew open and a gust of wind swept through the room, making me jerk from my distressing memories. My heart skipped a beat as it always did at seeing the likeliness of her features to my Celeste' s.

"Cora, always one for making an entrance." I gave her a warm smile, but I was only met with an icy glare. Seems I can do nothing right. "I wasn' t expecting you back so soon."

When she had agreed to help me and told me the council had already summoned her to perform a Blood Oath on an Alina Clarke, I could not believe my luck. She could go there without any suspicion and provide me with much needed intel.

"How did it go? Good I hope." I leaned my elbows on my chair arms and clasped my hands together as she took a seat.

"You could say that," she replied flatly.

My interest peaked and all I wanted to do was hurry her to tell me what I needed to hear, but I forced myself to be patient. "Go on."

"Firstly, I could not perform the Blood Oath because Alina, Logan' s mate, is not human," she said calmly as if she was reading the weather forecast. My eyes must have been bulging out of my head at this news, which encouraged her to continue. "She is a werewolf. A spell has been cast on her to mask her wolf. She did not know either."

That did explain why Logan was mated to her, but raised many more questions. "Well, this is a very interesting development. Why a spell? Who was hiding her?" I asked curiously.

"I do not know," she stated and my eyes narrowed to decide whether I believed her. "You asked me to look into her future, not her past," she answered, sensing my doubts.

"And... what did you find?"

She shuffled slightly in her seat and brushed a strand of her dark hair from her eyes. She hated this, I could tell, which only made me smirk more.

"If Alina helps Logan in this war, he will be victorious," she said, trying to hide her disdain in giving me such vital information.

I sat up straight. So, Alina was the key. She must be handled swiftly and then everything else will fall into place. The war will be mine.

As if reading my mind, Cora spoke quickly, "You do not need to worry about Alina. I have dealt with it already. She won't be a problem."

My arched eyebrows raised higher, willing her to explain herself.

"Alina will not tell anyone that she is a wolf. Logan has no idea and is likely to reject her as a human anyway. But if he doesn't, I have given his other love interest, Madeline, a potion which will make him forget Alina altogether. Madeline is under the impression that Logan will die in battle if he chooses Alina, so I have no doubt in my mind that she will go ahead with it."

I clapped my hands together deliberately and smiled, showing my pearly white canines. "I am impressed, Cora. You have done well."

She nodded but hatred consumed her frosty blue eyes. "Like I said, the girl is taken care of." Her look was warning me not to harm the girl. She forgot that my problem was not just with Logan but with all werewolves.

"It would seem so!" I replied. "So now, let's discuss the plan for our son." Her rage blazed at my use of 'our' but I ignored her. "He was shocked, as you can imagine, to hear that his mother was alive."

"And whose fault is that?!" she snapped.

"Yes, I know. He was not pleased with me either. However, this is his home and I am his father whether you like it or not." I watched her hands fist into balls and her jaw tense. "He wants to get to know you under his own conditions before he decides if he is willing to leave with you."

"That was not the deal!" She shouted and her power radiated from her body like a tidal wave.

"Now, now, Cora. I have not broken my end of the deal. I said you could have him, didn't I? But he is a grown man with his own mind and rightly so, he is sceptical right now. All I am suggesting is for you to spend a bit of time together here, so he feels more comfortable around you," I said without any detection of insincerity, a skill I have perfected over the years.

She eyed me suspiciously for the longest time before demanding coldly, "I want to see him. Now."

"As you wish." I nodded to my guard, and clearly one of Arius' buddies, to fetch him.

After a few minutes, Arius casually strolled into the room, his distinctive eyes darting between myself and Cora. She slowly rose from her chair as if any sudden movements might startle him.

"Hello, Arius," she said in the softest tone that I have ever heard. I wasn't even aware she was capable of showing so much love.

His eyes connected with hers and he seemed speechless for a moment, or perhaps, he was just really good at acting.

"You have no idea how many times I have dreamt of this moment. Of seeing you again." Her voice caught as she swallowed her emotions and tried to keep some composure. I wish I had some popcorn.

"So, you are my mother?" he asked, dully examining her features and looking her up and down.

"Yes. I hope I don't disappoint." She nervously chuckled.

He looked at me and his face was holding that unreadable expression that I find so infuriating. He returned his gaze to Cora and shook his head timidly.

She smiled.

"Forgive me but I only found out this news yesterday and it has been a lot to process," he said, which I guess did hold some truth.

"I know. I am sorry you had to find out this way and I am truly sorry that I wasn't around for you growing up. I would have given my life to have been there, but it was out of my control." She glared over her shoulder at me and I took a swig from my brandy, feigning innocence. "But I hope we can make up for lost time and get to know each other now," she added.

His eyes flickered to mine before he smiled back at her and replied, "I would like that. Perhaps you could stay here awhile?"

Good boy, I internally praised him. I could tell from her body language that she was hesitant, but she finally agreed.

"Wonderful! One big happy family." I clapped, pulling their attention back to my presence. "Cora, my guards will set you up in one of the guest rooms."

She nodded and started to the door before swiftly turning on her heels to face her son. "Would you mind showing me the way?" she asked.

"Of course not," he replied politely and led her out of the door.

I fell back in my chair, feeling elated! I'm not sure things could go any better. Actually, there is one thing that would give me great pleasure.

"Guards!" I shouted and one hefty man walked into my room. I didn't bother to learn their names. They were mere bodies to me.

"Summon Baylor, immediately!"

Chapter 46

Alina's POV

"Happy birthday to you! Happy birthday to you!" I forced out my best sing-song voice as I walked carefully into Chloe's bedroom holding possibly the worst homemade chocolate cake in existence. I no longer seemed to sleep, so when I suddenly remembered my best friend's birthday was the next day—which I had completely forgotten in my depressive state—I pulled myself together and spent the early hours of the morning ransacking the kitchen cupboards to bake what I hoped vaguely resembled a birthday cake.

Chloe sat up sleepily in her small bed and pulled up her eye mask, squinting at the morning light.

"Awww, babe! You're so cute!" she gushed as I set the cake down on her bedside table.

"Make a wish," I said, wrapping my arms around my body. She tapped her chin with her index finger and then blew out the candles in one single breath. I clapped my hands and sat crossed-legged on her duvet.

"Lina, you really didn't have to do that. I know how much you're hurting right now. The last thing you should do is make me a birthday cake."

"Wrong! I think it's a much better use of my time than wallowing in self-pity like I have been in the last two days," I said and gave her a small smile that did not reach my eyes. God, it hurt to even do that. "Is that why you've been so quiet about your birthday? Normally, you're shouting it from the roof tops at least a week before."

She leaned forward and gripped my hands in hers. "It just didn't feel right. I've never seen you like this, Alina. Not even after Michael. With him, it was like a typical dramatic marathon of ice cream, soppy rom-coms and cursing meltdowns, but this⋯ This is so much worse."

I lowered my eyes to look at our hands, fighting back fresh tears that were brimming at the edges. They just seem to keep coming!

"You're closed off. It's like you've mentally and emotionally checked out. You don't sleep or eat or smile or even talk about it. I'm worried about you." She squeezed my hands trying to get my attention, but if I look up and meet her sympathetic gaze, I know I will crumble.

"I'm fine," I lied and tried to portray the false bravery I so badly wished I had right now. She was right. I was closed off. I was forcing all my emotions and pain down into my gut because I was terrified of what would happen to me if I unleashed them. I had never felt physical or emotional pain like this in my life, not even after I lost my mum. At least in her death, I was given the peace of knowing she was no longer suffering. But with this⋯ there was no peace. Just the reality that I was never going to be enough for him.

"You're not fine, Alina. And it's okay. You don't have to pretend with me," she said kindly.

I shook my head and blinked back the tears. "No, Chloe, I

can't. If I allow myself to let go, if I fall apart, I will never get back up." My voice quivered with raw emotion. "I was really falling for him, Chloe, and he was just using me." A few traitorous tears fell from my eyes onto the duvet, and I quickly brushed my cheeks with trembling hands.

"Oh, my sweet, beautiful girl! You are so strong and you have been through so much. He doesn't deserve you. I just want you to know that when you do fall, I will always be there to help you back up… with prosecco in hand."

A genuine chuckle escaped my chest at the warmth and love I felt for my best friend at that moment. She really was one of a kind. I smiled through my tears, nodding my head. "Thank you, Chlo. Urgh, I can't believe I am crying on your birthday! I promised myself no tears today and it's not even nine AM."

"Hey, it's my birthday and you'll cry if you want to!" she joked and scooped a dollop of icing on her finger from the side of the cake. Before I could stop her, she licked it off.

"I wouldn't…" Too late. Her face said it all as she crinkled her nose and forcibly swallowed.

"Mmmm," she lied and I found myself giggling again.

"It was meant more for show than to eat," I explained. "I'll get you a decent one later from that bakery on Oxford Street you like."

She raised her eyebrows at me. "Does that mean you are planning on leaving the flat today?" she asked in surprise.

"Can't stay hidden away forever as much as I'd like to." I stood up from the bed. It honestly felt like I must start my life all over again and I don't even know where to begin.

"I still can't believe he hasn't called or texted. What a prick!" Chloe said in disgust.

It had been two days since my world shattered around me and, in all honesty, the total disregard for my existence hurt more than him sleeping with her. The fact that he didn't even think I was worthy of an explanation or an apology showed how little I meant to him. And what was the most pathetic thing of all? Even though I knew all this in my battered, broken heart, I still loved him with everything I am.

"Every time I think about him or want to hear his voice, I have to remind myself that if he wanted to talk to me, he would," I said sadly. "Enough. Let's not waste another minute of your birthday talking about him," I said with fake strength. "How are we celebrating?"

She smiled sheepishly and gave me a look that I know meant she's about to say something I won't like. "Well, Ryan has apparently planned a surprise for me today before all of this happened. But don't worry, I am so going to cancel him and we will—"

"What?! No way. Don't cancel because of me! That sounds so nice, you should be pampered by your man. Go, have fun!" I said, hiding my disappointment and misery.

"Are you sure? Because I will cancel him and we can do something together." She looked up at me with her big, dooey eyes.

"No Chloe, don't you dare!" I said firmly. "Do you mind if I jump in the shower?" I said, changing the subject and grabbing a towel off the back of the bathroom door.

I stood in front of the mirror and stared at the reflection of the broken girl before me. I don't even recognise myself as I pulled on my tiresome skin and ran my hand over the dark circles around my eyes. My hair was matted as I haven't attempted to brush it in the last few days. I took a deep, trembling breath to steady myself as another overwhelming flashback of Logan playing with my hair as I laid on his chest in bed popped into my mind.

'IT ISNT SUPPOSED TO BE LIKE THIS.'

A majestic voice murmured in my mind as if someone was standing right next to me, whispering in my ear. My head snapped up and I let out a loud gasp at the sight of my irises. They were still green but had a visible gold rim around them.

'ITS OKAY. TRY NOT TO PANIC.' The voice spoke again, only this time it was much clearer. I looked around the small room to double check I was alone. I stood frozen when I was faced only with my own reflection.

"Who are you?" my trembling voice said out loud.

'MY NAME IS XENA. I AM YOUR WOLF.'

"Ohmygod! My wolf?" I shouted, throwing my hand recklessly and knocking all of Chloe's cosmetics into the bathroom sink with a loud clatter.

"Lina? Are you alright in there?" Chloe called from behind the door.

Panic rose in me at being caught like this and I quickly picked up all her toiletries out of the sink whilst shouting, "Yeah! Uh, fine… just being clumsy!"

I heard her footsteps fade away and I sighed in relief.

'YOU KNOW YOU CAN TALK TO ME IN OUR MIND. THEN SHE WON'T HEAR.'

My golden green eyes widened, still not able to get accustomed to hearing another voice in my head.

"How?" I whispered aloud.

'JUST THINK ABOUT WHAT YOU WANT TO SAY AND DIRECT IT TO ME.'

My face creased in confusion as she made it sound so easy. But I closed my eyes and tried it anyway.

'Pancakes.'

'PANCAKES? AFTER EIGHT YEARS, THAT IS THE FIRST

THING YOU SAY TO ME?'

'Eight years? What do you mean? Oh, wow, I am actually having a conversation inside my own head with a wolf right now. Am I right? I'm not losing my mind. You are real?'

'YES, I AM REAL. I HAVE BEEN SILENCED AT THE BACK OF YOUR SUBCONSCIOUS FOR EIGHT YEARS. SINCE YOUR SIXTEENTH BIRTHDAY.'

My mouth gaped open in shock. I suddenly felt my body flow with the sadness and loneliness she had felt for years. Tears flowed down my cheeks as I feel so much empathy for what she must have been through all that time.

'WHY ARE YOU SAD?' she asked curiously.

'I'm just so sorry for what you must have been through. Trapped and unable to communicate for so long.'

'IT HAS NOT BEEN EASY FOR EITHER OF US. BUT WHEN WE FOUND OUR MATE, I FELT THE SPELL WEAKENING. I HAVE BEEN FIGHTING AGAINST IT EVERYDAY SINCE.'

My heart tugged at her mention of Logan.

'I'm sorry you never got to meet Elias.'

'I DID. THROUGH YOU. I SAW EVERYTHING THROUGH YOUR EYES. WE CANNOT GIVE UP ON THEM.'

'Xena, I am so very happy you are able to communicate with me, but you have to understand that Logan does not want me. There is nothing left to fight for.'

'I DON'T BELIEVE THEY WOULD DO THIS TO US. SOMETHING IS WRONG.'

I shook my head at her denial. She may have seen what was happening, but she hasn't been there or felt what I have had to the last week or so. She is blinded by their bond.

'Xena, you don't understand. I can't do this right now. It hurts too much.'

She went silent for a while and I watched as my eyes turned back to their normal shade of green. I had so many more questions for her but I could feel her grief in waves and she needed time to adjust just as much as I did.

Once I stepped out of the shower, I had a newfound energy and restlessness. It was like my limbs were itching to move. I craved the need to exercise to take away the internal pain I was feeling. I needed to run. To feel the burn, the exhaustion··· anything other than the heartbreak.

'Is this you?' I asked Xena in my head but she didn't reply.

I threw on my gym clothes and thought of the one person I wanted to work out with. Hannah. I texted her a quick message to check if she was working. She replied instantly:

Yes. Heading in now. You want a session? X

Yes please. But is Logan working today? X I needed to make sure there was no chance of bumping into him.

No. He is packing for his trip.

My heart stopped. How could I forget? He is going back to America tomorrow. Rage erupted inside me as I recalled our conversation in the bath··· *"I do not want to pressure you into making a decision about becoming my Luna, which is why we are still going through with the Blood Oath tomorrow. But you will come with me to America until you decide because I need to keep you safe. I can't leave you here alone."*

Liar! Where was his concern about my safety now?

I stomped out into the living room and stopped when I saw Darius lounging on the sofa. He had barely left my side since that day and only went home to shower and change. Chloe thinks he's weird and in love with me, but I know it's because he feels some kind of guilt about the way things happened and he has it in his head that I still need protection.

His eyes regarded me in surprise as he looked up from his phone. "You're dressed? This is progress."

I rolled my eyes. "I'm going to the gym. I need to release some pent-up aggression," I explained as I slipped my trainers on. I noticed Chloe and Darius shared an impressed look before he stood to join me at the door.

"Okay. I'll come with you."

"You don't have to," I said, grabbing my keys and phone from the table.

"I also have some aggression that needs releasing." He smirked. I knew he'd been to see Logan from the faded bruising and foul mood he'd come back in that day. He didn't tell me what had happened, and I didn't ask. I'm not sure I could handle hearing it.

When we arrived at the gym, I spotted Hannah waiting for me by the same studio door we went through last time. My heart ached at the memory of being with Logan in there, but I pushed it aside. Darius said he'd be over with the punching bags and to come and find him when I'm ready to leave.

As I was walking over to Hannah, Marcus came hurtling towards me.

"Uh, Alina, right? How are you?" he asked kindly, his warm face crinkling at the edge of his eyes and mouth.

"Yes, I am okay thanks. You?"

"Yes, great. Er, Logan isn't here today. Did you need to see him?" he asked.

"Oh, no! I am here to train with Hannah," I said quickly, pointing in her direction as she waved me over.

"Ah, okay! Well, have a good one!" he replied as he shuffled backwards about to grab another customer's attention.

"Hey, ready?" Hannah smiled as I approached.

"Yep, let's do this!" I replied and followed her into the room.

After two hours, I was covered in sweat and have pushed my body to the limits I never knew I was capable of. My limbs ached and my muscles burned, yet I still wanted more. I surprised myself and Hannah by how much stronger and more agile I seemed since our last session and I was starting to notice that she was becoming lethargic whilst I just wanted more. We were now onto hardcore martial arts fighting, where the only way out of a battle was to tap out in surrender. I had just managed to force Hannah to do just that for the second time in a row. She leaned over, resting her body on her knees, struggling to catch her breath.

"Bloody hell, Alina. I don't know where you've been hiding but you are one hell of a badass!" she panted.

I took a swig of the iced water and wiped the sweat off my forehead. "Shall we go again?" I asked.

"I'm sorry, but I'm going to have to take a breather. I also need to check in on some of my other clients, if you don't mind."

"No, it's fine. Thank you, Hannah. You're a great teacher."

"I don't think I can take all the credit, Alina. You're a lot stronger and faster than I remembered," she confessed whilst walking towards the door. I followed her out as she turned to say goodbye.

"I'm not going to go yet. I'll just jump on a treadmill or something. I could do with a good run." Even the words sounded alien to me as they leave my mouth, but it was what my body was craving.

Hannah shook her head and chuckled. "You are crazy, but go for it!"

I strolled towards the gym section but as I passed the huge caged ring in the middle of the room, I spotted a familiar man from last time I was here. Mr. Bodybuilder. I couldn't remember his real name but he was the one who fought Logan in the ring.

Suddenly, adrenaline spiked through my veins, and I wanted nothing more but to challenge him to a match.

'DO IT.' Xena's voice growled in my mind and I knew it was her energy spurring me on. She wanted a fight just as much as I wanted to feel anything but the internal pain of heartbreak. I walked up to the gigantic man and reached up to tap him on the shoulder. He turned and looked me up and down suggestively. Perv.

"Hi, my name is Alina and I would like to challenge you to a fight. In there," I said, pointing to the ring.

He burst out laughing before realising it was not a joke. "Go away, little girl. You're better off in the defence classes. They start in one hour." He smirked and turned his back to me.

"Oh, I get it. You're too afraid to fight a 'little girl' in case you are beaten to an inch of your life or is it that your mother raised you not to hit women? I'm pretty sure we are equal here and as I am the one challenging you, I can't see anyone objecting to it."

His eyes shone with amusement as he considered my words. "Let's make this interesting." He finally spoke up and his voice was hard and masculine like his body. "If I win, you have to agree to go on a date with me."

I rolled my eyes. "Fine." I held my hand out to shake his. I definitely wouldn't be losing this fight now.

We took our places in the ring and I bandaged my wrists just like I saw Logan do and glared at my opponent as he did the same. He refused the head guard and gum shield, unlike when he fought Logan. Clearly, he thought he didn't need it this time.

"Alina! What the fuck do you think you're doing? Get out of there!" Darius' voice bellowed from the side of the cage.

"Don't worry, Darius. I've got this." I winked at him and saw the utter disbelief on his face.

"Are you insane? Have you seen his size?"

I cracked my neck and rolled my shoulders. "Yep."

I walked to the middle of the ring to bump fists with the man, signalling the start of the match. We circled each other, sticking to the edge of the ring, neither one of us keen to make the first move.

'IM HERE WITH YOU, ALINA. WE CAN DO THIS.' Xena's determined voice pushed me on and gave me the courage I need to swing first.

I missed and he smirked. I attacked him again. My fist raised but he dodged easily, and I felt a sharp burn in my stomach as his fist met my rib cage. I fell to my hands and knees in pain but quickly pushed myself back up. He was chuckling when I lifted my right leg up to kick him in the stomach, but my eyes widened as he grabbed my ankle and twisted so my whole body rotated in the air and I landed on the mats with a hard slam onto my back. I struggled to breathe as the wind was knocked out of me and he strolled over and leaned down by my face.

"Give up yet, girlie? I'd rather not take you out for dinner black and blue. But if you insist," he snarled.

"Alina, tap out now!" Darius' worried voice yelled from the side of the ring.

"Aw, or you could get your boyfriend over there to come and protect you." The man's hot breath on my face had my nose wrinkled in disgust.

Anger bubbled in me as I remembered all the times I had felt helpless or out of control. All the time, I had been treated like a useless human who couldn't protect herself. But who am I kidding? I can't take this brute on?

'WE CAN! SHARE CONTROL WITH ME. LETS TEACH THEM ALL A LESSON.'

'How?'

'JUST LET ME IN. FEEL THE ENERGY SPREADING OVER YOUR BODY? DON'T FIGHT IT.'

I closed my eyes, taking deep breaths and allowing the electricity of power to flow through my veins. When my eyes darted open, everything was brighter, more focused. I locked in on my opponent and gave him a smirk as he returned it with a confused frown. Without warning, I rolled my body up onto my shoulder blades and kicked him with both feet with as much strength as possible. The impact with his chest threw him unexpectedly against the cage wires. Jumping to my feet, I didn't allow him to recover as I lunged forward pounding my fists into his stomach and then threw the biggest right hook that smacked his cheekbone. I could swear I heard a crack as his face whipped to the side and blood squirted from his mouth. I stood back panting but keeping my defensive stance waiting for him to retaliate. He wiped his mouth and spat more blood onto the mats. His eyes glistened with excitement as he realised I'm not messing around. He dived at me, fist raised, but this time I'm ready for him. I elegantly dodged every advance until I've danced around him and I leapt onto his back, pulling my arm tightly around his throat and cutting off his air supply. I pulled back one of his arms awkwardly behind him, nearly breaking his arm in the process. He dropped to his knees as he tried to get free from my hold, but I squeezed even tighter until his body fell flat to the ground and I am on top of him with my deathly grip turning his face a shade of beetroot. Veins were popping from his neck and he finally tapped out before he passed out. I abruptly climbed off him, panting heavily.

The sudden chorus of chanting and clapping filled the room and I was pulled back into the present as I glanced around at the shocked and impressed spectators.

That felt fucking unbelievable!

Mr. Bodybuilder stood up clumsily and approached me with a deadpan expression. After a few seconds, he held his hand out in respect. I shook it with a broad smile.

"Fair play, girly. The only person who can fight me like that is Logan."

I swallowed my hurt just at the mention of his name and then climbed out of the cage.

"What the hell was that, Alina?" Darius' voice trailed after me as I made my way through the crowd who gave me pats on the back and praise. I shrugged, not wanting to talk about it. "Where the hell did you learn to fight like that? Did Logan teach you?" He continued to interrogate me and I snapped.

"Don't mention his name to me," I growled, and he recoiled at my aggressive tone. I walked out of the gym with a new sense of self-belief, but above all else, power.

Chapter 47

Logan's POV

"These are the last boxes we have," Madeline said, dropping the flat pack cardboard onto the living room floor. The apartment was in disarray. Items, clothes, bubble wrap and boxes everywhere. I hated it. The mess and chaos of it was giving me anxiety and I needed fresh air. The last two days had been strange, to say the least. There seemed to be this tension between Maddy and myself but I don't know why. Every time I tried to get close to her, she acted distant but tells me everything was fine. And then there was the weird dreams.

When I close my eyes at night, I'm met with those exotic green irises that haunt me. I feel such a connection to them but I have no idea who they belong to. Last night, I woke drenched in sweat as I dreamt I was swimming in a lake with the pearlescent moon hanging low behind me and a complete feeling of bliss. I felt a calming presence there with me but every time I turned to find them, there was nothing there. An angelic voice kept calling to me… "Logan! Logan!"

My panic and frustration rose when I was unable to find who it belonged to. I would try so hard not to wake up knowing I hadn't found what I was looking for, but I always did.

"I think I'm going to head into work," I said, standing as I throw the last bubble-wrapped ornament into a box. "To say some last goodbyes and tie up any loose ends with Marcus."

Maddy just nodded, barely noticing me, far away in her own thoughts. It seemed like everyone was feeling the impact of the upcoming battle. We had waited for many years for this and now that it was finally upon us it only seemed natural to be nervous. There was a lot at stake.

Everything was coming together nicely for the battle. I'd sent Fredrik and his mate, Sloane, as well as her brother and a few others back to our old territory to get a head start on the maintenance before the other wolves arrived. Building work on the new pack house started months ago but I had no idea what state the territory would be in. I hadn't even attempted to return after the attack years ago. I told myself it was for our own protection, but really it was just too painful.

Our flight leaves tomorrow morning and everything was sorted, yet I couldn't help the feeling that I am missing something. My fight with Darius had put me on edge and we still had not spoken. I hope he would come to his senses soon and joins us, but I would not force him. Everyone had a choice. I've made that very clear.

Strolling through the heavy entrance doors of the gym, I couldn't help but feel a wave of sadness. I was really going to miss this place and the people I had come to care for over the years. I walked straight out to the back offices and found Marcus behind his desk going through a mountain of paperwork.

"Hey, man," I said, smiling fondly at him as I approached my own empty desk.

"Logan. What are you doing here? I said I'd email you the paperwork to save you from coming back in."

I tried to tell Marcus I had no interest in him buying me out of the business and that he could carry on with it without giving me any money, but he wouldn't take no for an answer. Stubborn old man. I couldn't let him buy me out using all the profit he had worked so hard to make over the years, so instead, I agreed to be a silent investor and give him back ninety percent of the business. He reluctantly agreed after lots of persuasion.

"Just needed a break. Think I would rather stab my eyeballs out then have to pack another box."

Marcus chuckled and pulled out his hidden whiskey from his drawer that he used to keep for those bad days but now it was only used for celebrations. "Fancy one?"

"You know me too well," I said with a grin.

We cheered to the business and our friendship.

"I know I've said it many times before, but I am truly grateful to you, Logan. What you did for me probably saved my life in more ways than one." Marcus' watery eyes shone as he took another gulp of his drink.

"You don't need to thank me, Marcus. I saw a good man in a bad situation and I was only too happy to help."

He smiled and put down his glass. "I'll miss you, mate. You had better come back and visit. This place won't be the same without you."

I nodded, struggling to hold my own emotions back.

"You know, Daniel has already approached me about taking over your classes. You trained him so well and I think he'd be a good fit, although his ego took a battering this morning against Alina."

My eyes snapped up to his smirking face at the mention of that name again. "Alina?"

"Yes, she was here this morning. Challenged the ogre to a one-on-one and beat the crap out of him. I like her even more now." He chuckled and talked about her as if we had known her forever. What was going on?

"Is she still here?" I suddenly asked, hoping to put a face to this name.

"No, she left with your cousin a few hours ago. You alright?" he quizzed, looking at my shocked expression.

I didn't bother answering and marched out to the gym to find Daniel. I spotted him at the back of the room doing some weights. I could swear the guy would live here if we allowed it.

"Daniel." I approached him from behind and he smiled at me in his mirrored reflection. I could see a nasty bruise forming on the side of his face and a cut on his lip.

"Logan, my man. I was hoping to catch you before you leave." He put the weights down and walked towards me, massive arms stretched out wide to pull me in for a mighty bear hug.

And that was when I smelled it. The most mouth-watering scent all over him. It was divine. But when I realised it was mixed with his own musky, sweaty stench, for some reason, it made my skin crawl and I wanted to rip him apart.

I composed my dark thoughts and ask him sternly, "Who can I smell on you? You smell like a girl?"

He stepped back confused and took a whiff of his underarm. "What? I can't smell anything." His creased face opens into a broad smile. "Oh, it must be that little Spitfire I battled earlier. Alina, I think her name was. Feisty thing. Hot as fuck too. She fought nearly as well as you do."

Elias growled in my head. It was the first time he had even made himself known in days. I was starting to get worried at his silence, so hearing him flooded me with relief, although I had no idea why he was upset.

"Looks like it from the state of your face," I replied mockingly.

"I wear my battle wounds with pride. Never thought I'd see the day I was beaten by a girl." He sneered.

We said goodbye and I wished him luck with his new position, which caused him to grin from ear to ear.

Intrigue got the best of me as I headed towards the security room. I locked the door so as not to be disturbed and started rewinding today's CCTV footage. I paused when I got to an image of a petite girl on top of Daniel's back in the cage. I squinted my eyes, concentrating on trying to recognise her, but all I could see was the back of her body and a high ponytail of sandy coloured hair.

I rewound it back another ten minutes or so and pressed play. I was mesmerised as I saw the girl walking up behind Daniel and tapping him on the shoulder. He turned and she was clearly saying something to him as he burst out laughing, but turned his back on her again. She must have said something else as he swivelled around and gave her his full attention. After a while, they shook hands before she turned, giving me a full view of her face.

I paused the video and stared open-mouthed. She was gorgeous. No, she was breath-taking. Her perfectly heart-shaped face was dainty but her features were striking. She had bright green eyes and the fullest lips I had ever seen. Her long wavy hair was pulled back from her face into a high ponytail and her tanned skin looked smooth and inviting against her tight black gym outfit. She was enchanting but I still had no idea who she was. I pressed play and watched the entire fight with my heart pounding, palm sweating and dick pulsating. Fuck me, she was hot.

At first, I saw red as Daniel punched her and flicked her onto her back with ease, but then something changed and she moved so gracefully around the ring and delivered lethal blows with vengeance.

When she had him at her mercy on the floor and he reluctantly tapped out, I didn't think I had ever felt so turned on. Who was she?

As I let the recording play out, my eyes watched with fascination. The way she moved, the flick of her hair, the way she smiled at everyone's congratulations with modesty drew me in. And then I saw my cousin. Trailing behind her, animated in whatever he was saying. She turned and I couldn't see her face, but from the look on Darius', she was pissed off with him. He recoiled back at her words and followed her out of the door silently. And then they were gone.

I must have watched the tape back at least ten times before I decided I must find out who she was. But then what was the point? Why should I? I have a girlfriend. I'm moving to America. I'm ending a war. I'm becoming an Alpha of a pack. I have enough on my plate without adding this mysterious woman into the mix. And I could tell, she would only cause me trouble. I sighed as I leaned back in the swivel chair and ran my hands through my hair. Something inside me wouldn't let this go. I told myself that I'm going to leave it up to fate to decide. I would ring Darius and if he answered, I would ask to meet the girl. And if he didn't, I would leave it alone.

I held my phone to my ear and listened as the phone line connected. My nerves started to grow at each agonising ring. The longer I waited, the more I found myself praying for him to answer.

The line went dead.

Well, I guess that was that then.

Madeline's POV

As soon as he left the apartment, I burst into tears. Tears and emotions that I have been finding so difficult to bury. This was also wrong. I had done an unspeakable thing and the guilt was eating me alive. I couldn't bear to have him touch me or try to comfort me when I know I don't deserve it. I had never felt so lonely in my life.

Seeing Logan and Darius, the only boys I grew up loving and caring for, at each other's throats and wanting to murder one another made me realise the extent of my actions. I was so naïve to think this wouldn't affect anyone but Alina.

When Logan kissed me after, hope spiked through me that we would be able to make this work. But that was short-lived when all I felt was shame and sadness. I didn't want him like this. He didn't love me. Not the way I needed him to. And the realisation that I took away true love from him caused me to pull back and run to the bathroom before he saw the tears flooding from my eyes. I kept trying to remind myself that I did this for him. To save his life. To save everyone's lives. But I couldn't pretend that the last two weeks hadn't happened, even if Logan had no memory of them.

He was happy with Alina. I know that now, because when I look into his eyes, they were empty. They hold no light or love for anything. He was back to being fixated on revenge against Lucius and nothing else.

As I sat here in the middle of our apartment packing up our life together, it truly felt like I'm saying goodbye to the life I used to live. The tears came relentlessly as I realised the truth. He is not mine. He never was.

But that didn't change what needed to be done. As much as I could barely look at my own reflection right now, if I allowed him to die in battle knowing I could have prevented it, I would never be able to forgive myself.

I drew up a plan in my head. The battle was maybe a week or so away once we get to America. In that time, I can hold it together, but I will keep my distance from Logan, intimately anyway. He doesn't need that on his conscience once I get the witch to give him back his memories. Plus, I don't even think I could go through with it even if I wanted to. It just didn't feel right anymore. Once the battle is over and we are victorious, I will find Alina and explain everything. Hopefully, she will give him another chance.

With my mind made up and my plan set in stone, I felt slightly lighter. I didn't care what would happen to me once the truth was out as long as I got the chance to make things right again.

Chapter 48

Cora's POV

"Channel your inner emotions, use them to feel your power but do not let them control you," I said as I walked meticulously in a circle around my son as he floated a few inches from the ground, eyes closed, focusing on his magic.

Lucius was right about one thing. Arius was a phenomenal being with great power, but he was also dangerous as he didn't know how to use it correctly. Due to his father's controlling and selfish ways, he had not been properly schooled and had no idea of his true potential.

"Very good. Now, focus on the bird. Feel its energy. Listen to its heartbeat."

His eyes opened as he concentrated on the white dove flying frantically around the room trying to escape. His pupils dilated a vibrant violet colour and I felt pride knowing it was a part of me inside him.

"Focus on its movements without watching it. Use your senses to pinpoint every action and then predict its next."

A purple glow started to shine from his aura as his magic intensified.

"Good. Now, manipulate it. Use your powers to hold it still, calm it," I commanded, never taking my eyes off Arius. The bird's flapping ceased and I turned to see that its wings were spread out wide, frozen in mid-air. Its eyes darted around the room but its heartbeat slowed as Arius calmed it with his powers.

"Excellent," I said proudly. He was learning some of the most complex magic I had ever taught very quickly. It was impressive.

Suddenly, the bird's neck was snapped in half and it fell lifelessly from the air and hit the floor with a thump. My eyes turned sharply to Arius, who came down from his levitation with a grin.

"What was that?" I snarled, anger rising at his change in direction of the spell.

"What?" he asked innocently.

"We were practising body control and binding magic," I growled, taking a few angry steps towards him.

"Yes, and I controlled its neck to snap. Cora, you do know we are about to go to war. Being able to control and snap the neck of a wolf with my mind would be of great benefit to me," He gave me a devilishly handsome smile and my anger faded.

"Please call me mum," I said carefully.

He turned and regarded me before stating, "We do look a lot alike, don't we?"

I smiled as I took in his features again and my heart burst with love. "Yes, we do and for that I am very glad." I took a seat behind the wooden table where my book of dark magic was resting.

"Why? What exactly happened between you and my father?" he asked, leaning on the table next to me. In the short time we have spent together, we have grown close already and I could hand on heart say that they had been the best days of my life. As much as I wanted to tell him the truth about his father, I didn't want to hurt him.

"It's a long story and one that does not need to be repeated.

Let's just say, it was no fairy-tale," I replied coldly.

He merely nodded, knowing not to push me on this, and reached over to the hefty leather-bound book of spells. "Is it true that you actually wrote this yourself?" he asked, clearly impressed.

"My sister and I, yes."

He stoked the gold letters and attempted to open it, but I slammed it shut with my magic.

"You are not ready yet," I said sternly. I was reluctant to teach my son the powers of dark magic until I was sure that he could control them and not allow them to take hold of him.

He huffed in irritation. "I am more than ready. I have been waiting my entire life to be like you. Please, teach me." His voice was soft and pleading but I noted the frustration in his tone.

"My son, you are destined to be a very powerful warlock, but with that power comes responsibility. You do not want to be like me. Magic is one thing, but dark magic is an entirely different entity. One must know who they truly are before they can use it to aid others. I do not want to see you use it against people who do not deserve it. I have made that mistake many times over and the darkness consumes your soul," I said, thinking sadly about the Alpha who no longer remembered his true mate by now, as well as many other innocent lives I have ruined in my three hundred years.

"I know who I am," he said defensively.

"Do you truly? Because I see the power you allow your father to have over you. You walk in his shadow instead of creating your own. He does not control you, you know. You are far stronger than he has ever been and you have a kind heart under that hard exterior. I can see it."

His emotionless mask slipped slightly and I saw the vulnerability and softness that I knew he possessed.

He stood abruptly and walked around the table towards the barred castle window. "He needs to believe he controls me," he said quietly, so I had to sit up straighter to try and hear him. "I know who I am and I know what I want. My father fears me because he knows I have more power. He has tried to suppress that side of me for so long to keep control. But I am ready. You being here is the sign that I needed." He turned and his stunning blue and brown eyes were determined. I saw what a strong and passionate man he really was.

"Then let's begin," I said, flipping the book cover over with a twist of my finger.

Alina's POV

Darius grunted as he threw his phone down on the sofa. Someone was trying to call him and my gut was telling me it was Logan. Sadness overwhelms me again at the thought that he wanted to talk to him and not me. Darius moved from his position next to me to kneel in front of my stretched-out body to check on the bruises.

"Let's have a look." He pulled away the bag of frozen peas and his eyebrows furrowed. "The bruising is actually going down nicely, but I still think we should take you to the hospital and get you checked over. You could have a broken rib or something," he fussed.

"I'm fine Darius. Honestly. It doesn't even hurt anymore, it's just a bit sore," I reassured him, but he applied the peas back to my ribs for good measure.

At that moment, Chloe came crashing through the door, arms full of designer shopping bags and a tiara on her head that read birthday girl.

"Christ! Bought the whole damn shop?" Darius teased her as she struggled to fit through the door and dropped all the bags on the floor.

"Actually, my very generous and wonderful boyfriend treated me to ALL the shops." She giggled and her face glowed with happiness. I smiled, knowing she deserved to be treated like the princess she was.

"Ooh, let me see!" I said faking enthusiasm as I sat up from the sofa. That was when she noticed my bruising as the frozen peas crashed to the floor.

"What the— Alina, oh, my god, what happened to you?" she screamed, running towards me like I'm about to take my final breath.

"Chloe, I am fine. Darius, tell her I'm fine."

He raised his hands as if he doesn't believe that I am.

I groaned in frustration at the pair of them. "I just had a little MMA match at the gym. You should see the other guy!" I smirked at Chloe's shocked expression.

"Other guy?"

"Yes. Alina picked the biggest, butchest man in there to bare knuckle fight. And she won!" Darius chirped up, giving me a sideways glance of pride.

"What? You won? How? Sorry, I mean... yeah, how?"

"I don't know. Adrenaline I guess." I shrugged. "Now, show me what's in the bags!"

Chloe didn't need to be asked twice as she ran back over to them and started pulling out an array of brightly coloured outfits. I "Oohed" and "aahed" over them and Darius stood abruptly.

"Okay, that's my cue to leave. I will be back later," he said, heading to the front door.

"No. Sorry, mister. It's girls' night. I'm the birthday girl and I want my best friend all to myself," Chloe insisted as he walked past her.

"I can't leave Alina by herself, especially not at—" he started, but I interrupted him.

"Darius, come on. I am fine. Please, just one night with Chloe. I promise to text you every few hours," I said, batting my eyelashes at him.

We all held our breath and awaited his decision.

"Fine, but text me every hour without fail until you go to bed." He sulked.

"Deal." I gave him my most serious face. I know he was just being protective because he thought my life was still in danger from Lucius. But I'm sure Lucius would know by now that Logan was back with Madeline and wanted nothing to do with his 'human' mate.

"That guy needs to get a life! He acts like he's your boyfriend... or worse, your dad," Chloe said after he left.

"He's just worried about me. He's been a really good friend, Chloe. I would like it if you two tried to get along."

"I get along with him just fine when he's not being a controlling freak, which is most of the time," she clipped and I rolled my eyes. "So, plan for tonight. We're going to crack open the prosecco, pump up the music, and dance on the sofa wearing all these ridiculously expensive clothes."

Chloe's enthusiasm and excitement was infectious and I made a decision right then and there to push every negative emotion deep down inside and give my girl the best version of myself even if it hurt like hell.

After a few hours and three bottles of prosecco, we were in full on karaoke mode, singing 'I'm every woman' at the top of our lungs and dancing around the room. The copious amount of alcohol helped to dull the ache of my heart, but every couple of minutes, I would be hit with a memory or a lyric from a song that made me think of Logan, pulling my eternal torture back to the forefront. It was exhausting. We were both wearing over the top and overpriced designer dresses that you would only wear to a sleazy nightclub and feather bowers around our necks.

"Oh, god. I need a wee break. Back in five," I said as I stumbled down the hall towards the bathroom.

Just as I entered, I heard a doorbell ringing and Chloe called out, "Hurry, that must be the Chinese takeaway."

I sat on the loo and typed a quick update to Darius.

All fine. One hour on, two more glasses down. About to eat a Chinese then go to bed. Love ya, you big goon. X

I smiled as he replies immediately.

Stop drinking, you're turning soppy. D x

I stood up and sorted out my dress. I looked ridiculous in a skimpy black mini dress with sheer panels. Not something I'd ever choose for myself, but I had no doubt Chloe would pull it off. I pulled the flush and washed my hands, feeling the warm fuzzy effects of the alcohol. I hadn't been this drunk since... the night I met Logan.

Images flashed in my mind of him pushing me up against the bathroom door. Of his touch, his smell, his voice. My body defied me as I felt wetness pool between my legs at the memory. I hated that he could still have this effect on me.

'ITS BECAUSE HE IS OUR MATE.' Xena purred in my head, feeling his effect and longing for him just as much as I did.

'Then where is he?' I bit back, not meaning to sound so aggressive, but my hormones were all over the place.

She whimpered in my head and retreated.

"Shit," I said out loud. I opened the door and immediately froze. It wasn't just Chloe's scent that I could smell in the room.

My heart started pounding in my chest as the smell of damp and firewood burned my nostrils and grew with each step I took towards the living room.

Fear took over when I saw Chloe standing in the middle of the room with a sickly pale, blonde-haired man standing behind her, holding her to his chest with his hand around her mouth. Her eyes were wide and she looked like she was about to faint.

"Alina, isn't it? It is so lovely to finally meet you." The man's voice gave a false sense of friendliness and he smiled, revealing very sharp canines. Vampire.

"W-who are you? Let her go. It's me you want," I said quickly, my voice quivering. I went to grab my phone and internally cursed myself when I remember I left it in the bathroom.

"Apologies. I am so rude! I forgot to introduce myself. My name is Baylor and you're right. I am here for you. But when I saw your pretty little friend here, I just couldn't help myself. Her blood smells so inviting." He bent his head lower into the crook of her neck as Chloe screamed into his hand and writhed against him.

"No! Stop, please!" I screamed as I took a few panicked steps towards them. He froze as his teeth graze her skin and looked back up at me. His eyes shimmered with evil.

Suddenly, two more muscular men walked into the apartment and surround me with a menacing look, and I gulped audibly. Their eyes were hungry for my blood and I could tell all it would take was one command from this Baylor and they were going to kill me.

'NO, THEY'RE NOT. NOT YET. THEY THINK YOU POSE NO THREAT. THEY THINK YOU ARE HUMAN SO ACT LIKE IT.'

Tears started to swell in my eyes and I looked at the man closest to me. "Please, please, don't kill me," I pleaded.

A sadistic laugh rippled around the room from Baylor. "I thought a she-wolf would have more courage than that. But I suppose you have never even shifted."

My eyes widened as I realised they know my secret. But how? No one knew... No one except—

Before I could even finish my thought process, I felt a sharp sting in my neck and watched as one of the men removed the needle. The room started spinning and I hit the tiled floor with a thud.

Chapter 49

Alina's POV

An agonising pain sliced through my head as I hit something hard and rolled on to my side. I blinked frantically but darkness was all I could see. My short, quick breaths felt hot and restricted as I realised I had a black hood covering my head. My whole body ached, and I attempted to move, but my wrists and ankles were bound together, causing a burning sensation with every movement. I could tell by the vibrations and rumble of an engine that I was in the back of a van or truck. I couldn't breathe. Where were they taking me?

The shudders from the vehicle came to a halt and I heard doors opening and shutting.

'PRETEND YOU ARE STILL UNCONCIOUS.' Xena growls in my head. I squeezed my eyes shut even though I know they could not see my face and focus on making my muscles limp. I swallowed a scream as I felt cold hands wrap around my ankles and drag me violently along the cold, metal floor of the van.

"I got this one. You grab the human," a deep voice said as he held my body over his shoulder.

Human? Chloe?

I let my arms swing with the rhythm of this creature's strides, trying to act as if I was still drugged. Keeping my breath shallow was the hardest part. I felt a change in the temperature around me from the chilly night's breeze to a warmer, more tepid environment, but it was not long before we were descending a flight of stairs and the bitterness of a winter's night was back.

I was laid down on a hard, cold surface with the hood still tied over my head. My stomach retched at the smell seeping through the fabric, my mouth was dry. A distant thud echoed across the ground, ricocheting into my ear.

"Tie that one up over there. This one needs the wolfsbane cuffs." I felt the rope on my wrist cut free.

Wolfsbane?

'DON'T LET THEM—' Xena started but the hood was whipped off my head so abruptly and I blinked around in surprise. Locking my eyes with one of the monstrous men who had kidnapped me, my heart pounded in my chest.

"Looks like someone wanted to join the party early," he snared, crouching down beside me. He reached round the back of his jeans and pulled out a pair of silver handcuffs and I suddenly felt Xena's energy flow through me.

Without thinking about the consequences, I lifted my bound legs and kicked his hand hard, so the cuffs went flying through the air. He fell back in surprise before turning like the speed of light after them. I took the opportunity to crawl forward and grabbed a small piece of broken glass lying on the floor beside me. I quickly tuck it into the side of my dirty dress just as I hear him approaching me from behind.

"Fucking bitch!" he yelled as I felt a powerful blow to the back of my head and everything went dark.

***

Something clicked my senses awake—heart pounding, mind wide awake, the sound of whimpering and snuffling in the room. I tried to lean up onto my elbows and the sight of a small pool of blood on the floor caught my attention. I lifted my cuffed hands and felt the back of my head. It was wet. A sticky wet.

Movement across the other side of the room made my eyes widen in shock and relief. Chloe was shuffling up against a concrete wall, tears flowing as she caught my gaze. Her hands were tied with rope to a radiator and her feet were bound together with duct tape.

"L-Lina?" she whimpered, more tears flowing and leaving trails through her makeup.

"Chloe, are you okay? Have they hurt you?" I asked, trying to sound as calm as I could. She was clearly on the edge of a breakdown, and I couldn't just as well join her.

She shook her head timidly. "W-who are they? Why have they done this to us?" she cried and I felt the guilt pang in my heart. It was all my fault that she was in this mess. I should never have come back to live with her.

I closed my eyes and leaned my head back against the cold stone wall. How was I going to explain this?

Just at that moment, a large steel door in the corner of the room creaked open and I narrowed my eyes as that vile man called Baylor entered the room and shut the door behind him.

"Good morning, ladies. I hope you both slept well," he said in a friendly tone, but his eyes bore into us with so much hate.

"What do you want from us? Why are you doing this? If it's money you want, I can get it. My dad is a successful stockbroker and..." Chloe talks a million miles a minute but stopped when his evil laugh erupted around the room.

"So, you haven't told her?" His eyes were sparkling as he

looked at me.

"Told… told me what?" Chloe stuttered as she glanced from him to me.

"Chloe I—"

"Your friend, Alina has got in with the wrong crowd recently. Or should I say the wrong 'pack'?" He spat the word like it was poison.

"I don't understand," Chloe muttered, her eyes darting between us.

"Oh, you poor human. You know I was naïve like you once. And then I was saved and given the power and strength to join the elite species of this world. I think you would make quite a fine addition to our cause," he said with a grin whilst picking up a strand of Chloe's hair between his fingers and rubbing them together.

"Leave her alone! She has nothing to do with your 'cause'. Let her go! You've got what you wanted," I shouted at him, anger rising at seeing him touch my friend.

He stood abruptly and took aggressive steps towards me. I gulped at the malicious look etched all over his face. "Let her go? So she can run back and inform your little wolf mate? Now, that would be too easy. We have much bigger plans for you. It is sad really, your little friend here getting caught up in all of this drama." He peered over his shoulder to take another look at Chloe.

"She won't tell Logan. And even if she did, I doubt he would even care. He has rejected me, and he does not want me as his mate. We haven't even spoken in days. He won't even know I'm gone," I said and my voice cracked at the truth that he wouldn't come looking for me. "Killing me will only solve one of his problems."

Baylor's eyes narrowed as he tried to read me. This was obviously news to him but he recovered quickly. "Well, we shall soon find out how true that is." He stood and headed back to the door, but before stepping out, looked back at Chloe and then to me. "You have until midnight tonight to decide your friend's fate. Either I turn her or drink her dry. Either way, I will enjoy having her."

The door slammed and locks turned. Silence filled the hollow cube of concrete. I looked at Chloe with tears brimming in my eyes. Her pale, terror-stricken face said so much.

"I-I'm so sorry, Chloe. This is all my fault. You shouldn't be here."

"W-what did he mean? W-what is happening? Am I going to die?" she hyperventilated, and I watched as her body started trembling.

"No. I won't let him hurt you. I swear. We will find a way out of here."

She took some deep breaths and tried to calm herself.

'Xena?' I tried to mind speak but I didn't get anything back.

"He's a… a vampire, isn't he?" Chloe's small voice asked as I scanned the room looking for a way to escape. One way in, no windows. No furniture. Just the cold, bare stone walls.

"Yes," I said softly and watched as her eyes widened and her breathing became erratic again.

"And… and L-Logan? He's a vampire, too?"

I shook my head quickly. "No, he's not. He's… He's a werewolf… and so am I."

Chapter 50

Logan's POV

"Urgh, I hate queuing. What's the point in all of this technology checking into flights faster if it doesn't actually work," I grumbled, tapping my foot and crossing my arms. I have never been the most patient person in the world, but today I was more agitated than usual. I had an awful night's sleep again, full of disturbing nightmares. This time, the voice wasn't calling to me but to Elias. I was in wolf form sprinting through an eerie wood after the majestic voice, but I could never find it. Something was more sinister in this dream than the previous. The voice was desperate. Seeking my help.

I just needed to board this flight and get home. I'm sure it is just anxiety over the upcoming war and having to organise and train so many wolves in just a matter of days. But we were ready. At least I thought we were.

I glanced down at Madeline who was staring into space and constantly bending and straightening her boarding pass. She looked as tired as I felt. She was wearing her cargo trousers with Doc Martins and a black knitted cropped jumper. Her hair was pulled back into a messy bun of ice white curls and she wore a bit of makeup but not too much. I hated it when she covered her natural beauty with all that shit. But her eyes were dull and the dark circles under them reflected her mood from the last few days.

"Hey, are you okay?" I asked softly, touching her arm to bring her out of her daydream.

"Huh? Yeah... um just tired," she said weakly.

Something was so off with her. I couldn't put my finger on it but it was like she had just given up. But I had no idea what she had given up on. Gone was that sassy, confident and funny girl I used to know. I knew the pressure of the next few weeks was getting to her. Becoming a Luna was not an easy thing.

"Maddy, I know all of this is hard and you're worried and scared but we can do this... together." I squeezed her hand as she looked up into my eyes and I was shocked to see the tears swelling in them. "What's wrong?" I said with concern.

"I-I can't do this. This isn't right," she said with a shaky voice as she turned out of the queue with her suitcase in tow.

I quickly caught up to her and spun her around by her shoulders. "What do you mean? What can't you do? Go to America?"

She shook her head whilst looking down at the floor. "No, not that. I can't keep lying to you. Pretending everything is fine when it's all such a mess." She sobbed.

I was confused. Once again. Why did it always feel like everyone knew something that I didn't?

Vibrations from my pocket distracted me and I pulled out my phone to check who it was. Darius. I ignored it and put it back in my pocket. This was much more important.

"I don't understand, Maddy. What are you lying about? What's a mess?" I asked carefully.

"Everything. Us. Our future. It's all a lie, but I… I did

something. Something terrible," she stumbled through her tears. People started to look at us as we stood in the middle of the airport as she had some kind of emotional breakdown.

The vibrations began again. I sighed and retrieved my phone. Darius again. I gave Maddy an apologetic look as I answered the call.

"Darius," I said flatly. Perhaps he changed his mind and wanted to come with us.

"LOGAN! Where are you? Are you with Alina?" His panicked voice had me on edge immediately. Once again, about that woman.

"At the airport. No, I don't even know the girl. Why would I be with her?" I said, irritated.

"Stop fucking around you, dickhead. Are you seriously not with her? You don't know where she is?"

"I've told you, I don't. What's going on?" I asked aggressively.

"She's missing. I went round to her friend's apartment this morning and they were both gone. Her phone was left there. Something's not right."

I sighed. Why was he wasting my time with this? "Maybe they went out and she forgot her phone. Anyway, I really don't see why this is any of my concern."

"What?! You're fucking kidding me, right?" he bellowed and I could feel his rage through my earpiece. Before I could reprimand him for talking to me with so much disrespect, Maddy snatched the phone from my hand and I glared at her.

"Darius? What's happened?" she asked, the tears were gone and she was now on high alert. I vaguely heard him telling her something about leaving because of a girls' night, no more texts, leaving her phone at home, neither of them there. Maddy's eyes paled in panic and she paled slightly.

"We'll meet you at your house. We're on our way," she said with conviction, and I started to argue.

"What? We will miss our flight! Maddy, what are you doing?" I said bewildered, trailing after her as she marched out of the folding doors of the airport.

She stopped and turned to look at me. She took a deep breath and her grey eyes connected with mine. "We can't leave. You have to find her. She could be in danger."

I stepped back, still staring into her sad eyes. "Why?" I said quietly, but I knew the answer before it even left her lips.

"Because... she's your mate."

***

I think I'm in a state of shock. I know I have somehow managed to move my limbs to get in and out of a taxi, but apart from that, the last half an hour had been a blur. Maddy tried talking to me. I saw her lips moving and the concern etched on her face, but I couldn't hear anything over the shrill ringing in my ears. It was like the world had faded away and all I could do was repeat the words over and over in my head.

I have a mate. I have a mate.

I looked up as Maddy knocked heavily on Darius' front door. How did we get here so quickly? I suddenly snapped out of my shock-induced coma as the door flew open with force and Darius' face was creased with panic but turned to anger as he registered me. He turned on his heels dramatically, leaving the door open for us to enter.

"Tell me again. What's happened?" Maddy asked calmly.

I stood awkwardly in the door frame that separated the living room from the kitchen, not knowing what to do with myself.

"She wanted to have a girls' night in with Chloe because it was her birthday. I didn't want to leave them because... well you know. But she's so stubborn! She said she'd text every hour, which she did, but then she went quiet. Her last text was at 11:00 PM and it said she was going to bed after their takeaway, so I just presumed…" he said and he started pacing and pulling on his hair. "When I still hadn't heard anything this morning I went round there. The Chinese takeaway was left outside their door. I broke the door in when there was no answer and it was as if the night had just stopped abruptly. Wine glasses still half full, clothes everywhere."

Maddy nodded in understanding but I just stood frozen. All I felt was numb.

"Was there a sign of forced entry? A note? Signs of a struggle?" she asked as Darius shook his head at every question.

Suddenly, he turned to me, eyes blazing with fury. "This would never have happened if it wasn't for you!" he yelled, pointing a finger in my direction.

"I don't…" I started but I had no words. I didn't understand any of this.

"No!" Maddy shouted unexpectedly, and we both turned in her direction. "It's not his fault. It's mine," she said calmly. Too calmly.

"No, it takes two to do what you both did. It's just as much his fault as it is yours. No more because he is her mate!" he spat at me.

"He doesn't remember," she said quietly.

"What? What are you talking about?" Darius interjected and I couldn't help but glare at her as well. She was right. I don't remember anything when it came to my so-called mate. What was I forgetting?

"You have to try and understand my position. The witch told me he was going to die if he stayed with Alina. I had to do something. I had to protect him and the future of our pack," she whimpered.

"Maddy, what did you do?" Darius gritted through his teeth.

My heart nor head were not ready for the words that left her mouth.

"He's under a spell. I gave him a potion to forget Alina altogether," she whispered.

"WHAT!" Darius and I bellowed together, making the whole house shake.

She cowered back with tears in her eyes but looked up at me. "I-I'm so, so sorry. It was wrong. I… I was so desperate to p-protect you." She sobbed and I felt Elias clawing at the surface. We may not have any memory of our mate, but the betrayal of someone we trusted most in this world had us seeing red. I lunged forward and grabbed her by the throat, pulling her up off her feet.

"How could you?" Elias growled through me.

"I-I'm so… rry." She choked out and my grip tightened, cutting off her oxygen. Her face was getting redder by the second.

"K-kill m-e. I des-er-ve it."

"Logan! Enough!" Darius' voice boomed behind me.

I threw her body against the wall violently and watched her slide down, struggling to fill her lungs with air again. I started to rampage through the house knocking furniture and shoving items out of my way.

"Where are you going?" Darius shouted after me.

"To find my mate," I roared as I reached the door.

"And how do you suppose you do that without your memories?" he barked back.

I froze, my hand on the doorknob. He had a point. I had only ever seen her on a CCTV tape and I had no idea where she would be.

"I… can help," the small voice of the traitor whispered.

"I think you've done enough," Darius glared at her. She was gripping her red-marked neck but was standing back on her feet. I scowled at her.

"I can get the witch to give you back your memories."

We all exchanged a look of understanding. I would be able to track her much easier with the mate bond intact.

"Then what are you waiting for?" I snapped.

Chapter 51

Cora's POV

"Dark magic draws on malevolent powers, to cause destruction and misfortune. To injure or kill. It creates power from the hate and anger inside of the user. You must focus on your darkest thoughts, memories, and emotions to be able to successfully perform these spells," I tried and explained to Arius as he lashed out yet again on the table, hitting his fists as he failed another attempt at dark magic. "You are not allowing your mind to access your emotions. You are too guarded," I added.

"I am angry now, so why isn't it working?" he said sarcastically.

"Because you are feeling it too much. You must be in control of your anger to channel it into your power."

He paced the room, running his fingers through his long, messy hair. He had been practising dark magic for nearly twenty-four hours now. He refused to stop until he was able to perform one of my spells successfully. I knew he was starting to tire, as I was too, but he was not giving up. It was admirable.

Quick as a flash, he turned to me, unique eyes sparkling. "Show me," he said, as if he was just being enlightened.

"What?" I asked, confused.

"Perform a spell on me. So, I can see what I need to do," he said excitedly.

"No. I can't," I said, shaking my head. I could never cause my son any pain.

He moved urgently over to my book, flicking through the pages until he found what he was looking for. "This one. Perform it on me so I can see its destruction," His face lit up at the thought of it.

I glanced over the page. Chaos magic. This spell required the witch to tap into and utilise the chaotic forces of the universe. Once used on a target, they can manipulate and reconstruct a person's reality.

"I'm not sure, Arius. This spell can really mess with your mind," I said cautiously.

"You said my mind is guarded. That I cannot channel my anger and hate. Make me see it so I have something to work with," he urged.

I sighed and eyed him carefully. "Fine, sit down."

He gave me a dazzling smile like a kid waking up on Christmas morning. Taking a seat in the wooden chair, he cricked his neck on each side and shook his arms out.

"Ready?"

"Ready," he said confidently.

"If it becomes too much just give me a sign. You will feel consumed by the darkness, but remember to clap your hands if you need it to stop." For the first time in my life, I was nervous about casting dark magic against another person.

"Got it. Cora, I'm ready."

My heart momentarily sunk as he called me by my first name yet again. "Okay," I said, taking a deep breath. I closed my eyes and focused on my own anger and the hate buried deep inside me. It was easy to do. I have a lot of it. Once I felt the power flowing through my veins, I opened my eyes and Arius looked taken aback as my power radiated, my hair splayed in the air and eyes glowed purple.

I began muttering the spell, focusing on his mind and pulling the darkest images to the forefront. Beads of sweat started to form on his forehead and his breathing became erratic. His eyes turned red as his vampire side took over. I projected his darkest memories in front of him, forcing him to relive them. I could not see what they were, but by the way his face crippled with pain and he screamed at the top of his lungs, I know it was haunting. He started to convulse in his chair and fell to his knees.

"No, no, please. Stop, father. I'm sorry." His voice was soft, almost fragile, as if it and his heart would break any minute.

I ran over, kneeling before him, but he couldn't see me. He was consumed by his new reality. I gripped his hand, needing to see into his mind, needing to join him wherever he was.

I saw it all. My son, maybe no older than eight years old, was held down by four vampires in the dungeons whilst Lucius flogged him relentlessly with a leather whip, slicing open wounds across his bare back.

"Father! Please, I'm sorry!" he cried out and tears flooded from my eyes. Lucius turned and grabbed a wooden stake from the wall and strolled towards him with a threatening grin. He pushed the stake into Arius' shoulder blade and his skin sizzled and burned at the contact as the most haunting cry echoed from the young boy.

"Next time, you will kill when I tell you to."

"Yes… yes… father," he spluttered as Lucius removed the wooden spear.

My poor boy.

I pulled us back from the memory as I broke the spell. Arius was heaving on all fours on the stone floor whilst I fell back, hands covering my mouth. I reached out to touch his shoulder, but he shrugged me away and stood upright.

"What did he do to you? Did he do that often?" I asked, anger rising.

"Nothing. It wasn't real," he snarled at me but was unable to look me in the eye.

Rage manifested itself inside me as I thought of the abuse and torture my son had suffered at the hands of his own father; someone who was meant to show him love and affection.

"That wasn't nothing. You were just a child. My innocent child."

"I am NOT yours!" he snapped and he turned to glare at me and for a moment all I see was the image of his father's face.

"I am so sorry, Arius. You will never know how sorry I am." My voice choked with emotion. "Let's leave this place together. I'm here now and I can protect you. We could start a new life together and practise magic and..." I said, but stopped at the cold look in his eyes.

"And why would I do that?"

"Because you will be safe with me. I will never treat you the way your father has. I am your mother and I love you," I said allowing the free-flowing tears to roll down my cheeks again and again.

"You... are not... my mother," he spat and I recoiled at his tone.

"Arius." I tried to walk towards him but he took the same number of steps back and my heart shattered.

"I will never go with you. My mother died at the hands of werewolves and now it is my chance to avenge her death. My father may be a monster, but they made him that way. They took away my only chance of having a happy childhood. To feel love from my parents." A single tear left his eye and fell to the floor. What lies had Lucius been feeding him?!

"That's not true! My sister died at the hands of wolves, yes and so did her unborn son! But you are my son, Arius. Your father has lied to you your entire life!"

"No!" he shouted. "He has been lying to you!" He stormed out of the room and slammed the door behind him.

I fell to my knees, head in my hands and cried like I did the day I lost my son for the first time. After a few minutes, my sadness turned to hate as it swarmed around my body and all I wanted to do was march into Lucius' office and rip his heart from his chest. The darkness within me was beckoning; wanting blood that I had denied it for over thirty years. But I knew that if I wanted any chance to be in my son's life, I could never be the one to kill his father.

A bright glow suddenly appeared in front of me and an illusion of Madeline projected into my mind. She was using a witch to send me a message via telepathy. Clever girl.

'Cora, I need your help. Alina is missing. We expect Lucius is behind it. I know what your premonition says but we cannot let her die. Please, we need your help. Meet us at 15 Baker close as soon as you possibly can. Thank you.'

The image faded and I blinked away the last remaining tears. I told Lucius not to mess with the girl, but Arius was right. Why would I believe a monster? Of course, he would go after her. She was the only thing standing in the way of his victory.

Well, I think it's about time I chose a side in this war.

Chapter 52

Alina's POV

"Whoa... bloody hell!" was Chloe's response after I had told her everything that had happened over the last few weeks. She was scared at first, but when I explained that wolves weren't like they were portrayed in the movies, she soon calmed down and bombarded me with questions, many of which I didn't actually know the answer to myself. It made me realise how much I still had to learn about myself and this life that had been forced upon me. That's if I ever got the chance.

There was no way of knowing how much time had passed or how long we had been down here for. No one had come to check on us or even given us any water or food. All we had was a bucket in the room to use as the toilet, which was no easy task when your legs and hands were bound. Chloe flat out refused to use it, saying it was too disgusting.

"So, if you and Logan are like soul mates or whatever, why did he go back to Madeline? It doesn't make any sense." Chloe shuffled uncomfortably up against the concrete wall.

"I don't know. I guess he was never really planning on choosing me in the first place, especially as he thinks I am human and wouldn't be the best fit as a Luna," I replied sadly.

"Well, that's bullshit! If he doesn't want you as a human, he sure as hell doesn't deserve you as a werewolf!" she said with her sassy Chloe tone that I love so much.

I smiled weakly at her, knowing she was right, but my heart still ached for him.

"So your wolf's name is Xena. That's unusual but I like it. It's pretty. What is she like?" Chloe asked, eyes sparkling with interest.

I felt a genuine smile spread across my face at the opportunity to finally tell someone about her. "She is amazing. She sounds so strong and powerful, but I haven't met her yet, so I don't know what she looks like."

"You mean you haven't turned into her?" Chloe asked carefully.

"Shifted? No. And for some reason, I can't communicate with her right now. I think it's to do with these things," I said, holding up my wrists, which were shackled together with silver cuffs.

"Do you think it will hurt? When you finally do?" she asked, looking slightly worried.

"I don't know. I haven't exactly been to werewolf school and learnt about any of this. I mean, up until a few days ago, I thought I was just an average human girl."

She nodded her head in understanding and looked around the room. "How are we going to get out of here?"

I joined her by searching every crevice with my eyes but there was no sign of any way to escape. "I don't know."

Abruptly, the locks turned and the door opened. I froze when I saw a familiar creepy man enter the room, but it was not who I was expecting. It was the King of the Vampires himself. I recognised him from the time we met in the park. He was still smartly dressed in a black tailored suit, but his face was more menacing now; no longer disguised as a businessman and revealing his true nature through his hostile red eyes and dagger-like teeth.

He looked Chloe up and down with a smirk and then his eyes fall on me. "Alina. We meet again." His sickly voice sent a shiver down my spine and my body tensed as he took a few steps towards me. Crouching down so he was at eye level, he reached his repulsive hand out and ran his fingers down my cheek. His skin was ice cold and I struggled to move away from his reach. "It's such a shame, to have to kill such a beautiful girl but you are the enemy. And killing you will bring great distress to a certain Alpha." He smiled widely, showcasing his pearly white teeth.

"I wouldn't be so sure about that."

His ruby red eyes shone with amusement and his skin crinkled around the corners of them as his smile widened. "Ah, yes! He ran back to his childhood sweetheart, Madeline. That must have hurt. I suppose I can tell you now though, as you are about to die anyway. Your lover boy is under a spell which made him forget all about you."

My eyes widened as everything fell into place.

"Cora, she owes me a favour, you see. And it was exactly what I needed to be able to capture you. And now I will torture you, kill you, and film it all so your mate can watch it back when I ask Cora to restore his memories."

I could hear my heart pounding in my ears as the tears started to escape from my eyes. No. I can't let this happen. Now I know what Logan and I had was real and this wasn't his choice. I can't let my death cause him insufferable pain.

"You're a monster!" I heard Chloe's shaky voice from behind him.

He didn't even turn to acknowledge her as he said, "I get that a lot." He stood quickly as the door opened again and Baylor walked in carrying a camera on a tripod. I held my breath and I thought I was going to be sick.

"Don't look so worried. We are not going to kill you… yet. Just going to have a little fun."

The next thing I knew, I was being dragged across the floor by my hair until I was in the centre of the room. I screamed out in agony as Chloe watched on in horror.

"Please! Stop! Don't hurt her," she cried.

"Shut the human up. We can't have her ruining our little homemade video now, can we?" Lucius laughed.

Baylor strolled over and effortlessly punched Chloe in the face, knocking her unconscious. My body started trembling, anticipating the horror of what would happen to me next. Baylor casually walked back over to the camera and pressed record. The red light shone brightly. Lucius stood in front of me, blocking me from the camera lens.

"Logan. Your kind once took the only thing that I ever really cared for and loved in this damned world. I think it is only right that you suffer the same fate before I kill you." He stepped sideways so I was in full view of the camera. "Such a terrible shame that you were unable to protect your mate. I thought better of you, Logan. But her she is. At my mercy. Unfortunately, I am not in a forgiving mood." He sneered.

Suddenly, he turned and his black, polished shoe connected with my face, knocking me backwards as I felt blood gushing from my nose. I whimpered and cried as the pain spiked and I brought my chained hands to my face.

Before I could react, I felt the stinging sensation on my scalp as he fisted my hair and brought me to a sitting position. Lucius' face was close to mine as he gripped my jaw with his other hand holding my head still. His demonic eyes blazed with hunger as he watched my blood flow down my face. I was glued to the spot as he bent his head forward and licked my blood from my chin up to my nose.

He pulled back and licked his lips as if I was the best thing he had ever tasted. Then he pressed his harsh lips to mine forcefully before releasing me. I fell back down to the concrete floor, a quivering mess. I felt violated and disgusting.

"She tastes divine. I shall enjoy having her before I stab her in the heart. Don't worry, I will let you watch that, too." I heard his sly voice speak to the camera again. "Good. Send it to his phone. Let's make him feel helpless and confused. Give him a preview of what's to come." He chuckled and left the room.

Baylor started packing up the camera and I took the opportunity to have him alone.

"B-Baylor? P-please, I need water," I said as my mouth dried up.

He stopped his task and studied me for a few moments. After what felt like forever, he walked over to me and pulled me to my feet. I wobbled slightly and then got thrown over his shoulder as he started to walk towards the furthest corner of the room. Whilst hanging upside down, I caught a glimpse of something silver in his pocket and carefully removed it. A key.

He placed me on the ground and pushed a wooden slat away from the wall that I hadn't even noticed before. It revealed a hole in the wall and a rusty metal tap. He turned it on and gestured for me to drink.

Bending my head awkwardly to the side, I let the arctic water wash away the drying blood and hydrate me at the same time.

"Thank you," I said quietly.

He stood abruptly, grabbed the camera equipment, and left the room, slamming the steel door behind him.

I crawled along the filthy floor towards Chloe who was still laid unconscious on the floor. "Chlo!" I lifted my cuffed hands, which were still gripping the key tightly, to her throat to check for a pulse. Still alive. I lay back down next to her body, staring up at the ceiling. I wasn't going to die without a fight. The key was too small to open the basement door. I examined it closely and realised it matched the same size hole in my cuffs. Now, I just needed Chloe to wake up.

Madeline's POV

"Thank you for your help," I said to the witch, who I had met a few times over the years, as I saw her out of Darius' house.

"No problem. Although I feel like I should warn you. You should be careful when dealing with Cora. Her reputation precedes her." She gave me a warning look and I just nodded and gave her a warm smile as she walked out the door.

"Madeline!" Darius' voice shouted urgently from the dining room. I raced back inside and stopped dead when I saw no other than the dark witch herself standing in the dinky room.

"Hello, my dear." She smiled kindly, but she seemed on edge. Sad even.

"Cora, thank you so much for coming so quickly." I walked towards her and stopped by the table.

"I was surprised to hear from you but it seems that I am not all that welcome." Her crystal blue eyes glance over to Logan and Darius, who were both standing aggressively, arms folded and staring daggers at the woman from the other side of the room.

"I told them. About the potion. We need to reverse it

immediately. Alina could be in danger," I said evenly, trying to take control of the situation before one of them explodes. What if she can't do it? Or won't?

She nodded her head once whilst saying, "Ah."

"Please, Cora. We need your help. This was all a mistake. I should never have given Logan that potion. He should be with his mate if that is what he chooses. No matter what the cost. I see that now." I glanced over to Logan but his stone-faced expression remained fixed on the witch.

Her eyes bore into mine as though she was trying to read my mind. "I will help you but you may not want my help after I confess my part in all of this," she replied calmly.

"We already know it was you who gave Madeline the potion." Darius gritted through his teeth.

She turned to stare at the two men. "Yes, I gave her the potion but I did so under false pretences." Her head whipped back to me and I saw a flicker of regret in her eyes. "I made Madeline believe that Logan would die in battle if he chose to be with Alina. That is why she was so desperate to change her mind. When, actually, my visions revealed quite the opposite."

I stumbled back and felt the colour drain from my face. She lied to me.

"WHAT?!" Logan's Alpha voice dominated the room and I felt myself cowering.

"Logan must be with Alina if he is to have any chance in winning the war. She is the powerful she-wolf he is destined to be with and from a strong bloodline," Cora explained.

The room started spinning as I gripped the back of a chair for support.

"Alina is human!" Darius growled and Logan snapped his head

towards him as we all realised that Logan had forgotten all of this.

"No, she is not. She had a masking spell placed on her as a child to hide her wolf. But when she met Logan, the spell was broken. I felt its effects when I was with her for the Blood Oath. Which she didn't need obviously. I know you don't trust me, but if Alina dies at the hands of Lucius, the war is already over." She remained so calm and collected whilst the three of us seemed to be crumbling at her confession.

So, I did all of this for nothing! He was always supposed to be with Alina and by lying to me, I nearly killed the entire pack as well as Logan. Shame and anger bubbled inside me as I couldn't believe I ever trusted this woman.

"Why? Why did you deceive me? I thought you wanted Lucius dead as much as we do!" I shouted at her. For some reason, I felt a strange connection with this woman and her betrayal hurt more than I cared to admit.

"Because… Lucius has my son. The son I thought I had lost."

Our eyes locked as I recalled her tragic flashback.

"He blackmailed me to help him sabotage you all and find out about Alina's future. He promised my son in return."

"So, he knows she is a wolf?" Darius asked in panic.

"Yes. I am afraid so. He more than likely already has her."

"So why should we trust you now? After everything you've done. You could still be working for him and could do anything to Logan instead of giving him back his memories." Darius eyed her suspiciously.

"I have come to realise that the influence Lucius has over our son is too great. The only chance I have of saving him is to help Logan end Lucius altogether."

"Wait! You have a son with Lucius? I thought he was married to your sister?" Darius bellowed.

"It is a long story and one we do not have time for," she snapped, her patience wavering. "Would you still like my help or not?"

I glanced over at Logan, who hadn't uttered a word but listened intently this entire time. His handsome features were harsh and unforgiving as he glared at the witch in front of him. Only he could make the next move.

"I want my memories back. Do it."

"I am afraid it will not be a quick fix. It could take a few hours to restore them all and you will be unconscious throughout."

"We don't have a few hours!" Logan hissed.

"Then I suggest we do not waste any more time. Go upstairs, lie on the bed and remove your T-shirt. Let's get started."

The two of them had a stand-off for a few moments and the air was thick with both their power. Eventually, Logan pushed past her and stomped up the stairs with Darius close behind.

I turned to climb the stairs but stopped when I felt Cora's hand on my arm.

"My dear, you should leave. When Logan wakes, his memories will be back and he will realise the extent of what we have done. There is no telling what he will do," she whispered.

I forced my arm from her grasp angrily and narrowed my eyes at her. "I am well aware of what WE have done, and I will face the consequences of my actions."

***

It had been two hours since Cora put Logan under the spell to restore his memories. Anyone would think he was just having a peaceful nap except for the odd twitch or his face creasing with pain. Darius, Cora, and I sat silently spread across the room. We were all avoiding eye contact with one another, and the tension increased with every passing minute. I had been trying to prepare myself mentally and emotionally for Logan's fury when he awakes, but I know that it was pointless. If he let me live, I would be grateful.

Unexpectedly, Logan's phone beeped on the bedside table, making us all jump at the sound. Darius reached for it and I glared at him.

"What? It could be Fredrik about the territory or even Alina." He opened the message and his eyes looked like they were about to bulge out of his head. His knuckles whiten as he gripped the phone.

"It's a video… from Lucius."

Both Cora and I were by his side in a flash as he clicked on the video. My mouth went dry and my heart started pounding as the video played out. He has her. He's going to kill her. She was terrified. I must do something. This was my fault.

Darius obviously had the same train of thought as he jumped up from his chair. "We can't wait for Logan. We have to find her now."

"I agree," I said and looked at Cora. She was our only hope. "Do you know where he would be keeping her?"

She shook her head and my heart dropped.

"I would have thought of his castle dungeons, but I do not recognise that room. I could do a locator spell. If you have something of hers here? A piece of clothing, a hairbrush?" she asked frantically.

Darius ran to the bathroom and returned clutching a hair tie. "Will this work? She left it here."

Cora took it from him and delicately untangles a strand of hair that was wrapped around it. "Perfect," she whispered like it was gold dust.

After ten minutes, we had a location. A deserted farmhouse outside of London. Darius was the first rocketing down the stairs.

"Darius! Darius!" I caught up with him just as he reached the bottom. "I think you should stay here with Logan."

"What? No. I need to save Alina."

"As much as I want to believe that Cora is on our side now, we can't leave her here alone with our Alpha," I said firmly and I saw the turmoil register on Darius' face. "Let me go. I will find her and keep eyes on her and as soon as Logan wakes, you can both join me." I grabbed his hand and squeezed it. He took in my face, seeing how much I needed to do this.

"Okay, but don't attack alone. If the place is surrounded, wait for us. Do not do anything stupid!" he said sternly.

"I won't." He nodded and I felt Cora's presence behind me. I turned and she placed her hands in mine and closed her eyes for a few seconds.

"Be safe, my child," she said when she opened them again.

I gave her a small smile and sprinted out of the door towards my car. It would take at least an hour to get there, but seeing as it was already 11:00 PM, the roads should be deserted.

I took a second to look up at the iridescent full moon hanging low in the night sky and said a silent prayer.

Please, Moon Goddess, don't let me be too late.

Chapter 53

Alina's POV

"Argh... my head... fucker!" Chloe grumbled as she came out of her debilitated state and tried to reach her hands up to her face but failed when the rope attached to the radiator restricted her.

"Are you okay?" Her right cheek was turning a nasty shade of purple and green, and her skin was swollen above her cheekbone.

"The more important question is, are you alright? I was sure they were about to kill you." Her eyes scanned my bruised body for any serious harm.

"I'm fine. They didn't really do anything but take a video of me," I lied, not wanting to cause her any more distress than necessary. "Chlo, listen. I have a plan and I need you to get on board because it's the only one I've got."

She nodded eagerly and I pulled out the fracture of broken glass from my dress with a mischievous grin. "Hold still," I said as I started to hack at the rope that held Chloe's wrists together. It was a tiring and painstaking process, but finally, the yarn frayed and Chloe was able to pull at the rest. She rubbed her sore wrists with a small smile.

"What about you?" She eyed the steel handcuffs.

My eyes twinkle as I revealed the small key.

"How did you…"

"It doesn't matter. I think it's to unlock these."

Chloe quickly grabbed the key from my palm and I hold my arms out, heart pounding. Please. Please let this work.

The key fit. She turned it. With a clunk, the cuffs were off.

We looked up at each other and grinned. "Okay now, untie the duct tape, but as silently as you can. We don't know how soundproof that door is."

As we both work meticulously to remove the duct tape from our ankles, I started to feel a prickly heat spread across my body. The temperature was close to freezing down here, yet sweat was pearling on my forehead. It must be the adrenaline I could feel coursing through my veins.

"Done," Chloe whispered with a triumphant smile that I knew would soon disappear.

"Okay. Now, you see that wooden slat over there?" I pointed in the direction Baylor had taken me to the tap.

"Yeah…"

"Behind it is a small hole in the wall. I think you are small enough to fit in it." I tried and gave her a look of authority, but I knew she would fight me on this.

"No way! Hide? And leave you out here alone?" she whisper-yelled.

"Yes. Chloe, you are human and Baylor said he was going to turn you or kill you before midnight. It must be nearly that now, so we don't have much time. If he's on his own, I can take him. Xena will help me," I said confidently, but really, I was masking my nerves. If Lucius came back, I would be screwed. I still hadn't heard from Xena since I removed the cuffs, but I could feel her presence. She was furious and restless; pacing up and down in my mind.

"Okay," Chloe's small voice squeaked.

I stood up and helped her to her feet before we ran over to the corner of the room. Chloe crawled behind the wood and was very snug with her head crammed to her knees, but she just about fit. Her frightened eyes gaze up at me and I felt my own courage crumble.

"I love you, Lina," she whispered.

"I love you, too. Whatever you do, do not come out. No matter what happens or what you hear. You come out and we both die, do you hear me?"

She nodded awkwardly and I gave her a final smile as I pulled the slat back, concealing her. Frantically, I gathered up all the duct tape and rope and hid it behind my back. Sitting on my knees so they couldn't see my freed legs, I stashed the cuffs and my arms behind me. I was sweating profusely now, and I felt lightheaded. Suddenly, I crippled over as an agonising pain rippled through my body. What was happening?

I pushed myself back up to a sitting position with difficulty and gritted through the torture as I heard the locks turn and the door flew open. Baylor strolled in with a smirk that soon faded when he only saw me. He was alone.

"Where's the human?" he shouted as he spun on his heels, searching the revolting room. I said nothing but grinned at his panic. He clocked the wooden slat and stopped. "Really? You can't hide from your future maker girly," he laughed as he took calm steps towards her hiding place.

This was my chance, and I didn't hesitate to take it. I leapt onto his back; my arms locked around his neck just like I did with Daniel in the ring. I squeezed as hard as I could and wrapped my legs around his waist.

He chuckled. Without warning, he threw himself backwards on the solid concrete floor. My back slammed down with his rigid body on top of mine and the air was knocked out of me from the impact. My grip on him loosened and he used it as a chance to turn around at the speed of light. His hard body was pinning me to the ground and a strand of his slicked back blonde hair fell forward, tickling my face. He grinned, red eyes dancing with excitement.

"Lucius was hoping to have his fun with you first, but I'm sure he won't mind if I have the honour," he whispered into my ear, and I felt my body judder, repulsed by his touch. Xena roared in my head at being in such an intimate position with someone other than our mate.

I felt him pushing my dress up to my waist and starting to unbuckle his belt with one hand as he gripped my wrists with his other up above my head. He froze. My eyes glowed gold and his stare flicked up to my wrists in his hand. No cuffs. I smirked at him and felt Xena's power flood through me.

I lifted my head violently and crashed into his nose as hard as I could. He fell to the side of me in agony and I jumped to my feet.

Then that excruciating pain spiked through me again, but this time it was more intense.

'LET ME OUT! GIVE ME CONTROL! DON'T FIGHT IT!' Xena roared in my mind.

I fell to all fours as I released a heart wrenching scream. I focused on her energy and allowed her to take over. I heard the vile sound of my own bones cracking and rearranging as my dress ripped. The pain was unbearable. I felt like someone was pulling me limb from limb, stretching me.

I opened my eyes and couldn't believe what was happening. Long, white hair grew from my arms and my nails elongated. My hands became humongous paws on the concrete. I threw my head back and let out an earth-shattering howl.

The pain dissolved and I could see through Xena's clear and focused eyes, Baylor staring at us in total disbelief.

"It can't be··· your···" he started, but Xena pounced on him and wrapped her jaw around his arm and bit down hard. He let out a shrieking hiss and punched us relentlessly in the ribcage, forcing Xena to eventually let go.

They glared at each other from a distance before both bounding into the air and colliding. Xena clawed and bit at his pale body, but a resounding howl from not far away distracted us. Another wolf was here.

Baylor took the opportunity to bite down on Xena's shoulder, infecting her with his venom. Her roar erupted through the air, and she turned her head and grabbed his arms, ripping it from his body effortlessly.

He fell back from the harrowing pain. We honed in on our target and her teeth pierced through his neck. With one ruthless snap and twist, the vampire's head was ripped clean off and flew through the air. Xena didn't stop tearing his body apart, limb from limb.

Panting heavily and with the vampire venom seeping through her veins, she stumbled to the metal door that was left ajar.

'Keep going Xena. We've got this,' I encouraged her as she climbed the stairs and we found ourselves in an old, derelict farmhouse. Commotion outside drew our attention and we padded through the open front door.

There was a large crop field opposite the house and men could be seen darting through the tall grass at inhumane speed as they were chased by a large, grey beast. Xena's protective nature kicked in as she dived into the field, ripping a vampire in half as she did.

Madeline's POV

Hiding in the towering grass out of sight, I examined the abandoned farmhouse from a distance. There were no lights on except for the main lobby and I could see at least six vampires standing guard around the veranda. I was still in my human form, so I know I could not get any closer without them smelling me. Everything seemed calm. Nothing amiss. No sign of Alina.

Suddenly, the air around me prickled and all the small hairs on my skin stood to attention. I felt Nina on high alert in my mind.

The ground vibrated as the most powerful and exceptional howl I have ever heard rang out through the night.

It was one of an Alpha.

Nina took control as I involuntarily shifted at the call. Vampires stared at each other and started to make their way inside the farmhouse towards the howl. We had to stop them. Nina released her own warning howl, and the vampires turned back as they saw my large grey wolf emerge from the crops. Their faces lit up with incentive as they glided towards us. We bolted back into the crop field.

Time for a game of cat and mouse.

Chapter 54

Logan's POV

"It's done." I heard a faint voice echo in my head. "When I break the spell, he is going to be very confused and disorientated, but as soon as his memories flood back to him, he will lash out. He will not be in control of his emotions and you will need to do your best to calm him down."

"No shit," a familiar, deep voice replied. Something in my mind clicked and I blinked my eyes rapidly, trying to get my bearings.

"What?! Where am I?"

"Hey man, you're at my house. Just take it easy, okay?"

I felt Darius' firm hands on my chest, keeping me flat. I looked around the room frantically and saw the dark witch standing by the side of the bed.

"What's going on? Why's she here?" My head began to throb as I struggled to sit up. "Where is Alina?" Panic was rising in me like a flooding dam.

"What's the last thing you remember, Logan?" the witch asked carefully.

"What? I don't know. I was having a drink with Maddy and then…" I tried hard to unscramble my thoughts, but they seemed like a puzzle that I must slot together so I could see the bigger picture. One by one, memories of the last few days emerged. Darius punched me, packing up the flat, watching Alina on the CCTV without any idea who she was, being at the airport, Maddy's confession and Alina was missing…

My breathing was becoming erratic. Little by little, I could feel my eyes widening and I knew they were turning black as Elias clawed to the surface. I fixated my gaze on Cora and before I could stop myself, I grabbed her by the throat, and threw her across the room into the wall. I felt black hair sprouting on my arms and my heart was racing in my chest.

"WHAT DID YOU DO?!"

She didn't react, but her eyes turned purple in warning.

"Logan, calm down. We need her help." Darius' steady voice tried to calm me.

"YOU ARE THE REASON SHE'S MISSING! IF ANYTHING HAS HAPPENED TO HER, I WILL KILL YOU… AND YOUR SON," I bellowed and punched the wall by the side of her head.

Suddenly, I felt all the heartache and sorrow I must have caused Alina. She thought I didn't want her. She thought I didn't care about her.

I gripped my hair as tears form in my eyes. I couldn't remember the last time I cried but just the thought of Alina coming in harms' way and thinking I didn't care had me at breaking point.

"Logan. We know where she is. Get your head in the game and we can go. Maddy has already gone."

I snapped my head up to his and saw regret in his eyes. "You sent her alone?" I barked.

"She wanted to go. We couldn't leave you alone here. Don't

worry, she won't attack. She will wait for us."

He misunderstood. I didn't trust her to go alone. When I find Madeline myself, I will kill her.

***

"How do you know this isn't a trick? That the witch hasn't planned all of this and is working with Lucius," I gritted as the car zoomed through the desolate roads out of the city.

"We don't. But we don't have any other options."

"I've fucked up. What if she doesn't forgive me?" My voice didn't sound like mine.

Darius gave me a sideways glance from the driver's seat. "It's not your fault, Logan. I've been pissed at you myself, but now I know. She will forgive you."

"Thank you, Darius. For sticking by her. And for punching me in the face." I gave him a feeble smile. I meant it. If it wasn't for Darius' help, I don't know how Alina would have gotten through it all.

"Don't thank me. I failed. I couldn't protect her," he berated himself.

"No. I didn't protect her. It was my job," I said sternly.

We continued for about ten minutes in silence.

My body was itching to get out of the car. I felt my skin tingle with anticipation. If anything happened to her… If she was killed…

I gulped back my emotions. I need to keep a clear head right now.

Unexpectedly, the overwhelming feeling took over my body and I started trembling and grunting in the passenger's seat.

"Logan? What's wrong?" I could hear Darius' panicked voice, but I couldn't focus on anything but tried to maintain control.

Elias was going insane and growling in my head. Every few

seconds, one of his grizzles would escape my mouth. I battled him in my human form, going through so much torment as it suddenly clicked what was happening.

Alina was shifting for the first time and Elias could sense her wolf. The closer we sped towards the location, the harder it was to keep dominance. Elias was striving on instincts alone and he didn't care about anything but her. My eyes cast over black as my control was slipping. She shouldn't have to shift alone. I should be there.

"Logan? Hang in there. We are nearly there."

That was when I heard it. The most enchanting and powerful howl called to me as I glanced up at the full moon. Darius swerved the car over hastily as he heard it, too. Black hairs sprout from my skin as I leapt out of the car and allowed Elias full control. I thundered down the road in my gigantic wolf form with Darius' wolf, Gunner, hot on my heels.

Elias' paws pounded the ground for what felt like miles and, for some reason, he seemed to know exactly where he was going. He could sense his mate was near and was eager to be with her. To see her for the first time.

We finally arrived at a long, rocky off-road lane and Elias lifted his snout in the air and sniffed desperately. So many scents. But amongst them all, we could smell the familiarity of Madeline's wolf, Nina, and a heavenly smell. Alina's wolf.

Elias didn't waste any time as he hurtled down the lane which opened out to a large farmhouse surrounded by fields. Rapid movement could be seen as the tall grass swayed and lurched in different directions. The blur of pale skin and now and again grey fur was seen from where we stood.

'WE BOTH CAN'T JUST GO RUNNING IN THERE. WE DON'T EVEN KNOW IF ALINA IS IN THERE,' Darius said

through mind speak, but Elias was impatient and so was I. We wouldn't waste a second longer without finding her.

'*SHE IS,*' I replied as Elias sprinted into the bushy, green jungle of crops.

As we landed, we saw a vampire stop in front of us and his demonic eyes enlarged at the size of my black wolf. Elias growled and ripped his throat out in seconds. We dashed between the stems following that irresistible scent until we saw another vampire five metres ahead of us. He was walking backwards, hands raised in surrender. But it was not me he fears. A majestic, dazzlingly white wolf, a similar size to Elias, prowled towards him gracefully, baring its teeth in a growl. Sensing or smelling Elias, the magnificent wolf's head turned, and we locked eyes with a set of golden irises that shimmered in the moonlight. She was exquisite.

'*MATE!*' Elias roared in my head.

But out of nowhere, the vampire took his chance to jump onto her back and bit into her neck. She howled in pain, and we were racing towards them. Before we could reach her, a flurry of grey fur leapt through the air and ripped the vampire from the white wolf's back. They crashed and tumbled into the crops, hissing and snarling as they clawed and bite at each other.

Elias got to the white wolf just as her legs gave way and she fell to the ground. Her furry body shuddered and trembled as she turned back to her human form. A naked Alina lay in front of us. I forced Elias back and shifted, bending down on my knees to cradle Alina in my arms.

She was falling in and out of consciousness and that was when my heart stopped at the sight of all the deep vampire bites all over her body. Her beautiful green eyes fluttered open and she looked up at me.

"L-Logan?" she whispered.

"Yes, it's me. I am so sorry. Stay awake. Stay with me."

Her eyes shut momentarily but she forced them open again. "You… have to… help her. Help Madeline."

My eyebrows creased in confusion as I lifted my head to see the grey wolf who just saved Alina pinned to the floor by two vampires.

Madeline?

I glanced back down at Alina, whose breathing was becoming ragged and I could feel her slipping away. I couldn't leave her. I couldn't help Madeline and forsake holding her. I shook my head.

"P-please," she stammered before her head fell backwards unconscious and her body went limp.

"Alina? Alina?" I shouted frantically, shaking her gently. A painful howl echoed from Nina as she was dominated by the two vampires, but I couldn't bring myself to let go of Alina.

Suddenly, a luminous orange glow radiated from Madeline's wolf and the vampires were thrown off her by an invisible force. She fell in the dirt whimpering as the glow faded and she passed out. Gunner ran through the plants and dealt with the two vampires effortlessly and then transformed back into his human form, running over to Nina who was still lying motionless in the soil.

"She's still breathing. She's going to be fine," Darius called to me as he checked her pulse.

I still had Alina huddled in my arms, her body close to my naked chest, and I could hear her heartbeat weakening. "Darius!"

He ran over and looked petrified when he saw the state of his friend.

"I have to suck the venom out, there's too much of it in her system. Her wolf can't fight it on her own."

He nodded as I lay her down carefully. "Let me help." He kneeled on the other side of her.

Elias growled at the thought of another man's lips on our mate.

"Logan, it will get the venom out faster if we both do it."

I gave him a tight nod. He was right, even if I hated it. We worked relentlessly sucking at her bite marks, drawing the venom out and spiting the disgusting tar on the ground. After a minute or so, I started to feel dread. It wasn't working.

'MARK HER!' Elias growls in my head.

'No, it could kill her in this condition.'

'IT WON'T. IT WILL GIVE HER WOLF THE STRENGTH TO HEAL HER.'

Darius looked up as he realises, I have stopped. "What?"

"This isn't working. Her heartbeat is getting fainter. I— I have to mark her."

Horror reflected in his eyes as he realised it was the only way. Marking shouldn't be done like this. It should be loving, intimate, and consenting. But I didn't have a choice. I can't lose her.

I brushed her filthy hair away from her face and kissed her lips tenderly. "I'm so sorry, Alina. Please forgive me."

Bending down, my face in the crook of her neck, I started kissing and licking her marking spot gently, hoping it wouldn't cause her too much discomfort. I hesitated as my teeth slowly start to break the skin.

"Wait!" A voice sounded from the tall grass and the witch appeared. "I can remove the venom as long as it has not reached her heart! You don't have to forcibly mark her. There is another way."

My eyes narrowed at the traitorous woman. I still didn't trust her.

"Please. We don't have time. Let me help. Remember I need her to live just as much as you do."

I nodded my head for her to approach, but held Alina protectively in my arms again.

Cora's eyes turned purple as she started to chant and guide her hand over Alina's body, summoning the poison to leave her. After a few minutes, Alina started to convulse and splutter as black tar bubbled in her mouth.

"Quick! Turn her on her side. She is expelling the venom!" Cora shouted.

I did exactly that as the thick tar leaked from Alina's mouth onto the ground. When she had finished, her eyes fluttered slightly and she mumbled something incoherent.

"Alina. Shhh, it's okay. You're going to be okay," I soothed, kissing the top of her head.

"C-Chloe. She's… Chloe" she muttered a little more clearly before she passed out once more.

Darius was on his feet in a blink of an eye and running into the farmhouse. After a few minutes, he came out carrying a shaken-up Chloe bridal style.

"We need to leave. It won't be long until Lucius shows up and these girls need to rest," Cora said.

I stood lifting Alina in my arms and walked to Madeline's car at the end of the dirt track. I slid into the back seat with Alina on my lap, never letting go of her. Darius placed Chloe in the passenger seat and she quickly looked around at a passed-out Alina in my arms. Her dirty hands flew to her mouth and her eyes filled with tears.

"Oh, my god, Alina. Is she going to be alright?"

"Yes," I said confidently as I stared back at Chloe.

"She saved my life," Chloe stuttered as the tears started to flow and my heart swelled with pride. "Oh… um… you're naked!" Chloe blushed and quickly turned to face the front.

I couldn't help but smile.

Darius poked his head through the driver's door. "The witch said she will take Madeline with her. Apparently, she put a protection spell on her which is what caused her to pass out. I'm not sure though. I think Madeline should come with us."

Anger still festered at what Madeline had done, but I no longer wanted her dead. She had just saved Alina's life and the witch had lied to her. However, I wasn't ready to see her or forgive her anytime soon.

"I think that's a great idea. Let the witch have her," I hissed at Darius and he regarded me with a surprised expression but didn't argue. He left to speak to Cora, only to return and started the engine, getting us far away from this hell hole.

I took a moment to take in all of Alina's stunning features as she slept safely in my arms. Even though her skin was covered with dried blood and dirt, she still looked so beautiful. And at this moment, I have never felt so scared in my entire life. So scared that I came so close to losing her because nothing in my life had ever meant as much to me as she did.

I hugged her close. "Alina, my life began and ends with you," I whispered into her temple, hoping she could hear me in her dreams.

Chapter 55

Logan's POV

It had been nearly twelve hours and Alina still hadn't woken up. I was starting to panic that the witch had done something to her, but Darius tried to reassure me that she had been through quite an ordeal and her body needed to repair itself. I hadn't left her side, not even to shower. Darius and Chloe brought me food and water, but I barely touched them. I couldn't until I knew she was okay.

Chloe explained what Alina had done, hiding her in the cubby hole and attacking Baylor herself. How her first shift was brought on because he was about to…

Bile rose in my throat and my gut twisted at the thought. I'd watched the video Lucius sent to my phone. My phone was no longer. Now I have even more reason to get my revenge on that monster, and I cannot wait to get my hands on him.

I kept replaying the first moment I saw Alina's wolf over and over. She has a white wolf, which only meant one thing—she has Alpha in her bloodline, but not just any Alpha. She had to be part of the Alabaster bloodline. They were the rarest and most powerful of our kind for centuries. To be mated to one was a huge blessing. The last Alabaster Alpha was before my father. Alpha Alec. He was the Alpha of my pack, the Blood Moon Pack. He was known for his ruthless and domineering leadership and his hatred towards vampires. In fact, some say he was the one who started this war between the species when he killed Lucius' wife and unborn child. But as far as I know, he had no children, which was why my dad became the next Alpha after he died in battle. He had been ruling for over two hundred years and my dad had been his Beta for the last fifty years.

A soft knock on the bedroom door pulled me from my thoughts and I smiled warmly as Chloe entered. She seemed a little on edge around me, probably because she knows what I am. Ah, that's another Blood Oath I need to sort out.

"Any change?" she asked, walking over and perching on the edge of the bed, holding her best friend's hand.

I shook my head and leaned forward, resting my elbows on my knees.

"You should get some rest. Or take a shower at least. I can stay with her."

"Thanks, but I'm okay," I replied, rubbing my eyes.

"You're just as stubborn as she is," she snorted, looking lovingly at her friend. "You know I should break your nose for what you put her through, but seeing as you were under a spell, I suppose I can let it go." She smiled but it didn't reach her eyes. I was riddled with guilt every time I thought about the last few days.

"Was she really hurt?" I said quietly, already knowing the answer. Even if she didn't love me, the mate bond would have made it insufferable.

"Yes. She was broken. I'd never seen her like that over a guy before. Obviously, now I know that you're not just a guy but her destined person… wolf, whatever." She flapped her hand in the air carelessly. "I was really worried about her but I think finding out she

The Last Alpha

had a wolf and talking to Xena provided her with some comfort."

My eyes broadened and Elias purred. "Xena?"

"Yes, that's her wolf's name." She smiled and I mirrored hers. "She thinks you slept with her though."

"Who? Madeline? I didn't… I—"

"I know. Darius told me. But Alina is going to need a minute to get her head around all of this. She knows you were under a spell but she can't just forget all the pain it caused her."

"I understand," I replied sadly. She was right. Alina had every right to be upset. She walked in on what she thought was me cheating on her and then ignoring her. "You know, I think I will take that shower after all. Do you mind?" I asked.

"No not at all," I stood up and walked towards the door. "Oh, Logan?"

I spun round and had to hold back a laugh at the menacing glare coming from such a petite human.

"I am happy you get another chance together, but if you ever hurt my friend again, I will castrate you and your wolf."

"Deal," I said with a smile.

Alina's POV

"So, I've decided to end things with Ryan. I know. I know. You think I'm crazy, but after my near-death experience, do you know how many times I thought about him? None! So, he is clearly not the one for me! I want a love that I can't live without!"

Chloe's voice filled my head before I even opened my eyes. I tried not to smile, giving away that I was awake as I enjoyed listening to my friends rambling too much.

"I told Darius and he said I was bonkers, and he felt sorry for the poor guy, saying that if I was waiting around for Prince Charming, I would be waiting forever as there is no such thing. I told him to go fuck himself. I honestly don't know how you can be friends with that lump!" she huffed.

"Oh, he's not so bad once you get to know him," I husked out, my throat dry.

"Alina? Oh, my god, you're awake! Thank goodness!" she screamed and jumped on top of me, hugging me like her life depended on it.

"Chlo! I can't breathe!" I wheezed and she immediately released me.

"Oh, shit, sorry! I'm just so glad you're finally awake."

"How long have I been out?" I pushed myself up against the headboard. I was back in the comforting surroundings of Darius' guest room.

"About thirteen hours. So not that long. But when you left me to deal with those two morons alone, it felt like forever!"

My heart flipped in my chest. Logan. He was there. He was here? I can still smell his enticing musk lingering in the room. "Logan is here," I said more to myself, but Chloe squeezed my hand and smiled.

"Hasn't left your side. Well, until now to have a shower, but apart from that!" She giggled, but I could barely manage a smile.

I felt sick at the thought of seeing him again after everything that had happened. What if things have changed? Did he even know who I was? I'm not sure I was strong enough right now to see him if he didn't have his memories.

Just then, the door flew open and a dripping wet Logan stood in the doorway with only a white towel hanging low around his waist. I gulped audibly at the sight of him. My body yearned for him immediately. How was it possible that he looked even fitter than I remembered? His black curls trickled droplets of water onto his shoulders and chest. His tattooed, toned arms and chest looked more muscular and ripped than before and those eyes… Lord, give me mercy. Piercing blue eyes bore into mine as the sexual tension in the room pulsed. He remembered.

"Um… I'm going to give you two some privacy," Chloe mumbled, climbing off the bed and squeezing past Logan's huge frame in the doorway. Neither of us acknowledged her, fixated on each other.

He took a few steps into the room and shut the door behind him. My heart sped up. I had gone over all the things I would say to him if I ever saw him again a million times in my head. But now that he was here, standing right in front of me, I went blank.

Suddenly, I felt the need to match his power. His dominance. I pulled back the covers to reveal my bare legs and climbed out of bed. I stood tall, in only an oversized white shirt and met his lustful stare. His jaw ticked and the desire swarmed in his eyes as he looked me up and down. I felt it, too, as my arousal started to grow, but I was also angry. Angry that all of this happened. Angry that I almost died. Angry that he forgot about me. Angry that he slept with her.

He took a few deliberate steps towards me until he was so close that I could see his chest rising and falling as he tried to control his breath. The glistening droplets of water zigzagged down his beautiful skin.

Momentarily, my self-control faltered as I took a glimpse at his lips, which soon turned upwards into a smirk when he caught me. Before I could stop myself, I slapped him across the face. It wasn't hard enough to cause impact but his face registered surprise.

"You promised you'd come back," My voice wobbled, my

emotion getting the better of me.

His eyes search mine and I saw how much regret and sorrow resided in them and it pulled on my heartstrings. He didn't deserve that but I was angry. Angry at how much I still wanted him. How much I still needed him.

"I'm so sorry, Alina. I never slept with her, I promi—" he started, but I dived at him, wrapping my arms around his neck and standing on my tiptoes as I crashed my lips against his. He froze for a split second but quickly wrapped his athletic arms around my body and deepened the kiss. His hands explored my body like no time had passed between us. They felt strong and familiar. They felt like home.

We pulled apart and rested our foreheads together. "No talking, I just need to feel you. I need you to erase the pain away," I whispered as my eyes connected with his. He leaned forward and kissed me slowly. Savouring every touch, every taste. He was the most delicious thing I had ever tasted and I wanted him. Now.

I pulled back to start undoing the buttons on my shirt painfully slowly as his eyes roamed my body hungrily. The way he looked at me made me feel like I was the most beautiful thing on this earth and all my insecurities melted away. I let the shirt fall to the floor and stood naked before him. He pulled away his towel and let me take him in. Holy fuck.

Gently, he picked me up and laid me on the bed, but instead of climbing on top of me, he sat to the side and leaned over so our breaths tickled each other's faces.

"Do you trust me?" His deep voice made my wetness grow and it felt like the biggest question in the world as he held his breath, awaiting my answer. Call me crazy, but even after everything, I did.

"Yes." I breathed and he kissed me passionately, his tongue invading my mouth, possessing me completely. He moved down my jaw line and throat, kissing tenderly and making goose pimples decorate my skin. It was as though he was kissing away every wound that had long since healed and every touch by another.

He reached over to the bedside table and took a swig of the iced water. My eyebrows arched in question, and he gave me a devilish grin as he replaced the glass. He lay down by my side and angled his mouth over my breast. I inhaled sharply as I felt the cold, wet sensation of an ice cube on my skin. He rotated it skilfully around my nipple with his teeth as it hardened under its touch. I moaned in pleasure at the sensation of the freezing ice mingled with his warm breath on my skin.

He glided over to my other breast and gave it the same tentative care and delight. Once he was satisfied with his efforts, he trailed the ice cube down my stomach, and I felt the baltic droplets running down my sides as the cube melted slightly. The whole act was the most erotic thing, knowing he was not actually touching me himself but still giving me immense pleasure.

When he went to my pubic bone, he sucked the ice cube into his mouth completely and pushed it against my nub with his tongue. I writhed about on the bed at the intense feeling and his strong hands held my hips in place. He moved it gently against my centre until it had completely dissolved from its warmth and replaced it with his icy tongue. He licked and flicked his tongue across me, sending shivers of ecstasy up my body. I gripped his hair as he started to speed up his rhythm and I could feel myself on the edge of a mind-blowing orgasm. My legs started to shake and my back arched off the bed as I released all my built-up emotions into my climax.

Once my body started to come down from its natural high, Logan crawled up the bed and scooped me up in his arms.

"I love you, Alina," he muttered drowsily just before I felt the weight of his arms relax and I know he had fallen asleep.

Chapter 56

Logan's POV

I woke up with a sense of blissfulness and felt Alina's fragile yet strong body in my embrace. The soothing beat of her heart and her skin against mine calmed me. She was safe here in my arms. I opened my eyes slowly and I was surprised to see her green iris watching me. I chuckled.

"Have you been watching me sleep?" I asked with a cheeky grin.

She blushed slightly but smiled back. "Well, I did have a pretty decent rest, I wasn't feeling that tired."

I must have passed out! "Oh, shit. Sorry. I haven't had much sleep recently," I tried to explain, but the amused look on her face told me she was not annoyed. "How long have I been sleeping?" I said, gazing out of the window, seeing the daylight had faded into night.

"A few hours."

"And you've been watching me the whole time?" I said with a laugh.

"Yep. It was hard to believe you are actually here. I thought if I closed my eyes again, I might wake up and it would have all been a dream," she confessed softly and my heart broke a little at her words.

I shuffled back down the bed a little, so I was face to face with her. "It's not a dream. I am here and I am not going anywhere. I'm afraid you're stuck with me," I said, meaning every word.

"That's if you'll have me," I added, and the nerves started to build. She was the only woman who had ever made me feel nervous.

She studied me for a few seconds, and I started to feel panic rising. This was the talk. The talk we needed to have. No matter what, I wasn't fucking this up again.

"You hurt me, Logan. You broke my heart." Her eyes watered but she fought back the tears.

I took a deep breath to control my own emotions. "I know it wasn't your fault. I know you were under a spell and you forgot I even existed, but the pain for me was real. I thought you didn't want me. I thought you just used me until I signed the Oath and then ran straight back to Madeline." She jolted up in panic. "Oh, my goodness, Madeline! Where is she? Is she okay?"

I sat up, reaching for her hands to calm her. How this woman could even care about someone who nearly ruined her life was beyond me. "She's okay, I think. She is with Cora, the witch."

"The dark witch? Why?"

"I didn't want her here. Not after everything she did to us."

Anger flashed across her eyes. I wasn't expecting this. "She saved my life! Her wolf took on half a dozen vampires just to give me a chance to escape and then she attacked one that nearly killed me and nearly got killed herself! And you sent her away?!" she shouted.

"Yes, she did, but she also poisoned me, split us up and nearly ruined the entire pack's future because of it!" My voice rose to match hers. I couldn't believe we were arguing over that woman.

"Logan, you can't blame her for doing what she thought she

needed to keep you and the pack safe. She wrote me a letter before I was taken. Explaining everything YOU failed to tell me." She pointed her finger at my chest.

"What? What letter?" I growled.

"She told me about the witch's premonitions and that you would die in battle if you chose to be with me," she choked out and I realised that she still didn't know the whole truth.

"Alina, the witch lied to Madeline for her own gain. The premonitions weren't true. Apparently, you are the key to all of this. You are who I am supposed to be with to win the war."

Her eyes widened in surprise. "Even more reason to forgive Madeline! She was manipulated and used by that witch! Hang on. Is that why you want to be with me now? Because you need to be with me to win the war?" She jumped out of the bed still naked, and the moonlight illuminated her golden skin, making her look like a Greek goddess. Albeit, an angry goddess.

"No, Alina! Of course not! You're not thinking straight. I wanted to be with you before I even knew the premonitions weren't true. I chose you, remember?" I tried to reason with her.

"Oh, lucky me!" she snapped, her voice laced with sarcasm as she paced the room. I sighed at my choice of words. So much for not fucking this up again.

"Alina, please. Come here." I softened my voice and pulled back the covers for her to return to bed.

She stopped pacing and glared at me, but I could see her face lighten slightly. She sulkily strolled back over and climbed in. I scooped her up into my lap so she was straddling me. I have to avoid allowing my gaze to travel down and staring at her sexy as fuck body otherwise I will get too excited.

Not the right time, Logan.

"Alina, please listen to me. From the moment I laid eyes on you at that party, my whole world shifted. You awakened a part of me I never even knew existed. You make me happy beyond belief and I am so grateful to the Moon Goddess for bringing you to me. For making you mine and me yours. I know this has been anything but easy and I know there will always be a risk in being together. But I would take every risk to be with you. You are my universe, and I would give it all up for you. If you don't want this life, if you don't want to be a Luna, fine. I don't care. I will lead my people into battle, but after, I will leave it all behind. As long as I have you." My heart pounded in my chest as I realised how truly vulnerable I have just made myself, but I needed her to know. I was serious.

She reached up and stroked the outline of my face with her small hand and I nestled into it, kissing her palm.

"I will take any risk to be with you. I love you, Logan." She smiled as a single tear slid down her cheek and I felt like my heart was about to burst with happiness.

I wiped away her tears with my thumb before I captured her lips in mine and wrapped one arm around her waist and the other in her hair. Our tongues entangled together and so many emotions flowed between us. I tried to pour all my love into our kiss, feeling every unspoken word. Her hips started to grind on top of me and I felt myself growing rock-hard. She drove me crazy. I swallowed her moans and they mix with my groans as she increased her speed, rubbing herself against my erection and I swear I could explode right there. I gripped her hips and lifted her so my tip was in line with her sweet centre and looked into her mesmerising eyes.

Goddess, I need her.

I glided her down onto me inch by inch until she was full of me and I felt her tight centre clenching around me.

"Fucckkk." I gritted out as she threw her head back, taking me in. She deliberately lifted herself up and down at that same painstakingly slow speed and gripped my shoulders as I completely filled her again. I leaned forward and kissed and sucked at her neck whilst she continued her sensual attack on my dick. There was no feeling better than this in the world. No feeling better than being inside her.

We both moaned into each other's mouths as I encouraged her to increase the speed by gripping her hips tightly. I could feel myself getting closer, but I didn't want this to end. I looked into her eyes, and I was shocked to see that they were completely golden. FUCK! I've never been so turned on. Her power radiated as she rode me, taking complete control, and I felt an overwhelming urge to mark her.

I allowed Elias to share control with me as she was doing with Xena, so the four of us could share this experience. Our movements became more vigorous and possessive from their influence.

She bent her head into my neck and started to kiss and suck my marking spot. My heart drilled in my chest as I did the same to her and felt her teeth graze my skin. I extended my own canines to show her I am ready and we both bit into the others neck, sending the most indescribable pleasure coursing through our bodies. We cried out into each other's necks as we barrelled over the edge and reached our own orgasms, seeing stars together. When the feeling slowly started to fade, I released her and licked the bitemark to help her heal quicker. She copied me and then we just gaze into each other's eyes as our bodies steadied.

I ran my thumb over her newly formed mark and smirked. "You are mine now."

She grinned back, glancing down at my own fresh mark she created. "And you are mine."

"Always."
"Always."

Chapter 57

Lucius' POV

"Where is my SON?!" I threw yet another crystal glass at my office wall. I had already tortured three of my warriors for information about Arius' whereabouts, but none seemed to know anything or they were extremely loyal to their friend. Since finding my only trusted liege in pieces in that basement and those two bitches gone, I have not been able to control my fury. This was not meant to happen. How did it happen? And now, my own son and his wretched mother were nowhere to be seen! If they played any part in this, they are both dead.

"W-we have warriors out searching for him, your majesty," the warrior stuttered, taking a few steps backwards as I reached for another glass and filled it up with liquor. My hands trembled as my emotions got the better of me and I knew I needed to calm down. If I could not get my anger under control, I would end up doing some irreversible damage. Luckily, even though vampires feel their emotions intensely, they can also turn them off. Like a flip of a switch. However, this gave control to the demon inside and the human part of our being is blocked out. Great in times of war, but not when you need to think clearly.

Suddenly, another warrior abruptly entered the room without knocking. Normally, I would have him whipped for such disrespect, but I overlooked it when I saw the urgency on his face. He bowed quickly before saying, "My king, your son has returned. He is in his bedroom, showering."

Showering? He disappeared for hours on end when we have lost our only leverage against the Alpha and returned to take a leisurely shower.

Rage boiled inside of me and I allowed my eyes to blaze as I flipped that switch. "Bring him to the dungeons immediately," I said with calm vindictiveness.

***

Arius walked coolly in front of two guards who have escorted him down to the dungeons. When he entered the filthy torture room, he showed no emotion. Once again, his face was blank like a robot. I will break his resolve today.

"Father," he greeted me coldly, meeting my burning red eyes. He lifted his chin slightly higher into the air to show me he was not afraid and broadened his shoulders.

Fool.

"Where have you been?" I asked icily. When he didn't answer, I took two steps towards him, and our noses were nearly touching. "I won't ask you twice," I growled.

He kept his gaze on mine and answered calmly, "I went for a run and a walk in the city. I am not a prisoner in this castle as far as I know, and I did not think it would be a problem."

I narrowed my eyes at him. I know he was lying but his face gave nothing away. "Where is Cora?" I tried a different angle.

Something flickered across his eyes and I knew that something had happened. Something he did not want to reveal.

"She has gone," he replied, keeping his voice neutral.

My eyes widened. "What do you mean… gone?"

"You were right, father. She wanted to leave and asked me to go with her. I refused and she was upset."

I turned and took a few steps back and forth. This was not good news. I thought we would have her here for longer. Something must have happened.

"What did you do? Why would she leave so soon?" I glared at Arius once more. His face creased slightly as I saw him struggle to remain calm. Good, I needed him to crack to get the truth.

"Nothing," he said.

Wrong answer.

I punched him brutally in the stomach and he crippled over from the force but stood back up right with no reaction.

"I will ask you again. Why did she leave?"

"Like I said, father, she wanted us both to leave. To get away from you, and I refused. She got upset and left." His eyes met mine and showed me that there was some truth to what he was saying, but I know there was more to the story.

"When was this?" I bit back.

He hesitated "Yesterday morning."

"WHAT?! And you are only just telling me this now?! Why?"

He didn't answer, which made the demon in me want to rip out his tongue, so he is never able to speak again. "ANSWER ME, BOY!" My fangs elongated in anger.

"I don't know," he said quietly, and put his hands behind his back as if he was preparing himself for the next physical blow.

I froze. If Cora left yesterday morning and Alina escaped last night, that could not be a coincidence. There were wolves' scents all over the dead bodies of my warriors. They would not have been able to find her location without Logan's memories returning or… Cora's help.

"DO YOU HAVE ANY IDEA WHAT YOU HAVE DONE?!" I screamed at him.

His eyes widened slightly in shock at my outburst, and I saw a look of confusion register on his face.

"BECAUSE OF YOU AND YOUR INABILITY TO KEEP CORA HERE, SHE HAS HELPED THE WEREWOLVES. SHE HAS GONE AGAINST US."

His distinctive eyes looked lost and he shook his head in disbelief. "No… no she wouldn't." he stammered.

"You fool! Of course, she would. You were the only thing keeping her here and helping us and you let her go! And now Alina has escaped, and BAYLOR IS DEAD!"

His mouth dropped open as he realised what had happened and it made me even more furious. But torturing him seemed to have no impact. He doesn't learn and kept failing me. He clearly no longer cared for himself, but I am sure he cared for his friends.

"BRING THEM IN!" I roared at the guard at the door, and he nodded and opens the steel door. Two of Arius' closest warrior buddies were dragged in, chained up with blood dripping down their faces from the beatings my guards had already given them. Arius' eyes widened as he turned to see them.

Growing up, Arius was kept very isolated from others, but I did allow him to make a few friends with some of the villagers' children when he was a child. These two were his closest friends and he had gotten them into the warrior training programme many years ago. I always told him it was a weakness to care about others. He was about to learn that the hard way.

"Father! What is this?" he shouted as the guards dragged the men over to the far side of the room and lay them each on a torture bed, shackling their arms and legs to the frame.

"This, Arius, is your punishment," I said with a smirk as his face was crippled with fear and anger for his friends.

"Father, please. I am the one who you should punish. This is my fault. Give me the punishment," he pleaded.

The two men groaned and pulled against their restraints as they realised what was about to happen.

"Oh, my dear son, I have tried that many times, but it seems you just never learn. So, I am trying a new approach." I smiled heartlessly. I walked over to the wall that held all my various torture mechanisms and picked off the wooden spear, one of Arius' favourites. I strolled towards him and placed it in his hand as he looked at me, baffled. I smirked as he suddenly realised that I expected him to perform the torture.

Shaking his head, he said sternly, "No. I will not do it."

Just as I thought. At least it gave me an excuse to cause him some more physical pain. I snatched the spear and rammed it into his shoulder and he fell to his knees as the wood sizzled against his skin. I dug it in a little harder, so it started to pierce his skin and he hissed at the pain. I quickly removed it and placed it back in his hand as he glared up at me from the floor.

"No," he repeated and dropped the spear.

So be it. I nodded to the guards who swiftly gripped either side of his arms and pulled him back against the wall, fastening his neck in a choker to keep him from interfering.

"Looks like I will have to do it myself. Shame. I was giving you the opportunity to go easy on them but now they have me." I chuckled, picking up the wooden spike and walking towards the men.

"FATHER!" I heard Arius bellowed behind me, but I focused on the brown-haired man lying pathetically next to me. I think his name is Ren. I lifted the spear and stabbed it into his thigh. The ear-splitting scream resounded around the room and intensified as I twisted the spear in his leg and left it there, melting his flesh.

"FATHER. STOP. THIS. NOW!" Arius screamed.

I picked off a silver knife next and walked over to his other friend who was bulky and known to be a good warrior. I didn't want to kill this one as he would be useful in the war, so I choose wisely what I could afford to lose. I held his hand still and rapidly chopped off his little finger and blood squirted in all directions. I threw the finger to Arius' feet and laughed as the man cried out for mercy.

Arius' tall and muscular body was uncontrollably shaking with anger and his breathing was in pants.

"What shall we go for next, Arius? The whip or wooden pellets?" I asked calmly.

"Fuck you!" he gritted through his teeth.

"Now, now. That is no way to speak to your father. I was only trying to give you a choice." I smirked. "Wooden pellets, I think."

I picked up the bag of small wooden spikes and the hammer. I placed one on the bare chest of Ren and hammered it into his flesh. The man thrashed on the table like a fish out of water. I went to take another one from the bag, enjoying myself so much.

"Er··· Your majesty··· I think..."

I turned my head to the guard who was interrupting me, only to see Arius levitating off the ground, eyes glowing purple like his mother and power radiating from his body. Both guards have stepped back in alarm and the choke around his neck was the only thing keeping him from rising higher. His face was so full of hatred and madness, even my demon felt fear.

He suddenly lifted his hands and a powerful surge rush through the air and hit me in the chest, knocking me back against the wall. It felt like my heart was restricted as I tried to breathe in gulps of air. Before I could get my bearings, a bright light shone in front of me and I was momentarily blinded. I blinked rapidly and my heart pounded as I looked around my old castle. I was back in my home I shared with Celeste all those years ago. I was standing in the foyer and screams and cries of pain and suffering could be heard outside the iron castle door.

I looked up and saw Celeste as clear as day smiling at me with evil in her eyes.

"No mercy," she whispered and started to walk away with the guards behind her towards the safe room.

I screamed after her to stop, knowing her fate, but my screams were silent. I couldn't go to her. A force pushed me out into the barbaric fighting, and I found myself attacking and defending as I make my way through the swarm of wolves and my people fighting callously. After a few minutes, I paused and looked up at the balcony.

Tears stung in my eyes knowing what I was about to witness and not being able to do anything about it. Celeste stood on the ledge of the stone barrier with Alpha Alec behind her with a knife to her throat. His eyes locked with mine and he grinned heartlessly.

I looked at Celeste and she had tears rolling down her cheeks as she started her chants and air whipped around them. She was going to sacrifice herself. He realised what she was doing and stabbed her through the heart, but it was too late. I watch helplessly as her body falls from a great height and hits the floor. Alpha Alec was clutching his chest as blood spread across his top and the look of pure horror reflected on his face as he fell after her.

I screamed.

The blinding light returned and then I fell forward onto the floor, clutching my chest as my heart pummelled. I looked up in complete shock to see Arius standing above me, no longer glowing. His face was hard, and he glared down at me like I was nothing.

I looked around and saw that the two men and the guards were no longer in the room. Realisation dawns on me that Arius had just used dark magic against me to save his friends. I clumsily stumbled to my feet, legs still feeling shaky, and gave him my most dazzling smile. His eyebrows creased in confusion.

"Looks like we won't be needing Cora after all," I said with a smirk and patting him on the shoulder.

Chapter 58

Alina's POV

Logan, Chloe, Darius, and I were all crammed into Chloe's little one-bedroom flat trying to go through our belongings and what to take with us to America. Once I told Chloe I was leaving and so soon, her little face had crumbled completely, and I found myself asking if she wanted to come with us. I guessed as a soon to be Luna, I could make those kinds of decisions without consulting Logan, but I was still nervous to tell him that she was coming. I shouldn't have been because he thought it was a great idea, seeing that she needed to do a Blood Oath and would be left unguarded here. Darius was not so thrilled.

"Please try and remember that you only have two suitcases for whatever you are bringing. We can get the rest shipped out later," his bored tone warned Chloe as she ran frantically around the flat grabbing pretty much everything in sight that she 'couldn't live without'. She rolled her eyes and picked up her blender from the kitchen top. "Er… no! You cannot take that! Necessities!" he yelled.

"This is a necessity! I have to have my morning smoothie every day!" she shouted back trying to wedge it into the already overflowing suitcase.

"We have blenders in the US, you know! We can buy one there! Necessities means clothes, toiletries, personal items. That's it!"

"Oh, shut up and come and sit on top of my suitcase so I can zip it up!"

"You are kidding, right? Just take the bloody blender out!" He threw his hands in the air as if he was talking to a brick wall.

I walked down the hallway into Chloe's room where Logan was neatly folding most of my clothes and putting them into my own suitcase.

He looked up at me with a grin. "How long do we have before they murder each other?" he asked.

"Umm, probably about five minutes if we are lucky." I giggled as he abandoned the packing and turned to wrap his arms around my waist and started nuzzling my neck.

"Mmm, that's plenty of time," he whispered seductively into my skin. We have not been able to keep our hands off each other in the last twenty-four hours and it had caused Darius to become very frustrated at the fact that we are getting nothing done and were no closer to getting back to America.

I smiled at his affection but tried to pull back so I could look him in the face. "Logan, as much as I would love to take you up on that offer, we really do need to pack! Our flight is in a few hours and so far, I am taking…" I looked over at my suitcase and what he had managed to get back.

"A pair of shorts, a toothbrush, a few tops and… ah lots of sexy lingerie." He smirked.

"Sounds perfect."

He chuckled as I swat his arm and walk over to the drawer Chloe let me use for my clothes.

The Last Alpha

"You know, once we get home, we can go shopping and you can buy a whole new wardrobe of clothes and anything else you might need. So just take things that you really want," he said simply as he fell onto the single bed that looked ridiculous under his huge body.

I eyed him carefully as I started to fold the rest of my stuff and pack. "Is there something you want to tell me? Like how you suddenly seem to have so much money?"

He smiled and my core tightened at the youthful and cheeky look he gave me. Why was he so bloody gorgeous?

"I don't know what you mean," he said coyly.

I rolled my eyes. "First, the posh hotel. Then the flights to America. Now the 'we can buy you a whole new wardrobe and anything you need'."

"What makes you think I haven't always been rich?" he asked with a twinkle in his eye. He was enjoying this.

"Because you lived in a lovely but small two-bed flat in East London that you rented and you worked in a gym," I said, stating the facts.

"I own the gym," he corrected me.

I rolled my eyes again. "And how do you come to own a gym at the young age of…" I suddenly realised I didn't know how old he was when he first came to London.

"Twenty-one." He smirked.

My eyes bulged from my head. Right.

He sat up on the bed and looked at me a little more seriously and took one of my hands. "My father was the Alpha of the biggest pack in America. Perhaps the world. With that, he had a lot of business that kept the pack running as well as the savings passed down to him from the previous Alphas. When he died, I inherited it all. And once you are my Luna, it will all be yours, too."

I gulped audibly. I did not see that coming.

He smiled at my stunned reaction. "So, like I said, pack light and we will buy you everything you need when we get home."

Home. I noticed that was the second time he had called it that. It was strange, knowing I had never been to this place, but it felt right. I hadn't felt like I'd had a home for a long time and no matter where this place was or what it was like, I knew I would love it.

I stopped and looked around the room. If that was the case, a lot of my stuff could be replaced, and it would be nice to start afresh. There was only one thing I needed to bring. I kneeled and reached under Chloe's bed and Logan leaned over to see what I was doing.

I pulled out my mother's old jewellery box and sit it on my lap as Logan's eyes scanned the box with interest and he raised an eyebrow at me.

"This was my mothers. I loved it as a child and she gave it to me on my sixteenth birthday. I keep all of my precious memories and items in it." I ran my hand over the worn leather lid and smiled. Logan and I hadn't really talked much about the elephant in the room. How was I a wolf? I had come to terms with the possibility that I was probably adopted.

"Can I?" he asked gently, reaching his hand out for the box.

My smile widened at his interest in my childhood and I was more than excited to share my happy memories with him. I climbed up onto his lap and opened the box.

I pulled out an old newspaper clipping of me dressed as an Egyptian for a school carnival when I was about ten years old. He snatched it out of my hand to take a closer look at the black and white photo.

"Look at you! You are adorable!" he gushed and I blushed a little. I think I look terrible in my homemade costume and terrible black wig but he clearly saw something I don't.

Next, I pulled out the note my dad wrote to my mum and handed it to him. I was interested in seeing what he thought and whether, as a werewolf, this would hold any meaning. He read it carefully and I saw his face soften.

"What's this?" he asked.

"It's a note from my dad to my mum. I found it amongst her things when I had to sort out our house after she passed. What do you think it means?"

He read it again and I could see he was intrigued by it. "I'm not sure. I mean it's clearly a love note, but the phrasing 'my full moon'…"

"Is that something a wolf would say?" My eyes lit up with hope and he gazed into them and smiled.

"Maybe," he said kindly.

I took it from his hand and read it again myself. I felt his body tense under me and looked up to see him holding the tiny, silver key that I still have no idea what was for.

"Whose is this?" he asked and his voice sounded strange.

"I don't know. I found it under some corner of a jewellery box fabric recently. I don't know if it had always been there or if someone had put it there. Why? What's wrong?"

He lifted it closer to his face and froze when he saw the moon crest on the handle. "This… This here…" He pointed at the symbol and looked into my eyes. "This is the crest of my pack. The Blood Moon Pack…"

Chapter 59

Logan's POV

I twiddled with the miniature key with our pack crest on my fingers as Alina's head rested on my shoulder. We were speeding through the familiar, diverse landscape of Oregon. My home. The broad deep-green swath and lush farmlands sweep past my window in the cab and I inhaled, feeling a mix of emotions at being back.

As we drove away from the rugged Pacific coastline and towards the West, I started to see the faraway alpine mountains in the distance and the roads were nestled with thick, old growth of fir trees. Don't get me wrong, I loved living in London. The impressive and futuristic lifestyle was exciting, but nothing could beat the true beauty of the sheer wilderness that Oregon had to offer. I was disappointed that Alina was not awake to take it all in but the jet lag had knocked her and she needed to rest. I reminded myself that I had forever to explore these lands with her.

I smiled at the thought.

I glanced back down at the little key again. What was this? And how did it come to be in Alina's possession? I was convinced it was from my pack. The crest was identical to the ones we used to use to seal important documents with wax. I used to enjoy drawing it as a boy, sitting in my father's study whilst he worked. I hadn't pushed Alina to talk about her past or how it was that she was a wolf as I knew she had a lot to come to terms with so quickly, but this just raised more questions.

After we discussed the key, she showed me a picture of her mother and father and five-year-old Alina in their arms. They all looked so happy. I felt as though I had seen her father before but had no idea where or how. He looked familiar and his stocky and broad build was one you would link to a werewolf. Her mother was beautiful and looked just like Alina, but I didn't recognise her at all.

I needed to get answers. I knew it would mean a lot to Alina to find out about her history and who her parents really were, but it was also important for the pack. If her family had some connections with our pack, they would need to know. I need to know.

After what felt like hours, we finally started to drive up the steep, beaten roads towards the mountains and the serenity of lakes upon lakes came into view. We were nearly home.

I shook Alina awake gently and she rubbed her sleepy eyes and looked around dazed. "We are nearly here. I didn't want you to miss the first moment you see your new home," I said with a smile, but I could feel my nerves mounting.

I really hope she liked it. I was also unsure as to what to expect myself. I haven't been back here for nine years. I sent some of my most trusted wolves here a year ago to tidy the place up a bit and create a burial ground for the ones that were killed all those years ago. Even though many of the bodies had been burnt by the vampires, some bones were still found and we felt it was only right to honour those who had died even if we no longer had their bodies. I also paid for the work to begin on the new pack house. I didn't want to demolish the old one, but I also knew I could not live there after the horrors that happened. I wanted the pack to have a fresh start. I plan to turn it into a pack hospital and home for any orphaned or injured wolves.

Alina's vibrant eyes scanned the scenery and her mouth gaped open. "It's stunning!" She breathed and climbed over me to get a better look out the window. I chuckled as she looked like an excited child and wrapped my arms around her, kissing her shoulder. We stayed in silence as we both took it all in.

The car started to slow as it reached the pack territory and became dense with the evergreen forest that sat at the bottom of the mountain. The driver halted and nodded at me in the rear-view mirror. This was where I told him to stop.

Alina turned to look at me, confused.

"Out we get," I said, opening the door handle and lifting her to her feet. She spun around but all she could see was the breath-taking landscape of lakes, forest, and the road we just drove up.

"We are here?" she asked, puzzled. I walked over to the boot and got our suitcases out the back before paying for the cab and he started to reverse back down the road, leaving us alone. I walked over to her and held her hand, leading her towards the forest.

"What about our suitcases?" she asked.

"I have mind linked Darius. His car will pick them up in a few minutes." I stopped abruptly as we stood across the invisible territory line and turned to face her. "You are now standing in your new territory."

She looked down at the floor and then back up to me with a beaming smile and my heart expanded.

"I thought, if you wanted to, we could make this a moment to remember and run through our lands together. In wolf form," I said carefully. I wasn't sure how she would feel about shifting again but her smile told me she was more than happy.

"Really? As Xena and Elias?" she asked, clapping her hands.

Elias purred in my head at the thought of running with Xena in their new home as Alpha and Luna. "Yes. If you are okay with shifting again?"

She nodded. "Is there a way to make it hurt less?"

I smiled and stroke her face. "Each time you shift, it will hurt less and less and will soon just feel like second nature."

"Okay. How do I··· um··· start it?" Of course, she shifted because of the full moon and impending danger last time. This would be different.

I pull my shirt off over my head and started undoing my jeans. She took off her jumper and her leggings and stood before me in her underwear. I wriggle out of my boxers with a mischievous grin and watched as she blushed slightly at the sight of me. Still so innocent. She took her underwear off as well and I flushed her body against mine as the mild, cool air blew around us.

"When you feel Xena coming to the surface and asking for control, just relax and let her take over. The more you fight it, the longer and more painful the change is."

She nodded and I gave her a brief kiss on the lips before I took a step back and shifted effortlessly into Elias. I mounted over her tiny frame and she smiled as she reached her hand up to stroke my side. Elias purred and nudged his head into her, eager to meet his mate properly.

She giggled. "Alright. mister!"

She stepped back and closed her eyes, focusing on Xena. After a few seconds, she cried out in pain and fell to her knees. My heart pounded at seeing her suffering but I know she could do this. Her bones cracked and grew as her white fur sprouted all over her body. Within seconds, she was standing nearly as tall as me in wolf form.

She took my breath away as a human, but my goddess, she was some wolf!

Her golden eyes locked with Elias' deep sapphires and she elegantly strolled towards us and brushed her head against Elias' neck affectionately. I could feel his emotions and how much he loved her and wanted to protect her.

'You are incredible,' I said to Alina in mind link.

'We can mind link?' Her surprised voice echoed in my mind.

'Since we marked each other, you became part of the pack, so now you can mind link any wolf in the pack,' I explained.

'And you're only just telling me this?!' She acted annoyed, but I could hear in her voice that she was smiling.

'Ready for our first run?' I asked.

'You mean, are you ready?' She smirked and Xena bolted off into the forest at a ridiculous speed.

'Oh, you are on!' I growled, sprinting after her.

***

Fucking hell, she was fast!

Elias could just about keep up with her, but it was definitely the fastest he had ever had to run. Xena enjoyed taunting him by slowing down enough to let him think he was about to catch her before sprinting off again. By the time, we were getting close to the pack house, Elias was becoming aggravated and impatient and so was I. We decided to play dirty. Darting in a different direction, we hid behind a large bush and spied on Xena as she stopped, realising we had disappeared.

'Logan?' Alina mind linked me. Xena spun around in a circle, trying to sense us and sniffed the air. She started stalking towards the

bush and our excitement grew. Once she was about two metres away, Elias leapt over the bush and tackled her to the floor, pinning her down. She growled fiercely until she realised it was us and Elias bent down and licked her face. She purred and wriggled teasingly beneath him, which made us more than horny. He pushed her to the floor harder and she nipped his neck flirtatiously. That was it!

'Shift!' I growled in mind link and felt her body start to change. I quickly took control and shifted back to my human form, picking a naked Alina up from the floor and slammed her possessively against a tree. She cried out at the impact, but I quickly covered her mouth with mine and thrust inside her before she knew what was happening.

"Ah, Logan! Yes!" she cried as I started pounding into her relentlessly, Elias still present, wanting to take out his sexual frustration. too. Her fingernails extended and she pierced the skin on my back as she dragged them across it, making me growl out as the pain mixed with pleasure. This was wild, rampant, animalistic sex and I loved every minute of it.

"MINE!" I growled as I increased the speed even more and started hitting that spot that made her scream my name over and over. Her body started to spasm as she reached her orgasm and I felt mine coming too. I held her to me firmly as I thrust inside her one last time and cried out her name.

I kissed her with so much passion as we tried to regulate our breathing and when I pulled away, she was grinning like a Cheshire cat.

"Well, that was unexpected," she cooed.

"That was for running away from me." My voice was still deeper than usual, with Elias reluctant to retreat to my mind.

Suddenly, her eyes glowed golden and when she spoke, I knew it was Xena from her majestic voice. "You need to get faster then, Alpha." She smirked.

"Next time you run from me, I will be the one to fuck you. Not Logan," Elias' voice vibrated with arousal.

"Promise." She enticed him. Fuck.

I was still inside her and my dick is hardened again, so I smashed my lips to hers and started fucking her senseless once again. Like I said before, I couldn't get enough.

When we have finally had our fill of each other, we walked hand in hand towards the clearing ahead. I stopped when I saw the clothes folded neatly by a tree, thanks to Fredrik. I walked over and handed Alina her clothes and started to put my own on. Once we were both dressed, I took her hand once more and took a deep breath.

"You seem nervous," she said, looking up at me through her long, dark lashes.

"I am," I replied honestly. "I haven't been back here since I lost everything, and I am worried about what memories it's going to bring back. I also really want you to like it here and feel like it is your home. So yes, I am nervous."

She smiled and squeezed my hand supportively. "I already love it here and wherever you are is my home."

I returned her smile and looked towards the old, abandoned pack house I could see in the distance.

"Then let's go home."

Chapter 60

Alina's POV

I was blown away. This place was incredible. Not only was it picturesque and full of so much natural beauty, but it was also enormous. The forest that Logan and I just ran through must be at least a hundred acres and then the buildings in the little town were modern and impressive. Logan had clearly spared no expense in the architecture and rebuilding.

The new pack house was at least four storeys high, modern with a large glass panel running up the height of the building in the middle. It gave it an open feel and I couldn't wait to get inside and see it. He had also instructed the building of around eighty houses on the territory for wolves to live in luxury. But the building that really drew me in was the old pack house. It looked slightly out of place amongst the new contemporary buildings, but it still held its own elegance. It was clearly worn and battered by the climate and no one had taken care of it for the last nine years, but I felt a connection to it. I wanted to go inside but I was trying to be mindful of how all of this would feel for Logan.

He was still gripping my hand as he talked to some of the wolves who had been here for the last week getting things ready. He was clearly pleased with what had been done and I could see his shoulders have relaxed slightly.

"The pack house is nearly finished. Yours and Luna's room is ready, and we are just furnishing the other rooms in the house now," Fredrik informed Logan with a broad smile. He looked like a completely different person to the man I met that first night at the party. He looked happy and carefree, and I no longer find him intimidating. I guess finding your mate could really change you.

"Excellent. Thank you, Fredrik. You have done a great job here. Everything looks exactly how I wanted it." Logan patted Fredrik's shoulder in praise and I could swear the man blushed. "Have you picked a room out for you and Sloane yet?"

"No. We have been staying in one of the houses that's made up ready as we weren't sure where to go," he said, shuffling his feet.

Logan sighed. "Fredrik, as my Beta, it is required that you and Sloane stay in the pack house. But if you prefer to have—"

"No. We would be honoured to stay in the pack house." Fredrik's eyes lit up and I saw how much this meant to him. It was very sweet coming from such a butch and masculine man.

"Then go and move your things onto the second floor. You have the entire floor." Logan grinned and Fredrick looked like he was about to faint.

"Thank you, Alpha," he said and ran towards the brown-haired girl who was busy helping load the trucks with rubble. He picked her up, startling her completely and spun her around before walking towards the pack house.

"Well, you just made someone's day," I said with a smile. "So where do we stay?"

"The top floor of the new pack house is all ours." He

grinned.

"And what about the old pack house?" I asked carefully.

He looked over towards it for the first time and I saw sorrow in his eyes. This was hard for him. "I'm not sure yet. I think we should turn it into a hospital or something. What do you think?" He looked down at me and I was a little taken aback that he was asking my opinion.

"Um, I don't know. Can we go and have a look at it? Only if you are ready," I asked, not wanting to push him into it too soon.

He looked up at it again and for a minute I thought he was about to refuse. "Okay. I suppose it is better to get it out of the way now than when everyone starts arriving," he said seriously.

I wrapped both my arms around his bicep as we started to walk towards the mansion. We stepped up onto the veranda and paused at the front door. It was hanging on by its hinges and the white paint was chipped and crumbling. There were faint red, brownish marks all over it where someone had tried hard to scrub away the blood stains but had failed. Logan tensed and closed his eyes.

"We can do this. Together," I said confidently, and he opened his eyes and nodded once before pushing open the door.

We stepped into a large lobby area that had an impressive staircase in the middle leading up to an array of floors that spiralled as you looked up. All the furniture were still they were, and it gave off an almost eerie vibe to the lives that once lived here. I took a sideways glance up at Logan as his eyes scanned his surroundings and I could hear his heart drumming in his chest.

"Are you okay?" I asked quietly.

"Yes. It's just… strange. Being back here," he said calmly, but his voice was thick with emotion.

We carried on walking through each of the expansive rooms on the ground floor quietly. Every now and again, Logan reached out and touched something or brushed the dust off an item. When we got to an upturned rug that was once concealing a trap door, he froze, staring at it. The vacant look on his face showed me that he was having a flashback of some kind and I stood silently next to him, never letting go of his hand.

"This is how we escaped," he said after the longest time. "The warning alarms were going off all around the territory and my parents had gathered as many younger wolves as they could into the pack house. My father told me to start sending them through the trap door that leads underground through the mountains and out into a stream. I did as he said and once most of them were gone, the fighting was at our door. He pushed Madeline and Darius down and then turned to me. I wanted to stay. I wanted to fight," he said weakly and his eyes were watery. He suddenly sniffed and his voice changed to one of strength. "I wasn't given a choice. But now, I have one. I will fight this time and I will end Lucius."

My heart beat rapidly at the thought of the battle. The scared human part of me wanted to beg him not to fight, to not go ahead with this battle, but I know that was not an option. I needed to be strong. For him and for our pack.

"Yes, you will."

He leaned over and kissed me on the lips gently. "Thank you. Let me show you upstairs."

We spent an hour or so looking around and discussing what we might do with the place. I agreed it wouldn't feel right to knock it down when it held so much history and so many memories, even painful ones. But it also didn't feel right to turn it into a hospital. To make it a sterile and cold environment.

We reached one door on the top floor, which Logan explained was his family's floor. "This was my father's office. I spent a lot of time here as a child."

I raised my eyebrows at him. "That sounds fun."

He chuckled. "As the next Alpha in line, it was my duty to learn from a young age. It wasn't always a barrel of laughs but we made the best of it." He clearly thought very fondly of his father. I wish I could have met him.

We strolled into the office, and everything has been untouched since that day. There was even an opened liquor bottle and abandoned glass on the grand, mahogany desk. Logan walked over to it and lifted it with a small smile. I casually meandered around the room looking at the collection of books in the bookcase and the photos on the shelves. There was one of a young Logan with his parents and another of Logan as a baby in his mother's arms. I wanted to cry at how beautiful it was, but I pulled myself together.

I got to the end of the wall where a large landscape photograph was hung. It had maybe two hundred people in it, all staring at the camera with wide grins. I spotted Logan's parents near the front and his mother was heavily pregnant, obviously with Logan, as he had no siblings. But that was not what caught my eye. The man who stood tall and regally next to his dad had piercing green eyes and white shoulder-length hair. He looked important. And then I looked to his side and gasped.

"What?" Logan came to my side and looked up at the photograph. "What is it?"

I lift a shaky finger and pointed to the young man next to the leader. There is no denying it, it was a younger, more attractive version of my dad.

"Is that…" Logan's voice trails away.

"My dad," I said in a whisper.

Logan pulled his phone from his pocket and called someone, but I completely zoned out and didn't hear his conversation as I continue to stare at the image.

"Fredrik is on his way. He is a few years older than me and is in this picture too. He might know something," Logan said, hugging me from behind and pointing at a small boy at the side of the crowd. After a few minutes, Fredrik and his mate Sloane barged into the room.

"Fredrik, do you remember who this man is?" Logan asked, pointing at my dad in the photograph.

He walked closer and stared at it intensely before nodding. "Yes. That was Alpha Alec's son, Clarke," he stated, not realising the implication of his words.

Son?

"Son? What do you mean? I didn't think Alec had a son?" Logan asked, baffled, and I was glad he was able to talk as I stood in shock.

"You were born not long after this picture, so I expect by the time you were old enough for the stories to be shared with you, Clarke was gone." Fredrik tried to explain but he was not making any sense.

"Sorry for asking, but why is this important?"

"Fredrik, that man Clarke? He is Alina's father."

Fredrik's head snapped at me and it was clear that he couldn't quite believe it himself.

"Can you please explain to us what happened? Why didn't I know about him?" Logan's urgency for answers was evident.

"Why don't you both take a seat and I will tell you what I know."

Logan and I sat in the chairs opposite the desk, not even caring about the amount of dust residing on them and he reached for my hand as Fredrik began.

The Last Alpha

"Alpha Alec had a son with a woman who was not his mate. He would not take her as his in the hopes that he would find his true mate, but he still wanted his son. Clarke grew up here on the estate. Alec was a great Alpha to his people, from what I have been told, but he was not an emotional man. He did not give his son much attention or love, but instead tried to train him to be the next Alpha in line. Clarke was well liked by the people and a lot of the older women cared for him and gave him the parental love he craved growing up, so he never became hard-hearted like his father. When this picture was taken, Alpha Alec had just declared war against the vampires and King Lucius. Little did he know that his own son had found his true mate and she was human."

He stopped to let all of this information sink in, but my mind was spinning and I felt like I was listening to a story that was completely unrelated to me. How could this be my father? Next in line to be Alpha? My grandfather was Alpha Alec.

"When Alpha Alec found out that Clarke's mate was human, he wanted him to reject her, believing a human mate could not be Luna. Clarke refused and Alec banished him from the territory. No one heard from him again and Alec signed the next Alpha role to your father, Logan."

Silence filled the room. No one knew what to say. I suddenly became terrified that Logan would hate me. That I was a descendent from Alpha Alec and would have been in line for his role if my grandfather had accepted my mother. I turned to look at Logan with tears in my eyes.

"I'm sorry," I said quietly.

His eyes widened at my distress. "What are you sorry for?"

"That… that I am related to Alpha Alec. That…"

"Shhh. Don't be silly. Alina, I don't care who you are related to or what it means. You are my mate and I feel blessed to be mated to another Alpha." He smirked as he said Alpha as I realised that was what I was.

I nodded as he wiped away my tears and I felt stupid crying in front of Fredrik and Sloane. Sloane walked over and passed me a tissue with a smile. I haven't had the chance to speak to her yet, but I could tell she was a sweet girl and we were going to get along.

"I hope you don't mind me asking, Alina, but is your wolf white?" Fredrik asked.

I nodded my head slowly and he rubbed the back of his head with his hand and smiled.

"You know what this means, don't you?" he said, looking at Logan.

Logan grinned back.

"What? What does it mean?" I asked curiously.

"Alabaster wolves, which is what you are, Alina, have a special gift. When they have mated and marked with their true mate, they can share their power and strength with them, causing both wolves to become the most powerful breed of wolf alive. As long as you are together, you can fight better, run faster, have immense strength, more so than any other wolf."

I turned to Logan. "So that is why we have a better chance at defeating Lucius?" The pieces of the puzzle were all slotting together.

"Yes. I knew you were an Alabaster wolf as soon as I saw Xena, but I had no idea you would be related to a previous Alpha of my own pack!" He seemed happy about this revelation, but I was still uncertain.

"So, my dad must have changed his name and made his last

name Clarke instead? I knew him as Richard Clarke. But one thing doesn't make any sense about all of this. If he was mated with my mum, knowing how strong the bond is, how could he just get up and leave her one day? And why did they spell my wolf to not emerge."

No one had an answer.

"I don't know, Alina." Logan broke the silence. "But we will try and get to the bottom of it. I promise."

I took another glance over at the picture of my dad. Did I ever really know him at all?

Chapter 61

Alina's POV

It had been three days since Logan and I arrived and every day, I find more to love about this place than before. From the idyllic scenery to the new arrivals that kept flooding into our territory. I would never tire of seeing the look of awe and hope on their faces when I give them a tour of their new home. I have never felt so much pride and optimism for our futures.

I kept catching Logan staring at me with a strange look on his face as if he couldn't really believe this was all happening. That we were here.

"Luna, two new wolves have arrived at the border. They have a young child with them also. Which house shall I put them in?" Sloane skipped into the new pack house kitchen as I was stocking the fridge.

A huge grin spread across my face as I turned around and saw her digging into the bag of grapes on the table. Sloane and I hit it off immediately. She was headstrong and independent but with a big heart and we had a lot in common.

"I will come and meet them now. And please, give up with the Luna thing. It's weird." I chuckled. I was starting to get used to some of the pack calling me Luna, but it felt very strange when it came to people I thought of as my friends.

"Sorry, no can do. You are my Luna and so that is what I shall call you." She winked and popped another grape into her mouth.

I rolled my eyes but smiled.

"Oh, and Alpha Logan asked me to take you shopping later, so let me know when you are ready to leave." She smirked mischievously as I gestured to all of the food I was currently putting away.

"But I have just been shopping," I started.

"Clothes shopping!" She had a twinkle in her eyes, clearly very much looking forward to dragging me around the designer shops that she would no doubt be well acquainted with. Chloe and Sloane had quite an eye for fashion and had bonded well over their shared love for the latest trends. Although Sloane's taste was more edgy and darker than Chloe's, they seem to have become firm friends, too. "Chloe is coming as well."

"Of course, she wouldn't give up the chance to buy new clothes! Okay, well, I was hoping to head back to the training grounds later," I said disappointed.

The last few days, Logan, Fredrik, and I had been spending most of our time training with any willing and able wolves to prepare for the battle. Even though I lack the experience of the men, Xena seemed to be a natural leader and fighter and, as I can share control with her in my human form, I have taken the lead in training the female wolves.

"We can still go! Go deal with the newbies and I will meet you on the grounds after. Then we will do a bit of retail therapy! The perfect day!" Sloane jumped down from the bar stool with a grin.

"Okay. Thanks, Sloane!" I said, walking towards the main entrance of the pack house.

The Last Alpha

I still couldn't quite believe that this was my home now. Sometimes, I had to pinch myself just to check I wasn't dreaming. It just all felt too good to be true. Logan. America. The pack. This house.

But then, the reality of the situation always hit me soon after. We were about to go to war. With the vampires. And only one of us will survive. Them or us.

I shook my head at the thought and plastered a warm smile on my face as I saw two wide-eyed people walking towards me behind Fredrik. The woman looked in complete shock as she glanced up at the huge pack house and carried a young boy in her arms. The man, I recognised. He had been at the meeting in Ruislip Woods, the first stranger to commit his loyalty to Logan.

"Hello! My name is Alina. Welcome to the Blood Moon Pack. You must be exhausted, so I will take you straight to your house so you can settle in and then we will give you a tour of the territory when you are ready," I said, holding my hand out to the man.

"Thank you, Luna. That would be wonderful. This place is···" He released my hand and looked around again. "Quite special."

"Yes, it is. And we are so pleased and grateful for you choosing to join us here," I said and held my hand out to the timid woman.

Her eyes darted from mine to my hand and back to my eyes before she quickly shook it and curtsied!

"My Luna, we are the ones who are grateful. You have saved our lives," she said weakly and I noticed a tremble in her voice. Was she scared of me?

I placed my other hand over the top of hers to force her to look up from the floor. "Please, call me Alina. You deserve this just as much as every other wolf. You are home now."

Her eyes clouded over with unshed tears and she gave a small smile.

"And who do we have here?" I said, looking down at the three-year-old boy cuddled into his mother's chest.

"Oh, my goddess, I am so sorry we have not introduced ourselves. My name is Rohan, and this is my mate, Fiona, and our son, Nico."

I smiled at them all and looked down at the boy. "Tell me, Nico, do you like swimming?" I asked and the little boy's eyes lit up as he nodded his head enthusiastically.

"I thought you might. Please follow me and I will take you to your new home."

I started walking towards the more elite houses on the estate that were fitted with small swimming pools in the back gardens. They were meant to be saved for wolves of a higher rank, but there was something about this family that pulled at my heartstrings. They had been through tough times; it was clear from their modest clothing and very little belongings they had with them. It was time to change their luck.

I pulled out my ring of keys and took one off and handed it to Rohan as his mouth gaped open when he saw where we had stopped outside.

"Here we are. Enjoy." I grinned.

"But··· Luna... we can't... We don't see—" he started, stumbling over his words as Fiona's hand went to her mouth and silent tears ran down her cheeks.

"Nonsense. Rohan, you were the first man to stand up and declare your loyalty to Logan at the meeting. That is not something I will ever forget. You and your family deserve to be happy here and start a new life. I am sure Logan will want to find a place for you to be in his inner circle amongst the warriors."

He gulped as tears welled in his eyes also, but he stood taller and bowed his head. "Thank you, Luna."

I started to walk away to leave them, but I turned quickly and said, "If you both would like to attend training, the sessions start in half an hour and will last all day, but there is no expectation. Please take your time to get settled into your new home. And, Nico?" The boy looked up at me with a smile. "Go and jump in your new swimming pool!"

The little boy squealed and wriggled out of his mother's arms, running up to me and hugging my legs. "Thank you, Luna lady," he said with a slight lisp. Adorable.

I ruffled his hair as he ran back to his mum excitedly. I took a minute to watch the little family from a distance as they hugged each other and screamed with pure happiness. Being a Luna to this pack was the most rewarding thing in the world.

Logan's POV

I leaned on a tree in front of the old pack house. I still did not know what to do with this place and it was starting to bother me. The territory was taking shape and more and more wolves were arriving for the battle. We had nearly filled all of the houses and I'd realised that we were probably going to need to build some more. But that would have to wait until after the battle. Training was my top priority right now.

I was just about to head to the ground to start the first round when I sensed Alina's presence not far away. I looked over to see her walking with a new family towards the VIP houses. I recognised the man immediately and smiled at the memory of him in the woods. But it was Alina I couldn't keep my eyes off. She was smiling genuinely and chatting to them with so much warmth and confidence. The last few days, I have watched her flourish into her role as Luna of this pack and she kept catching me staring at her in admiration. I can't

The Last Alpha

believe I am so lucky.

Since finding out who her father and grandfather were, she had stepped up and taken everything in her stride instead of crumbling and feeling betrayed like any other would be.

We had talked about the fact that she is the rightful Alpha of the Bloodmoon Pack but she was refusing to take the title. She wanted to remain the Luna and run the pack as equals instead. I had tried to explain that we could both be given the Alpha role but she didn't want it. I think she was worried about taking something away from me, but in all honesty, all I feel was be proud. Proud to be able to call her mine. To be by her side. No title could change that.

I smiled as she gave the family the keys to one of the VIP houses and the emotion on their faces. She had a heart of gold. The little boy ran up and hugged her legs and my heart melted.

I casually walk up behind her, startling her as I wrapped my arms around her waist and nuzzled her neck. She smells amazing.

"Have I ever told you how incredible you are?" I said huskily.

She grinned. "And have I ever told you how generous you are?" She turned in my arms and holds hers around my neck. "You just made a lovely family very happy."

I shook my head. "No, that was all you."

She leaned up and pecked me on the lips, but it was over too soon, so I pulled her body tight against mine and leaned in again. She smiled as our lips touched. Once we pulled away, I looked down into her mesmerising eyes.

"Go on a date with me?"

Her eyes widened in surprise and her smile broadens. "A date?"

"Yes, a date. Tonight?"

"But... we have training and new families arriving every minute. There is still so much to do…"

"I have just realised that I have never taken you on a date. So forget about all of that. Will you go on a date with me tonight? Please?" I said with a sparkle in my eye.

She giggled in a giddy way and looked so bloody cute. "Okay, my Alpha. I will go on a date with you."

I grinned back at her. "Okay, let's go train these wolves so that I can have you all to myself later."

Alina's POV

"And he didn't say where he was taking you?" Sloane asked as she flicked through the array of gorgeous dresses hanging on the rack. We had come into the nearest city which was full of cute boutiques as well as a few designer shops.

"Nope. So, I just think something simple," I said, eyeing a black long-sleeved dress. "Like this." I held it up and both Chloe and Sloane wrinkled their noses and shook their heads.

"No way. This is your first date! You have to go all out!" Chloe waltzed over to a bright pink satin mini dress. "Like this! Imagine his face when he sees you in this!"

My eyes widened in horror.

"Cute but not her style," Sloane interjected. Thank god! "You should wear something tight fitting to show off your banging bod but you want to keep it elegant. He could be taking her to the Opera for all we know!"

"I doubt he's—" I started, but once again the girls started chatting as if I was not even there!

"OMG! Imagine that! I would love to go to the Opera! Need a bloody man to take me first though!" Chloe moaned.

"Oh, babe, your Richard Gere will whisk you away one day!" Sloane laughed.

"Richard Gere?! Oh, from *Pretty Woman*! YES purleaseee!" Chloe fanned her face.

"But in the meantime, you could have a little fun with a wolf…" Sloane winked and Chloe blushed. I looked at her, realising she had someone in mind.

"Chloe! Do you like someone?" I shouted.

"What?! No! I mean well… there is one guy… wolf… he is like an Adonis!"

"Who?" I shouted excitedly.

"I know who…" Sloane smiled coyly at us and Chloe narrowed her eyes.

"No, you don't…"

"It's Darius…"

Chloe actually chocked on her own saliva and burst out laughing. "Are you insane? That big Oof."

Sloane's face turned into a frown. "Oh, come on, Chloe, you have got so much chemistry and passion! Imagine how good the sex would be."

"Yeah, passion to kill each other! I wouldn't touch that man with a barge pole. Gross!" She laughed.

"Well, who is it then?" I asked, crossing my arms.

"I think his name is Joseph. He is one of Logan's best warriors. Young and fit. His body is to die for and the way he throws men around on those training mats… wahooo! He could throw me around any day." She giggled.

"Is that why you're so interested in watching the training?" I raised my eyebrows at her suggestively.

"Of course!"

I rolled my eyes and walked over to another clothes rail. A gold dress caught my eye and I pulled it out. It had a scoop cowl neck with thin straps over the shoulders and a criss-cross at the back. It cuts in a V shape at the back and flows down to the floor with a high slit up the leg. The fabrics felt expensive and chic. It was stunning.

"That is fucking insane!" Sloane came up behind me to see what I was holding. "Try it on immediately!"

"Girl, if you don't try it on, I will!" Chloe shouted, trying to take it from me.

My grip tightened and I pulled it to my chest. "Okay, okay. I will try it on, but don't you think it's… too much?"

"NO!" they both shouted in unison.

I smiled shyly and walked into the dressing room. A flashback of the last time I was in the situation entered my mind and I smirked. That green dress changed my life. Let's hope this one is just as significant.

Once I was in it, I stepped back and looked in the full-length mirror. It was incredible and fitted me like a glove. I pulled back the curtain and walked back into the shop to my friend's open mouth and wide eyes.

"Fucking hell!" Sloane stood up and walked around me in a circle.

"What do you think? Do you, guys, like it?" I asked hesitantly.

"I LOVE it! You look like a supermodel!" Sloane smiled and I rolled my eyes, not able to take the compliment, and looked over to Chloe. She had tears in her eyes.

"Chloe! What's wrong?" I said, running over to her and bending down to her level on the sofa.

"S-sorry! You just look so… so beautiful… And I am so proud of you," she stuttered, wiping her eyes. I pulled her into me for a hug as I tried to keep my own emotions in check. "Sorry I must be coming on my period or something." She laughed through her tears.

"So, you like the dress?" I smiled and she nodded.

"Okay. Looks like it's a winner." Sloane threw me Logan's bank card with a smirk.

Chapter 62

Logan's POV

"Right, men, we are here to talk strategies. You have been chosen as my most trusted warriors and will play a key role in the battle. I value all of your contributions and no idea is a bad one, so please feel free to share," I said, meeting every one of my men's eyes as they nodded in understanding.

Fredrik stepped forward and unrolled a large table map of our territory. "Ideally, we want to hold the battle away from the housing and families. The woods would be to our benefit, but also this large area of clearing at the back of the woods would be a great ground for battle. But we know the Vampires will try and attack where it hurts the most. The village." Fredrik explained to the others.

I took over to deliver the hard news. "So we will need to ensure that any wolves who are not able to fight and children are safe. We have built a safe room underneath the new pack house that can hold up to a hundred people. When the vampires attack, we will not have long to get them in there. It will be a matter of minutes," I explained and saw the concern in some of the men with young children's eyes.

"We need to have border controls every minute of the day and night from now on, as Lucius could attack any day. As soon as the pack warns of their presence, we will sound an alarm to alert the families to get to the safe room. I would like you, men, to pick six warriors to be in charge of getting them all there as quickly as possible. I know it will be difficult to do, but I need my best warriors ready for action straight away and not worrying about their families."

They nodded, but I could see how hard that would be for some of them.

"Hopefully, the vampires will enter through the forest, and we can bring the battle to them and push them to the clearing away from the village." Fredrik added.

"And what if they don't? What if they attack the village first?" Rohan asked, looking intensely at the map.

"We currently have around one hundred eighty warriors. We are expecting a few more in the next few days, but not many. I think our best option is to have designated posts for warriors around the territory. That way, when the battle begins, we will know where and the others can come and join the location."

Darius interrupted. "But how will we all communicate? I know any wolves who have always been a part of the previous Blood Moon Pack can mind link but there are lots of new members of the pack that have not been initiated yet. Does that not show weakness in our defence?"

It was a very good point. "We will need to hold a ceremony tomorrow and make sure all new members are initiated before the battle."

Darius nodded but then spoke carefully. "You know what this will mean? Alina will also need to be initiated as Luna."

"Yes, it does mean we will have to hold the Luna Ceremony before we would like, but I think she will understand." My gut twisted at the thought that she might not be ready. I didn't want to rush her or force her, but Darius was right. We needed to be a united pack to make our defence the strongest it could be.

"I have an idea about battle tactics." Joseph spoke up for the first time. He was an original member of our pack that escaped through the trap door though he was only about fifteen when he did. We had lost touch with him, but he had heard we were returning and he came straight back for his revenge. He was a clever man and a great fighter. One of the strongest. I was glad he was here.

Darius scoffed and I glared at him for being so rude. "Sorry, but how has this kid got any knowledge of battle tactics? I bet he has never even been in a battle."

"Darius⋯" I warned.

"Only as much as you have, I am sure." Joseph smirked back, which shut Darius up.

"Please, Joseph. Continue," I encouraged.

He stood up and leaned over the map, pointing to the middle of the forest. "Just here, there are bushes and bushes of prickly and overgrown gorse plants. It would be the perfect place to hide traps and wooden stakes on the floor. They grow for acres through the middle of the forest so we could use it as a wall and shoot arrows at them as they approach. We could also have our less experienced fighters up high in the trees with wooden spears and arrows. I also have a friend who works with firearms. He said he could get me about twenty-five guns that can shoot wooden pellets."

I smiled, impressed at the man's idea. "That is a great idea. Thank you. Darius, anything you would like to add?" I asked, enjoying watching him squirm.

"No." he sulked and folded his huge arms over his chest, looking away.

"Can I ask, Alpha?" Joseph regarded me again and I nodded.

The Last Alpha

"How many vampires will join Lucius in the battle, do you think?"

The room went silent and they all looked at me. Fredrik looked down at his hands. This was the only question I dreaded. But I had to be honest.

"I do not know. I have heard, within his castle and followers who back him, there are a few hundred, but there could be more joining him."

"So, we are massively outnumbered?" Joseph didn't say it accusingly, just as though he was stating the facts.

"Yes. I think we will be. However, many of Lucius' followers are newly turned vampires and will be easy to kill," I tried to say optimistically.

"Also, I think we should tell them about our Luna." Fredrik looked at me for approval, but I could have punched him in the face. It wasn't his place to say anything. Seeing the rage in my eyes, he quickly added, "If we are doing the ceremony tomorrow, they will soon find out. I think it would put all their minds at ease slightly."

"What about Luna Alina?" Rohan asked.

I sighed, running my hands through my hair. I really hope she isn't too pissed at me for this.

"Alina is an Alabaster wolf," I said and watched the men's faces morph with shock. Darius knew she was a white wolf, but he still didn't know how. "Her father was Clarke Snow, son of Alpha Alec Snow. The last Alabaster Alpha of the Blood Moon Pack."

"No fucking way!" Darius roared. Joseph grinned. Rohan looked like he was about to faint.

"And you two are marked and mated?" Rohan asked.

I nodded and smiled. *Yes, she is mine.*

"Then that means…" Darius said with a broad grin. "You two are fucking invincible."

I laughed out loud as he jumped around the room and the other men watched on at his hysterics.

"It will still be a challenging battle and we will be outnumbered, but I have every faith in us that we will be victorious. Please keep this information to yourselves for the moment. I need to speak with Alina about the ceremony." I stood and they all bowed their heads out of respect. Even Darius. "If you'll excuse me, men, I have a date to get ready for." I grinned as I walked out of the room.

***

I had moved my suit into Darius' room earlier so Alina could get ready with the girls in our room. Once I had showered and dressed, I looked in the mirror and tried to tame my unruly curls. They still fell forward into my eyes but Alina always said she loved them so I leave it. I shook out my arms and added my cufflinks to the white shirt that clung to my muscles. I hadn't worn a suit in years.

Suddenly, I felt butterflies in my stomach and a weird sensation spread through my body. Was I nervous? I took a deep shaky breath and walked out of the bathroom.

"Looking good, man," Darius said with a smirk as he followed me out of his room and down the steps to the main entrance. A girly giggle filled the air as we reached the bottom and I saw Chloe flirting and rubbing Joseph's biceps as he said something that made her howl with laughter again. Typical Chloe.

"Urgh, why did you put that guy in your inner circle?" Darius growled behind me and I turned to see him glaring at them.

"Because he is the next best fighter here after me. What's your problem with him?" I asked, looking up at the stairs, anticipating Alina's arrival.

"He is just a douche. Thinks too much of himself. I mean look at him. I bet he doesn't even know her name and will be on to the next one tomorrow."

I looked over my shoulder at Joseph and Chloe, who were now looking very cosy with his arm wrapped around her shoulder.

"I don't know. I think they look good together," I said, and Darius scoffed and folded his arms. I raised my eyebrows and smirked.

"Careful, Darius. Anyone would think you are jealous."

"Me? Jealous? Of him? Fuck off!" He stormed off and I stifled a chuckle.

"What's so funny?" I heard Alina's angelic voice from the top of the stairs and whipped around to see the most beautiful woman I had ever seen in my life.

She smiled sweetly as she descended the stairs in a striking gold dress that hugged her figure seductively and I felt my dick twitch. Her soft hair was tied up in a messy up do and curls cascading down her face and neck. She was glowing. And I forgot how to breathe.

"You look… incredible," I said as she reached me at the bottom step.

She beamed at me but slightly blushed as she looked me up and down. "You don't look too bad yourself, Alpha."

I held my hand out for her and felt her small hand wrap around my huge one and walked her out of the house. Chloe gave her a little thumbs up as we passed, and I had a car waiting out the front. I opened the door for her and then climbed in the back next to her myself.

The car started to pull away and out of the territory as Alina turned to look at me again. "So where does charming Logan take girls on his first date?" Her eyes twinkled with excitement.

"Well, seeing as this is my first date… I don't think I can

answer that." I smirked as her eyes narrowed.

"What do you mean··· your first date?"

"Well, I have only ever dated Madeline and we were already good friends before that, so we never really went on dates as such. It just kind of happened."

"But··· you never dated before?" she questioned, still unable to believe that she probably had more experience in the dating world than I did.

"Nope. I screwed around. I never dated."

She swatted my arms and I chuckled.

She looked out the window and suddenly went quiet and I felt the atmosphere between us change.

"What's wrong?" I asked and she quickly turned to look at me.

"Nothing," she lied and looked back out of the window.

"Alina, I know something is wrong. I can feel it through the mate bond. Tell me."

She looked uncomfortably at the driver and shook her head. I sighed and leaned forward, pressing a button to raise the privacy barrier so he could no longer hear or see us and turned to her.

"If you don't tell me what's wrong, I will turn this car around and take you straight up to the bedroom and force it out of you." I growl seductively and her head snaps to me in shock. I raised my eyebrows at her and she gulped.

"Okay. It's nothing. It's just··· are you happy··· you know just being with me?" Her cheeks flushed crimson and I was so confused by her question.

"What are you talking about? Of course, I am happy being with you."

"No, I mean··· in the bedroom?" she whispered the last part

and I almost burst out laughing but refrained when I see how serious she was.

"Alina, what are you saying? You think that I want to sleep with other people?" My voice rose as I realised that was what she was insinuating.

"I don't know! It's just that, under the circumstances of how we met… you and Madeline clearly enjoyed having quite an adventurous sex life with other people as well. And my ex told me I was boring in the bedroom, so…" She looked down at her hands, embarrassed and anger rose in me that she would even think about this.

"Alina, Madeline and I, near the end, we hardly ever had sex because I just wasn't into it. The reason we had threesomes and I watched her with other people was because it took the pressure off me and she thought it made me happy. It didn't. And if you think I would EVER want to sleep with someone other than you or even see you with someone else…" I clenched my jaw and balled my fist at the thought of someone else's hands on Alina. I was ready to kill someone.

"So, I'm not boring in bed?" she asked quietly.

I quickly pulled her by her hips onto my lap in one swift motion and she let out a small gasp. "You are the furthest thing from boring in bed. Fuck, it took every ounce of strength for me to get out of bed every morning because I want to stay there with you and take you again and again."

She smiled shyly down at me through her lashes and I wanted to fuck her right now. I leaned forward and kissed and sucked at her marking spot causing a moan to escape her lips.

"In fact, you turn me on so much that I want to fuck you right here in the back of this car," I mumbled against her skin and she rolled her head back, giving me access to her neck and chest as I planted kisses down her skin.

"We can't…" she whispered.

A growl rippled through my chest as I felt her start to grind over my dick. "Your body is saying the complete opposite."

She looked down at me with a smirk and I saw the golden ring around her eyes matching the colour of her dress. I raised my hand to cup her face and stroke my thumb along her lips as she parted them slightly.

The tension prickled as I stare from her lips to her eyes and then the stillness erupted with manic movements of me pulling her dress up around her waist and her unbuckling my trousers and releasing me. Our mouths moved passionately, kissing, sucking and biting each other's lips and necks as she took me into her warm centre and we both cried out. There was nothing slow about her movements as she rode me completely and I gripped her waist tightly, burying myself deeper. I turned abruptly so her back was on the seats and started pounding into her, feeling an overwhelming protective feeling I was not used to. Thinking of someone else touching her skin or hearing her moans had me pounding harder and growling.

"You are MINE!"

She moaned and gripped my shoulders as our bodies collided over and over.

"Say it!" I growled into her neck.

"I'm yours…" she breathed and I bit down into her marking spot again, causing her to scream out in ecstasy as we both saw stars. We lay there panting for a few moments and then I climbed off her and helped her sit up straight as she readjusted her dress. It was only then that I realised the car was no longer moving and we must have arrived. I leaned forward and kissed her lips.

"Don't ever think you are not enough ever again," I said

lowly and she smiled at me before I opened the car door and held my hand out for her to exit.

She climbed out and looked up at the restaurant I have picked. It was the best one in town and I wanted tonight to be special. She looked up at me with a huge smile and I took her arm in mine and we made our way through the entrance.

"Logan Black," I said to the waitress, who gave me a smouldering look and ignored Alina completely. That just pissed me off.

"Right this way, sir," she replied seductively and swayed her hips as she walked ahead in front of us.

I ignored her and looked down at Alina who was looking as though she was about to rip the woman's throat out.

That's my girl.

She led us out through the restaurant into the back courtyard where it was lit with fairy lights and candles. The only table stood alone in the middle and a violinist started to play a romantic melody as we walked out. I looked down at Alina with a smile as her mouth hung open.

"Do you like it?" I asked.

"You did all this?" She stepped forward and looked around. The waitress saw her for the first time and I notice her looking Alina up and down with envy.

I walked up behind Alina and wrapped my arms round her. "Do you like it?" I asked again.

"I love it. And I love you." She turned and gave me the most gorgeous smile.

"I love you," I said, pecking her on the lips. "Always."

"Always," she replied as the waitress cleared her throat behind us and I rolled my eyes, making Alina chuckle.

"If you would like to be seated. I will bring you over the wine," the waitress said, a bit more coldly than before.

We both took a seat at the table and Alina picked up a few of the scattered rose petals from the table and played with them in her fingers.

"How did you know white roses were my favourite?" she asked.

I smiled. "I have my ways."

She giggled. "You mean Chloe."

"She comes in handy now and again, yes." I cleared my throat as I prepared to bring up the next bit. "Alina, there is something we need to discuss but I don't want it to ruin our evening, so if you don't want to talk about it now, then we can do it later."

Her eyes narrowed at me and she looked nervous. "What is it?"

"The Luna Ceremony."

Relief flooded her features and made me wonder what it was she didn't want to talk about. "Yes, we can talk about it now. It's fine."

"Okay. So, today the men and I had a battle meeting and Darius made a good point of saying that with so many new members of the pack who haven't been initiated yet, we cannot mind link them all. This would be a disadvantage in the battle."

She nodded as the waitress came over with the wine and I waited until she had left before continuing. "The problem is, as we are marked and mated now, you must be initiated as the Luna first in order for the mind link to work for everyone. So we will need to do the Luna Ceremony as soon as possible."

She nodded again. "Okay, how soon?"

"Tomorrow."

She took a sip of her wine and put it down slowly, torturing me with her silence. She looked up at me and smiled. "I can't wait to officially be your Luna."

My heart somersaulted in my chest and I leapt out of my seat and swung her around, taking her by surprise.

"Logan! Put me down." She giggled as I put her back on her feet.

"Thank you," I said with sincerity. "I don't know what I ever did to deserve you, but I promise to always try to be worthy of you."

She kissed me before sitting back down. "Isn't the Ceremony meant to be quite grand? How are we going to plan that in less than twenty-four hours?" she asked in panic.

"Yes, it is a very grand event but we can't do it like that in these circumstances. So I was thinking that we could just hold a big BBQ and firepit dancing tomorrow night and then once the battle is over, we will do the grand ceremony properly. Does that sound okay?"

"That sounds perfect. It will be a great chance for all the pack to mingle and get to know the newbies as well."

"Newbies?" I chuckled.

"Hey! Don't take the piss, I take my Luna responsibilities very seriously." She put on her most serious expression and looked fucking adorable. "And on that note, there is one pack member who still isn't here."

I looked at her blankly.

"Madeline."

I rolled my eyes, not this again. We keep having this same conversation.

"Alina, let's not do this now. It's up to her if she returns."

"No, it is not because you sent her away. She probably thinks she is not welcome here. In her own home."

"She's not welcome here," I snapped and took a gulp of my wine.

"Logan." Alina gave me that look that told me to stop being a prick. "I really think we should contact her. Tell her if she chooses, she can come here."

"No," I said stubbornly. It was not even that I was holding a grudge for what had happened. It was more that I didn't want the dynamic to change. Everything was great. Alina and I and the pack were happy. Things were going perfectly. Just the thought of Madeline's presence here made me uneasy.

"I thought you said we were equals in this pack," Alina shot back, giving me a deathly glare.

"We are."

"Then don't you think we should compromise? I think she is part of this pack and she should be here. You don't want her here. So how can we compromise?" she asked, but I know she already has the answer, so I didn't bother saying anything. "We tell her she is welcome here if she wants to, but if she is happy with Cora, then so be it."

"That doesn't sound like a compromise to me," I sulked, leaning back in my chair. "You are too soft."

Alina threw her napkin on the table. Oops. That pissed her off.

"Tell me, Logan. What kind of leader do you want to be?"

The question caught me off guard as I looked into her challenging eyes.

"Do you want to be like my grandfather? The type of leader who was rigid and showed no mercy. That did not forgive or look past people's flaws? Or do you want to be the leader that protects his people and shows kindness, especially to those who are in pain or hurting the most?"

I sighed and leaned forward to hold her hand on the table. "Of course, I want to be the latter. But this is more complicated than that."

"I don't see how it is. She has shown she is sorry. She admitted to you what she had done and then got the witch to give you back your memories, knowing it meant she would lose you forever. She came to my aid when she could have left me there alone. She saved my life and nearly lost hers in the process. And she did all of that with a broken heart. I know she hurt you, Logan, but you've hurt her too. Don't you think enough is enough?"

I sighed and rubbed my hands down my face. I did not want to spend my night arguing about this.

"You are right. I know you are. But I don't know where she is or how to get a hold of her. Fredrik said he had tried her phone but it was dead. If she wants to come back, I will allow it. But I am not going to go out of my way to find her."

A small smile formed on her face. "See? A compromise. That wasn't so hard, hey?" She winked at me and I couldn't help but smirk at her.

My sexy, headstrong, stubborn as hell mate. You will be the death of me.

Chapter 63

Madeline's POV

Rays of mellow sunlight filtered through the verdurous canopy as the sun sunk down beneath the tops of the pines and I felt the last warmth of the day wash over my face. Once again, I was lying in my favourite spot on the mossy-green carpet of the forest floor, looking up at the branches overhead that were woven together almost like fabric. The brilliant colours of the leaves were golden hues and vibrant oranges, bringing warmth to the chilly autumn breeze. This was my happy place.

Cora thought I was crazy for spending all my time out here in the forest alone, but in all honesty, it had been my saving grace. Here, I was free to feel, to cry, to curse, to overthink. I felt like I may have lost my mind in these woods, but I have definitely found my soul.

When I first woke up in Cora's home, I freaked the hell out. The last thing I remembered was fighting two vampires who had attacked Alina's wolf and then I passed out. I honestly believed I had died and I had made my peace with it. But waking up to hear that Cora had spelled me before I left Darius' house and the way she had nursed me back to health (I refused her magical healing, I wanted to heal from my wounds the way I knew how) made me feel a love that I hadn't felt for many years. The love of a mother.

At first, the pristine and calming influence of her white house helped ease my mind, but soon I found it sad and cold. There were no personal items, no family pictures. Everything had a place and it made me realise even more that I no longer did. So the minute I felt strong enough, I ventured out into this evergreen haven and I don't tend to come back until the sun sets. Sometimes, Cora would join me for a few hours but she didn't seem too keen on the outdoors, so it never lasted long. But I knew she was lonely and enjoyed the company. Just like me.

I breathed in the earthy crispness of the forest's scent and sighed. Time to head back. I ran my fingers over the fuzzy, soft moss beneath me and relish in its embrace, knowing soon the floor will be a bed of crunchy leaves instead. I sat up slowly and took one last look around. I would miss this place a great deal, but I couldn't hide away in the forest forever.

Suddenly, a stunningly beautiful hawfinch landed onto a fallen tree trunk in front of me and bobbed its bulky orange-brown head in all directions, studying me as if I was an old friend.

"Hello again, Cedric," I smiled. This wasn't the first time I had seen this bird or this breed of bird in these forests. The first day I woke up here, there was one on the windowsill of the bedroom and yesterday, one was perched on a branch watching me for hours until it flew away. I know it was more than likely a different bird each time, but it made me feel like I had a companion, a friend. So, I decided to name him Cedric. Like I said, I have lost my mind.

The striking bird hopped forward slightly on its pink legs and its beady eyes focused on me.

"I am afraid it is time for me to go now. The sun is setting and Cora will have prepared us dinner. You can join us if you like." I opened my hand out flat and inched forward and waited. I was about to laugh at myself and stand up when the bird gracefully flew over and landed on my palm. My eyes widened in surprise, as I had never actually held a bird in my life. I took a few moments to study its striking features as it sized me up as well. "You are very handsome, Cedric. You may be the only person in the world who trusts me right now." I hesitantly raised my other hand and used my index finger to stroke it's back, half expecting it to fly away immediately, but when it didn't, my face lit up.

An animal moved in the distance and suddenly startled the bird as its wings expanded and it took off into the sky. I watched it fly up through the canopy and out of sight in awe. That was amazing.

I walked back to Cora's house with a spring in my step and a smile on my face for the first time in weeks, but it soon fell when I saw Cora's frail body hunched over her cauldron on the veranda as she banged her fist down on the table. She looked up at me as I approached and gave me a weak smile. She was slim before but she had lost more weight over the last few days and looked more skeletal than ever.

"Still no luck?" I asked and sat across from her on the glass chair.

She shook her head and sighed. "I can feel him. I am always just about to get through and then it is like he shuts me out and the magic evaporates."

Cora told me everything about what happened during her time at Lucius' castle and how she found her son. The only time I ever saw her smile was when she talked about him, so I asked about him often just to give her some joy. She had told me about how he was abused by his own father as a child and perhaps still was. I knew he apparently looked like a supermodel and had two different coloured eyes that made his beauty out of this world (I am sure she was just being biased). I also knew that he was half warlock, half vampire and extremely powerful. This last bit of information was one of the many reasons I had come to the decision to head back to America. I had to warn Logan and I had to convince Cora to come with me and help us.

Looking at the shell of the woman before me, I knew it was going to be a difficult task.

I reached forward and squeezed her hand. "I know he will come around, Cora. Just be patient."

She gave me a sad smile. "He doesn't even believe I am his mother. Lucius has corrupted his mind and poisoned him against me. I am not sure there is anything I can do."

I leaned back in my chair and looked out into the forest, trying to gain some inspiration to help this woman who I had come to care for.

"Cora, is there not a way of sharing your memories with him? Like you did with me? So he sees the truth."

"Yes, but I am not sure he will believe them. He could think I am spelling him or manipulating him."

I sighed. "What about his powers? Does he possess the same gifts as you? The gift of premonition?"

"I don't know. He didn't mention it. Even though he is very powerful, he is very inexperience in his witchcraft when I started teaching him. I am not even sure he has tapped into all his abilities. Why do you ask?"

"Because if he could, then surely, he would not be able to see your future as you are related. That could prove to him that you are his mother."

She pondered this for a while. "Maybe. But this would all take time. Time that we do not have."

She was right. Time was ticking. After saving Alina, Logan

agreed for Cora to take me with her. Even though it hurt, I understood why. He may never forgive me. Heck, I was not sure I would ever forgive myself. I know he did not want me around or part of his pack anymore and it had taken me a few days to decide whether I should honour his wishes or return home for the battle. I wanted to do what was best for him and Alina and stay away, but I also needed to fight in this war. He was not the only one who lost everything that day. My parents, my home, my future was taken from me, too. And I wanted revenge just as much as he did. I may not be the Luna of our pack, like we thought I would be, and I am okay with that, but I still cared about my people. I could not stay here and hide in the forest whilst they go to war with our enemy.

"I want to thank you, Cora. If it wasn' t for you, I would be dead. You took me in when I was at my lowest and showed me kindness. You are not the bad bitch everyone makes out you are." I winked at her and her infectious cackle echoed through the trees.

"Don' t tell anyone. I have a reputation to uphold." She smirked. "You do not need to thank me, dear. I owe you for my deception, so I would like to think we are even now."

I looked down at my fingers and started to fiddle with my nails as my nerves increased. "Actually··· there is one more thing I would like to ask of you." I looked up and met her icy blue eyes as she regarded me with curiosity. "I am going back to America to stand with my pack and fight the vampires. Please, will you come with me?"

Her eyes glazed over as her body tensed at my words. She showed no emotion and I had no idea what she was thinking, so I carried on talking.

"I know as much as you do, that we are not the type of women to sit back and let others fight our battles. We have a mutual hatred for Lucius. And even if you do not want to fight, surely, you want to be there to watch him fall."

"Madeline, you know I do. But it is more complicated than that."

"Because of Arius? That is even more reason for you to be there. Lucius will be using Arius in the battle for his powers. He will become the wolves first target."

Her eyes narrowed and her face showed instant rage.

"But with you there, you can counteract his magic, protecting us and him in the process."

She stood abruptly and walked over to the edge of the veranda, looking out into the enchanted woods. I held my breath.

"You are right. Lucius will do anything to win, including throwing his own son at the wolves and misusing his powers. I have to be there."

I tried and hid my glee at her words. With her on our side and blocking Arius' powers, we would be able to get to Lucius easily.

"Thank you, Cora. When shall we leave?" I have had no communication with anyone from my pack and I was unsure what the plans were or how long until the battle would commence, so I was eager to get back as quickly as possible.

"Soon. Start looking for flights," she said as she walked towards her front door and back into her house. I followed her, confused.

"Er, I thought you would, you know, do that finger clicking thing and teleport us there like you did with me from London?"

"No, I can't risk it. If Arius has worked out how to stop me from contacting him through magic, then he could also be able to track me when I use it. It is better to keep my involvement as hush hush as possible."

"Okay," I said finding it difficult to hide my disappointment at not being able to get there sooner.

The Last Alpha

She headed to her room as I flipped through my phone and started searching for flights. I threw my head back and groaned when I saw that the next flight from Sweden to America was tomorrow afternoon and would take nineteen hours to get there with one stop! She had best be right about this special son of hers, otherwise, we have just wasted two precious days for no reason!

Chapter 64

Lucius' POV

"Your majesty, I am afraid that we have not found them. They all seem to have vanished."

I turned, my eyes burning red and the guard cowered back slightly.

"Vanished? Tell me, how does a group of wolves simply vanish?" I snarled, baring my fangs at him.

"I-I do not know, my king. We have searched the whole of London and followed any leads but it has all been a dead end. It is like they have left the UK."

I spun around, glaring at him. "So have you checked the airports? CCTV? Flight details? ANYTHING?"

He bowed his head in fear as my anger erupted out of my body. It had been nearly a week since Alina escaped and Logan and his beasts had disappeared and my patience was wearing thin. These idiotic warriors of mine didn't have two brain cells between them.

"W-we are doing it now, my king," he stuttered.

I walked up to him menacingly as he stepped back towards the wall. "Don't bother, I will do it myself," I growled and just as I reached him, I extracted one of my nails and slit his throat on my way out. Just before I shut the door, I heard a thud as his lifeless body fell to the floor. I looked at the guard outside. "Clear that up!" I spat as I marched towards Arius' room.

At least one silver lining in all of this mess was that Arius' powers were growing and he had been tirelessly spending every waking moment locked in his room, learning new spells from Cora's book. It was the first time in his life that I was impressed. He showed great power and his purpose would now be more valuable in the war than ever before. He was the key to my victory.

I threw open his heavy, wooden door and barged into the room. I scanned the room quickly and found him sitting in a large, black velvet winged chair. His bedroom window was wide open even though it was the beginning of autumn and he's wearing nothing but a pair of grey tracksuit bottoms. But what intrigued me the most were his eyes. They were completely black like a demon; no sign of pupils or colour.

At that moment, a bird flew through the window and landed on his arm. A strange looking bird with a bulky brownish-orange head. Abruptly, Arius brought his free arm over to the bird and placed his hand on its head. I watch in fascination as he shut his eyes and when he opened them again, they have returned to their normal blue and brown shades. He released the bird and it flew back out of the window.

"What was that?" I asked, walking over to him.

He looked up but didn't stand to greet me. Still disrespectful, I see.

"A spell," he replied in a bored tone and got up, walking casually over to the thick leather-bound book that lay open on his desk.

"What kind of spell?" He was testing my patience every day at the moment, but I needed to keep in his good graces for the time being. I needed him to want to help me.

"One where I can control the birds' minds," he said, as if it was the most unimpressive thing in the world.

"So you were controlling that bird?" I asked, calmly trying to get more information out of him. This could be very useful in battle.

"Yes, I was the bird. I controlled its movements and I could see through its eyes." He flipped the pages over until he found another one that he started to read.

"Son, that is very impressive. Could you do that to a wolf?" I struggled to keep the excitement out of my voice as I thought of all the endless possibilities.

"I don't know. Haven't tried."

I frowned. "Why a bird then?"

He sighed, clearly getting annoyed by all my questions. "I wanted to check in on Cora. See where she was and what she is doing."

Annoyance brewed inside. Why was he doing that? He should not care about that woman. He turned to look at me for the first time and smirked when he saw my face.

"Don't worry, father. I was just checking that she isn't working against us. That she isn't helping the wolves." He turned back to the book. Once again, I underestimated him.

"And? Where is she?" I asked.

"She is at home in Sweden. Doing nothing but trying to contact me which I am blocking."

I nodded. "So she is not helping them?"

He paused as he read part of a spell before answering coldly, "No."

I breathed out a sigh of relief. It was one thing to have Arius on my side, but I was still not ecstatic about losing Cora. She was the most powerful witch and I did not want to go against her in battle.

"When is my birthday?" Arius suddenly asked, startling me by his strange question. Vampires don't tend to celebrate birthdays, as we have lived for so many centuries there was not much point. And honestly, I didn't know the date he was born.

"You know we do not celebrate birthdays. Why do you ask?" I narrowed my eyes at the back of his head.

"I need to know about it for a spell."

I walked over to the table and looked at the page. It was written in symbols and I had no idea what any of it meant.

"I don't know when your birthday is," I said honestly, walking away over to the chair.

He turned to look at me with a blank expression. "You do not know what day your son was born?"

My eyes blazed at his challenging tone. "No. Like I said, it is not important."

"But you know what day my mother was killed?" he asked, narrowing his eyes at me, showing no sign of fear.

"What is with all these questions?" I did not like where this was heading. I had always told Arius that his mother was Celeste and she was killed in battle, pregnant with his sibling. He had been a year old at the time when, in truth, he hadn't even been born.

Suddenly, a knock on the door interrupted us and I felt relief flood through me. "Come in!" I ordered.

"My king, my prince. I think we found something of interest to you." The guard bowed at us both and then smirked.

"This better be good," I snarled as we followed him down the hall to the grand ballroom that I only used as my throne room.

I took a seat on my throne and Arius stood broadly next to me and we heard her screams before we saw her. I felt Arius tense beside me. He never liked seeing women in hysterics. The double doors were heaved open and two guards dragged a black-haired girl into the room with her arms is wolfsbane cuffs.

"P-p-please," she cried as they threw her to the hard floor at my feet.

"And who do we have here?" I smirked as the girl's face looked up at me, tear stains through her makeup and sore, red eyes from crying.

"This is one of Logan's pack, your majesty. Her name is Emma."

She whimpered and looked down at the floor.

I climbed out of my throne and bent down beside her, lifting her chin with my fingers to look me in the eyes. "Hello Emma." I smiled.

"W-what are you going to do to me?" she mumbled in between her sobs.

I stood up and walked back to my throne, taking a glance at Arius as I did. His robotic expression was void of any emotion and he looked straight ahead. "Well, that all depends."

"On what?" she cried.

"On how much information are you willing to give me? You see, your Alpha seems to have disappeared. Do you know anything about that?"

She dropped her head back down as the tears flowed from her eyes and her straight black hair covered her face.

"We found her at the airport, my king." One of the warriors spoke up.

"The airport? How interesting. Going anywhere nice, my dear?"

The girl didn't speak but continued to whimper on the floor. I nodded to my guard, who pulled her back by the hair and extended his fangs.

"NO! No, please!" she screamed in fear.

"All you have to do is talk, Emma. And we won't hurt you,"

I said calmly, glaring into her eyes.

"A-America," she whispered, but I heard her.

"And why were you going to America?"

She whimpered again so my guard yanked her hair. "OW! Because that's where they have all gone. Back home."

My eyes widened. Back home? To the Blood Moon Pack. Of course. He was giving me a sign. An invitation to end all of this where it started.

"And Alina? Is she with him?" I asked, needing to know who killed my most loyal liege.

"Y-yes. They are all there now. The only one who isn't is… me and…" she started, but quickly changed her mind as soon as the words left her mouth. Interesting. Who was she protecting?

"You and…" I asked and she shook her head. I nodded to the guard who sunk his fangs into her neck as she screamed out in pain.

"Stop! Pleaseee!"

The guard pulled back as her blood ran down his mouth and my other warriors' eyes turned red in hunger.

"You were saying? You and…"

"M-Maddy," she whimpered as more tears ran down her face.

"Maddy?" I asked curiously. Who was that?

One of the guards stepped forward noticing my confusion. "Madeline, your majesty. Logan's former chosen mate."

"Ah, yes! Of course. The pretty girl who was dumped by our Alpha. So I see she has come to her senses and left the pack. Good for her. Obviously, she is still a wolf, so I cannot allow her to live. What a shame," I gloated as Emma's head snapped up to me with terror written all over it. "Where is she?" I asked and she shook her head.

"Father, perhaps we should focus on Logan and the pack. They are obviously preparing for battle and the longer we leave them alone, the more prepared they will be." Arius' voice boomed into the room and I could swear I detected slight panic.

I turned to meet his gaze but his face showed no emotion. "Don't worry my son. We will get to them all in due course. But you are right. That she-wolf is the least of my concerns right now. I will make it her privilege to be the last wolf killed and take my sweet time on her," I smirked. "Arius, perhaps you would like the honour of taking care of this one for me?" I gestured to the girl at my feet as she whimpered and pleaded, looking at Arius.

"Yes, father," he said flatly, and started walking towards the girl. She shrank away and started crawling from him. He picked her up in one swift motion and threw her over his shoulder, striding out of the room and down the corridor. Only her screams echoed through the castle as I leaned back in my chair and grinned.

Time to go to war.

Chapter 65

Alina's POV

"Come on, ladies! You have got this! Thumbs out, fists up, elbows in. One-two, one-two, two, one-two. Amazing!" I screamed as loud as I could over the groans and grunts in the room. I had around forty women in my session and seeing how some of them had never fought in their life before this week, they looked pretty damn strong. "Okay, take a five-minute breather and then we are going to pair up."

They all walked off in different directions to get a drink and I spotted Fiona in the corner looking extremely uncomfortable.

"Hey Fiona! Would you like to join us?" I said, approaching her and wiping sweat from my forehead with a towel.

"Oh, no. I think I will just watch for now. I'm not much of a fighter." She smiled timidly.

"I wasn't either before I started all of this. I am sure you will pick it up in no time," I encouraged her and gave her a warm smile. She shook her head and looked down at the floor. "Okay. Well, watching will help anyway. Why don't you take a seat on that bench and make some mental notes?" I suggested and she nodded and walked over.

After I got the girls to pair up and spar with each other, I decided that they were ready for one-to-one combat. Half of them punched the air and the other half looked like deers in headlights when I told them. I looked around the room and saw who the attacker could be. All the men were either in combat already or sparring in pairs with Logan and Fredrik walking amongst them shouting tips and directions. And then I spotted the perfect man for the job.

Jax.

He was taking a break in the corner, and he noticed me watching him and smiled. I waved him over. I have only met him a few times, but he seemed like a nice bloke and one of Logan's original pack members. He had been training with Logan awhile, so he knows what he was doing, but also isn't too intimidating.

"Hey, Luna. You okay?" he asked as he jogged over.

"Yes, thanks, Jax. I have a favour to ask of you though. I think my girls are ready for one-to-one combat, but they need to go up against someone that is skilled and won't hold back too much." I gave him a knowing look and he nodded.

"No problem."

I smiled and squeezed his shoulder. "Thank you." I turned to the girls and got their attention. "Listen up, ladies. Jax has very kindly offered to fight you all one-to-one. So, who wants to go first?"

"Luna, why are we fighting a man?" One of the younger girls shouted out.

"Because most vampires that will be in Lucius' army will be men and they will be ruthless. There is no point learning to fight each other. You need to know how to attack and defend against someone who scares you. No offence, Jax."

"None taken." He smirked.

"I will go first." Sloane stepped forward with a devilish grin.

"Okay, get yourselves ready," I said as we all made a circle around the mats to watch the fight.

It was a pretty good match and Sloane held her own well. When she shifted into her wolf, Jax stayed in human form pretending to be a vampire and she nearly had his throat a few times before I stopped them.

"Great match." Jax shook her hand at the end and she beamed proudly. "Who is next?" he shouted.

After a few fights, Jax was starting to tire and my girls were dominating, so I swapped him out and got Fredrik in. Things became a lot tougher for them then, so I allowed two girls against him which he secretly loved, showing the girls how they could work as a team to dominate and take down vampires. This inspired them and they started talking about strategies.

"Please don't get my Beta killed before the ceremony tonight." Logan came and stood next to me, watching the scene before him.

I chuckled and looked up at him.

"You have done amazingly well with these girls, Alina. They are fierce," he praised and I grinned proudly at them as they jumped on Fredrik's back. "Not as good as my men, though." He smirked at me cheekily.

"Oh, really? I have had to save your men's arses a few times, so far, from having their necks ripped out." I rested my hands on my hips and grinned at him.

"They are just going easy on them. Boosting their confidence."

I scoffed. "Whatever. Why don't you get in the ring instead then? Show us how it's done," I teased.

"Because no one will want to fight me. They are too scared." He winked and looked over at the girls again.

"I'll fight you," I said with confidence and his head snapped at me with a mischievous grin.

"You sure about that, Luna?" He stepped closer to me and looked down from his towering height, trying to intimidate me. I glared back up at him, pushing my body up against his.

"Stop the match!" I shouted without taking my eyes off him. "It's my turn!" I walked into the centre of the mats and the two girls moved away whilst Fredrik looked a little unsure.

"Er, Luna…" he started.

"Don't worry, Fredrik. I'm fighting Logan, not you."

Fredrik spun to look at Logan who was removing his shoes and clicking his neck with a smirk and stepped away from the mats. Suddenly, there was quite an audience around us, all eager to see how this would play out. Their future Luna and Alpha against each other.

"No shifting," Logan said as he walked into the middle of the floor. "I can't have all these men seeing your naked body after. I will kill someone." He growled and I burst out laughing.

"No problem." I closed my eyes and allowed Xena to come to the surface and share control. When I opened my golden eyes, I was met with Logan's darker shade of sapphire, showing me that Elias had come out to play.

"Hello, mate." His deep voice was no more than a whisper.

"Ready to get your ass kicked?" Xena purred.

"By you? Any day," he teased, and I giggled as we started circling each other and sizing each other up. Some of my girls were cheering me on at the side lines whilst the men were shouting for their Alpha.

He lunged, first grabbing me by the waist and throwing me down on the mat whilst leaning his body weight on top of me. Luckily, my arms were free and I quickly wrapped them around his neck and squeezed him until he turned slightly and I could throw him off.

The Last Alpha

I jumped up and kicked him straight in the chest, making him stumble slightly with a grin. I lunged forward fist first, aiming for his stomach, but he caught my hand and pulled it behind my back awkwardly and pressed my body up against his before leaning down and kissing me, making all the men roar.

I bit into his lip and smirked as he jumped back, releasing me and giving me the opportunity to kick him again and jump onto his back, strangling his throat.

"Oi, play nice now, little one." He growled as he tried to flip me off, but I hung on for dear life.

I knew this move and I knew what he would do next. Just before he went to flip backwards so I could land on my back, winded with him on top of me, I jumped off him and he realised it was too late as he fell back on his own back, knocking the air from his lungs. I calmly sat down on top of him, straddling his waist with a grin. I put my extended claws around his throat and said, "Check… mate."

But before I knew what was happening, he flipped me over so my stomach was on the mats and pulled me back by my throat and with his claws extended. "Too cocky, my mate!" He growled with a smirk plastered on his face.

The room erupted in roars and cheers as we both stood up and did a little bow, giggling. He swept me up and I wrapped my legs around his naked waist and kissed him passionately.

"Get a room, you two!" People hooted and shouted, but we didn't care. We were the only ones in the room at that moment. He pulled away grinning.

"I think we just might," he said, throwing me over his shoulder as he strode out of the grounds with me giggling and hitting his back.

***

The Last Alpha

"Come on, you two! The ceremony cannot begin without our Luna!" Sloane grinned as she poked her head around my bedroom door. Chloe was just finishing up my hair into a side plait that hung over my shoulder and some curls that loosely framed my face.

"It's all done! You look amazing." She winked at me in the mirror before I turned on the stool and walked over to the walk-in dressing room.

I still couldn't believe I have a walk-in dressing room! My pretty white dress hung on the door and I ran my fingers down the side of it and smiled. It was apparently tradition for the Luna and Alpha to wear white at the ceremony, which suited me just fine as it made me feel like I was honouring Xena. The dress was different to my usual style, with a boho vibe and flowing sleeves. It was girly and elegant, but I loved it.

"Stop staring at it and get it on, girl!" Sloane walked over, pulling it off the hanger.

I stepped into it and turned around so she could fasten up all the buttons down the back.

"I think I am just going to change quickly!" Chloe said, looking at herself in the full-length mirror. "This dress just doesn't feel right. I think I should wear the blue one."

"No! We don't have time! You look amazing, Chlo! We have to get down there like five minutes ago or Fred will withhold sex from me tonight and that is not happening for the sake of a dress." Sloane glared over my shoulder at Chloe.

"Oh, come on! We all know Fred could never withhold sex from you, he is obsessed with you! Empty threats!" I giggled and could tell Sloane was smirking behind me.

"Really? But this feels a bit too plain." Chloe was still studying herself in the mirror, scrunching her nose up. She was wearing a gorgeous red bodycon dress that stopped just below her knees. It had a deep V at the front which showed off her assets. But other than that little bit of skin, it was very classy for her and she looked beautiful.

"No, Chlo, you really do look amazing. Stick with the red." I smiled at her.

"And do you know what Joseph's favourite colour is…" Sloane teased in a sing-song voice and Chloe beamed.

"Okay, I'm ready. Let's not keep them waiting. Hurry up, girls!" Chloe raced from the room and Sloane and I burst out in giggles.

"Is it really his favourite colour?" I asked.

"No idea. But it got her out the door, didn't it?" Sloane laughed and pulled me by the end out after her.

Chapter 66

Alina's POV

When we reached the back garden of the pack house, my heart started racing. Logan had said we would keep it quite an informal and small event, but he didn't mention how pretty it would be. Candles lit an aisle through the grass towards a huge open fire pit in the middle and the whole pack stood under the trees that were lit up like Christmas trees with fairy lights and flowers. They circled the firepit, leaving only the candlelit walkway when they saw me approaching.

I looked forward and spotted Logan's tall, muscular frame standing by the blazing fire pit in a loose fitted white linen shirt that was open, revealing his broad chest and white trousers. His black curls were still slightly damp from his shower and fell over his eyes in that sexy way that made my knees go weak. He looked so damn delicious. He smiled, showing his pearly white teeth as our eyes locked. He looked the most relaxed and happiest I had ever seen him. The nerves evaporated. It was just me and him.

I reached the fire pit and he held out his manly hand for me to take, which fit perfectly with mine.

"You look stunning," he whispered in my ear as Fredrik

walked in front of us to start the ceremony.

"Blood Moon Pack, we stand here together tonight as one. One family. One kind. One pack. We have not had an easy journey, nor do we have an easy future, but together we are stronger than we ever knew possible. Tonight is the start of our new beginning. One full of hope, of promise and, most importantly, love. Not only are we welcoming new members to our pack, but also our Luna, Alina Clarke. I have no doubt in my mind that she will be the most wonderful Luna this pack could ever wish for and many of you will have already seen that in the last few days.

"Her kindness, generosity, support, and courage are reflected in all of us. Because as our Luna, we will look to her for guidance and wisdom. She will be the anchor to our ship. Before we start the ceremony, our Luna would like to say a few words." Fredrik turned around and winked at me as I wiped the tears from my eyes. I had no idea how sweet he could be. I looked up at Logan and gave him a reassuring smile as his face creased with confusion. He didn't know I was about to do this.

I stepped forward and scanned the crowd of faces. Many were familiar now but some are still new. Still unsure. I smiled at every one of them warmly. "Thank you, Fredrik. I know it is not custom for the Luna to address the pack during the ceremony, but I am not an ordinary Luna. I want to be transparent and honest with you all from the start. My hope for the future of this pack is to be full of trust and love and therefore, it is only right that you all know my story." I paused and caught Darius' eye in the crowd. He gave me an encouraging smirk and mouthed, "You've got this, buttercup!"

"Just a month ago, I had no idea I was a wolf. I had no idea supernatural beings even existed." The crowd erupted in gasps and whispers and I smiled, predicting their reaction. "It wasn't until I met my fated mate, your Alpha Logan, that my human life unravelled. Since then, I have experienced secrets, pain, suffering, passion, but most importantly, love. I have come to learn that as a child, I was spelled to keep my wolf from emerging. Meeting Logan broke the spell and now, I know who I truly am." I paused as I scanned the faces of my pack. I had no idea what their reaction would be to my confession and my nerves started to build again. Sensing my unease through our bond, Logan stepped forward and squeezed my hand, giving me the courage to continue. "My name is Alina Clarke Snow and I am the daughter of Clarke Snow. Many of you may know that name as the son of Alpha Alec Snow of the Blood Moon Pack. The last known Alabaster wolf."

Silence rippled through the air. It was like no one dared to breathe, as the only sound that could be heard was the gentle whistling of the wind through the trees. And then suddenly, everything changed.

An almighty roar exploded from the crowd as they howled and shouted in celebration. Many jumped and hugged each other. Their sea of bodies moved and collided like waves on the shore.

I released the breath I didn't realise I was holding and looked up at Logan with surprised, teary eyes. He was staring at me with a beaming smile and leaned forward and kissed my forehead tenderly. I let out a soft chuckle as the whole scene overwhelmed me. I finally felt accepted. I had found my family. My people.

The crowd calmed after a few minutes and looked back at me with awe and optimism in their eyes.

"Thank you for accepting me as your Luna. I promise to always do right by you all and treat you all as my family. Logan and I sincerely want to thank you all for being here and standing with us, not knowing what the future holds is scary, but together, we will prevail!" I shouted the last word with a laugh and the crowd erupted again!

"To our Luna, ALINA CLARKE SNOW!" Logan roared and the crowd chanted it back, making tears of happiness flow down my cheeks.

Fredrik stepped forward again, shushing the crowd after a few minutes.

"Let's get the ceremony started!" he roared and turned to gesture to Logan and I to step forward in front of the fire pit.

"Tonight, we are gathered here to pay tribute to our dear beloved Moon Goddess for gifting us with a new life. For blessing us with a new Alpha and a new Luna to lead us. Our Moon Goddess has chosen our next rulers wisely and carefully."

Fredrik turned to the small stand next to the fire that held a number of odd-shaped bottles that I hadn't even noticed until now. He lifted one with clear liquid and poured it into a glass bowl whilst saying, "We were made from the tears and blood of our mother. She gave us an exceptional gift of life that we are meant to appreciate and value every day."

He picked up some kind of flower I had never seen before and dropped it into the bowl. "She gave us mates to love, respect, admire, honour and worship so that we would not be lonely on this earth."

I watched as Sloane looked up at him and gave him a seductive wink and I giggled, looking up at my own mate. I don't think I have ever felt so happy in this moment.

He sprinkled some seeds into the bowl. "She gives us children to care for, tend to, cherish, and protect." Next, he picked up the most expensive looking bottle full of a gold liquid and poured it into the glass mixture. "The Goddess chooses an Alpha who is meant to lead, communicate, praise, discipline and protect his pack with his life." Fredrik turned to Logan, who stepped forward to the bowl. "Do you, Logan Black, at the age of twenty-six, accept the position of Alpha of the Blood Moon Pack?"

"Yes, I, Logan Black, accept the position of Alpha of the Blood Moon Pack. But I also share equal responsibility and leadership with my Luna."

Fredrik ran a knife over Logan's hand and Logan squeezed it over the bowl as red droplets fell. He stepped back and smiled at me with so much love and pride and my heart melted.

"A Luna is chosen to love, nurture, respect, support, and protect her pack with her life." Fredrik turned to me with a nod and I realised it was my turn to step forward. Taking a shaky breath, I held my hand over the bowl. "Do you, Alina Clarke Snow, at the age of twenty-two, accept the position of Luna of the Blood Moon Pack?"

"Yes, I, Alina Clarke Snow, accept the position of Luna of the Blood Moon Pack. But I also share equal responsibility and leadership with my Alpha." My voice sounded strong and confident even though I was shaking like a leaf. Fredrik ran the blade over the palm of my hand and I felt a stinging sensation as I squeezed my hand over the bowl. Watching my blood mix with Logan's and the concoction that Fredrik had created made me feel blessed, as if this was always meant to be.

"Now it is time to establish the pack as one with our Alpha and Luna together as destined mates. Alpha, Luna, please step up to the grail and grasp hands together, allowing your blood to mix and drip, not only signifying you as Alpha and Luna of our pack but also by blood as mates, creating a vow between the two of you and the goddess."

We followed his instructions and I glanced up into Logan's swirling blue eyes. It was crazy to think that only a month ago I didn't even know this man existed and yet it felt like I had known him my entire life. He was my soul mate. My person. He was my forever.

"I would like to say my own vows," Logan spoke before Fredrik could start and my eyes widened in surprise. I hadn't prepared anything! Was I meant to?

'You don't have to say anything but the traditional vows. Don't panic.' Logan's voice echoed in my mind through mind link.

"Of course, Alpha Logan." Fredrik stepped back to give the audience a view of him.

"I, Logan Black, promise in front of my pack and the Moon Goddess to love, honour and respect you as my Luna and as my mate. Alina, in you, I have finally found what I have never dared to dream of—the kind of love that is rare. Before you, I always felt like something was missing, a part of me that was never complete. Finding you meant finding my home, my peace. I always wanted you. Even when I didn't know what I wanted. Even before I met you. It was you. You were the missing piece, because without you, nothing makes sense. No matter what our future brings, we will always be okay because I love you. Always."

My eyes were so clouded with brimming tears that I couldn't see clearly. My heart felt like it was about to burst from my chest as I let his words sink in.

Fredrik went to step forward but I held my hand up to stop him and looked back at Logan with a smile. I knew what I had to say.

"I, Alina Clarke Snow, promise in front of my pack and the Moon Goddess to love, honour and respect you as my Alpha and as my mate. Before you, I was broken. I had fantasies, ideas about what true love meant and how it would feel, but none of them compared to the feeling I have when I am with you. Meeting you was unexpected, but it made me realise something. It made me realise why I had to wait.

Why we had to go through all of our past heartbreaks, all of our tough situations. Why we had to go through it all just to be where we were on that day we first met. The stars aligned and fate intervened, and I realised it was all worth it. Because you are my definition of love. You are my forever and my always."

His blue eyes glistened with so much emotion and, without warning, his free hand gripped the back of my neck and pulled me to his lips. He kissed me aggressively at first, but then it turned to one of passion and pure love. The crowd cheered and I smiled against his lips.

"I love you," he whispered as he pulled away.

"As a final act of commitment to your pack and each other, you will drink from the grail." Fredrik handed Logan the bowl first and he sipped from it before passing it to me. The bitter taste of the liquid burned my throat and I had to try my hardest not to cringe.

"I now present to you and our Goddess, Alpha Logan and Luna Alina of the Blood Moon Pack!" Fredrik roared and Logan raised our still entwined bloody hands in the air. The crowd erupted in cheers and chants and Fredrik poured the reminder of the bowl into the open fire pit. Everyone gasped as the flames blazed six feet into the air and changed between white and black embers.

"As your Alpha and Luna, we now invite any new members who wish to join our pack to come up to the flames and share your blood, committing yourselves to the oath and protection of the Blood Moon Pack!" Logan shouted over the fire and men and women all stepped forward, creating a line to start the initiation.

Logan's eyes sparkled at me, the enchanted flames dancing in the reflection of them. "To our new beginning."

Chapter 67

Logan's POV

"To our new beginning." I looked into her eyes and saw my entire universe. I had never felt so much euphoria and love than I did at that moment; surrounded by my pack, the pack I had rebuilt from the ground up, and looking into the eyes of my Luna, the woman I love. She was glowing. Her radiance projecting in all of the ecstatic and excited faces of our new pack members.

"It is an honour to become part of your pack, Alpha and Luna." Rohan approached us as he wiped the blood away from his hand. "I will fight to the death for this pack. You are now part of my family." He nodded at Alina with a smile.

"Hopefully, you won't have to," I said with a grin and shook the man's hand as his wife walked up beside him. She bowed in respect.

"Please. We want you to treat us like equals. No more bowing." Alina said softly to the shy woman and her face blushed, but she nodded and agreed.

Once everyone had been initiated, I turned to Alina. "It is time to do our first run through the territory as a pack. Are you sure you are ready for everyone to see Xena?"

She nodded. "Of course. I trust them all."

"Okay, then. Beloved wolves of Blood Moon Pack, we are now united and stronger than ever! It is time to share our first run together through our lands. Please join us!" I shouted, instantly gaining everyone's attention. I nodded at Sloane, who held up a blanket in front of Alina.

"What are you doing?" Alina whispered to her but I answered first.

"Only my eyes are allowed to worship your body. No one else's," I whispered huskily in her ear and she rolled her eyes.

"One of these days, I may have to shift unexpectedly. You cannot hide me forever," she said as she removed her dress.

"I can try." I smirked as I threw my discarded clothes on the ground and allowed Elias full control. I felt his paws hit the ground and looked over to see Alina shifting into Xena effortlessly. Looks like she had caught on quick. We scanned the pack as they started removing their clothes and shifting into their wolves.

'Ready?' I mind linked Alina.

'Let's go,' she said eagerly. We both darted off through the crowd as they parted for us to take the lead and we heard the thunder of paws on the ground behind us.

As we ran, wolves mind linked us, thanking us and praising us for this new life. I felt an overwhelming sense of pride that we managed to get to this point, but also fear. Fear that it could all still be taken away. Elias shook his head and growled at me for the thought, wanting me to stop tainting this special moment. So that's what I did. I shut it out and focused on the here and now. On feeling the wind whipping through Elias' fur as he manoeuvred and leapt through the forest with his mate by his side and his pack behind him.

Soon, we reached the large clearing at the back of the woods and both Xena and Elias stopped at the same time, as though we were in tune with each other. Gradually, all of the pack filtered through the trees and stood proudly behind us, waiting for our next move. The full moon illuminated the sky and acted as a beacon, guiding us.

Xena turned her head to gaze into Elias' eyes and brushed her head against his neck. They both threw their heads back and released a magical howl of happiness as every wolf in the pack did the same. Birds flew up into the air from the shock of the vibrations that rippled through the forest. Once silence occupied the night once more, we turn and sprinted back to the village.

Time to get this party started!

***

The atmosphere was electrifying, and everyone was in high spirits as they chatted around the fire pit, drinking beer and dancing as the flames warmed their bodies. I watched Alina from a distance, sitting on a log by the fire with a few women, laughing and chatting. She looked so carefree and happy, and a warm feeling spread across my chest. All I wanted to do was touch her, hold her, be with her, but this wasn't just about us. Tonight was important for all our pack and I need to leave her alone to mingle and have fun as much as it killed me. I strolled over to Darius who was busy flipping burgers on the grill.

"Couldn't get me another beer, could you?" His gruff tone made me raise my eyebrows at him. I picked one out of the ice box and snapped the cap off with my teeth before passing it to him.

"Cheers," he said before nearly downing the entire bottle.

"You alright, mate?" I eyed him carefully. I always knew when he was pissed off about something, but normally it was directed at me. He must have been the only one who wasn't happy tonight.

"Yeah, great," he replied sarcastically. He looked over the grill and took another swig and I followed his glaring gaze. Chloe and Joseph were sitting next to each other on a log around the fire and looked very cosy. She laughed at something he said and swatted his arm and Darius grunted.

I turned my back on them, so I was facing Darius and leaned on the table. "So… Chloe and Joseph, aye?" I said casually.

"What about them?" he said in a bored tone and flipped over another burger rather aggressively.

"I heard they were an item. Pretty smitten." I took a swig of my bottle to hide my smirk.

His head snapped at mine, and anger was evident in his brown eyes. "Who told you that? Did Alina tell you that?" he growled, and I chuckled.

"Why do you even care?" I said comically. It was too easy to rattle him.

"I don't! I just think she could do better, is all." He looked up at them again before passing a burger to a man who didn't ask for one.

"Er… I wanted a sausage, actually," the man started, but soon stopped when he saw the look on Darius' face. "It's okay, burgers are fine." He walked away and I chuckled.

"Could've fooled me. You've been acting like a jealous boyfriend for days now. What's the deal?" I pushed and he sighed.

"I don't fucking know, man. She drives me crazy. She's annoying and over the top and loud and never shuts up and… I can't get her out of my fucking head," he gritted through his teeth and my eyes widened. I wasn't expecting a confession so easily.

"Then tell her. Tell her you like her," I said calmly, taking a mouthful of burger.

"No fucking way. I would rather shoot myself. Like I said, she drives me crazy. It would never work."

"Maybe you just need to get laid. It's been a minute," I smirked, knowing it would wind him up.

"Fuck off. I get laid all the time."

"Oh, yea? When was the last time?" I raised my eyebrows at him.

He stopped flipping the burgers and his eyes widened. "Shit. It's been at least two months! How the hell did that happen? Fuck man, that is it! I just need to get laid! It's nothing to do with Chloe!" His eyes lit up and he ripped the apron from his body and shoved it in my hands. "Take over for me. I need to find a hottie to graft tonight. Can't waste any more time."

I laughed and nodded as he sped away scouring the crowds for his victim. "Idiot," I muttered under my breath as I started flipping burgers. I felt two hands wrap around my waist from behind and her smell engulfed my senses.

"Hey, beautiful." I lifted my arm for her to nestle under it as I continued with my new job.

"I thought I was the burger queen?" she giggled, watching me.

"Wanna take over?" I asked, handing her the spatula.

"No, I'm good. Never come between a man and his BBQ," she joked and I turned to put my arms around her waist.

"You can come between me and anything, anytime." I smirked and winked at her cheekily as her cheeks flushed pink. I leaned in and nuzzled her neck at her marking spot, feeling her body react to my touch.

"Logan… not here…" She tried pushing me back on my chest but I didn't budge.

"If you didn't already know, I am the Alpha here and I can do whatever I want, whenever I feel like it," I said huskily into her skin.

"Well in that case⋯" She ran her hands up my back and into my hair and tugged roughly, pulling my head back to look at her face.

"So can I." She grinned and pulled my head to her as she smashed her lips against mine hungrily and an explosion erupted inside me. Fuck.

I knew I needed to stop, otherwise I was about to take her in the forest and fuck her brains out and that wouldn't be a good look for our first night as Alpha and Luna. I pulled away, panting heavily.

"Not fair," I growled, and she giggled irresistibly and released me.

"Where is Darius, anyway? He was pretty adamant he wanted to be in charge of the BBQ tonight," she asked, scanning the crowds.

"Interesting story," I smirked, and got her attention straight away. I pointed the spatula at Chloe who now had her legs draped over Joseph's thigh and was hugging his bicep.

"What?" she asked, her nose creasing in that cute way it did when she was confused. "What about Chloe?"

"He likes her," I said with a cheeky grin, and waited for the dramatics.

"Who?" her eyes widened as she realises. "Darius? Darius likes Chloe? Shut the fuck up! Did he say that? I don't understand! Still doesn't explain why he's not here cooking."

"He was getting angrier and angrier watching them two together, so I took over," I said, shrugging as she looked over at Chloe again.

"And I also pointed out that he hadn't had sex for a while." Alina turned to me and grabbed my arm.

"What?! So he is going to have sex with someone else even though he likes Chloe and he hasn't told her. Logan! I could kill you! Why do you always have to mess with him?" she growled lowly to avoid causing a scene and I gave her my biggest smile.

"Because it's too much fun!" She hit me on the arm again and I chuckled. "Anyway, she's not into him so I have just saved him from heartbreak. Win, win!"

"You men are so clueless sometimes!" She started stalking off into the crowd.

"Where are you going?!" I shouted after her.

"To fix your mess!" she cries back and I laughed out loud. *Good luck with that, darling!*

Chapter 68

Chloe's POV

"So, have you ever been with a wolf, Chloe?" Joseph's green eyes twinkled with mischief as he took a swig from his beer. I looked up at him through my eyelashes and ran my finger down his bicep.

"I don't know what you mean," I flirt back, feigning innocence.

He smirked. "Let me be clearer then. Have you ever felt completely and utterly fucked to the point that you fear you will never walk again?" He lowered his voice so only I could hear him and my heart raced. Fuck, this guy was next level hot.

"I can't say that I have. Although I am pretty sure I have made a guy immobile before." I smirked back and swigged my beer bottle, too.

"Then you haven't been with a wolf." He winked, and I bit my lip. His eyes travelled down to my lips and I saw the desire swirling in them. He smiled, showing his perfect teeth and looked away. Why wouldn't he kiss me already? I hate having to make the first move but this guy was starting to wind me up to the point that I would jump his bones in front of everyone at this bonfire.

I looked up and saw Darius glaring at me over the grill, his face like thunder. Wonder what had pissed him off this time. It didn't take much. Logan stood next to him, smirking. So of course, the cousin rivalry continues. I narrowed my eyes at him, challenging him to look away first, and when he did, I felt a little wave of triumph. God, he really gets under my skin.

Only this morning, he annoyed me to the point that I physically took my shoe off and threw it at him. I don't even know what it is about him, but he just knows how to push my buttons. Alina said it was because we were so similar. Pfft. As if I am anything like that loud, insensitive, annoying hulk. I mean what man needs so many muscles, anyway? He should definitely just paint himself green for Halloween. Spitting image. I scoff at the thought.

"What are you laughing at?" Joseph turned and eyed me with a smile.

Shit. Now I look like a crazy person, laughing for no reason. "Oh, I was just thinking… how it is funny that I am the only human here."

"And why is that funny? We aren't going to eat you or anything. Well, maybe I will." He smirked and my heart flipped in my chest.

Yes, fucking please. Eat me up!

"Hey, do you know that Darius guy? Alpha Logan's cousin, isn't he?" He nodded towards the BBQ just as Darius ripped of the apron and shoved it into Logan's arms before storming off. Such a child.

"Yeah, I know him. Wish I didn't," I muttered and watched as he walked straight up to a semi-attractive brunette and started talking to her.

"I think he has a problem with me," Joseph said flatly, clearly not that bothered either way.

"Really? Why'd you say that?" I asked, still watching him as the girl laughed at something he said and touched his arm. A strange feeling heated up in my gut and I took a drink from my beer to settle it.

"Dunno. He just seems to hate me. Tried to be a dick to me in front of Alpha yesterday at the battle meeting. And caught him staring daggers at me a few times tonight. Maybe he likes you," he said with a sideways smile.

"What?! You are crazy. He despises me. Makes it very clear daily how much I annoy him. I am sure he is just threatened by you. You are one of the best fighters here." I narrowed my eyes as Darius threw his arm over the girl's shoulder and they walked towards the edge of the wood. Where were they going? Wait, why do I even care?

Urgh. Come on, Chloe. Focus on the hot guy you have right next to you. You are only acting this way because of the stupid dream you had last night.

I sighed as a flashback of Darius' huge body crushed mine against my bedroom wall as he ripped my pyjamas off my body and consumed me. Urgh! All because of Sloane and her stupid comments about thinking it was Darius that I liked. Saying we have chemistry and passion. Bullshit.

"Hey? Are you there?" I heard Joseph's voice disrupt my thoughts.

"Huh? What? Sorry, I just zoned out then. Think all this beer is starting to go to my head." I chuckled awkwardly.

"I asked you if you wanted to perhaps go on a date sometime? Once the battle is over. I don't really want anything to occupy my mind until after then," he said calmly and I felt like squealing.

"Yes! Umm, I mean, yeah, that would be nice."

Suddenly, the atmosphere around us all changed from carefree and fun to tense. Lots of people stood up in front of us to get a better look at what was happening.

"What's going on?" I whispered to Joseph, but his body started to tense and he sniffed the air. Without warning, he bolted up from the log, forcing me to fly backwards onto the ground, and started to push his way through the crowd. My heart started racing knowing something must be seriously wrong and I stood up to get a better look.

I saw five naked people in the distance and then Joseph stopped in front of them. Everything happened so fast. He ran at the same time towards one of the girls as she did the same and leapt into his arms. And the next thing I knew, they are fucking kissing! What the…?

Everyone cheered and whistled as the humiliation bubbled up inside me. He found his mate. Of course. And once again, I was alone.

Not being able to take any more, I ran to the woods as tears streamed down my face. I kept running and running with no idea where I was going or what I was doing. All I knew was that I couldn't stay there after that. I was already the pathetic human girl in a pack of wolves and now I was the rejected pathetic human girl. Just great. I tripped over a branch on the floor and fell face first into the mud.

"Ow, fuck!" I shouted as I sat up and held my ankle. Well, that would teach me to run in high heels in the forest at night. I heard twigs snapping underfoot and someone approaching. My heart started pounding. Why did I think it was a good idea to run into the woods at night alone? No good ever comes from a girl alone in the forest.

An enormous shadow of a man made me scream.

"Shhh, bloody hell, woman! It's only me! Stop screaming!"

I recognised that deep voice. "D-Darius?" He came into view and looked at me up and down like I was some helpless lost puppy.

"What are you doing here?"

"I came to check on you. To check you are alright. Which clearly you are not," he scoffed, pointing at my ankle and irritation bubbled within. See, five seconds in his company and I already wanted to punch him in the face.

"Great, I am just terrific, actually, so you can leave and pretend to stop caring. I am pretty sure you only came to gloat anyway." I tried shifting my body up to stand but fell back as the pain shot through my leg.

Darius grunted and bent down whilst rolling his eyes. He picks me up in one effortless movement, bridal style.

"What are you doing?! Put me down."

He sat me on a fallen tree trunk which was so big that I was directly at his height and my legs swung halfway down to the floor. He picked up my ankle and I was surprised by how soft his hands felt on my skin. My breath hitched as he bent down to study it.

"You have just twisted your ankle. It will feel alright in a few hours once you get an ice pack on it."

I stared at him in disbelief. Why was he being so nice to me?

"These, however," he said, pulling off my red Louboutin's. "Are not alright and a hazard to your health." He threw them over his shoulder and they flew into the darkness of the woods. Ah, there's the dickhead I know!

"No!" I screamed and held my hand out for them. "You idiot! Do you know how much they cost? They are Louboutins!" I glared at him and he frowned.

"Lou-bou whatys?"

"Oh, my god! You have to be kidding me! Go and get them! Now!" I shouted as he crossed his arms over his chest.

"Nah." He smirked.

The Last Alpha

"This is not the time to be screwing with me, Darius. I have just had my heart broken and now you have thrown my babies into the darkness to be ravished by predators!"

He scoffed again. "Enough with the dramatics, Cinderella. They are just shoes. Ridiculous shoes, if you ask me."

Rage boiled inside me and I clenched my fists together and tensed my jaw. "They are not just shoes⋯" I gritted through my teeth. "Get me down from here right now and I will go and find them myself."

"You know you should really be thanking me." He smirked, putting his hands at either side of my hips on the tree. My heart speeded up at his proximity. What was he doing?

"What on earth would I be thanking you for?" I growled.

"Well, I bet you haven't thought about that golden boy finding his mate in front of everyone since I threw away your shoes." His chocolate brown eyes sparkled with amusement.

"This is funny to you, isn't it? Oh, ha-ha, poor Chloe, rejected by a wolf in front of the entire pack. Well, fuck off Darius. I am not in the mood."

His eyes suddenly changed and all the amusement and mischief were gone. Instead, he looked tense. Serious even and I suddenly felt a prickly tension between us. "No, it isn't funny to me, Chloe. I came to check on you because⋯ I knew that must have been hard⋯ To see him with someone else."

His square jaw twitched and his eyes searched mine. I suddenly felt very uncomfortable at how close he was. I could smell his cologne and it was fogging my senses.

"I⋯ Why do you care?" I asked quietly and see some emotion flicker in his eyes. But just as quickly, it had disappeared and his smirk was back. He pushed away from the tree trunk.

"I don't. I just wanted to check you weren't about to do something stupid like run into the wilderness alone."

I narrowed my eyes at him. "So, you do care?" I gloated, realising he still admitted to caring somewhat about my safety.

Now it was his turn to glare at me. "Why are you always so difficult?" he snapped.

"Me? What about you?! You are the most annoying man I have ever met in my entire life!"

He turned and kicked the leaves on the floor with his huge combat boots as he chuckled. "I knew this could never work," he muttered under his breath, but I just about caught it.

My eyebrows furrowed together. "What could never work?" I asked curiously, all my anger dispersing. God, I felt like I was on some kind of emotional rollercoaster every time I was around this frustrating man.

"Nothing," he muttered. "I think we should head back now."

"Not until you tell me what you meant by that," I said folding my arms across my chest so violently that I lost my balance and before I could stop myself, I was falling to the ground. I let out a gasp as instead of the hard landing of the floor, I felt strong arms around my body and I was pressed up against a rock-hard chest.

I opened my eyes and they widened in shock as my face was inches away from his. I could feel his heart beating in his chest and his eyes were once again intense and full of⋯ desire? I wanted to look away but I couldn't. They were captivating and my body failed me as I felt my arousal grow just being in his arms. His jaw tensed as he took a deep breath in and closed his eyes but still held me tight against him.

"I— er, thank you," I said weakly as I tried and wriggled from his embrace. He loosened his grip and I slid down his toned body, feeling about the size of an ant against him. I started to hobble away from him. Being barefoot was not making it any easier against the prickly forest floor.

"He doesn't deserve you anyway." His voice comes out in a deep husk and did things to me that I do not care to admit. I froze at his words. Slowly, I heard his footsteps crunching behind me and then the warmth of his body against my back. I wanted to move or turn or run but something stopped me.

"You are too good for him so don't cry over him, okay?" His tone was soft but still deep and I gulped down unwanted feelings. I don't know what was wrong with me, but I was starting to feel things I shouldn't. That stupid dream. I need to get out of this situation, it was too dangerous.

My body tensed as I felt his fingers travel around my waist and slowly, he turned me to face him. I swallowed audibly as I looked up into his beautiful deep brown eyes. Why had I never noticed how many different shades of brown they were?

"Did you hear me?" he asked in a lower voice and his eyes flickered down to my lips and back up to my eyes.

I nodded my head slowly.

A small smile crept across his face and he lifted his hand and runs his fingers gently down my cheek. "Well, I never. Are you speechless?"

"W-what are you doing, Darius?" I asked in a low voice as his hand travelled down my neck, giving me goose pimples all over my skin.

"Why? Do you want me to stop?" His hand froze at the crook of my neck and he held my gaze.

My voice was out before I could stop it. "No." What am I saying?

His eyes travelled back to my lips and I bit my bottom lip involuntarily. He growled and my eyes widened. It was the most erotic sound I have ever heard and awakened a need inside me.

"Don't do that." His voice was thick with arousal and wetness pooled between my legs.

Oh shit, I am in trouble. Do I really want this annoying, arrogant, cocky but sexy as fuck man?

I shocked myself when I realised, I really do. A small smile played on my lips and I bit my lower lip again. His growl rippled through his chest and his mouth was on mine in seconds.

Fire ignited inside me as our mouths collided and fought for dominance. He bent down and wrapped one arm around my waist, pulling me up off the floor against his body and his other hand gripped my hair, deepening the kiss. My dress restricted me from wrapping my legs around him so I had to leave them dangling. I knew I should have worn the blue one! My arms went around his stocky neck and I threaded my fingers through his wavy auburn hair. My god, this was the best kiss of my life. We pulled apart when we both ran out of oxygen, panting heavily.

"What the fuck was that?" I said leaning my forehead against his.

"The fucking best kiss I've ever had," he breathed.

"What are we doing? We can't do this," I said trying to argue against my urges.

"Why not?" he asked still holding my body up with one arm, which in itself was bloody impressive and turning me on.

"Because we hate each other. We can't stand each other," I whispered and made the mistake of looking down at his lips again. I wanted to kiss him again.

He pulled his head back and took a deep breath. My heart sunk as he slowly put me down on my feet. "You are right. We can't do this. It will end badly."

My eyes narrowed at him. "Why will it end badly?" I pushed away from him, earning an aggravated look in return.

"You are impossible! You just said yourself we can't stand each other. Of course it will end badly. And I don't do relationships so…" He shrugged his arms in the air and let them fall back down to his side. How bloody dare he!

"Is that what you think this is? Me trying to trap you? Oh, wow! You are the last person on earth I would want to be in a relationship with." I picked up the hem of my dress and started marching (or I should say waddling) away trying not to put too much pressure on my ankle.

"That's not what that kiss implied!" I heard him shout behind me.

"Don't flatter yourself! It was a minor brain malfunction. A moment of pure insanity and it will never happen again!" I yelled over my shoulder before I realised how close he already was behind me. I screamed as he yanked me off my feet and started striding towards the pack house carrying me in his arms. "What are you doing? Put me down!" I hit his chest with my fists, making no impact whatsoever.

"It is too painful to watch you hobbling along on that foot. And I am sure you would love to have to walk through that crowd, barefoot and with your lipstick all smeared and try and explain yourself?" He smirked and I glared at him.

"Fine. Take me to my room, but I am warning you. If you tell anyone about what happened in there, I will rip your balls off."

He chuckled. "I'll take you to your room, alright…"

"Urgh. You are the most…"

"Gorgeous, sexy, irresistible man I have ever laid eyes on." He mimicked my voice.

"Actually…"

"Chlo! Are you alright? What the hell happened to you?" Alina came running over from the crowd, worry in her features as Darius lowered me to the ground.

"Oh, um…I fell in the woods. Twisted my ankle. Darius found me and was just taking me to my room." Her eyes darted between mine and Darius and a small smile spread across her face. Shit, she suspected something. "I am fine now, Darius. You can go," I said coldly.

He shook his head at me and walked into the pack house and I finally felt like I could breathe again.

"Are you sure you are alright? After you know, Joseph…" Alina asked.

"Yes. Oh, god that was nothing. I am fine. I wish him all the happiness in the world!" I threw my hands up in the air dramatically and she raised her eyebrows at me. *Stop acting weird Chloe. Everything is fine. She doesn't know anything.*

"And Darius?" she asked carefully, her eyes flickering to my smudged lipstick.

"Still a loser. I mean, his strength comes in handy when you fall over in a wood, I guess. But apart from that, still a waste of space," I said trying to keep my cool.

She eyed me suspiciously and nodded.

"I am going to go to bed now. Shattered! Can't keep up with you, party animals. Hah! Get it, animals… because you are wolves!" I faked a laugh and cringed at myself. I need to lock myself in a room for the next twenty-four hours, away from everyone until I have calmed down! "I will see you in the morning. Love you!" I shouted as I hobbled into the house and started making my way up the stairs to the second floor. Why didn't they install a lift?

Darius' POV

I slammed the door to my bedroom on the second floor and run my hands through my hair. Fuck! Why the fuck did I do that? She was the last person I need to sleep with. I actually seemed to like her, care about her even. And she was Alina's best friend. Way too complicated, way too many strings. I like my women unattached.

But that kiss… Man that was some kiss. It had taken every ounce of self-control to not flirt with her or make a move when I saw her in that red dress at the ceremony. I had always found her attractive. I mean, who wouldn't? Her petite frame made her so adorably small but she still had womanly curves in all the right places which she always flaunted in the trendiest clothes. Mousy brown hair that was always styled immaculately and amazing blue eyes. And those sharp lips that drove me crazy when she's talking but also crazy when I…

Stop it, Darius. Get a fucking grip.

I couldn't remember the last time a girl had occupied my mind like this. I mean, I had a thing for Alina when I first met her, but very soon I realised it was just friendship. She felt more like a sister to me. But the more I got to know Chloe, the more I found myself constantly thinking about her. Trying to be near her even if it meant annoying the hell out of her to get her attention. It was pathetic. I just needed to get her out of my head. Which was my plan until that plank found his mate. Even though I am secretly relieved. I hated seeing his hands all over Chloe. At least now, he wouldn't so much as bat an eye in her direction.

Now what? We just go back to annoying each other, bickering

every day, pretending the kiss never happened. That was the best thing to do. For everyone's sakes. I would get over this crush eventually.

'BUT SHE KISSED YOU BACK' Gunner's deep voice boomed in my mind. He liked Chloe's spunk, the way she put me in my place. She was not our mate, so of course, he was weary but he could see why I like her.

No I don't. It was just a fleeting moment.

But she did kiss me back… so maybe she felt the same way? She said she hated me but her body told me the opposite. This was such a mess.

I flopped back onto the bed and heard some kind of grunting noises from the stairs. Shit. It is her; I know it is. Shall I go out? Shall I help her get to her room?

I scoffed at myself, knowing that it was a terrible idea. I could hear a patter of footsteps on the landing close to my door and my heart raced. Don't do it. Don't go out there. Let her go.

I bolted across the room and yanked my door open aggressively just as she passed it and she jumped in surprise and fell on her ass.

"What the…!" She shouted, looking up at me from the floor and I couldn't help but laugh. "You made me jump, you dick!"

I laughed harder when I saw how much menace she was trying to portray on her face and failing. She pulled herself up and put up her middle finger at me as she started to walk away again. I grabbed her wrist and pulled her back.

"What are you doing?" She glared at me.

"You need to put an icepack on that ankle of yours otherwise it will be the size of an elephant's tomorrow," I said meeting her gaze.

She pulled her arm from my grip and I let her. "Thanks for the tip but I am sure I will be fine." She moved again.

"Suit yourself. I hope you like being bed bound because that is where you will be spending the next two days." I folded my arms across my chest and leaned against the wall. She stopped but didn't turn. "I have some ice in my room. I can make you an ice pack up to save you a trip back downstairs."

She turned and glared at me. "I am not falling for that trick."

"Okay, only trying to help. Good night then," I said and walked back into my room and closed the door.

I listened carefully and when I heard her sigh loudly, I knew I got her. A few seconds later, a knock on my door. I opened it with a smirk and she pushed past me into my room.

"Change of heart?" I smirked as she stood awkwardly on one leg.

"Just get the bloody ice pack, you moron, so I can go to bed."

I walked over to the freezer and pulled out a bag of ice, popping a few ice cubes in a flannel and wrapping it into a tight ball. "Sit," I ordered and gestured to my bed as I walked back towards her.

"No, thanks. I will take it and leave," she replied stubbornly so I wrapped my arm around her waist and threw her onto the bed and she lets out a squeal. She sat up abruptly and glared at me as I kneeled down on the floor in front of her. "What is your problem? Did your parents drop you on your head as a baby or something?"

"No, just trying to help a friend in need." I smiled sweetly. "And please don't speak about my dead parents in that way."

Her eyes widened and she put her hand to her mouth. "Oh… I am so sorry… I didn't mean to…" She stopped when she saw my shoulders shaking from the chuckle I was supressing. "You are sick!" she shouted as I held her foot still. She tried to pull it away from me but I tightened my grip around her calf and held the ice pack to her ankle. We stayed like that in silence for a few moments and the tension thickened once more. This was a bad idea.

My eyes hungrily roamed up her slender leg as the slit of her dress fell from her thigh. I slowly ran my free hand up her leg towards her thigh and back down.

"D-Darius··· Stop," she whispered huskily and her voice sounded so sexy.

"What if I don't want to stop? What if I want to do more?" I asked and her eyes widened.

"Like what?" she swallowed nervously and I smirked.

"Shall I show you?"

She thought carefully for a moment before replying seductively, "Show me."

My dick hardened at her words but I was still unsure how much she wanted this. I leaned forward and started placing kisses up her shin slowly and then onto her thigh. She let her head roll back as her breathing hitched. As I got closer to the top of her thigh where her dress restricted my access, I licked her skin causing her to jump at the different sensation.

"Shall stop?" I asked, my head so close to her centre and I wanted to taste her more than anything.

"I-I think we should," she said and my heart dropped. Disappointment must have shown on my face as I stood up abruptly and she climbed off the bed. I held out the flannel filled with ice and she took it from me carefully.

"Thanks," she said quietly and I walked to the door. I opened it for her without saying a word and stepped to the side to allow her to leave. I didn't dare speak; I didn't trust what would come out of my mouth. She walked past me and hovered by the door. She turned quickly and opened her mouth to speak but as soon as our eyes connected, it was game over. She dropped the ice as I slammed the door shut and pushed her up against it as my lips found hers. I had to lean down to reach her as I cupped her face in my hands and our tongues danced together. Her hands explored my body and she tugged at my shirt, trying to pull it up. I pulled away from her to pull it over my head swiftly and threw it to the floor.

"This doesn't change anything," she breathed between her pants. "I still hate you."

I smirked knowing how I was about to change that view completely. "Ditto." I smashed my lips against hers again before she could say anything else and pulled down the zip at the back of her dress. She shimmied out of it without breaking our kiss and I lifted her body up so I could hold her against the wall. Her little legs wrapped around my waist, and I felt her naked boobs against my chest. I walked us over to the bed and threw her down on it and took in her perfect body.

"Like what you see?" she teased, and I growled as my dick throbbed against my jeans. I climbed up the bed towards her, lowering my body onto hers, being careful not to allow my full weight to crush her and started kissing and nibbling her neck. She moaned suggestively and it sounded like heaven. "Is it true what they say about… sex with a wolf?" she gasped between her moans.

I lifted my head up and looked into her eyes with a mischievous glint. "Oh, yes… You won't be getting any sleep tonight," I said huskily and returned to her neck as she bucked her hips against mine, pulling me against her.

"This is a one-time thing so make it count then." She gave me a sexy smile and I bit a little harder than usual into her neck, drawing a bit of blood. She gasped out loud. Fuck, she was a human. I need to go easy on her.

"Shit, sorry! Did I hurt you?" I snapped my head up to look into her eyes, but they were full of desire and longing.

"No. Do it again."

I smirked at her response.

"Oh, and Darius? Don't you dare hold back."

That was it. I was a goner.

Chapter 69

Alina's POV

"I have something to tell you," Sloane said shyly looking down at the floor as we headed back to the pack house after our morning training session.

"What is it?" I asked softly.

A small smile painted her dainty face and she looked up to meet my gaze. "I'm pregnant," she whispered, looking around to check no one heard.

"What? Oh, Sloane! Congratulations!" I stopped walking and reached for her hand. "You are happy, right?" I said carefully.

"Of course!" Her whole face lit up. "Why wouldn't I be?"

"Well, it's just that you're so young and you haven't been with Fredrik for that long."

"I am a year younger than you!" She laughed.

"Exactly! We are young!" I said almost shocked at her reaction.

"Luna Alina, you still have a lot to learn about the ways of wolves," she mocked, shaking her head. My eyebrows furrowed.

"Once you find your true mate, it is the greatest blessing for the Goddess to grant you a child together. Many wolves fall pregnant straight away, but for some, it can take much longer. The Moon

Goddess grants us a child when she feels it is right, so who are we to judge her choices."

I wasn't sure how I felt about this news. Having lived a human life for so long, I wasn't used to the fast-pace way things seemed to move amongst the wolves. I had always expected to have children once I was married and settled down, probably in my thirties. Logan and I hadn't even discussed children yet. We had only been together for a month, surely, he would run a mile!

"What's wrong?" Sloane asked when she saw the panic on my face. I wish I was better at hiding my emotions. My face gave everything away.

"Nothing. It's just fast, isn't it? But honestly, I really am so happy for you and Fredrik! You will make the best parents!" I said with a huge smile and pulled her in for a hug.

She giggled. "Thank you. I am so excited. I really want to give this child the perfect, safe upbringing. The one I never had," she said sadly as she rubbed her flat stomach.

"I am sure you will. How has Fredrik taken the news?"

She rolled her eyes and scoffed. "He's elated, of course, but more protective than ever! I had to practically trick him into the shower this morning so I could sneak out to training! He thinks I should be bubble-wrapped for the next six months!"

My face creased again, confused.

"Wolves pregnancies are shorter than humans. Wow you really don't know much, do you? Don't worry, I will fill you in on it all."

"Do you think…" I paused, wondering whether I should say it out loud. "…Logan expects to have children so quickly?"

She raised her eyebrow in a suggestive way that told me her answer. "Put it this way… Have you and Alpha ever used protection?"

"No but I am on the pill, so⋯"

She stopped walking as we were halfway up the stairs to the second floor of the pack house and I turned sideways to look at her smirking. "The pill doesn't work on wolves, my Luna. As soon as your wolf emerged, it would have lost effect."

My eyes widened and I felt heat start to burn across my skin. What?!

"Don't worry." Sloane chuckled linking her arm with mine and continuing up the stairs. "Like I said, the Moon Goddess has a plan for us all. She will gift you a child when the time is right, so just enjoy all the hot newly mated sex until then."

Just as we reached the landing of the second floor, Darius' bedroom door swung open and a dishevelled looking Chloe walked out with last night's dress on. Her hair was matted and stuck up in all different directions and her makeup was smudged. She looked like she hadn't slept a wink and had love bites all over her neck and body. Her eyes bulged when she saw us both stood gawking at her with our mouths hanging open.

"Shut up! Don't say a fucking word!" She gritted through her teeth as her cheeks turned crimson and she ran down the corridor and into her room, slamming the door behind her. Sloane and I turned and looked at each other in disbelief and burst out laughing.

"I told you so." She giggled and I shook my head with a huge smile.

Logan's POV

"Come in!" I shout to Fredrik who was knocking on my father's old office door. I was starting to pack up any valued belongings or important documents from his study and asked Fredrik to meet me here so we could talk over our battle plan again. He walked in with a tense look on his face and huffed as he flopped down on one of the chairs. I raised my eyebrows at him. "Something wrong?"

"Women. Why are they so stubborn?" he growled, leaning his head back and looking up to the ceiling.

"I am guessing you mean one woman in particular?" I said whilst scanning the pages of the next pile of letters my father had kept. None seemed relevant anymore as many of the men who had written them were now dead.

He sighed again. "She's pregnant."

I froze and dropped the letters. I jumped up from my father's chair and nearly knocked him to the floor, pulling him in to a big bear hug. "Man! Congratulations!" I beamed at him and his face lit up and I saw how truly happy he felt about it.

"Thanks, Alpha. You know, I had given up all hope of having a family after Iona so this feels like a miracle. I'm still scared to go to sleep every night in case I wake up and find none of it is real." He chuckled but I could see the pure anxiety written all over his face.

I squeezed his shoulder, knowing what he meant. "It is real, Fredrik, and you deserve all this happiness."

He smiled at me but then frowned. "Problem is…"

"You are being overprotective?" I chuckled knowing it was exactly how I would be feeling if Alina were.

"Yes. I can't help it! I feel like I need to be by her side 24/7 and I am driving her crazy already. She actually tricked me into the shower this morning, making me think she was joining me when actually, she darted out the room and went to training!"

I laughed out loud, imagining the fury that would have caused him.

"I was on my way there to grab her ass and drag her back to the bedroom when you mind linked me."

"Good job I did then. Look, I know it's hard man but you have to give her a little bit of space."

He shook his head before dropping it back again and huffed. "She still wants to fight."

My eyes scanned his face as I realised what he meant. She wanted to fight in the battle whilst pregnant. Now I understand his frustration.

"I can't let her Logan. If anything was to happen to her and the baby, after knowing what it would do to me, I wouldn't survive it. Not this time," he said quietly and his voice was laced with emotion.

"I understand. Have you said all of this to her?"

"Yes! Like I said, she is stubborn. She has been a fighter all her life. Lucius killed her parents, too and took away her childhood. She wants blood but when I told her she is not thinking about the baby, she slapped me."

I supressed a chuckle, knowing Sloane was a feisty one which was why she was so perfect for Fredrik. But I had to agree with him on this one. He would be distracted in battle if she was there and I couldn't risk not having him on top form as well as risking any danger coming to her and the baby.

"I will sort it, Fredrik. Don't you worry." I winked at him as he looked across to me with hope in his eyes.

"She won't like it," he said flatly.

"She won't have a choice when her Alpha commands it."

I grinned and his face lit up. "Is everything ready for the battle?"

"Yes. Everyone knows their stations and the wooden pellets and guns from Joseph's man have arrived. We are keeping people out of the woods apart from the border patrols as the spears and traps have been set. We are ready." He grinned and my shoulders released their tension.

"Good. It is just a matter of waiting now and training our army

The Last Alpha

as much as possible." I walk over to my father's safe and tried another code. Failed. I sighed in frustration.

"Still not able to get in there?"

"No. I have tried his birthday, my mothers, mine. The date he met my mother. Nothing works."

"He likely changed it before the attack for safety. Have you tried the date he became Alpha? The day Alec attacked Lucius?" I tried to recall the date it was but I had no idea.

"Twenty-seven, eight, ninety-two," he added when he saw my hesitation.

I typed it into the keypad and laughed when the door popped open. "You are a genius!" I said and he smirked. I started pulling out files, a jewellery box and important pack documents. There was also a large stash of cash and a strange long tube made of leather. I pulled it out and saw the pack's crest on the side of it. I rolled it in my hands, looking for a way of opening it and stopped suddenly when I saw a tiny keyhole on one end. My heart raced as I scrambled through my pockets looking for the tiny silver key that I had been carrying around on me for days.

"What's that?" Fredrik asked walking over to me and eyeing the tube suspiciously.

"I don't know but I think I am about to find out." I put the key into the keyhole and it fit perfectly. I turned and pulled the lid off. I looked inside but could only see scrolled up paper. Pulling it out carefully and unrolling it, I scanned the handwritten letter until I reached the bottom and my eyes widened.

'Alina. Come to my father's study. Immediately. I have something important to show you.' I mind linked her and within minutes, she raced into the room.

"What is it? What's happened?" she asked in panic and I

walked her to the chair to sit down. I knelt down beside her and handed her the leather tube as her face creased with confusion. I placed the small key in her hand and her face snapped up to mine.

"It's from your father. It's a letter to you and your mother."

Her eyes watered immediately as she pulled the letter out of the tube with shaky hands. A sob left her lips as soon as she saw his handwriting. She looked up at me and I wiped the tears away from her cheeks with my thumbs.

"I know where I want to go to read this," she said in a wobbly voice. "To the lake. Thomas said it was my dad's favourite place."

"Okay, let's go," I said lifting her to her feet and putting my arm around her waist.

Alina's POV

To my two true loves, my darling Lucinda and Alina,

If you are reading this letter, then I am so sorry. It means I have failed and have not made it home to you both. I have posted you the key and hope that one day, you will find this letter so we can say our final goodbye.

Luce, my moon. Please don't hate me. I am sorry that I left the way I did but I know that if I told you where I was going and what I was doing, you would have begged me to stay. One look into your beautiful eyes and I would have crumbled. I would have stayed. But I had to do this. You know how much my people mean to me. My pack. I couldn't just leave them to face Lucius after it was my father's actions who caused all this madness. I had to do something. I plan to make it home to you very soon, my love. But if I don't, you need to know. You are the light of my life. You changed me and gave me indescribable happiness and a lifetime of love that many can only dream of. My only regret is not being able to see you one more time. I know the pain you will feel after I am gone will be insufferable, but you are strong, my love. You will survive. You must, for our daughter. She needs you. I know that this is not the end for us. Just the end of this lifetime. I will find you again in the next. I will always find you. But until then, goodbye, my moon. I love you.

Alina, my beautiful daughter. If you are reading this letter, then by now you know who you really are. Perhaps your mother has told you or perhaps it is safe for you now. Whatever the reason, I am sorry we had to hide it from you for so long. Please understand that your mother and I did it for your own protection. There was always a chance you would remain human as your mother was but we also knew you could be an Alabaster wolf. The world we live in right now is against our kind but with the gift of the white wolf, you would have had a target on your back. I hope you can forgive us.

I wish I was there to watch you grow up into the strong, resilient woman I know you will be. You are a true leader. Caring, powerful, intelligent. It runs through your blood. Don't ever let anyone take you for granted, my daughter. Whether you are an Alabaster wolf or not, you are special and deserve the world. You will make this world a better place, I can feel it. I wish I could be there to see it.

But fate is out of our control. Whatever happens to me, as long as you know I died a happy man full of pride and love for my family, I will be at peace. I love you, my sweet girl. Don't ever forget it.

Love your devoted husband and father,
Richard Clarke

I put the letter down and held my head in my hands and cried. I cried for the last nine years of never knowing what he had sacrificed. I cried for my mother and the pain his death must have caused her. She would have felt the bond break when he took his last breath. I cried for never having been allowed to truly know the real and wonderful person my father was. I cried because I finally had closure after all these years.

I felt Logan wrap his arms around me and pull me into his chest as we sat on the bank of the river. He kissed my hair and rubbed my back as I sobbed. Letting me deal with my grief but calming me all the same. After five minutes, I lifted my head and wiped my tears. We sat in silence for a few minutes.

"He knew he was going to die. I could feel it in his writing. Yet he wasn't scared," I said calmly and Logan looked at me with understanding. "I hope I have an ounce of his strength and courage."

"You do. His blood runs through your veins. You are strong, Alina. You have so much courage and compassion."

I gave him a small smile and looked out across the lake. It really was beautiful here and I felt connected to my father.

"What if we don't win, Logan? What if we fall like our father's did?" My voice caught.

He turned and cupped my face with his hands, forcing me to look into his eyes.

"We won't."

"W-what if we are not enough?" I stammered as a tear fell down my cheek.

"No matter what happens, it is all worth it to me. Being with you, loving you. It is all worth it."

I nodded and smiled at him sadly. "But we will win."

Suddenly, I heard a crunching behind us and saw Sloane and Chloe approaching. Logan smiled and whispered, "I'll leave you to it. Be careful getting back through the woods, okay? Mind link me if you need me."

The Last Alpha

I nodded and gave him a peck on the lips as the girls sat down and took his place.

"Logan mind linked me and filled us in. We are so sorry, Alina." Sloane wrapped her arm around my shoulder.

"You know, I actually feel relieved. I finally know the truth about what happened to my dad and as much as it hurts, I know he did the right thing. He did what I would have done, so if anything, I just admire him."

They both nodded and we sat in comfortable silence for a short while watching the birds diving into the lake to look for fish.

Suddenly, I turned to Chloe. "So, are you going to tell us what happened between you and Darius? Don't lie to me now." I raised my eyebrow at her and she threw her head into her hands.

"I don't know what happened! One minute we were arguing and bickering like cat and dog and then next thing I know, we are kissing in the woods! And then it all kind of escalated," she muttered, refusing to look us in the eye.

"Do you like him?" I asked with a smirk.

"No! God, he is still the most infuriating man I have ever met!"

"So you don't want to do it again?" Sloane teased.

"No! Yes… No! I don't know! Help me!" Chloe cried and fell back onto the grass behind us as we laughed.

"Was the sex good?" I asked with a giggle, finding it hard to imagine two of my best friends doing that together.

She rolled her head to the side and grinned. "Best sex I have ever had. Don't you dare tell him that though!" She pointed her finger at me and I chuckled.

"Okay, so you're clearly attracted to each other. Why don't you just relax. Don't overthink it and see what happens?" I said calmly shrugging my shoulders.

"No. It won't work. We cannot have a conversation without insulting one another." She shook her head.

"Last I checked, you don't need to talk when you're…" Sloane teased her again and Chloe threw a stick at her.

An ear-splitting ringing sounded through the territory and my heart started thundering in my chest.

We all jumped to our feet, looking at each other wide-eyed.

The battle alarm.

They're here.

Chapter 70

Logan's POV

'ALPHA, VAMPIRES DETECTED AT THE BORDER EAST SIDE.'
'ALPHA, VAMPIRES IN THE WEST OF THE FOREST.'
'ALPHA, VAMPIRES NEAR THE LAKE.'

The frantic voices of the mind links coming through from my border control stopped me in my tracks in front of the pack house.

"Sound the alarm!" I shouted up at men posted on the pack house balcony. They nodded and ran inside and within seconds, the alarm sounded, and chaos erupted. Women and children came running out of their homes with fear-stricken faces towards the pack house safe room. A few warriors grabbed younger children to get them there faster. Men run into the woods, shifting into their wolf's mid-air to the locations of the vampires but my head spun. This wasn't right. They were coming in from every direction, but how?

I looked up and saw mists of black smoke dotted around the village and then they appear as if from thin air. Vampires. Magic. The air reeked of it.

One appeared right in front of me and before it had a chance to turn around, I broke its neck with my bare hands as screams were heard in the village. Women and children were running towards me as Vampires appear in front of them causing them to change direction.

'VAMPIRES IN THE VILLAGE! ANY WARRIORS MINUTES AWAY, GET HERE NOW,' I sent over mind link as I shifted into Elias and took down two vampires who were about to grab two young girls.

My jaws were filled with the bitter taste of blood as I ripped into their flesh and tore out their throats. From the corner of my eye, I saw more of my warriors running into the village and taking down the vampires easily.

I froze when a swirl of purple smoke appeared a few metres in front of me and revealed a man I have seen before. The man who commanded the vampires from the top of that hill. His eyes glowed purple but his fangs protruded. A hybrid. He smirked at me, and I saw the amusement in his eyes.

Elias growled and leapt at him but before he landed, the man has vanished only to appear again a few metres away. Elias speeded towards him again with more ferocity but he was too quick. He suddenly appeared by the entrance of the forest and the smile on his face enraged me. He was playing with me.

Abruptly, he turned on his heels and his body became a blur as he bolted through the trees, deeper into the wood. He wanted me to follow. I let out a ferocious roar to alert my warriors to join me and raced in after him.

Alina's POV

"We need to get back to the village. Now!" I shouted as I grabbed Chloe's hand and the three of us started to run through the trees, jumping over logs and branches.

"Are they here? The vampires?" Chloe's voice was full of fear, and it spiked something inside of me. Determination.

Before I could answer, two puffs of smoke appeared in front of us and revealed two pale-skinned men with blazing red eyes scowling. We froze. I search the trees for any sign of more, but it seemed it was just the two of them. Easy.

Sloane shifted into her wolf as she jumped forward at one of them, but I stayed in human form allowing Xena control.

The second vampire ran at me and I dodged his advance, pulling Chloe behind me. "Stay here," I said pushing her back, so she fell to the floor. My fist connected with the man's ribs and then I spun and kick him in the chest. He staggered backwards in surprise and hissed at me, but I didn't give him a chance to attack. I punch his face with all my strength and then his stomach again as he crippled over, giving me a chance to jump onto his back. I locked my arm around his neck and grabbed the top of his head with my other hand. Snap. His lifeless body fell to the floor and I climbed off him. Sloane was still in wolf form with blood dripping from her jaws as she stood over the body of the other. I glanced at Chloe whose eyes were open wide in horror. I grabbed her arm and yanked her up and we started running again.

Once we got to the village, anger boiled within me. There were a few bodies of women and even a child on the floor covered in their own blood.

"OMG!" Chloe cried, covering her hand over her mouth.

"Get inside, NOW!" I screamed at her, pushing her towards the pack house.

She tripped forward as tears left her eyes, pleading with me.

"NOW!" I commanded in my Alpha tone without realising and she ran up the steps and into the house. I turned to Sloane's wolf.

The Last Alpha

"You, too."

Her eyes narrowed at me and she growled, shaking her head.

"You are pregnant Sloane. This is an order."

Before she could react, a haunting woman's cry echoed through the air and I saw Fiona running desperately between the houses.

"NICO!!" she shouted as tears glide down her face. I ran over to her and grab her shoulders as she looked up at me, terrified. "I can't find Nico! I can't find him!" she wailed and my heart started racing.

"I will find him. Sloane, take Fiona to the safe room now and then stay on guard by the door. I will be back with Nico."

Sloane shifted back to her human form and put her arm around Fiona to guide her inside. I close my eyes, allowing Xena to focus on any sounds in the distance. I heard a whimpering by the outskirts of the village and start to race towards it. "Nico!" I called but I still couldn't see anyone.

I sniffed the air and picked up his scent to my right. Running between two houses, I came across a log shed and bent down. In between two large logs, Nico's tiny body was curled up in a ball and shaking.

"Nico, it's okay. It's me, Luna Alina." I made my voice as soft and calm as I could. He turned his head slowly and his eyes widened in relief. "I've got you. I'm going to take you to your mother. Come out now." I held my hand out to him as he carefully took it and crawled out of the space. I picked him up and squeezed him into my arms, stroking his hair as he whimpered, "It's okay."

I turn around and gulped. Five black mists appeared, surrounding me and Nico.

Shit!

Logan's POV

Elias thundered through the woods but there was no sign of the hybrid. I slowed my pace realising I need to think clearly. I need to stop doing what he wanted. Most of the women and children were safe now. It was time to turn the tables and get them to do what we wanted. I paused and felt warriors approaching behind me. I mind linked everyone.

'EVERYONE TO THE GORSE. WE NEED THEM TO COME TO US,' I instruct as Elias started to run towards the gorse bushes in the middle of the forest. Where was Alina? Panic started to rise within as I know she was at the lake when the alarm sounded.

'Alina?' I tried and mind link her but heard nothing back. I know she was not hurt as I would feel it through the mate bond but her silence was worrying me.

We got to the gorse bushes and I shift back to my human form and looked at all of the wolves standing around me. More and more approached and I spotted Darius, Joseph, and Fredrik amongst them but no white wolf.

I looked up in the trees and saw lots of our warriors sat in the branches with guns, waiting. The wood was suddenly still. Anticipation filled the air. No one moved. Then I smelled it. The smell of dark magic and smoke. I narrowed my eyes over the gorse bushes and suddenly, hundreds and hundreds of vampires appeared, standing firmly to the ground with their beady red eyes piercing through the early evening dusk.

I scanned each of their faces. No emotion. Rigid robots of death. That was all they were. And then I spotted him. Standing in the middle of his army, wearing a full black suit and a smirk on his face. Lucius.

Standing next to him was the hybrid man, eyes no longer purple, showing the distinctive different colours of each one. His skin wasn't as pale as the other vampires but it was clear he was still one of them.

"Logan. How poignant to have chosen the same exact location I succeeded in my last battle. Thank you, it has brought back many fond memories." Lucius sly voice pierced through the air.

"But you did not succeed. FOR WE ARE STILL HERE!" I roared and my army threw their heads back and howled. I grinned as I saw his smile falter.

"Not for long, boy! I will enjoy tearing every last one of you to shreds. But don't worry, I will save you till last and rip out your mate's heart for you to watch before I do your own. Just like I did with your mother and father." He snarled and something inside me snapped.

I shifted into Elias, releasing an earth-shattering roar and leapt over the gorse bushes towards him as his army of vampires raced towards us.

My anger fuelled me as I viciously ripped through every vampire I came across. Eager to get to their maker. I could hear wooden pellets whizzing through the air as vampires hissed in pain and the snarls and growls of wolves fighting them.

Suddenly, I felt a huge impact on my side and was knocked to the floor as a vampire climbed onto of my fur and bit into my shoulder. I howled at the pain of his poison as I threw him off me and he hit a tree but then, in a split second, another one was on me. I turned to see Fredrik's wolf stride into the air and knock the man off me. But before I could move, two more were grabbing at my fur, digging their extended nails into Elias' skin. I whipped my head around to see the same happening to many of my wolves. We were outnumbered. We were losing.

Where was Alina?

Chapter 71

Alina's POV

The menacing faces smirked at me showcasing their sharp fangs as they stalked around Nico and I. I slowly lowered him to the ground so I would have my hands free if they attacked and he hid behind my legs, gripping on to me for dear life. There was no way I was going to let them hurt him. But I had never been against this many before. Alone.

My heart pounded in my chest as I heard Logan's voice echo in my mind, '*Alina?*' I knew I couldn't answer. It would give them the perfect opportunity to attack if I was distracted.

Bending lower, I took my attacking stance and eyed them all wearily, trying to judge who would attack first. As long as they didn't all attack at once, I might have a chance. I needed to take at least one or two out immediately and I could only do that as Xena. I took a quick glance down at Nico and tried to show him with my eyes that it was going to be okay.

"Close your eyes, Nico," I whispered and he squeezed them shut before I shifted into my enormous white wolf. Shock registered on their faces at the sight of me and gave me the window I needed. I dived forward and ripped out one of the vampire's necks and then kicked the one next to him with my hind legs, sending him flying through the air. The other three ran at me at once and I only managed to get a hold of one of their arms. I tugged ruthlessly and ripped the limb from his body but the other two were on top of me, their claws digging into my fur.

Out of nowhere, a brown wolf flew through the air and ripped one off me, giving me the chance to fight the other fairly. After I managed to tear it's head off, I looked up to see the brown wolf still struggling against the vampire. From the corner of my eye, the vampire who I had catapulted into the air was hurtling towards Nico who was curled up on the floor. Xena sprinted towards the boy and stood protectively over him as the vampire collided with her body forcing us to roll together on the floor. Xena managed to bite into his leg as he fell back. She stood up but the vampire attacked her own leg in return causing her to howl before she leaned down and ripped his head off.

I shifted back to human form and ran towards Nico, picking him up in my arms as a deafening howl erupted from the brown wolf. I turned and saw the vampire had his hand in the wolf's chest and my eyes widened in horror. Letting go of Nico again, I raced over and snapped the vampire's neck before it could pull out the wolf's heart.

I kneeled as the wolf shifted back to its human form and gasped, covering my mouth with my hand. Rohan.

"Daddy?" I heard a small voice behind me, and Rohan turned his head as a tear fell from his eyes. Nico ran over and fell on top of his father's chest crying. Rohan lifted his hand and placed it on his son's head.

"Shhh, it··· it's okay," he muttered, struggling to speak against the pain. I looked down at his stomach and the hole that was oozing with blood. I quickly put my hands on it and pressed hard to try and stop the bleeding and Rohan winced. He looked up at me and shook his head. My eyes spiked with unshed tears.

"No… it's to… late. Save my son," he whispered and I started shaking my head.

"No, I can get help and we can get you inside and…" I said frantically but his eyes stopped me.

"There isn't time. More will come… You… will be outnumbered. Take my son. Get him to safety," he pleaded as he struggled to keep his eyes open. The tears flowed from my own.

I nodded slowly knowing he was right. He winched as he took off a ring and put it in Nico's hand. "My son, this is now yours. Wear it… with pride and with courage. It is a reminder of how much I love you and your mother. Look after her for me, won't you?" he said as he stroked the boy's hair.

"Okay, Daddy." He sniffed and hugged his dad again.

I nodded at Rohan and pulled Nico from him as he started to fight against me, trying to get back to his dad. I held him in my arms and started to walk back to the pack house as Nico stretched his arms out to his father on the floor. "DADDY!!"

Sobs escape my lips as I picked up the pace and ran to the pack house and hand Nico to Sloane.

"Are you alright? What's happened?" Sloane's eyes widened as she sees my face.

"Get him to his mother and lock the doors. That is an order, Sloane. I have to go." I turned and raced out into the forest, shifting back into Xena as I felt Logan's panic through the mate bond. He needed me.

Logan's POV

I heaved off another two creatures but two more latched on. I growled and bit into one of their legs and pulled him off me. Suddenly, a majestic roar shook the trees and all the wolves' heads snapped up. She was here. I saw a flurry of white fur leap over my head as she ripped through the vampire on my back and then into another on Gunner's back. Momentarily, all the fighting seized as the vampires stared at Xena in shock and the wolves used the opportunity to quickly gain back control. I stood up from the ground and she came to stand next to me as we looked over at Lucius. His eyes were wide with surprise which quickly turned to rage.

As if hit by some kind of force, I felt a surge of energy course through Elias' body. I looked at Xena and she was staring at me. She felt it, too. Suddenly, we were moving together like a dance. Her actions matched mine and we were completely in sync as we annihilated any vampire in our path with ease on our way to Lucius. I had never felt power like it.

We were just a few metres away from the devil himself when a mighty gust of wind swept through the air and as soon as it hit us, our bodies froze. We could not move. Magic was holding everyone, vampires and wolves frozen in time. My eyes were the only thing I had control of. They darted to Xena who also stood like a statue, her front legs in the air as she had been about to leap.

An evil laugh rippled through the air. My eyes flickered to Lucius who seemed to be the only one able to move except for the man standing next him.

"I expect you haven't met my son, Arius." Lucius chuckled as he patted the man's shoulder and started to walk towards me. Son? Something clicked and I realised that he must be Cora's son. I gulped as I realised how powerful he was, controlling hundreds of wolves and vampires all at once.

Lucius was in front of me now and panic rose at how easily he could kill me. Kill any of us in this moment. He smirked as if reading my mind and walked over to Xena. My heart pounded in my chest.

"A white wolf." He clicked his tongue as he stroked her fur as rage brewed inside me but I still couldn't move. I was helpless.

"This must be Alina." He stood on his tip toes to look up at her eyes and laughed. "I thought I had killed the last Alabaster wolf when I murdered Clarke Snow with my bare hands. It appears I was wrong. Easily rectified." He pulled out a silver blade from his pocket.

"This was the blade Alpha Alec used to kill my wife and unborn son. It feels only right that I use it to kill his granddaughter, don't you think?"

No! No, I can't let this happen. I looked at Arius to see how I could get his attention but his eyes were already on me and our eyes locked. I connected with something. Emotion. He wasn't sure about this. About what his father was about to do. He suddenly broke the spell and I could move. But Darius' wolf was closer. He bit into Lucius arm that held the blade and Lucius dropped it to the floor. Gunner snarled but before I could do anything, Lucius had grabbed the blade with the speed of light and stabbed it into Gunner's side. He released an agonising howl and Lucius dissolved into a puff of black smoke only to appear again next to his son. Gunner fell to the ground whimpering, and I saw red.

Xena felt it to, and we rampaged through the crowd before us at Lucius, only to be sent flying through the air by a huge force from Arius' hand. Elias' back hit a tree and fell to the ground. Arius levitated into the air and moved his hands together elegantly as a storm brew around him. The power he radiated was terrifying. What was he going to do?

But before anything could happen, we were all blinded by a bright, luminescent glow that surrounded all of the wolves. I looked up to the source of power and saw a woman with long black hair sprayed in the air as she rose off the forest floor.

Cora?

Cora's POV

As soon as we set foot in the territory, I knew something was wrong. I could feel Arius' power. Madeline looked at me with wide eyes as we walked through the desolate village at bodies of wolves on the floor. Coughing and spluttering came from one man as Madeline raced over to him. I walked slowly behind her and could see that he was in a bad state. Madeline scanned his body and her eyes widened at the huge wound in his stomach. He had already lost too much blood. He would be dead in a matter of minutes.

"We have to go," I said sternly, trying to pull at her arm.

She pulled away and glared up at me. "We can't leave him like this. There must be something you can do." her beautiful grey eyes pleaded with mine but I shook my head sadly. Her eyes clouded over with emotion and she looked back down at the man. "What's your name sir?"

His eyes roll back in his head and then he coughed up another load of blood. This was pointless.

"Madeline, we have to go. Now."

She went to get off the floor but the man grabbed her arm in desperation. He was scared. She looked back up at me and I knew what she is about to say.

"You go. I will stay with him and then follow you… after." She gulped. Her heart was too big for her own good, it would get her killed one day. I tusk but don't argue with her. I didn't have time. I closed my eyes and focused on Arius' magic and with a click of my fingers, I was in the middle of the forest.

In front of me, I could see an army of wolves and vampires all standing as still as statues. Some looked like they had been in mid-fight when they were frozen. The air vibrated with dark magic and I looked up to see Arius projecting control over all of their bodies. He had come a long way from controlling birds, I was impressed. Then something broke the spell and mayhem broke out. An agonising howl erupted from a wolf and Lucius appeared next to his son with a smirk on his face and blood dripping from the blade he was yielding. Two huge black and white wolves were thundering through the fighting towards Lucius and Arius. But just before they reached them, Arius lifted his hand and they flew through the air. My eyes widened as I saw Arius cultivating his magic as a storm raged around him. No. Not this spell. I had to stop him.

I started my chants as a white glow erupted from my hands and created a protection barrier around all the wolves from his magic. I felt myself levitate into the air and flew towards my son who was looking at me with shock and anger. We hovered a metre apart, glaring at each other, our magic colliding and causing a huge amount of electricity between us. Purple and white sparks filtered through the air as we each tried to hold onto our control.

"You don't have to do this, son! You are not like him! You have a choice!" I shouted over the howling of the wind.

His eyes narrowed slightly. "I have never had a choice. They did this to me first. They are the reason my life has been how it is!" he shouted back.

"You have been fed lies, Arius. They have done nothing to you! Your father raped me, stole you from me, and abused you. Raised you to be like him. But you are not like him. You have a good soul. I know it. You are better than this. You are better than him!" I shouted, not breaking eye contact with my powerful son. I saw the doubt I needed to see flicker in his eyes. "Let me show you the truth. Please," I said softly as I reached my hand out to touch his cheek. He looked unsure but didn't pull away.

Once my hand touched his skin, he closed his eyes and I shared my past with him. I left nothing unturned or hidden. Celeste's death, Lucius raping me, his birth, the pain of believing he was dead, my meeting with Lucius when he told me he was alive, the dungeon when I first saw him.

We have begun to slowly glide down to the ground as I felt him give up on his spell. He opened his eyes and tears threatened to fall from them. I stroked the side of his face and smiled sadly. He knew.

And then I felt it. An excruciating pain through my chest and my eyes widened. Arius' eyes mirrored mine and I heard him scream, "NOOOO!" as I fell into his arms and the blade was pulled from my back.

I looked up to see Lucius holding a large bloody knife with a sadistic grin. But I didn't care. My son knows I am his mother. I will die happy.

I looked up into my son's exquisite eyes as tears fell from them onto my face. "Don't cry, my child. I am happy. Knowing you have the truth and you will do the right thing. Be the man I know you are. You may not have known love your entire life but I have loved you from the moment you entered this world. I will never stop loving you, my son. Take that with you." I reached up and caressed his face once more and he closed his eyes. I felt my chest rise for the final time as I took my last breath in his arms.

Chapter 72

Lucius' POV

I watched on helplessly as Cora and Arius were floating out of reach in the air, power surrounding them both and a storm raging around them. The sky had turned as black as the devil's soul and bolts of lightning illuminated a pathway of violent rage. A clanking sound boomed through the dark clouds. Doubt consumed me as I observed my son, hoping he was powerful enough to defeat her. The traitor witch.

Anger boiled in me as I scanned the forest floor and every wolf was encircled with a glowing aura protecting them from any attack by my warriors. Not that anyone was fighting any more. Everyone's eyes were transfixed on Arius and Cora; their magic sucking the life out of the atmosphere.

My eyes widened in horror as Cora reached out and touched Arius' face. He closed his eyes and his power faded as they both started to drift to the forest floor. She was spelling him. She was winning. If she won, then they won. You stupid boy. I saw red and I let the demon inside me take over.

In a split second, I had shimmied behind her and stabbed the blade into her back, making sure it pierced straight through her beating heart.

I held it there for a few seconds and twisted it before pulling it out forcefully.

"NOOOO!" Arius' voice boomed through the air. She fell forward into his arms as he kneeled to the ground, cradling her frail body. I stood in shock at the pure love between them. What was this?

Her eyes searched his and she smiled. She started to whisper something to him and all I could do was watch on. Why was he listening? Why did he care? She was trying to overpower him. I saved him. Her hand reached up and touched his cheek as she took her final breath. Her arm fell with a thud onto the forest floor and her body went limp in his arms. No one moved. This wasn't what I was expecting.

I turned around to slowly scan the warriors behind me. The wolves no longer had their protection aura but still my vampires were not attacking them. They were all watching Arius intensely. The wolves stood menacingly, huffing and grunting in anger at the scene before them. Yet, they didn't move. I turned back to Arius who was still knelt holding Cora's body and his shoulders were heaving up and down. Carefully, he placed her body on the ground and stood up, not taking his eyes off her.

"You lied." His voice was low and full of rage.

I narrowed my eyes at him. Was he talking to me? When I didn't answer, he lifted his head and met my gaze. I had never seen such a threatening look in all my years on this earth as the one I was faced with right now.

"YOU LIED!" he shouted again, directing all his anger at me.

I shook my head carefully as I put my hands up in surrender.

"What are you talking about, son? Don't listen to her. She betrayed us. She was messing with your head. She was about to kill you! I had no—"

"CHOICE? YOU HAVE ALWAYS HAD A CHOICE! You chose to rape her. You chose to make her believe her baby was dead. You chose to abuse me all my life. You chose to lie to me. You choose to go to war against the wolves. You chose to kill the only person who has ever cared about me. My mother. Everything has been because of YOUR choices." His eyes blaze between red and purple as his demonic side battled against his dark magic, fighting for control.

I gulped down my fear. "Son··· none of that is true." I kept my voice low and calm, not wanting to upset him anymore than he already was.

"DON' T LIE TO ME!" He lifted his hand and I felt a huge force wrap around my throat, choking me.

My hands snapped to my throat to try and pry off the attack but there was nothing there. I felt myself struggle for oxygen and my blood was pulsing in my head. Arius stepped over Cora' s body and walked towards me dangerously. I choked out, "P-p-please, my son," as I reached my arm out to him asking for mercy.

"I have never been your son." He spat at me and started to walk away.

Just as I felt darkness clawing at me, the pressure was gone. I fell to my knees, gasping for air as I held my throat. I wanted to go after him, stop him. But my throat was too sore and my body too weak.

He bent down and picked up Cora' s body in his arms, her head hanging as the ends of her long black hair brushed the forest floor. For a moment, I wanted to cry as it reminded me of when I held Celeste that haunting day.

"Warriors of the night, I no longer hold any allegiance to the King of Vampires. He is not worthy to rule our people and is nothing but a coward who hides behind others. He does not care if you live or die, you are all mere pawns in his game. I am giving you a choice, unlike this monster who has ruled us with fear and cruelty. Follow me and things will be different. Or stay and meet your end just like your king." He glanced at me and only hatred was evident in his eyes.

"Arius…" I wheezed out as I stood to my feet shakily. "What are you doing?" He didn't answer me as he turned and started to walk away into the woods carrying Cora. "ARIUS!"

Panic rose within me as I look around at my warriors who were all glaring at me. "What are you doing?! Fight, goddammit! I am your KING! Kill these beasts!" I pointed my arm at Logan and Alina's wolves as they sniggered at me.

My eyes widened as vampires start to shimmy into black puffs of smoke and disappeared. They were abandoning me. My own men.

I went to shimmy myself to get away from this situation but my feet were fixed to the ground with an invisible force. Arius. I cursed under my breath as I try to struggle free from its hold.

A sinister laugh echoes through the trees as my head snapped up to see a naked Logan with his arms folded across his chest. "My, my… I did not see that coming." He smirked and started to take slow steps towards me. I pulled at my feet more ferociously, trying to escape but I couldn't move. "I would give up if I were you, old man."

I stood tall to mask my fear and he was only a metre away as his eyes danced with amusement and malice.

"Look around." He chuckled and my eyes scanned the battlefield as the last of my vampires who have remained loyal and stood with me were being ripped apart by the wolves. "It's over." His eyes twinkled as I swallowed.

"This is really how you want to win this war? You really think people will respect you when they hear how you killed the Vampire King as he was unable to defend himself?" I snarled back at him.

He smirked. "The war is not over, old man. Your kind still exists. However, you are my own victory and how you die does not matter to me. As long as you are no longer breathing, I will be a happy man."

Before I could utter another word, I felt an unbelievable pain in my chest as Logan's extended claws pierced my skin. I gripped his arm with both my hands, trying to pull him away but he was too strong. I looked down as his hand sunk into my chest painfully slowly and I screamed out in agony. Everything started to spin and black dots appear in front of my eyes as I felt his fist squeeze my heart.

An image of Celeste laughing in our bed, rounded stomach under our silk sheets, entered my mind.

"Any last words?" I heard a faint voice before me.

"I-I love you, Celeste." I felt a sharp tug and an emptiness where my heart used to belong; the heart that stopped beating long ago.

Celeste, my love. I am coming.

Logan's POV

I ripped his pulsing heart from his body and threw it to the ground. I watched as the life drained from his eyes and a small smile played on his lips. It angered me that he has the audacity to smirk even in death. I gripped the sides of his head and tore it from his body as it fell to the ground. I throw the head on the floor next to his heart, panting heavily as I fell to my knees. I finally had our revenge.

I felt dainty hands glide around my neck and Alina's body hugging me from behind as uncontrollable sobs escaped my lips. Years of anger. Years of pain. Years of torment. It all evaporated from my body with each shaking breath. I tried and got myself under control. I leaned my head back onto Alina's shoulder and looked up to the sky.

The Last Alpha

I did it father. I did what you wished.

I leaned down and grabbed the hair of Lucius' mangled head and stood up tall, turning to my pack. I lifted the head in the air and the forest shook with thunderous howls full of meaning. I dropped it and pulled Alina into my arms, breathing in her scent through her hair to calm me.

Feeling as though I had enough control over my emotions to address my pack, I pushed her behind my body to hide her nakedness and she wrapped her arms around my waist.

"Blood Moon Pack, today marks a day that will stand in the history of our kind for generations to come. Today is the day that we took back our lives! We rid the world of a monster. But this will not be the end. We may have won this fight, but we have not yet won the war. We do not know what the vampires will do next without their king. But I do know that we will need to be cautious." Many of the pack nodded their heads as I spoke. "But tonight··· Tonight we celebrate!" I shouted in my Alpha tone and heard the delighted howls and celebrations from our pack members who fought so bravely.

I looked over my shoulder at Alina who was smiling up at me with tears in her eyes.

Alina and I ran over to Darius' body that was being lifted by a number of warriors. My heart pounded when I saw blood covering one side of his body.

"He's going to be okay. We need to get him back to the pack house before he loses anymore blood," Fredrik said rubbing Alina's arm as she covered her mouth with her hand.

I nodded, swallowing my own emotions.

'Alpha and Luna, come quick in the east of the woods. It's Madeline,' a warrior mind linked me and Alina's eyes expanded as unease loomed in my stomach.

The Last Alpha

Madeline? She's here?

Alina shifted into Xena gracefully and darted off through the trees. I groan before following her. So much for celebrating.

We reached a small clearing deep in the forest and shifted back into our human forms as we approach a few men circling a tree. One turned and stepped towards us and nodded in respect. I scanned the forest floor around me and saw the remains of three or four vampires. It was hard to tell as their bodies were snapped in all directions or torn to shreds.

"What happened here?" I asked in a gruff voice.

"We don't know, Alpha. We found Madeline here alone, sobbing over the witch's body. These vampires were already dead." He looked over his shoulder back at the tree. "She won't move or speak to any of us."

Alina stepped forward and I growled realising she was still naked in front of these men. I grabbed her arm to pull her back and she glared up at me.

"Not now, Logan." She growled with determination on her face.

I released her reluctantly as she walked towards the tree. I followed protectively behind her, glaring at the men to look away. And then I saw Madeline. Curled up at the bottom of the tree trunk wearing only a black T-shirt and hugging Cora's dead body. She was sobbing hysterically as she rocked the woman in her arms. My head whipped around frantically, looking for any sign of Arius. He must have been here. This could be a trick, an ambush.

"Where is he? Where is Arius?" I roared. It came out more aggressively than I liked, and Madeline's face looked up to mine. Her eyes were puffy and her face held so much pain.

She shook her head and a sob escaped her lips.

Alina ran towards her and bent down next to her. "Madeline?

Madeline, it's me, Alina. Where is Arius?" she said softly as she placed one of her hands on top of Madeline's.

"He's… He's gone," she whimpered and fell into Alina's arms.

Alina looked up at me in shock as she hugged her tightly. "We need to get her back to the pack house. She is in shock," Alina said as she looked around at the horrifying scene in front of us. I nodded and walked forward and picked up Madeline in my arms.

"No. Cora. I can't leave her. Please," she cried out as I stood up and started to walk towards the pack house. Alina nodded to the warriors who picked up Cora's body carefully.

"It's okay, we've got her. She is coming with us," Alina said reassuringly and Madeline sniffed into my chest.

So many questions popped into my mind. Why was Madeline here? Did she come with Cora? How did she get her body? Where was Arius? Did Madeline kill those vampires?

I looked down at her broken face and she looked so small and helpless.

Now was not the time to question her. She needed to rest.

Chapter 73

Madeline's POV

His grip around my wrist was so tight my hand started to get pins and needles as he cut the blood circulation off.

"It's okay. I'm not going anywhere. I'm staying right here," I reassured him as I stroked his dark brown hair away from his face. He was a handsome man, probably in his late thirties although it was hard to tell. His body violently shook as he coughed up more blood. My face creased, imagining the pain he must be in right now. I didn't recognise him from our old pack, he must have been a new member.

"Shh, it's okay," I soothed trying to keep him calm as his eyes widened and then snapped shut forcefully as another surge of pain shot through him. He had lost so much blood. It was everywhere and he was looking paler by the second.

"Tell... Fiona... that I love..." He coughed up more blood through his mouth and rolled to his side.

I quickly scooted above his head so he would rest on my lap when he rolled back down. A tear escaped my eye as I smiled down at him sadly, "I am sure she already knows but I will tell her. I promise." This man had someone who loved him and he loved her. How was this fair?

"I'm so⋯ cold," he whispered as his body violently shook on the dusty floor.

I fought back a sob as I could tell these were his final moments and he was spending them here like this, with me. It wasn't right. He should be with his loved ones. I closed my eyes and I ran my fingers across his face, hoping it would give him some comfort. I started singing softly, the gorgeous lyrics to carry you.

I opened my eyes and looked down at his peaceful face. He was no longer in pain. I released the sob I was supressing as I gently closed his eyelids and put both hands on the ground beside his head. I sucked in a deep breath and carefully placed his head on the floor and stood up. My heart broke as I walked away from him.

I reached the entrance of my childhood woods as my body shook from the shock of what just happened. A man just died in my arms.

No more. This had to end today.

I picked up speed as I raced into the forest, the sky vanishing above me, only a few fragments of deep blue remained through the canopy. It had been years since I had run through these trees, but they called to me as if they remembered me. The air was rich with the fragrance of leaves but damp to. Suddenly, it was as if the day had shifted to night as violent storm raged in the sky. The wind howled and the trees creaked, bent, and moaned as their limbs were ripped away and their leaves became confetti in the gale. My heart started to flutter as the air thickened with the pain of war. With fury. Something was wrong. Only immense power could manipulate the elements like this. Cora or her son.

And that was when I saw them. Four vampires walking through the forest with hostile expressions. I quickly ducked behind a tree, pushing my whole body up against it. I held my breath hoping they hadn't seen me. Silence. I waited a few more moments before forcing myself to take a glance back in their direction. There was no one there.

I released a breath as I turned back only to be face to face with evil itself. His red eyes burned into my soul as he hissed inches from my face, his rancid breath coating my skin. Fangs protruded from his mouth and a scream escaped my lips before I could stop it. He gripped my hair at the top of my head and threw me forward to the ground.

The dirt and leaves of the forest floor cushioned my landing and I looked up to see I was surrounded by them, all hissing and snarling at me hungrily as if I was the most delicious thing they had seen. I gulped and felt panic rise. I needed to shift. I looked down at the floor and closed my eyes focusing on Nina as one stepped forward towards me.

"You look good enough to eat, darling. What's a little wolf doing out here alone?" His sickly voice sent a shiver up my spine. Just as he bent down to get a better look at me, I felt my wolf take over and I took a bite out of his face as my snout emerged and teeth sharpened. He fell back in agony holding his torn flesh as Nina sprinted away. They were hot on our tail as we dodged and jumped through the forest. The rain started to fall. No, pour mercilessly, torrential even. It made it difficult to see but I willed Nina on.

We leapt over a fallen tree trunk and as we were mid-air. A rock-hard body bulldozed into our side and knocked us to the ground. We stood up, growling and snarling as the vampires had us circled once again. Fear rose in me as I could not see a way out of this alive. So be it, but I was not going down without taking some of these bloodsuckers with me.

Nina pounced at one of them, biting into his arm. Shaking our head side to side until we felt his flesh rip away in our mouth. Another jumped on Nina's back and wrapped his arm around Nina's throat. This was it. Nina roared out, anticipating the snap of our neck but it never came. The weight of the vampire's body was suddenly ripped off us and we watched as it flew into the air and all his limbs were torn from his torso in one go by an invisible force.

Nina's head whipped left to right frantically, searching the forest for the attacker but there was no one in sight. The other vampires did the same, spinning on their heels, fear evident in their wide eyes.

I took my chance and jumped at one, ripping its throat out in seconds. The other two redirected their anger at me, remembering that I was their original target as one punched me so hard in the stomach, I heard one of Nina's ribs cracked. Involuntarily, I shifted back into my human form from the pain and curled up on the forest floor. Both, vampires stalked towards me licking their lips, eyes scanning my naked body.

And then my entire world changed. I smelled him. *MATE.*

A blur of movement rocketed in front of me taking down one of the vampires with it as the other retreated in shock. And then it was back, taking the last vampire at the speed of light and all that was left of him was his gut-wrenching wail that lingered through the air. Then it was silent once more.

I scurried to my feet, holding my ribs as I searched between the trees, squinting against the heavy downpour. My heart was pounding in my chest. The heavenly aroma of rosewood once again filtered through the damp forest air and my whole body tingled. I turned quickly, searching for my saviour, my destined mate. Nothing could have prepared me for what I found.

A few metres away from me was the most desirable man I had ever seen. He was over six feet tall, with short black hair that was styled effortlessly. It looked so shiny as it glistened in the rain. His body was athletic, and his muscles were visible as his drenched black T-shirt clung to his chest and stomach. His face was chiselled and his features oozed striking masculinity as his mouth parted with his deep breaths. He looked like the ultimate bad boy. And then I noticed his eyes.

No.

One crystal clear blue iris that raged like the sea. The other a deep brown full of the riches of the earth.

They bore into my soul as if he could see my darkest secrets, my inner pain. I started shaking my head as I took a few steps back. I tripped on a branch and stumbled backwards but before I hit the ground, I felt an arm around my waist and a hand supporting my head. I looked up into his hypnotising eyes as my skin exploded at his touch. My breath hitched. We didn't move; him holding my naked body in his arms as the rain danced across our skin. He looked down at my lips fleetingly and then back up to my eyes. His expression gave nothing away.

"Who— who are you?" My voice came out as a whisper as the wind swept it away.

"I think you already know." His voice was deep and seductive.

I gulped and shook my head slowly. No. It couldn't be.

My heart spoke his name before it left my lips, "Arius…"

I stood up and pushed him away from me, but my body immediately craved his touch again. I wrapped my arms around my chest self-consciously. His eyes flickered down my body before he quickly removed his black T-shirt and pulled it over my head. My eyes bulged at his gesture and my cheeks flushed pink as they roamed his now naked torso and took in his tempting physique. His body was a gift from the gods.

When my eyes travelled back to his face, I could swear I saw a ghost of a smile playing on his lips. And all my senses snapped back to the present.

"Get away from me!" I shouted as I backed up against a tree trunk.

Hurt flashed across his face but just as quickly it was gone and his expression stony once again. He took another step towards me and I pushed myself up harder against the tree. I had nowhere else to go as terror coursed through my veins.

His face hardened as he watched my body tense and fear registered on my face. "Why are you afraid of your own mate?" he asked lowly.

"I know who you are!" I glared at him, ignoring the desire that was raging through my body. His eyes glazed over, and his jaw ticked. "You're his son… You're a hybrid. You're the enemy." My voice faltered as he stepped closer again and rested his hands on either side of my head against the tree, caging me in. I was completely at his mercy. If I ran, he could kill me. His power radiated from every fibre of his body. He was the devil himself and he was my mate. Why? Why would the goddess do this? I swallowed down the tears that were threatening to spill. Something flashed across his face, and it softened slightly.

"You do not need to fear me. I won't hurt you."

I looked down at his lips and fought the urge to reach out and trace them with my fingers. The rain eased and I blinked rapidly as it gave me a clearer view of his face that was only inches away from mine. He was painfully beautiful, yet darkness lurked within. Warning me. I searched his unique eyes. Oh, how I wish I could believe that to be true. But I can't. I won't.

"You are HIS son. The man who murdered my entire family. My pack. You are one of them. You will always be my enemy," I said quietly but the determination was evident in my voice.

His body tensed and anger changed his expression to one that made my heart stop. He looked purely evil yet all I felt was turned on. What was wrong with me?

"You know nothing," he growled through his teeth and his nose brushed up against mine. Just that mere touch sent sparks across my skin. I could feel his breath fan my face and my arousal grew but I would not give in to it. This could never happen.

"I know enough. I know how you hurt the only good person you had in your life. How you shut her out when all she wanted was to be a part of your life. How you chose that monster over her." I glared back at him as my anger built. His eyes darted between mine as he seemed to be losing control of his own emotions. His lips thinned as he held back whatever it was that he was trying so hard not to do or say.

Suddenly, his hand was wrapped around my throat. It is not aggressive but firm holding me in place as I lifted my chin up and my face away from him and balanced on my tiptoes. His nose rubbed up against my cheek and he inhaled. Wetness pooled between my legs and I cursed my damn body for reacting to his touch.

"Like I said, you know nothing," he growled.

Something caught my eye over his shoulder as moonlight shone on an array of jet-black hair by the bottom of a tree. My eyes widened in horror as I saw Cora's pale body lying on the floor.

"Cora?" I shouted and shoved Arius off me. He let me as he staggered back and I ran to her.

My hand slammed over my mouth as I realised that she was dead. Her pale skin was void of the vibrancy it once had and her lips were turning a shade of grey to match. I turned and screamed at Arius who stood topless, hands in his pockets as he looked down at his dead mother.

"What did you do to her?! How could you? She was your mother!" I cried in rage and pain.

His eyes snapped to mine and I saw hurt and anger on his face. "You really think that little of me? That I would kill my own mother?"

I opened my mouth to speak but I didn't know what to say. Did I think that little of him? I didn't even know him or what he was capable of. He was Lucius' son after all. But deep inside of me, I knew he wouldn't have done this.

Suddenly, the trees shook, and the floor vibrated as all of the packs howls of victory thundered through the forest. Arius' fangs extended in defence and his eyes flashed red. I took a step away from him. He regained control when he saw the fear on my face.

"You… you should go." I muttered, realising the pack were on their way. They would find him soon enough and goddess knows what would happen.

"You are coming with me." He stepped towards me menacingly, but I put my hand up to stop him.

"I am not going anywhere with you." I glared at him and he glared back. "Take one step closer and I swear, I will reject you right here and now."

His eyes narrow at my words, and he looked down at Cora.

"She stays with me." I added. "She was my friend, like a mother to me when I needed her most."

His face softened slightly just as both our heads whipped around at the sound of thundering paws in the distance.

"Go!" I shouted at him, panic rising in me. Why was I worried? They would try and save me from him. But did I want to be saved? I suddenly realised I wasn't protecting myself but protecting him.

He stood his ground, not moving, just staring deep into my eyes.

"Go!" I shouted again as their footsteps were getting closer.

"I will come for you." His tone was demanding but it felt more like a promise than a warning and my heart fluttered. With a click of his fingers, he vanished behind a swirl of purple smoke.

I sunk down to my knees and wailed out the pain and frustration I was feeling inside. Scooping Cora into my arms, I buried my face into her chest and cried. I couldn't stop.

Why, Moon Goddess? Why him?

Chapter 74

Alina's POV

I stretch my limbs in the enormous king-size bed with a smile plastered on my face. This seemed to be how I woke up every day now. Blissfully happy. I turned my head and took in Logan's relaxed face inches from mine. His lips were slightly parted as he softly snored and his thick black eyelashes fanned his cheeks. His floppy curls fell over his face and onto the pillow and I couldn't stop myself from reaching out and twirling one around my finger.

I smiled as he stirred in his sleep and his arm reached over my body, pulling me into him possessively. He nuzzled his face into my neck and sighed. A giggle escaped my lips as his stubble tickled my skin and sent tingles through my body.

"What are you so happy about?" His gruff morning voice made my insides flutter as I turned in his arms to caress his beautiful face.

"I always wake up happy I think you're the reason." I smiled sweetly at him as his ocean blue eyes fluttered open. He leaned in and his strong lips were on mine, giving me the best wake up present possible. I pulled away quickly and his eyebrows creased in annoyance.

"I'm sure I have bad morning breath," I said sheepishly, trying to climb out of the bed to head the bathroom.

A firm grip around my waist yanked me back onto the mattress and Logan climbed on top off me so I was unable to escape again.

"Don' t you dare wake me up and run away from me, Alina," he said in a husky voice and his eyes rested on my lips while he licked his own. "I have warned you before about what happens if you run from me."

The temperature rose through my body as his words excited me but I pretended to play it cool. "I must have forgotten," I said seductively.

"Then let me remind you." He threw my arms above my head as he held my wrists together with one hand and his mouth explored my neck, leaving a trail of kisses and bites along my skin. I moaned and ground my hips up against his naked groin, only the silk of my night dress acting as a barrier between us. His other hand roamed my body as he caressed my breast and nipple through the sheer fabric and then down the side of my body until he reached the hem of the dress. He pulled it up so it was around my waist as he moved down my body, licking and kissing through the silk.

I arched my back as his mouth connected with my centre and he blew warm air on my delicate skin. "Ohhh, yes, Logan!" I moaned out as I closed my eyes and threaded my fingers through his hair. His tongue worked its magic on my sweet spot and within minutes I was falling apart around him. Before I had a chance to regain my senses from that mind-blowing orgasm, he thrust inside me and devoured my cries out with his mouth.

Tearing the night dress down the middle, he pulled me up as he sat back on his heels and bounced me up and down effortlessly. I would never tire of this. Of him. The feeling of him filling me completely. I gripped his shoulders, digging my nails in as he increased his speed and soon, we were both crying out each other' s name as we came hard together.

We fell back onto the bed with a satisfied giggle and he pulled me onto his chest. I could still hear his heartbeat pounding under my head as I traced my fingers over the outline of his tattoos. I leaned my head up and rested my chin on one of his hard pecks as I ran my finger around the impressive artwork of a wolf howling up at a full moon.

"Why do you have so many tattoos?" I asked and he smirked down at me through his lashes.

"You are only just asking me that now?" He chuckled as he drew circles over my bare back with his fingers; the sparks from his touch giving me as much pleasure as I know mine were giving him. I raised my eyebrows to show him I am waiting for answer. "Because I like them. To me, they are a form of art and what better way to tell the story of my life than on my own skin."

"They tell the story of your life?" I said surprised as I studied each one with new interest.

"Yep, this arm is the story of my ancestry. My parents' wolves here." He pointed to two black wolves with their heads entwined sweetly on his bicep. "A token to the day my father became Alpha here." A man that I now recognised as his father was sat upon a throne wearing a crown. "Our pack crest and symbol of the Blood Moon." He pointed to the tattoo on his right peck. "And my other arm is full of memories I have of my childhood and since the attack." I turned to examine the arm that was wrapped around my back and noticed a forest scene on his shoulder, a fighting symbol that I recognised from his gym in London and some Latin words running down his forearm.

"What does this mean?" My finger traced the swirling letters.

"The axe forgets, but the tree remembers," he said quietly, deep in thought. "It is a famous quote about karma. It seems to have come true." He grinned at me with a twinkle in his eye.

I smiled back and rested my head once again on his chest. "Why have you left this blank?" I asked, running my hand over his left peck.

He shivered under my touch. My eyes connected with his and he smiled so lovingly at me, I felt myself melting under his gaze.

"I want to show you something," he said carefully as he sat up, forcing me to fall off him onto the mattress. He strolled over to the walk-in wardrobe, giving me a glorious view of his naked body. After some shuffling around in his wardrobe, he enters the bedroom again with a canvas in his hands.

I sat up curiously as I study his face. "What is it?" I asked as a faint blush crept up to his cheeks. Is this Alpha seriously blushing? A small smile played on my lips as he shuffled on his feet awkwardly.

"I' ve never told you this but I love to paint. When I lost my memories of you, I kept having a reoccurring dream every night of your eyes and a lake. I could feel you there with me but I could never find you until the moment Cora put me back under a spell to regain what I had lost. The first memory that came back to me was you standing in that lake looking up at the moon. It has always been such a special moment for me. It was the moment I realised I love you and would die for you. That is why every night I revisited that moment. Even though I couldn' t see you, I knew you were there."

My heart fluttered in my chest at his words.

He gave me a coy smile as he turned the canvas around and I gasped. There was the most stunning painting I have ever seen. A huge full moon was in the background, its reflection rippling on the surface of the water surrounding a woman with green eyes looking up at it. She stood in the middle of the lake, naked from the waist up, the top half of her body exposed and hair falling down her back. The way he had drawn her, through his eyes, she looked like the most beautiful woman. I blinked a few times and crawled to the end of the bed to get a better look at her face. My eyes flicker up to his and his smile broadened. She was me.

"This is going to be my next tattoo if you like it. Right here, above my heart," he said as his hand went to his right peck. I gulped down my emotions. No one had ever done anything as romantic as this for me before.

"I love it!" I shouted as I jumped off the bed and into his arms as he chuckled and dropped the canvas to the floor to wrap his arms around me.

"Phew! For a second there, I thought you were about to kill me." He laughed as I pulled my head back to look into his eyes.

"Well, for a second there, I thought you had drawn another woman so…" I joined in with his laughter.

"I only have eyes for you. Always," he whispered as he kissed me on the lips.

We climbed back into the bed, savouring our alone time for as long as possible before the business of the day took over. Being Alpha and Luna seemed to be taking up lots of our time apart as I deal with the needs and care of pack members and Logan meets with his warriors and border control. He was still on high alert as he knew Arius and the vampires were still out there. We had heard nothing in the last week and even though it was a relief for me, I could tell it was troubling Logan.

"Are you worried?" I asked before I could stop myself. I wanted Logan to be able to open up to me about things that perhaps he couldn't show to anyone else. He needed to seem strong and fearless as their Alpha but I wanted him to know that with me, he could be himself.

He sighed as he twirled my hair in his fingers. "Yes. If we were just dealing with vampires here, then I wouldn't be. We have strong border controls and we are more than prepared for vampire attacks but…"

"Arius," I finished his sentence before he could.

"He is a hybrid, Alina. That means he is potentially the most powerful being alive now. And I don't know what his plan is. That's what worries me."

I nodded my head in understanding. "But he did leave Lucius to be killed by us. He even cast a spell to make sure Lucius could not escape. Maybe he doesn't want a war. Maybe he will leave us alone."

"I hope you are right. But I have a feeling that he will be back. And I know we cannot prepare for it. You saw how the vampires appeared from thin air. That was his magic, they went undetected by our border control. He is powerful and I want to keep this pack safe. But against him, I am not sure how," he said so honestly it tugged at my heart. I looked up at him and stroked his cheek.

"We will deal with whatever happens together. We cannot go through our lives living in fear again. I will not allow it. We take each day as it comes. Your people love you because you are already proving to be the best Alpha. And I love you even more."

He smiled down at me. "Thank you. You always know exactly what to say."

I giggled. "Role of a Luna, is it not?" I winked at him and he tickled my sides.

Suddenly, there was a knock at the door and he groaned loudly. "Go away!" he grumbled as I hit his shoulder, smirking.

"Come in!" I shouted pulling the covers over us up to my neck.

Sloane poked her head around the door. "Sorry to interrupt but the florist is here with the flowers and the caterers are setting up downstairs." She shot me an apologetic look but I smiled back at her.

"Okay. Thanks, Sloane. I will be there in ten minutes."

She left, shutting the door behind her and Logan was instantly back to groping me as I pushed him off and climbed out of bed.

"Come on! You heard her!"

He groaned as he pulled the covers off him and sulked into the shower. "Join me?" He winked as the water glided over his body, tempting me.

I rolled my eyes and pushed my urges deep down inside. "We both know that is a terrible idea if we ever want to leave this room today."

He pouted which made me giggle and suddenly I felt a little lightheaded. I gripped onto the sink until it passed but Logan noticed.

"You okay?" His voice was laced with concern.

"Yes, fine. Just felt a bit lightheaded for a moment. Just need to eat something," I said with a small smile.

This was not the day to get ill. This evening, we would be holding a ceremony to honour and say goodbye to all those who fell in the battle. Two in particular that held a special place in my heart for their bravery. Rohan and Cora. I had arranged everything with no expense spared. The fallen heroes were to have the best possible send off and it would be emotional but a night of celebration. That was what they deserved.

After I showered, alone, and got dressed, I headed straight down to the kitchen where the caterers were busy setting up. I had hired human cooks as they would not be staying to cook for the evening and were just dropping off all the food and doing some last-minute dishes here this morning. Everyone knew they had to be in their best behaviour. I smiled as I walked in and saw Sloane was already directing them to all the appliances and storage. She really was the best Beta.

Seeing that she had everything in hand, I headed outside to the back lawn to check on the florist. They were unloading hundreds of gorgeous bouquets from a van and walking them down to the ceremony that was being set up under the two large oak trees where Logan and I held the Luna Ceremony.

I smiled as I watched Madeline, running between the florists, directing them to the right areas. To say we had come a long way was an understatement. I would even go as far as to say that we were becoming friends though we were still a little wary of each other. Sloane had welcomed her into the group with open arms as Fredrik had such a close relationship with Madeline already. Chloe on the other hand was being a little more sceptical. I told her not to be as it was clear that Madeline was a very different person to the girl I first met in the clothes shop. She was still stunning and confident around others but something in her had changed. She seemed gentler but also broken. I couldn't help but feel a little responsible although she had tried her best to reassure me that it had nothing to do with me.

She had taken Cora's death very hard. For the first two days after the battle, she kept herself locked away in her room on the second floor. Sloane took food and water to her but she had never moved from the bed. Then on day three, she emerged and came looking for me. I was surprised, to say the least, when the first thing she did was apologise profusely about what she had done. I was even more surprised when she told me that she thought I was the best Luna this pack could ever have and that she was so pleased that Logan was so happy. She then went on to say that she was going to leave and become a rogue. She didn't want to burden us with her presence but I forbade it. I ordered her to stay, much to Logan's annoyance. He had not been so forgiving.

She had also tried to speak to him but he had refused to see her. Again, surprisingly, she understood and did not push him on the matter. Like I said, she was different. Hearing how she held Rohan in her arms as he died broke my heart and I thanked her for staying with him when I couldn't. He didn't deserve to die alone.

I have tried checking in on Fiona and Nico everyday but she is beyond distraught. I deliver food to her and her son and sometimes stay and play with Nico but she never said a word. Just stared into space with puffy eyes. I am starting to really worry about her.

"Hey, Luna, the florist wasn't sure where you wanted the lilies so I just told them to put them over by the chairs for the moment until you were available," Madeline said as she walked towards me.

I smiled at her warmly. "Thank you, I will go and sort it all now."

She looked around as the ceremony area started to take shape and let out a shaky breath.

"Hey, how are you holding up today?" I ask as her grey eyes met mine.

"Okay, I think. I just need to stay busy. Thank you to you and Logan for making this so special. Cora would have loved it," she said as the tears threatened in her eyes but she quickly blinked them away.

"You two were really close, weren't you?"

She nodded twice before looking down at the ground. "I know we hadn't known each other for a long time but we just had this connection. We got each other. She reminded me a lot of my own mother. I just wish I could have been there when she··· you know." She choked out and fanned her face. "Sorry. I promised myself I would hold it together until tonight."

"Don't apologise. Cora was a very special woman. Without her help we may not be here today. We will celebrate her life tonight and you can say goodbye to her properly. The witch community have responded to our invitation and many are coming to show their respects."

"That is great. Thank you, I know she had some close friends among them." She suddenly seemed nervous and I could tell something was on her mind. "Do you think··· do you think Arius will come?" Her eyes searched mine and I saw something cross her face··· Fear?

I wouldn't lie and say the thought hadn't crossed my mind as well. Cora was his mother after all, even if he only found out seconds before her death. Madeline had made it clear that she didn't want to relive whatever happened in the woods. From the look on her face right now, she was terrified of him.

"Honestly, I don't know. At least we will have the witches here if he does." I tried to reassure her and ease her concern.

She nodded and clapped her hands together.

"Right. What can I do to help?" she asked and I smiled before giving her a to-do list to keep her busy.

After speaking with the florists, I headed back inside to the kitchen to make up some food to take over to Fiona. As I opened the fridge and the potent smell of uncooked meat hit my nose, I heaved uncontrollably. I slammed the fridge shut but it was too late. I ran past Sloane and into the downstairs toilet just in time before I puked my guts up.

Once I felt like I had nothing left to give, I stood up shakily and splashed my face with cold water, only to see Sloane's amused expression behind me in the mirror.

"I'm fine. I am just not feeling too great today. Don't worry though, I will be fine for tonight," I said confidently as she lifted one eyebrow at me. "What?"

She chuckled and walked towards me with open arms. She pulled me into a tight hug and whispered in my ear, "Congratulations, Luna."

My body tensed and eyes widened as I realised what she meant.

Chapter 75

Logan's POV

I Left my room with a spring in my step and practically jumped down the stairs three at a time. Nothing was going to change my mood today. I could just feel it in my bones, today was going to be great, although hard. I had lost more warriors than I had bargained for in the battle and devastatingly two women and one child who hadn't made to the safe room in time. But today was about celebration and honouring their lives. We wanted to make it as happy event as we could for their loved ones and for them watching down on us.

I stopped on the second floor and decided to check in on Darius before I head out to the border control. He had been bed-ridden, pack doctor's orders, for the last week and I could tell it was starting to do his head in. Not to mention the fact that Chloe had not left his side. I knocked before entering, hoping I wasn't about to walk in on something that would haunt me forever.

"Oh, thank god! You can deal with this stubborn moron! I have reached my limit." She practically screamed at me as she threw a towel down onto the bed.

"Hello, to you to!" I smirked as her eyes narrowed at me, obviously not in the mood for sarcasm. Darius rolled his eyes at her from his position in the bed. He was shirtless with a large bandage wrapped around his waist. Lucius had stabbed him with a silver blade laced with wolfsbane so it had taken a lot longer to heal than any other wound would for a wolf.

"No one asked you to be here anyhow," he gritted through his teeth but she definitely heard him.

"You, ungrateful prick! Fine, get out of bed, fuck up your healing and run a bloody marathon for all I care!" She went to walk away from him but he grabbed her wrist and yanked her back so she fell onto his chest on the bed.

He smirked at her before saying, "Oh, but you do care that's why you're so mad."

She pushed off him and stood up but I could see she was fighting the urge to smile back. "Yes, asshole, I do care about you. Lord knows why! So just stay put until tonight alright?" Her voice softened as he pouted his lips and blew her a kiss. "You are impossible." She giggled and left the room.

I gave my cousin a knowing look as I walked over and perch on the side of the bed.

"What?" he asked, looking slightly embarrassed.

"You really like her, don't you?" I teased but I honestly want to know. I have never seen him like this over a girl before.

He rolled his eyes at me. "Like is a strong word. Tolerate is more appropriate," he said flatly.

I laughed. "Come on, mate. Give it up already. Everyone can see how much you two are into each other!"

His head snapped to me and his eyes lit up at my words. "Do you really think she's into me?"

Goddess, this man is such an idiot sometimes. "Why else would she be so concerned about you? You should have seen the state she was in when we brought you back here unconscious. She hadn't left your side for the entire week." I scanned the room and saw all her belongings thrown around messily. "And it looks like she's moved in."

He couldn't hide his smile any longer. "Yeah, I guess. But, Logan, you know me. I don't do relationships. I am no good at them and with her, it's even more complicated."

"Why?" I asked curiously.

"Because I can't hurt her. It's best that this doesn't turn too serious so neither of us get hurt."

"Darius, you can't go through life scared of getting hurt. That is no way to live. If she makes you happy, then that is something worth exploring surely." I tried and reason with him.

"Anyway, tell me what's going on. I am dying of boredom in here. Well, when Chloe isn't around anyway." He smirked, and I shook my head.

"Nothing much. We are just busy setting everything up for tonight. I am about to take a shift on border control." I shrugged.

"Lucky bastard. So, no sign of the hybrid?" he asked.

"No. I don't know whether that is good or not. We have invited some of the witch community tonight to pay tribute to Cora. She was like a celebrity amongst them."

"Urgh. I hate witches. They really freak me out." He shook his shoulders and the winced at the pain it caused him. He pulled himself up on the bed, so he was resting against the headboard. "You know, Maddy came to see me yesterday." He eyed me cautiously.

"Oh, yeah," I replied casually. My mood was too great today for even her name to ruin it.

"Yeah. She really is sorry, you know," he said carefully, judging my reaction.

She had asked to speak to me a few days ago but I had refused, and she had been keeping her distance from me since, respecting my space. It wasn't that I was even holding onto a grudge anymore, I just wasn't interested.

I sighed. Maybe I would feel better if I aired it all out with her. Especially now that Alina had ordered her to stay here even when she wanted to leave. She wasn't going anywhere, and I couldn't ignore her forever.

"She's different, Logan. I don't know how or why but something in her has changed. I think you should hear her out at least."

"I will. I'll go and see her in a minute."

Darius grinned like a Cheshire cat. It had always been the three of us since we were pups, and I was sure it had affected him more than he let on.

We sat and chatted for a few more minutes before I made my way downstairs. Alina and Sloane were nowhere to be seen so I headed out into the backyard to see how the preparations were going and bump straight into Madeline.

She stepped back awkwardly and looked down at the floor. "Oh, uh, so sorry, Alpha," she said respectfully and went to walk around me.

"Wait," I said and she froze. "Can we talk?"

She glanced up at me sideways and a small smile spread across her face. "I would like that," she said softly.

I smiled back and gestured to the bench at the veranda. Once we both sat down, looking out over the lawn, it became awkward again. How was I going to start this? I didn't have to as she started to speak.

"I know you probably don't believe me, and I fully understand why, but I just want to say again how truly sorry I am about everything. What I did… It was so wrong and there is no excuse for it.

I was thinking about the pack and myself and I couldn't see the truth." I turned to look at her as she looked down at her fingers on her lap. "You don't know how happy I am to see you truly in love. Before we were together, we were friends. Best friends. And all I have ever wanted was for you to be happy. I tried to make you happy for years and failed. Seeing you with Alina this week and how amazing you two are together has made me realise that you were never truly happy before."

I went to interrupt her, but she held her hand up to stop me.

"And that is okay, Logan. I won't lie and say it didn't hurt when you chose her because it had always been us. When we talked about the future, it was always me and you. But hand on my heart, I can say now that I understand. You were right. We were never meant for each other, and we would have never made each other happy."

I sighed and nodded once before looking back out at the people busy with preparations, unaware of the closure happening between two past lovers. "What you did was fucked up, Maddy, and it is going to take a while for me to forgive you and trust you again. You intentionally came between me and my mate and honestly, I wasn't sure I would ever be able to be in the same room as you again without wanting to rip your face off."

She laughed and I smiled.

"I wouldn't blame you if you did," she said with a chuckle, but I could hear the regret in her voice.

"That aside, I have made mistakes, too. We are not perfect. I am sorry, Maddy. I never meant to hurt you the way I did. I really tried to ignore my feelings for Alina when I first met her, but I just couldn't. I hope one day, you get to experience those feelings with your own mate."

A single tear slid down her face and she quickly wiped it away.

She looked over at me with a sad smile. "Maybe one day."

We sat in a comfortable silence for few minutes.

"You should be really proud, Logan. Of all of this. What you have rebuilt here is special. And for defeating Lucius. You really did it. What you had always dreamed of achieving and more. Your parents would be so proud of you."

I smiled as I watched the pack members laughing and interacting. I looked back over at her. Darius was right, she had changed. There was something different about her. Sadness perhaps but it had changed her. She seemed softer, yet tough. As if she was accepting all her flaws and past mistakes and using them to rebuild herself again.

"Thank you, Maddy. I know Alina has asked you to stay. If it is what you want, I think you should. You belong here just as much as any of us."

She nodded carefully and sniffed. "That means a lot. Thank you."

I stood up and looked back at her. "I'll see you later."

"Yep. See you later," she said with a smile.

I walked away feeling a massive weight lifted off my shoulders.

Chapter 76

Alina's POV

I stared at my reflection in the mirror. It was fair to say I had been through all the emotions today. Denial. Shock. Anxiety. Excitement. Anxiety again. And now gratitude. I had taken several pregnancy tests with Sloane to prove her wrong but in fact, each one only proved her right. I was pregnant with Logan's baby. With our own little pup and my heart could burst. It was something I hadn't thought I wanted yet but now it had happened, I couldn't be happier. I had hardly seen Logan all day as he was busy with the preparations and the security of the event which gave me an opportunity to come to terms with the news and prepare myself for telling him. I had no idea how he would react. I hope he would be happy. But in all honesty, I was scared. This was fast and I wouldn't blame him if he freaked out.

The bedroom door opened and my eyes connected with his as he ran his finger through his hair. He was sweaty and shirtless, indicating he had just been patrolling the border as Elias.

"You look beautiful," he said walking over and bending down to kiss me on the cheek. I smiled at his gesture knowing it was a lie as I had spent most of the day throwing up and no amount of makeup could change how pale and tired I looked.

The Last Alpha

"Thank you. Everything okay with the border?" I asked, swivelling around on my vanity stool.

He rubbed his hands up and down my arms. "Yes, everything is how it should be. No signs of anything strange, so fingers crossed." He gave me a small smile before walking into the bathroom and turning the shower on.

I follow him in feeling my anxiety rising again. Do I just come out with it? Do I lead up to it?

"I spoke to Madeline today," he said as he stripped down and walked into the shower.

My eyebrows raised at him in surprise and I leaned back on the sink. "And how did that go?" I asked carefully. I really wanted us to all put what had happened behind us and move forward with our new lives. There was no point in holding onto resentment or anger. It would only eat away at our souls.

"Good. She really did seem sorry," he said whilst shampooing his hair and I nodded at him. "But I am not ready to forgive and forget. However, it's a start. I hope one day we can be friends again. She does seem to have changed," he said thoughtfully.

"She has been through a lot. I think it would change anyone," I said softly.

"We all have," he responded and I smiled again. He was right. The last two months had been a whirlwind for us all. And now there was a baby on the way about to cause its own chaos, I was sure.

"Logan… I have something…" I said quietly as he stepped out of the shower and wrapped a towel around his waist. The sight of him stopped my thought process as I licked my lips hungrily. He chuckled and walked towards me.

"You have something…" he repeated with a cheeky grin knowing the effect he has on me.

Suddenly, Fredrik mind links us both, *'Alpha, Luna. The witches are arriving.'*

Logan's eyes widen. "Shit. They are early!"

"Don't worry. I am ready. I will go down and greet them. Just come down when you are ready," I said calmly and he gave me a loving smile.

"I'll be in five minutes!" he said and I nodded whilst walking away. "Alina, you were about to tell me something?"

I looked over my shoulder at his confused face. "It can wait. Now, hurry up!" I grinned back at him before leaving the room.

The ground floor of the pack house was swarming with bodies as our pack members mingled and chatted to the witches and warlocks. They seemed friendly enough, curtsying and thanking me for the invitation when I greeted them. One woman with red fiery hair that cascaded down her back in tight curls walked through the door and her presence immediately caused many of the witches to turn and bow to her out of respect. Her eyes scanned the room and when she saw me, she smiled politely and walked towards me. She gave off an aura of importance as she bowed her head to me.

"You must be Luna Alina. It is a pleasure to finally meet you." Her voice was regal and confident. I tried to not let her intimidate me and stood a little taller, bowing my head to her also.

"I am sorry. Have we met before?" I asked as she looked me up and down carefully.

"No, my child. But I have heard lots about you. My name is Margret Visla. But people call me Maggie. I am an elder witch and member of the enchanted council."

I gulped as I realised she was practically a royal in the eyes of the enchanted. "It is a pleasure to meet you, Maggie. Thank you for coming to pay your respects."

The Last Alpha

Her eyes flickered over my shoulder to the man approaching behind. I felt a strong arm wrap around my waist protectively and looked up to see Logan's tight expression as he looked the woman over.

"And you must be the famous Alpha Logan. On behalf of the council, thank you for putting an end to Lucius' reign of terror. He was nothing but a demented soul who needed to be stopped." She smiled slyly at him and I felt his body tense.

"I have always wondered why the council never stepped in and dealt with him themselves," he said almost accusingly and my eyes widened. What was he doing? We just got rid of one enemy, let's not make another! But I was surprised when a cackle escaped her lips and she smiled back at him.

"Believe me, we wanted to. But it is against our laws to intervene with personal vendettas. He was revenging his wife and unborn son just like you were revenging your father and your pack." Her eyes sparkled as she looked back to me.

Before I could stop myself, the words were out of my mouth, "Then what do you do?" I quickly apologised for my tone. "I am sorry. I didn't mean it to sound… It is just that I am fairly new to this life and I…"

She held her hand up to pardon me and smiled warmly, "The council is made up of one member of each supernatural species that is classed as an elder. That means we have been around for over five hundred years and are here to keep balance on earth. Above all else, we protect the supernatural from exposure to the humans and we only intervene in matters of an extremely serious nature."

Logan scoffed and scowled at her but she ignored him. "Cora was a very good friend of mine. I hope my being here to pay my respects is not unwelcome."

The Last Alpha

"No, of course not. You are very welcome," I said quickly, nudging my elbow into Logan's side. He nodded at her once.

"Thank you. Could you please tell me if a wolf by the name of Madeline is here?" she asked courteously.

"Yes, she is just over there, speaking to those women," I said pointing over to her direction.

Maggie bowed her head and walked in that direction and I looked up to Logan with a confused expression. He simply shrugged it off and before I could say anything, Fredrik and Sloane approached us. Fredrik's arm was tightly wrapped around her waist just as Logan's was around mine and she rolled her eyes at me which made me giggle quickly.

"Do you think these men will let us walk anywhere alone tonight?" she joked and gave me a knowing look. Panic rose as I wondered if she thought I had told Logan and was about to say something.

"We are just mere beasts protecting our hearts." Fredrik grinned at Logan who chuckled back. "You wait, Luna. This is nothing on how Logan will be when you are carrying his pup."

A blush crept up onto my cheeks and I saw Sloane nudge into him.

"What?" he said in irritation and I quickly changed the subject.

"Do you think everyone is here now? Shall we make a start?" I looked up at Logan and he nodded at me with a sad smile.

He stood up on a few steps of the stairs and coughed loudly to get everyone's attention. The chatter died down and everyone turned to glance our way.

"Ladies and gentlemen, thank you so much for coming to pay your respects to our fallen heroes this evening. Tonight will be difficult but it should also be one filled with love and celebration for their lives. If you would all please make your way outside, we will start the ceremony in due course," Logan addressed the audience and they all start to shuffle through the back doors into the beautifully decorated garden.

Everyone took their seats on the wooden chairs, decorated with white lace and Logan and I took our places at the front. There was a wide aisle through the middle of the chairs for warriors to carry the coffins down.

A respectful silence filled the air as they wait for us to start. Logan went to step forward but I gripped onto his forearm when I saw Fiona and Nico's chairs were still empty. He nodded in understanding and we waited a few more moments. Just as I was about to give up hope, I saw Fiona dressed entirely in black carrying Nico in a little suit down to the front of the assembly. She took a seat in her chair and kept Nico on her lap. Her netted black veil covered her face but she nodded her head at me to show she was ready. I smiled at her warmly and looked at Logan.

"Going to battle was always a risk. A risk that would cost lives. The lives we lost that day will forever hold a special place in our hearts and the history of our kind. They gave their lives in order to give us back ours. And I for one will be eternally grateful to have known them and to have fought beside them. Their memory will live on through the stories we tell of them to future generations. They are the reason we stand here today."

He stepped back as the violins and harp started to play, filling the air with a beautifully haunting melody. The first two coffins started to make their way down the aisle, carried on the shoulders of warriors. Logan read their names out as they were placed at the front. And so, the ceremony continued as Logan and I took it in turns to read the names of the fallen pack members as more and more coffins were laid on the ground between rows of flowers.

The Last Alpha

The next two were brought down and a lump in my throat formed. I read out the names. "Five-year-old, Keely Maines." Loud sobs escaped a woman in the crowd as her mate wrapped his arms around her. "Thirty-eight-year-old warrior, Rohan Chevalier." A tear ran down my cheek as Fiona nestled her face into Nico's little body and her shoulders shook. I tried to look away but when I saw his little hand caress his mother's cheek so attentively, I fell apart.

I felt Logan wrap his arm around my shoulder as he prepared to say the last name on the list. "Cora Anderson."

The warriors started to carry her coffin down the aisle and witches and warlocks stood up as it passed them. Once it was laid on the grass, they sent sparks from their fingers, shooting up into the sky as fireworks exploded against the black canvas of the night.

Once the melody had finished, we invited some of the family members to come and say a few words and a final goodbye to their loved ones. Fiona stood and held Nico's hand as she walked towards Rohan's coffin. She said her own silent farewell and leaned over to kiss the lid of the coffin before walking back to her chair. Lastly, I look over at Madeline to encourage her up to the front. She took a deep breath and closed her eyes before standing and taking her place.

She scanned the faces in the crowd nervously and looked over at Cora's coffin. "I did not know Cora for very long. But in the time I had with her, I connected with her on a deeper level. Many only knew Cora's reputation as a ruthless dark witch who caused many pains and sufferings. That may have been true once upon a time. But what many don't know about her is that she fought so hard to try and change that. She dedicated the last thirty years of her life to trying to atone for her sins. The woman I came to know was caring, forgiving, and above all else she loved the ones closest to her with a fire and passion that only a true mother could possess. She gave her life for those she loved. She gave her life to put an end to evil. She was my friend and a truly special person. I will miss her dearly and only hope that her soul can now rest in peace knowing she died saving others."

Suddenly, a powerful gust of wind blew through the air and we all bend down or cover our eyes until it settled. As the puff of purple smoke faded away, shocked gasps of terror were heard from the crowd as Arius appeared halfway down the aisle. He was wearing a dark black suit with a black turtle neck jumper underneath. His black hair was styled back away from his face and I saw the exquisite different coloured eyes that had always been hidden by the violet or red he normally had. His face was cold and hard as he scanned the crowd and it rested upon Madeline. I saw her gulp in fear as he continued to stare at her intensely before he looked to Logan and I.

Logan's body tensed beside me as he put his arms across my front to push me behind him protectively. I gripped on to his hand and pulled it down to my side. I was his equal. Not his damsel.

No one dared to move as Arius took deliberate steps towards Cora's coffin. When he reached it, he ran his hand over the lid but still showed no emotion. I needed to control this situation. Logan was not in control of his emotions right now; I could feel his rage through the mate bond. I could not let any more harm come to my people.

"Arius, thank you for joining us to pay your respects," I said carefully, trying to keep the fear hidden from my voice.

He looked up at me and our eyes connected, but I felt no emotion. And then he smirked. "It appears my invitation got lost in the post." His eyes twinkled but I saw the evil lurking behind them. He was testing me, seeing how we would react. Would we retaliate or would we stay calm?

"I am sorry. We did not know how to contact you. Of course, you are welcome. Cora was your mother after all."

Logan whipped his head at me in surprise but I ignored him, keeping my gaze on the man in front of me. Something flickered across his face but I could not quite register what it was.

"That is why you are here, is it not?" I asked sternly and his eyes travelled over to Madeline before going back to me. Strange.

"Cora was my mother although this fact was kept hidden from me all my life. However, I had grown close to her in the last few weeks. I believe she would want to be laid to rest in her woods in Sweden. I am here to take her body." His voice was commanding and was not seeking permission. Everyone's eyes widened and I felt panic inside. If this was all he wanted then we should keep the peace. But it could be a trick.

"Let him take her," a small voice echoed through the air and all our heads turned to Madeline. She was staring straight at Arius with a determined look. "He is right. Cora would want to be home, not here. Let him take her."

I turned back to Arius as his gaze moved from Madeline to mine. I nodded once and he looked at Logan. Logan nodded again.
Without a word, Arius held his hand out to the coffin and another gust of wind filtered through the air as both himself and Cora's coffin disappeared.

Everyone remained in silence, unsure what to do next. Logan mind linked me. *'This could be a trick. A distraction. They could be about to ambush us.'*

I scanned the trees surrounding us but nothing seemed out of place. Logan asked for a report from the border patrol through mind link.

'Nothing Alpha. No sign of any vampires. He came alone.'

My body relaxed slightly as someone called out from the pack. "What now? Is he gone?"

Logan spoke up first. "Yes, he came alone. We should remain on high alert but there seems to be no threat. Why don't we all head inside for food and drinks as the warriors and families bury their loved ones?" he said with a smile and I felt the tension in the air evaporate. We paid our respect to the families before heading inside and starting the buffet.

Madeline's POV

I took a seat on the veranda and held my head in my hands. My heart was still pounding at seeing him again. I hated how my heart fluttered when he looked my way. I needed him to leave before anyone realised what we were. Goddess knows how the pack would react to such news. As much as it tore at my heart, seeing how everyone reacted in his presence helped me to make my decision. I had to reject him. It would hurt like hell and I may not survive it but it would be better than the alternative—being mated to a demon. The last week had been torture. Some days I would feel everything at once. Other days, I felt numb. I don't know which was worse.

"Are you, Madeline?" A frail voice caused me to sit up straight as I saw a small woman dressed in black standing next to me. Her eyes were puffy and she looked pale and weak.

"Yes. Can I help you?" I asked softly. She looked like she needed someone's help.

"My name is Fiona," she said quietly and gave me a pained smile.

My eyes widened as I recalled that name. "You are Rohan's mate." My voice came out as a whisper as she nodded sadly.

"I just wanted to thank you. For being with him in his final moments. You will never know how much peace that has brought me knowing he didn't die alone," her voice caught at the end and tears welled up in her eyes.

I stood up and walk over to her, putting my hand on her shoulder as she looked into my eyes. "You do not need to thank me. He was a brave man and I could tell he had a good soul. His last moments were peaceful." She released a sob at my words. I pulled her into my chest as her body shook. "He loved you very much. He wanted me to tell you that but I know you already know."

She pulled away from me and wiped her eyes. "Thank you. I best go inside and find my son."

I nodded my head and gave her a warm smile. My heart went out to her for such a tragic loss but she was stronger than she thought. She was a mother, she had to be.

I watched as she walked into the pack house as people started to sit down at the tables. I couldn't go in yet as I was still too shaken. A chirping noise behind me pulled my attention. I turn to find a hawfinch bird perched on the fence of the veranda. My head cocked to the side as I wondered what on earth a bird like this was doing in this country. They were native to Europe.

"Cedric?" A small smile played on my lips. "Are you following me?"

Suddenly, it spread its wings and fled off into the entrance of the woods. I squinted my eyes after it and gasped when I saw two glowing purple eyes staring at me from the darkness of the forest.

'*MATE*' Nina growled in my head and I gulped. He was waiting for me. Summoning me.

I checked no one was around before I walked into the forest following the bird. The crunch of leaves underfoot was the only sound as I stepped deeper into the woods. The enchanted eyes have vanished. I stood still as my heart raced in my chest. Unexpectantly, I felt his presence behind me and his breath tickled my neck, sending a shiver down my spine. I jumped forward and turned to face him.

His sexiness took my breath away as he stood broadly in his black suit and his beautiful natural eyes bore into mine. My body and wolf wanted to run into his arms, kiss his lips, ran my hand through his hair. But I am stronger than my desire.

"I, Madeline Damaris from the Blood Moon Pack hereby reject..." I didn't get to finish my sentence as his hand slammed against my mouth and his arm snaked around my waist holding me to his body. His face was thunderous as he glared down at me.

"Ever try and reject me again, little wolf, and your pack will feel the true wrath of my power. I will kill every last one of them," he hissed and I gulped in fear. "Understand?"

I nodded as he slowly removed his hand from my mouth and looked down at my lips and back up to my eyes. His grip around my waist tightened as if he was scared that I would run away.

"Why? Why do you even want me as your mate?" My voice came out with a quiver as I searched the eyes of this mysterious man. It made no sense. We were enemies.

"You will change your mind. It took me some time to come to terms with it, too. You will want me eventually." His voice was so low and seductive and I watched his lips as he spoke.

"What do you mean? You knew?" My eyes widened in surprise.

A small smirk played on his lips. He nodded and released his grip on me. The hawfinch landed on his shoulder and he reached up and stroke it. "I believe you know my friend, Cedric?" His eyes sparkled with amusement and I gasped.

"That was you? The whole time?"

His face turned serious and he stepped towards me again as the bird flew away.

"I knew you were my soul mate the first time I saw you at the ambush in Ruislip Woods. Ever wondered who stopped that vampire from ripping your throat out? I have been keeping an eye on you ever since." He traced his finger over my bottom lip and I tried to ignore the sparks it caused on my skin. He was there? I don't remember seeing him. "Madeline..." His voice was like silk as my name rolled off his tongue sensually and I felt my core tighten. He bent his head towards me until his lips brushed against mine. I felt sucked in. Drawn to him.

Suddenly, I snapped out of it and push his chest. "No!" I shouted as anger boiled inside me. His face flashed with his own rage at my rejection.

"I am a demanding creature, Madeline. I am cruel, unreasonable, and impatient. But I am feeling generous. I will give you the same amount of time I had to come to terms with the fact that you are mine. You have three weeks and then I will come for you and no one will stop me." He lifted my arm and waved his hand over my wrist as a gorgeous gold bracelet with a blood red ruby in the middle appeared.

"This is so I know where you are at all times."

I pulled at the bangle but it wouldn't budge. "You are a psychopath!" I spat at him and he grinned.

"I prefer the term creative." His face turned serious again as he grasped my wrist and pointed at the ruby. "If you ever need me... for anything." He gave me a seductive look. "Rub the ruby and say my name and I will come to you."

"I won't.... need you," I growled at him and he chuckled.

"We'll see. Remember... three weeks." He smirked and disappeared in front of my eyes, leaving me alone in the woods once more.

Chapter 77

Alina's POV

The room was full of chatter and laughter as wolves and witches dug into their meals and the drinks started flowing. I smiled as I took a seat at the head of the main table with Logan next to me and looked at the faces of the ones I love. Now more than ever, I was grateful for them all.

I sniggered as I saw Darius and Chloe bickering as she tried to cut up his food for him and he told her he was more than capable. I glanced over at Fredrik and Sloane who were grinning at each other with so much love as he rested his hand on her belly. I caught Fiona's eye and she gave me a small smile which I returned as Nico took a huge mouthful of his dinner, making noises of appreciation.

Madeline entered the room, looking somewhat flustered. We caught each other's eye and I mouthed "Are you okay?" She gave me a warm smile that didn't reach her eyes but nodded as she took her seat. Looking around at all of these people who have become my family made me realise how lucky I was to have found them all.

My life may have turned upside down in the last two months but I wouldn't change it for the world. I finally knew who I truly am. I am Alina Clarke Snow, an Alabaster wolf raised in the human world by the most selfless parents who loved so deeply. I am the rightful Luna of the Blood Moon Pack, the last pack standing in the world and I would die protecting anyone of my people. I am a mate to the most loyal, loving, and gorgeous man who I love with every inch of my soul. And I am soon to be a mother to the future of our kind, my little pup.

I leaned my head onto Logan's shoulder and let out a contented sigh. He smiled down at me.

"You okay?" he asked as I lift my head to look into those gorgeous eyes that I could spend eternity getting lost in.

"More than okay." I smiled and gave him a peck on the lips. "Can we go for a quick walk?"

He eyed me suspiciously and then a wide grin spread across his face. "Absolutely." He nuzzled my neck and I giggled. If he thought that was what I meant, he was in for an even bigger shock.

We strolled hand in hand towards the bottom of the garden to my favourite tree. Once we were sheltered under the dangling branches of the Red Alder, I pulled at his arm to stop him and he turned to look at me.

"Logan, I have something to tell you and…" I stumbled over my words as the nerves increased.

His hand came up to my face and his thumb caressed my cheek as his face creased with concern. "What is it? You are worrying me," he said.

"Before I tell you, I just want you to know that I understand if you need a bit of time to… you know, to process it. Or if you freak out. Trust me, I had a little freak out myself," I said quickly as his eyes burned into mine.

"What's going on, Alina? Whatever it is, you can tell me," he pleaded and I smiled up at him.

"I'm… pregnant," I said softly and studied his face for his reaction.

His blue eyes widened slightly and then an enormous smile lit up his entire face. He dived at me, lifting me off the floor and spinning us around as I giggled into his neck.

"Really? You are really sure?" His voice was higher than usual and he looked so excited.

I nodded at him as my face hurt from smiling so much. "You aren't upset? Or freaked out?" I said carefully.

He laughed and squeezed me into his body again. "You have just made me the happiest man alive, Alina. Why would I be freaked out?"

I shook my head in disbelief.

"Wait, did you freak out? Are you freaked out? Do you not want this baby?" He suddenly pulled me away from him to look into my eyes as I saw hurt register on his face.

I shook my head quickly. "No, I mean, I was shocked, and this has all happened so fast but… I am happy. I want your babies more than anything else in this world!" My eyes teared up as I saw such genuine happiness on my mate's face.

He kneeled down on his knees and hugged my waist before kissing my stomach and looking up at me. "Right here, I have my entire universe in my arms. You and our baby. You will never know how hopelessly in love I am with you both."

"I think I have some idea." I smiled down at him through my lashes as I ran my hand through his curls knowing I felt the same way.

"I love you," he whispered.

"I love you."

"Always."

"Always."

THE END

ABOUT THE AUTHOR

Aura Rose is a British romance author who is a true romantic at heart with a wild imagination. Her stories will make you fall in love, shed some tears, laugh out loud, scream at the pages, have you on the edge of your seat but most importantly, leave you begging for more. Her dominant, sexy male leads will do anything for the women they love. The female leads are sassy, strong, confident and never damsels in distress. Her stories are filled with real human emotion and you cannot help but become invested in the character's journeys.

Visit Dreame to Read More Story by Aura Rose

Dark Love (Sequel to The Last Alpha)

His Lost Tribrid

Her Silver Eyed Mate
www.dreame.com

ABOUT DREAME

Established in 2018 and headquartered in Singapore, Dreame is a global hub for creativity and fascinating stories of all kinds in many different genres and themes.

Our goal is to unite an open, vibrant, and diverse ecosystem for storytellers and readers around the world.

Available in over 20 languages and 100 countries, we are dedicated to bring quality and rich content for tens of millions of readers to enjoy.

We are committed to discover the endless possibilities behind every story and provide an ultimate platform for readers to connect with the authors, inspire each other, and share their thoughts anytime, anywhere.

Join the journey with Dreame, and let creativity enrich our lives!

Sneak Peek - **Dark Love**

Chapter 1

Madeline's POV

The pulsing bodies thrust up against each other to the beat of the pounding music. The energy was loud and seductive as I weaved my way through the crowd of people grinding on the dancefloor. The neon beams darted across the room like swords of light illuminating people's euphoric faces. I found a place that felt right and closed my eyes, allowing my body to sway to the music. The feeling was freeing.

I started to glide my hands up and down my body seductively as I felt my desire to be touched by someone. No, not just someone. Him. My thoughts filled with images of his strong hands, his tempting lips, his toned and muscular body. I felt arms around my waist, a man grinding his groin up against my ass, but my eyes didn't open. I imagined it was him. My body burned for more as I ran the man's hands up and down my body for stimulation. But then the music stopped. Everyone stilled as if they were frozen in time.

My eyes flew open as I searched the crowd of statues frantically. Then I locked eyes with those majestic irises that made my heart race. One ice blue, one deep brown. He stood still glaring at me with a heated gaze through the sea of bodies. I gulped. He took slow, calculated steps towards me as his body towered over mine. I looked up at him through my dark lashes. He smirked as he leaned into me, whispering in his alluring, deep voice, "Ready to make a deal with the devil?"

I shot upright in my bed, my body damp from sweat under my night clothes. It was just a dream. It was always just a dream. I took deep breaths as I rested my hand over my heart, trying to calm my heavy pants. I looked down and caught sight of the gold bracelet with the magic ruby fastened in the middle still stuck on my wrist. This damn thing. This was the reason he could come to me every night in my dreams. To torment me.

I pulled at the gold band forcefully and tried to snap it off with all my might. It was no use. It was too robust. A constant reminder that he was not going to leave me alone.

I studied the blood red ruby for the millionth time. It was so beautiful; deep and enticing as black ink swirled around inside it. Anger rose in me at feeling so trapped. So helpless.

I contemplated rubbing it and saying his name so he would appear in front of me and I could give him hell for never letting me get a decent night's sleep or better yet, reject him as my fated mate.

I shook my head and fell back on my pillow as I huffed out in frustration. No, I couldn't put the pack's lives in so much danger. He warned me what he would do if I ever tried to reject him again.

Suddenly, a knock at my bedroom door startled me from my thoughts. "Come in," I called, sitting up in my bed as the door opened and Sloane came in and plonked herself down. She was starting to show and the little bump on her stomach made my heart melt. I was so happy for Fredrik to have found such an amazing second chance mate and to start his own little family. He deserved all the happiness in the world.

"What are you still doing in bed?" She raised her eyebrows at me and I looked over at my alarm clock. I groaned when I saw the time was already mid-morning.

"Sorry. I've not been sleeping very well. It was a rough night." I yawned and she eyed me carefully.

"Perhaps you should go and see the pack doctor. You don't look too good," she replied, putting her hand on my forehead.

"I'm fine. Honestly, just weird dreams and I find it hard to switch my mind off at the moment," I pulled the covers off me and walked towards the bathroom.

I wish so badly that I could tell someone what was really going on with me. But honestly, shame and fear stopped me. How could I tell the people I was working so hard to rebuild relationships with after my wrong doings that I was mated to our enemy? To Lucius' son. A vampire and warlock hybrid. They would never look at me the same way again. And who knows what chaos it would cause. I had to sort this mess out myself but I didn't have the first idea how.

Suddenly, I really missed my best friend, Emma. She would always be there to listen. I was starting to grow more and more concerned as I hadn't heard from her for over a month. She should be here with our pack.

"Okay, well as long as you are sure. I came to get you because I realised you were going to be late," Sloane called from her position on the bed.

My eyebrows furrowed in confusion before I realised what day it was. Shit. Luna Alina's birthday.

"Oh shit! Of course, give me ten minutes and I will be down. Thanks, Sloane." I poked my head around the door and smiled at our Beta before she left my room.

Hurriedly, I showered and dressed casually in a pair of dark jeans and a black high neck top before doing my make up. I applied my foundation, bronzer, and signature smoky eye. Just as I was about to leave my room, I looked up at the calendar hanging on my wall. My heart drummed in my chest. Three weeks and three days. I crossed today's date off and hope rose in me. Perhaps, he wasn't coming for me after all.

I raced down the stairs of the pack house to the ground floor. Hearing the laughter and happiness echo from my friends in the dining room, I took a deep breath before plastering a smile on my face.

Logan had spared no expense to shower his mate and our Luna with a brunch banquet, decorations and presents as my eyes scanned the lavishly decorated room. Everyone was already seated at the large table with the birthday girl at the top and Alpha Logan stood behind her chair.

"Madeline!" Alina beamed as I walked towards her. She was radiant and glowing. I bent down and kissed her cheek.

"Happy birthday! You look amazing!" I smiled genuinely as she blushed. If anyone would have told me three months ago that my then boyfriend's destined mate would turn out to be one of my closest friends, I would have laughed in their face and told them they were mad. But here we are. I stood up straight and nodded at Logan, the man I used to love. He grins back at me and I walked over to take a seat next to Fredrik at the table.

"Now that we are all here, I just want to make a quick toast." Logan's deep voice commanded the room and we all gazed up at him. He picked up his glass of champagne. "To our Luna and my perfect mate, everyone here loves you more than you will ever know. Happy birthday, Alina!" He bent down and kissed her lips before raising his glass.

We all picked ours up and cheered to our Luna. I won't lie and say that sometimes being in the same room as your ex and his true love is a little overwhelming, but I am dealing with it. It actually helped seeing them so happy together, knowing they belong together. And now, they were expecting a child. It was like a fairy tale. Whereas my love life was more like a nightmare.

"Madeline, you will back me up on this. Please, can you tell Chloe that wearing matching outfits tonight is so…" Chloe lowered her knife and fork and glared at Darius as he tried to find the least offensive word. "…unnecessary."

She scoffed and rolled her eyes before looking at me. "It is not matching. I just bought him a suit that is the same colour as my dress," she explained and I tried and hid my smile. That sounded pretty matchy to me. Chloe was the only one in the group who still seemed a little weary of me so taking Darius' side on this wasn't the best idea.

"That doesn't sound so bad." I shrugged whilst digging my fork into a piece of fruit.

"See! So will you stop your moaning and trust me. I know fashion and you will look great!" She grinned back at Darius who glared at me for not having his back.

"We will look ridiculous! I bet Logan and Alina aren't even matching!" he raised his voice so the top of the table heard him.

Logan turned his head with a smirk. "I am wearing the same colour and style masquerade mask as Alina." He shoved a mouthful of his brunch in his mouth before smirking. He knew how to wind a situation up so well.

"Did you hear that? The same colour masquerade mask not entire suit! They are practically married and were not even⋯" He quickly stopped as the whole table went quiet and the atmosphere tensed.

"We're not what?" Chloe hissed. "Not even together?" She threw her napkin onto the table and stood up abruptly. "Sorry, Alina. I have suddenly lost my appetitive. I will meet you in your room when you're all done." Before storming out of the room.

Darius leaned back in his chair and rubbed his hands through his messy auburn hair. "Just great," he gritted.

"Well, you handled that like a pro." Logan chuckled and Alina hit his arm, tutting.

Darius glared at him across the table as Alina stood up.

"It's your birthday! Stay and enjoy your brunch and you have presents to open." Logan held onto her hand, keeping her at the table.

She looked torn, wanting to stay and celebrate her birthday but also worrying about her best friend.

I stood up abruptly and nodded at her. "It's alright, you stay. I'll go and check on her."

Alina's face creased with uncertainty, knowing Chloe and I were not particularly close, but she nodded and sat back down all the same. Darius gave me a thankful look as I left the table and the dining room. I stood still in the lobby, using Nina's wolf hearing to try and pinpoint exactly which way Chloe went. I got the faint sound of her footsteps and her heartbeat at the back of the house. I strolled out onto the veranda and saw her sitting with her arms folded across her chest on the swinging bench. I cautiously approached and she looked up at me, surprised to see me of all people.

"Mind if I join you?" I asked softly.

She shrugged and I took that as an opportunity to sit down. We sat in silence for a few moments just looking out over the lawn and into the forest. We were now well into autumn and the trees were beginning to look bare, with only a splatter of vibrant orange and yellow leaves hanging on.

"Has he always been like this?" Chloe asked in a clipped tone.

I turned to regard her pretty face as she continued to gaze ahead. I tried to think back to a time where Darius had had a meaningful relationship in his life but only one stood out. His mother. He was such a mummy's boy growing up, always following her around, needing her attention. Logan used to tease him about it all the time but I always thought it was sweet. When we escaped the vampire attack on our territory all those years ago, he not only lost his mother that day but the only stable relationship he had. I thought about all the string of short-lived affairs or on-night stands he had when we were in London. He even had a fling with Emma at one stage. That was weird. But he had never been committed.

"Like what?" I asked carefully, not wanting to say the wrong thing.

"So detached. So closed off… It's like we take one step forward and two steps back on a daily basis. It's exhausting," she confessed and wrapped her arms tighter around her body.

I looked out across the lawn again. "Yes. I guess he has always found it difficult to form deeper connections with girls. Sorry, I know that's probably not what you want to hear."

She sighed. "Why though? What is he so afraid of?"

"Getting hurt," I said instantly without hesitation. I realised that actually, that was what I was most scared of, too.

She laughed in frustration. "Aren't we all? But you can't live your life in fear of getting hurt. You would never experience love that way." She quickly turned to me with wide eyes. "I am not saying I love him! God, we barely even like each other!"

I chuckled, knowing that was a lie. "I think you like each other plenty!" I said and she gave me a small smile. "If it is any consolation, I have never seen Darius like this about anyone before. You push him and scare him but it's a good thing. He needs it. And yes, he can be a dick sometimes but if you have even the smallest feeling that it might be worth it, don't give up on him."

She looked at me and her face softened. "Thanks. The funny thing is… I am not even sure what I want from him myself. We fight like cat and dog but my god, the passion. I have never experienced anything like it. But I'm scared…" She looked down at her hands and she suddenly seemed so vulnerable and small.

"What are you scared of?" I asked gently.

She met my gaze as she said, "Of letting him in. Getting close to him and then losing him. What if he finds his true mate?"

I saw all the worry and fear in her eyes and it reminded me of my own when I first found out Alina was Logan's destined mate. I sighed heavily. "I don't know Chloe. I am probably the wrong person to ask."

"No. You are the only person I can talk to about this. You have been there. It happened to you," she said quietly and my heart dropped as I saw pity in her eyes.

"I suppose, but every situation is different. Logan and Alina are truly perfect together. I can see that now. Not all mates are though…"

An image of my own mate entered my mind and I shook my head. The three weeks he had given me to 'come to terms with the fact that I was his' had only made me more certain that we can never be together. He was my enemy. Our species were at war. I could never love him.

"Do you think you will ever meet your own mate?" Chloe's question surprised me and I gulped down my panic. But when I looked into her eyes and saw how vulnerable and open she had been with me today, I felt the urge to tell her. To reveal my secret. Could I trust her?

I pushed a lock of my icy blonde waves behind my ear. "I already have," I muttered quietly.

She gasped and her eyes bulged.

"It is complicated, and I have struggled to understand why the Moon Goddess chose him for me. He is not a good person. It has been really hard to deal with and I need to find a way out of it. So please, can you keep this between us? You are the only person I have told." My grey eyes pleaded with hers.

She grabbed my hands and squeezed them with care. "Of course. I am so sorry, Madeline. I always hoped you would find happiness one day with your true mate."

I smiled at her sadly. "So did I."

Printed in Great Britain
by Amazon

36254931R00342